The People the Fairies Forget

Cheryl Mahoney

Stonehenge Circle Press

Stonehenge Circle Press

ISBN-13: 978-1-68012-629-7

ISBN-10: 1-68012-629-6

First Edition

Cover images courtesy of flareimages/Shutterstock (Tarry) and NatUlrich/Shutterstock (Marj)

Dedication

For the Writers of Stonehenge

Nothing has made me appreciate all that I've learned from you like revising this novel. Thanks for all your wise advice to add more tension, visceral reactions or body language—and for being there when I just needed to hear, "we love it, write more!"

Contents

Book One: Sleeping Beauty's Servant

...she considered that, when the Princess awoke, she would feel considerably embarrassed at finding herself all alone in that old castle; so this is what the Fairy did. She touched with her wand everybody that was in the castle...As soon as she had touched them, they all fell asleep, not to wake again until the time arrived for their mistress to do so, in order that they might be all ready to attend upon her when she should want them.

Charles Perrault

~ ~

Chapter One

I don't generally have much use for royalty, but I do appreciate the amount of food they serve at their christening celebrations. Lots of stories are told about what happened at the christening of the fair Princess Rosaline of Waldisan, but I might be the only one who'd mention the way the buffet table in the great hall positively sagged beneath the expanse of fruit, roast meat and fine pastries. After better than a thousand years of attending parties, I was pretty bored with christening curses and all that they entail. But I could still get enthusiastic about a good soufflé.

On my fourth trip to the table, I secured myself a leg of lamb, three rolls, a mound of grated carrot, six slices of pie and some beautiful red and green apples. Balancing my platter carefully, I pushed through the crowd in all their silken finery to hunt out a seat. My previous seat would be long gone by now. The crowd probably would have made way if I had wings, but unlike a lot of much flashier fairies I could name, I usually chose to blend in when I was among humans. My shaggy brown hair hid my pointed ears, so I could avoid all the shocked looks and silly questions that happened when people met a fairy who wasn't female and sparkly, with gossamer wings.

After dodging a lot of wide skirts and ridiculously long sleeves, I finally sank onto a padded bench along one wall, with a long exhale of relief. The seat was enough out of the crush of the crowd that no one would knock into me or my plate. The only disadvantage was that it looked straight at the table laid out for the other fairies in attendance.

I intended to ignore the fairies and devote myself to my meal, but as I bit into my leg of lamb, I noticed that the other occupant of my bench was staring at the fairies in open-mouthed wonder. I chewed, swallowed, and gave him a nudge. "Better eat; you don't want that meat pie on your plate to go cold."

The kid was maybe fifteen, and I didn't need magic to know he was a farmer's son. Smelled like hay. The rough cloth of his clothes marked him as a commoner anyway, and the wide eyes suggested he'd never been to a royal party before. They don't usually invite farmer's sons to royal parties, but they tend to throw open the gates at christenings. He turned that wide gaze on me and said in hushed awe, "I've never seen a fairy before!"

I glanced reluctantly at the fairies' table. "I expect not." That crowd wouldn't talk to a farmer's son.

The royalty had provided the usual set-up for their magical guests: places of honor, gold plates, hovering servants, and so on, *et al*, *ad nauseum*. I preferred my bench. When you've got a place of honor, everyone's so busy bowing at you that you can't have a decent conversation or properly feed a decent appetite. Besides, the farmer's son seemed likely to be better company. I recognized all five fairies sitting at the table. They were all sparkly and winged, and were the usual ones who turned out for royal christenings. They were never much use for a decent conversation under the best of circumstances.

"Eat your meat pie," I said again, picking up one of my rolls. "Ever been to a royal party before?"

"No," he said, as I had expected, and lifted the meat pie in one hand while he went on staring at the fairies. "I heard they're going to give magical gifts to the princess."

"Sure, that's why they were invited," I said, and crunched into my roll. Crumbs rained down on my shirt. "So tell me, if you could have any magical gift, what would it be?" I asked around a mouthful of sourdough.

"To talk to horses," he said promptly.

"Ooh, that's a good one," I approved. "Just horses?"

"Yeah." He finally tore his gaze away from the fairies to grin at me. "If I could talk to chickens, I couldn't eat them anymore."

Comments like that kept me going to the commoners' parties. The royalty could afford more elaborate food, but commoners often had better sense. Also, commoner girls are more likely to be willing to dance. Good food, good company, a spot of dancing—that's a good time in my book.

So far, this party had excellent food, good prospects for good company, and there might be dancing later...but it all depended on whether the evening was still continuing cheerfully by then. It's always hit or miss with royal christenings. I kept going to them, but sometimes I wondered why.

The farmer's son finally started eating his pie, and I went through the lamb (perfectly cooked), the grated carrots (a smidge too much pepper), most of the rolls and two apples by the time the royal herald appeared on the stairs at one end of the hall. They had an enormous staircase over there, which was clearly designed as a place for heralds to stand and blow trumpets. This herald came out onto the landing in his scarlet uniform and launched into a long run of fanfares. Nice volume on it, though I'd heard better trills.

The crowd murmured and exclaimed and shushed each other. A few unfortunates got caught out talking after everyone else was quiet, and eventually there was relative silence. The farmer's son, about to bite into a pastry, set it down untouched. I did my best to chew quietly.

The herald cleared his throat self-importantly, tugged once on his coat, and announced in a ringing voice, "Honored guests, friends and countrymen, ladies and gentlemen, I present their most excellent Royal Majesties, keepers of the royal welfare, defenders of the nation's peace, most honored and celebrated heirs of the mighty throne, sovereign lords of the sundrenched lands..."

And so on and so on. I stopped listening halfway through, and only remembered too late that I had meant to listen for their actual *names*, buried somewhere in the middle of the titles.

Kings and queens tend to run together for me, especially when their stories are similar. You know. He was kind, she was beautiful, they wanted a child for a long time and were distraught not to have one, and then lo and behold a daughter was born. I did remember the princess' name, or part of it. Her first name was Rosaline, and there may have been a Eunice somewhere in among her eleven others. They'd said all twelve names during the christening ceremony, before the banquet.

I tuned in my magical senses when the herald finally finished and the King and Queen came forward, Her Majesty carrying the princess wrapped in a silk blanket. I didn't care about their titles, but I was curious to see if I'd find anything unusual in their auras.

It's hard to explain what an aura looks like, considering it deals in senses you humans don't have. They don't exactly 'look' like anything; it's more a metaphorical impression, but visual images are the best way I've found to explain it.

So how'd their royal majesties look? He came across like a stalwart oak tree, one with a hollow trunk. That probably meant he'd be a decent king if circumstances never forced him to crack his strong appearance. The queen came through as a lily, decorative with no thorns. I couldn't get any real read on the princess; her character was still too young, unformed and nebulous.

Not *un*interesting readings, but not unusual either. Royal training tended to produce oak trees and lilies (though sometimes you see the genders reverse those qualities).

I glanced over at the farmer's son, magically speaking, and found him coming through as a wide green pasture, sunlit and straight-forward. He'd probably be good with horses.

I turned back to the royalty, easing off the magical focus to listen to the Queen's speech as she stepped forward to address the crowd. "Thank you all so much for coming," she said with a gracious smile. "We are deeply touched by your presence and your kind wishes for our beloved daughter. And we especially want to thank our dear friends..." She turned towards the table with all the sparkles and wings, and introduced each fairy to the crowd. I gave a mental shrug and went back to crunching another apple; I already knew the fairies' names.

Finally the Queen concluded, "And we are so honored that our fairy guests have offered to bestow their own special gifts upon our daughter."

At that, I sat up straighter and put down my apple core. I always pay attention to magical christening gifts, just to see if someone's become more creative since the last time. Next to me, the farmer's son was leaning forward, eyes wide and shining again.

Their Majesties descended to the foot of the stairs, where the last step formed a raised platform. A silk-swathed golden cradle was already in place, and the queen laid the princess in it as the fairies left their table to approach.

"How do you suppose they know what's best to give her?" the farmer's son asked in a whisper.

My lip curled in spite of myself. "Tradition, mostly." But maybe, just once, someone would do something different.

Asafoetida came fluttering up first, flapping lilac wings and shedding lavender sparkles everywhere. Someone was going to get stuck with a lot of sweeping up after this. Asafoetida stopped in front of the cradle, clasped her hands together, and saddled the poor kid with an "angelic disposition." Turmeric was next, showing more creativity in her blue and green sparkles, but none at all when she bestowed "beauty to charm the coldest heart." When Wintergreen decided "magnificent skill at dancing" was what a girl needed above all else, I gave up and turned to my pie in disgust.

The nobility never asked me to give a gift to their offspring. Though really that might be just as well. They probably wouldn't like what I'd come up with.

Saffron gave her gift fourth ("voice like a lark"—honest), and as she was backing away and as I was just getting to the really good crunchy bit of the pie crust, the whole event took a turn for the worse. Apart from the pie.

A sudden clap of thunder sounded through the hall and echoed off the walls, punctuated by an explosion of acid green sparks. I sighed in resignation as black smoke billowed up in the middle of the room. All the humans pushed back towards the walls with cries and exclamations, while the queen flung herself over the cradle and the four fairies clustered around her. The farmer's son nearly jumped out of his seat and I narrowly managed to grab hold of the edge of his plate to keep his pastry from falling underfoot.

When the smoke cleared, a tall woman with bat-like wings and serpent-like hair stood in the center of the room, facing the stairs, the fairies, and the princess. She sparkled in a black and purple way.

That was Echinacea. I had been half-expecting her, like you expect the last of your figs to turn up rotten just when you desperately need to make a pudding.

The shoving to back away redoubled at the sight of her, everyone shrieking and shouting and making hysterical demands for someone to do something, even though no one seemed to have a clear idea about what needed doing. I could have told them that there wasn't anything *to* do, but no one would have listened.

"Don't worry, she's not here for the onlookers," I told the farmer's son, whose eyes had gone wide with fright this time. "She'll want witnesses to tell the story."

He dragged his gaze to me, looking not in the least reassured. "How do you know?"

I hesitated. "I've…heard stories." I'd seen it happen. Many, many times.

Echinacea fixed the crowd with her gaze, eyes glittering and hard, and everyone fell suddenly silent. Could have been a spell, but I could see there was no magic at work. Just force of personality. "Someone," she said, voice rolling through the hall, "forgot to invite me."

That's how it always happened. Someone always ended up forgotten on the invite list. Someone besides me, I mean.

And the result? Curses, every time. Me, I say there's nothing like a curse to ruin a good party, but not everyone feels that way.

Confidentially, Echinacea had dropped a curse on Rosaline the moment she arrived, so the rest of us wouldn't have time to prevent it. I had felt the magical shudder run through the room at practically the same moment as the first billow of smoke. When Echinacea spread her arms, launched showers of purple sparks everywhere and intoned, "I shall have to enact payment for this slight," it was strictly for effect.

Rosaline was already cursed to prick her finger on a spinning wheel and drop down dead

This might have bothered me more if I'd had any expectation it would actually come to pass. Neither the pre-existence of the curse nor the unlikeliness of it taking effect stopped Echinacea from reciting a long, rambling poem on the subject. It had at least three seriously stretched rhymes, and I finished my last two slices of blueberry pie before she was done.

After announcing the particulars of her revenge, Echinacea stormed out with an exit as overdramatic as her entrance. Almost before the thunderclouds cleared, the last remaining fairy came prancing forward.

That development was even more expected, at least if you'd been to as many christenings as I had. I could barely stifle a groan. Good Fairies actually drew straws before christenings about who got to give their gift last. They all *loved* being the one who swept in to save the day after an Evil Fairy made an appearance.

The last fairy on this occasion, I am sorry to say, was Marjoram. I am even sorrier to say that I had known her for centuries, and sorriest of all to admit that she's my cousin. More or less. Fairies don't relate to each other in quite the same ways humans do.

"Do you think she'll save the princess?" the farmer's son asked, face scrunched with worry but eyes big with hope.

I stared at him, not surprised but still wondering. Why did commoners feel so reassured whenever they saw a woman with sparkles and little wings? It wasn't as if the Good Fairies ever did anything to help someone like them. "Yeah," I said finally. "I expect so."

I turned back to watch the drama around the cradle. The other fairies had clustered around Marjoram in an overpowering cloud of multicolored sparkles. She looked puffed up with importance, cast a shower of pink glitter over the princess, and announced, "By the powers of Good, Benevolence and Kindness, I have changed this curse so that it will not end in death. The princess will prick her finger on a spindle, but she will merely fall into an enchanted sleep, to be awakened someday by a kiss."

And that, of course, required absolutely no creativity at all.

The queen, who reached into the cradle to snatch up her daughter, didn't look much happier at this news. But the rest of the crowd started murmuring to each other, and while it wasn't a happy murmur anymore, it was a less frightened one.

The farmer's son leaned back on the bench and scratched at his hair. "So I suppose she'll sleep for a hundred years until a prince comes along and—"

"Did anyone say anything about a hundred years?" I snapped. I'd been hearing this for *so* long. After it was over and people stopped being terrified, they always remembered the same stories. "Or a prince?"

He blinked, clearly confused by my reaction. "Well, no. But I've heard stories too. Isn't it always a hundred years?"

I sighed, fiddled with my last roll. "Yeah. It always is." The roll didn't look all that appetizing anymore.

Up on the dais, Marj bestowed a few kind looks and a few air kisses, then popped out in a cloud of pink smoke and glitter. She left first and most dramatically, but the other fairies followed soon after.

I couldn't see much use in staying either. After this, there would be no dancing, no toasts to the princess' health, no cheerful conversations over a few more helpings of dessert. The party was sure to be ended early. I could already feel that the mood of the crowd, though reassured since Marj's appearance, was not celebratory anymore anyway. I took another look at the royals' auras—the queen was positively wilting, and if the king didn't do something about the cracks already forming in his metaphorical oak tree, the repercussions were going to be much worse than one ruined party.

That meant it was time for me to go. Before I did, I glanced at the farmer's son again. "You going to eat that pastry?"

He looked down at his plate like he'd forgotten about it. "Oh. No, I guess not…"

"Good. I'll buy it from you." I dug into the pocket of my trousers, and pulled out a handful of gold coins.

His eyes positively bugged out. "*What*? I can't—"

I held the coins up, and nodded towards the crowd. "See that man over there with the peacock feather in his hat? That's the Royal Horsemaster. Go buy yourself an apprenticeship." With my other hand, I held up a finger. "But there's one condition. You have to promise me, if they throw a party for the princess' 16th birthday, *don't go*. In fact, take a trip that week."

The farmer's son looked even more stunned now than he had been by the fairies in all their sparkly glory. "I...all right, but..."

"Good." I dropped the coins in his hand, picked up the pastry and headed for the door.

I knew exactly how this would play out, and it was going to ruin a lot of lives. Helping one person redressed the balance a little.

At least, I knew how this was *intended* to play out. Assuming no one interfered.

I could just walk away. I had walked away from similar situations often enough. And maybe I would have walked away this time too—if it hadn't been Marjoram. But no one aggravates me like Marj. And I wasn't going to sit around for the same old thing for one more time.

Pastry in hand, I walked out of the hall, saving my transporting for when I was out of sight. Not all of us are melodramatic.

We're all good at finding each other, if the one we're looking for doesn't try to hide. It was easy for me to orient on Marj, on the edge of my awareness like a sparkly itch. I probably shouldn't mention what her aura looked like to me; it's hard to find a polite metaphor. I focused on the itch, and popped after her.

I landed knee-deep in flowers in some meadow, which was exactly the sort of place she *would* decide to go. Marj was sitting on a rock, gossamer wings spread to the sunlight.

"Why is it," I demanded, kicking a few flowers as I clumped towards her, "that you can never tell anyone anything useful?"

She looked at me coolly through lowered eyelids. "Why, Tarragon, I have no idea what you're talking about."

"Cut the act, Marj," I said, sitting down at one end of the rock. "We've had this conversation before. The christening. Rosaline. Why do you never comment when they all start mentioning a hundred years?" I took a bite out of my pastry, sending up a puff of powdered sugar.

She drew up her knees and wrapped her arms around her ankles, demonstrating flexibility that probably defied physics. "It's tradition, Tarry; you know that. It's always a hundred years."

Tradition—an excuse for being irrational, on the grounds that we've always been irrational. "That tradition only started because you and your friends never manage to tell people that it doesn't *have* to be a hundred years."

She smiled at me, sweetly and patronizingly. "We both know the hundred year tradition is a *bit* more complicated than that. And besides, I didn't hear you mention other time options either."

I snorted. "As if they'd have believed me. Royalty always looks at me slantways and dismisses me completely." And how was it my responsibility to explain *her* spells?

"If you'd just magic up some wings and a little sparkle…" Marj raised one hand, fingertips glowing pink.

I slid back to the far end of the rock, spilling sugar from the remaining pastry. "No, thank you, it's against my deepest principles." Me, with sparkles. The very idea gave me shudders. Contrary to what may seem evident, sparkles are not an inherent part of a fairy's physical form. Sparkles are a choice, and I choose otherwise. "They'd have believed you if you told them the spell on the princess could be broken sooner."

Marj flicked her fingers, sending a shower of gold sparkles cascading down to hit the rock under her but miss me. "Oh, I suppose, except it sounds so…unimpressive to say that the princess will fall asleep and could wake up any old time. That wouldn't create a sensation at all."

The remarkable part is that Marj honestly didn't notice that was a shallow and selfish motivation.

"What I really cannot fathom," I grumbled, "is why you think you're helping them so much by putting the princess to sleep for a century. It's better than dying but it's not good news. Her parents will never see her awake again after she stabs herself on the spindle."

Marj smiled an elusive smile. The more elusive the smile, the more dangerous. "Perhaps."

Wonderful. It really was every bit as bad as I'd feared. I squinched my eyes shut, counted to three, took a deep breath and said, "Marj, I'm going to tell you this *one* more time. It is not *nice* to put an entire castle under a sleeping curse."

She sniffed. "As if you know anything about Goodness and Niceness. I am a certified Good Fairy, an official practitioner of White Magic. I know exactly what I'm doing."

"You and your Good Fairy clique..." I gritted my teeth, and against my best instincts tried yet again to explain what ought to be obvious. "It's all well and good being considerate of the princess, but none of you give any thought to anyone who isn't royalty. You're not being Good to those castle workers you're knocking out until a prince deigns to rides up."

She just gave a shrug. "Their duty is to serve their princess. They serve her by being there while she sleeps."

Which was just wildly missing the point. "They have *lives*, you know. Goals, and families, and...love affairs, even. You may not believe this, but it is possible to fall in love without crowns or enchantments."

She smiled again, her favorite self-assured smile that always made me want to smack her with something heavy. Possibly a hippogryph. She smiled that smile, and in the face of my perfectly valid, completely factual argument, she said, "Maybe."

Maybe. What is a person supposed to do with that? A sane man would probably throw his hands up and go looking for another party, but I have a bad streak of stubborn and I'd been listening to this nonsense for one too many centuries. And truthfully, if I hadn't expected things to go this way, there would have been no point in seeking Marj out to begin with. So instead of departing for happier scenes, I asked, "Would you be interested in a wager on that subject?"

She was.

Chapter Two

Let's jump on ahead sixteen years, less a few weeks. That's not long, when you live for centuries. Princess Rosaline's sixteenth birthday was fast approaching, and the results of her curse with it. Curses nearly always strike on sixteenth birthdays. Magical cosmic forces gather and the universe is in the right alignment and...well, it's nearly always on sixteenth birthdays.

Knowing that, I interrupted my usual round of parties to head back to Waldisan, to the castle of the fair Princess Rosaline (of course she was fair; it was one of her christening gifts), because I had a wager to win and a point to prove.

Marj and I were debating a simple question—whether commoners could have true love too. It sounds ridiculously obvious, right? But the stories were only ever about certain kinds of people, and Marj and her ilk refused to believe anyone else could matter. So we were betting on the subject, and I was bound and determined to *make* her see that an ordinary love affair could survive against magic and royalty and unearthly beauty and all that other nonsense Good Fairies traffic in.

I wandered the castle, looked over my prospects, and looked forward to my gloating rights.

As I wandered, I avoided the parts Marj and her friends liked, the royalty's portions. I wouldn't find the kind of people I needed there. Instead I strolled through the servants' area, in an unassuming guise as a castle servant of vague rank, watching for anyone who looked to be in love.

I considered the guardsman making cow eyes at one of the upstairs maids. Or the stable boy taking advantage of the shadowed corners of his realm. I might have chosen those, or a few others. I had options, but I didn't feel confident while reading any of their auras, and I like to rely on my gut—as long as I can be sure I'm not confusing hunger and instinct.

I walked on, and told myself not to worry. I'd been to parties at endless castles, and never yet seen one that didn't have at least few people in it who were in love.

I stepped out of the dim stable and into the fresh air of the courtyard, where a flock of kitchen girls were gathered in the sunshine. I drifted that way, hoping for new possibilities. Some of the girls had to be romantically involved with someone. Maybe even with the goatherd who was sitting on the stoop in their midst. I knew he was a goatherd because there was a baby goat sitting next to him, and also because I'm magical. Magic also told me his name was Jack, which made him eligible to figure as the hero in a lot of stories Marj would turn her nose up at. There *were* stories about non-royalty, but only a very specific kind of story, and not the true love kind.

I spotted an open edge of a sun-warmed step and claimed it before anyone's skirt could get in the way. Leaning back on my hands, I stretched out my legs and settled in to eavesdrop. No one in the group knew me but none of them noticed that, thanks to a minor spell. Not an invisibility spell, just a don't-take-much-notice-or-think-about-it spell. Keeps people from reacting to the pointed ears too, if my hair isn't enough to hide them, saving me all the bother of explanations.

As I picked up the thread of conversation, the head cook was relating the story of the princess' christening in thrilling tones. A woman clearly fond of her own cooking, she punctuated the narration with waves of one large hand. The story had grown more dramatic over the years. Echinacea was uglier, the smoke was darker, the general horror was greater, you know how it goes.

It was all so much how it usually went that I was genuinely taken aback when the cook followed the usual with, "There's some who say that it has to be a prince that wakes the sleeping princess or that it has to be true love's kiss to break the spell, but I was there, and all that fairy said was a kiss. Could be anyone." She punctuated the statement with a nod and a snap of a pea she was shelling.

No doubt Marj would have found it unsensational to explain that anyone, royal or not, fond of the princess or not, could wake her up any time. Why make life easier for anyone if you can make a sensation instead? I grimaced, and consoled myself with a handful of shelled peas stolen from the nearest bowl.

The goatherd tilted his head, eyes narrowing in thought. "If it's that simple, when the princess falls asleep can't they—"

A horrified female chorus went up, making me jump. "If, Jack, say *if*!"

"Don't ever say *when* she falls asleep," a blonde serving girl scolded him. "Do you want to bring bad luck on us?"

"Or the King's wrath, more likely, if it gets heard," another said darkly, and flung a few peas into the bowl on her lap with extra force.

I scratched behind one ear and wondered how badly the King's aural oak tree had cracked by now, and how much that was affecting his ruling and his country. I hadn't gone by to check. Who wants to see something like that? I shrugged, tossed a pea up in the air and caught it in my mouth. It's a talent.

"Leave Jack alone," another girl broke in on the hubbub, and an edge in her tone made me think I should pay attention to this one. I looked sideways at her and concentrated—Emmy; that was her name. "He's only been bringing his goats to the castle for a few months. You know people talk about the curse more here in the castle than anywhere else, and it's spoken of even less in other countries like Perrelda."

I nodded, satisfied with my own power of observation. I had thought Jack's inflections were different from everyone else's, although the difference between a Waldisane accent and a Perreldan one is slight.

"Is that why you're so curious, goat boy?" the blonde asked, nose in the air.

Jack straightened, putting his shoulders back. "Goatherd, I prefer, miss," he said with exaggerated politeness. "'Goat boy' makes me sound like a satyr, which I don't think is what you meant."

I grinned, and snagged another handful of peas. The goatherd had at least some nerve, and that meant some potential. And I didn't fail to notice that the blonde sniffed disdainfully, but Emmy smiled at him.

See, I *knew* I didn't need to worry. But I'll admit that both the peas and the new prospects were making my stomach feel better.

"All I was going to say was," Jack continued, "if it only takes a kiss, *if* she falls asleep, couldn't somebody just kiss her and wake her up again?" He stretched his legs out in front of him, scratched the baby goat's head with one hand and reached the other hand into Emmy's wooden bowl. She slapped his hand before he could get any peas, and he grinned and withdrew it again.

"The princess can't wake up for a hundred years," another girl said. "She's supposed to sleep for a century." Right on cue for that idea. I suppressed a sigh and reached for more peas. Thanks to my spell, nobody stopped me.

"The fairy didn't say anything about a hundred years, either," the cook put in, which was so unexpectedly reasonable of her that I turned my head to look at her in surprise. A pea I had tossed in the air hit me on the nose, giving me a new reason to be glad no one was noticing me right now.

"Well, maybe someone kissing her would work then," Jack persisted. "Why wouldn't it?"

"Jack, you're too practical to deal with fairy curses," Emmy said with a half-laugh. "They're never solved by practical solutions. Besides, there must be more to it, or why would their majesties be so worried?"

In theory, a practical royal had to exist—but I hadn't met many.

"She's not going to fall asleep anyway," the cook said, jaw set. "Their majesties have banned spinning wheels and burned every spindle that was in the kingdom. So that's that." She broke another peapod with a sharp snap.

"That must have been an amazing bonfire," Jack offered. "All the spindles, I mean."

I remembered that—I hadn't attended, but I'd heard about it. I hadn't attended because I'd been certain this wouldn't be a fun, dance around and roast something to eat, kind of bonfire. Those were the only kinds I went to.

"It was enormous," Emmy said, voice going soft. "I was just three but I remember it...maybe because I couldn't understand why my mother was sad, when it all seemed so exciting to me. But my family worked in cloth, the spinning, weaving, dying, all of it. That all ended when the spinning wheels were burned."

Exactly why that bonfire was not going to be a fun time. Also, as I said, royalty: not practical.

"They couldn't spin, but couldn't they do the rest?" Jack asked.

She shook her head. "It all starts with thread. The best way is to spin it yourself, or buy it from nearby. With no one in the entire country able to spin, the price of thread from across the borders rose to the skies. My parents lost their cloth business and could only work in the laundry in the last few years before they died, and today everyone in Waldisan buys their cloth from Perrelda." She sighed, then half-smiled. "But at least I have a job not likely to be interrupted by a curse. My mother wanted me to learn cooking because she thought people would always need to eat."

A wise woman. I would have liked to meet her.

I didn't especially want to meet Jack's baby goat, but the goat decided right about then that she wanted to meet me. Take-no-notice spells don't always work on animals. "Shoo," I told the kid, as she came nosing over towards me.

She bleated at me. If she made enough fuss, someone was going to start paying attention to the disturbance, and then to me too despite the spell. I hastily shoved a snap pea at her. She shook her tiny horns, but fell to nibbling the vegetable.

By the time I paid attention to the conversation again, they were back to the princess and her curse.

"It's like a story, isn't it?" Jack remarked. "An old legend, maybe."

"You wish we were in a story, don't you, lad?" the cook said with a wink. "In stories, the goatherd always turns out to be a prince in disguise, breaks the spell and marries the princess in the end."

Yeah, the stories could never just be about an *actual* goatherd.

"Maybe I don't want to marry the princess." Theoretically he was saying that to the cook, but he was looking at Emmy.

I focused carefully; it was faint, but she was blushing. He'd been coming here for a few months—I wondered how long they'd been dancing around each other. My bet was all of those few months. And I was feeling more and more confident about my bet with Marj too.

"You have your stories wrong anyway," Emmy said, brisk tones at odds with her blush. "Jacks don't turn out to be princes. Jacks are always clever knaves who win their way in the world by their wits."

Now that was nice, she'd been reading those stories Marj wouldn't like. Jack, on the other hand, frowned at the comment. I looked closer, magically speaking. I'd already picked up some general aural impressions, but now I made more of an effort to puzzle out what picture I was getting from the goatherd.

The best I can describe Jack's aura would be as a sailing ship. Mixed metaphor for someone who clearly wasn't a sailor, but that was the impression. Specifically, a big grand sailing ship, one with its sails set slightly awry. Unless I was mistaken, that comment about Jacks being clever had set a few more sails flapping untidily.

So—good potential, not a lot of confidence. Compared to plenty of arrogant princes I had met, this didn't seem like too big a failing.

Especially since he at least had enough confidence to smooth out the frown and follow-up with a casual tone and the question, "Do Jacks marry princesses often?"

Emmy's eyes flicked to him, and then back to her vegetables. "Sometimes. Sometimes they marry commoners."

He pressed the point. "Kitchen maids, for instance?"

Her lips curved into a smile. "Sometimes."

Oh, I liked these two.

I clasped my hands around one knee, leaning forward to focus in on Emmy's aura. Cloth was an obvious metaphor, but it fit her. Maybe a banner, one flexible enough to twist in the wind, but dependable and hard to tear apart too.

I didn't have a multitude of solid evidence, but the auras looked promising and my gut had a good feeling. And I'd eaten enough to feel sure I wasn't getting mixed signals.

I swallowed my last handful of peas and slipped away from the group into a shadow, where I shifted my take-no-notice spell into a full invisibility one. Made me inaudible too, to avoid the disembodied voice issue. Then I conjured up Marj.

She wasn't happy about coming. She was invisible to everyone but me, but still popped in with extra sparkle. She hovered a foot off the ground, little wings flapping madly—a meaningless gesture, considering they weren't actually holding her up. She had her hands on her hips, and stared at me through narrowed eyes. "What do you want, Tarry? I was stringing flowers into garlands with the girls."

Would *you* want to put your fate into the hands of someone who considers that activity the height of recreation? "We made a wager, remember? Time we followed up on it."

"About Princess Rosaline, you mean?" She folded her arms and backed off on the glare. "Naturally I remember. The time has gone by so quickly." She glanced around the courtyard, evidently taking it in fully for the first time. Her nose wrinkled in disapproval. "Why are we here? This is the *common* part of the castle."

I swear, that woman could set my teeth on edge faster than anyone I'd ever known. "Yes, Marj, it's the common part. Where else would I go to look for commoners to win our bet with?"

"But it's so...*very* common." She glanced down, and her sparkles began vanishing an inch before they hit the packed-earth floor. That would save someone a lot of sweeping later.

"It's extremely common," I agreed, because it wasn't like I could argue the point. "So's that goatherd over there. He's very common, and he's the one I've picked."

"A goatherd," she said, sounding as though she'd never heard of the concept before. "Really."

I bit back a retort and just said, "Mm-hmm. He's in love with that kitchen maid he's sitting next to."

Marj shook her head doubtfully, and ruffled her wings. "You really think that they're Truly in Love? And you're sure he's not a prince in disguise, or possessed of a magic talisman?"

I indulged in an eye roll. "Yes, I do think they're in love, and of course he isn't, you can see that for yourself."

Princes just ooze princeliness, even when they're in disguise. And barring a strong concealment spell, one magical being is always alert to someone else's magic. That pretty much ruled out the talisman theory.

"He is rather good-looking, I suppose," Marj said after a moment's furrowed-brow study. "And she's pretty enough."

Sure, Jack was good-looking, in a brown-eyed, sandy-haired sort of way, and Emmy had striking black hair. I thought it was more significant that he seemed like a pleasant fellow, and that she had some snap to her blue eyes. "Marj, where did you get the idea that only beautiful people can fall in love?" I asked through gritted teeth. There it was again—the stories were only about a certain kind of person. Even though you could look around and see that love was so much broader and complex and not reserved for just the chosen few.

Marj ignored the question, nodding to herself and remarking, "Yes, I suppose this will do. If you're sure." She clapped her hands together, setting off a spray of gold sparkles. "Then we're ready for when the curse befalls the princess. You remember the stakes of our wager?"

I sighed loudly. She didn't need to treat me like an idiot. "Of course I remember. When you lose, you have to lift the sleeping curse you're planning to hit this castle's inhabitants with." The curse that, among other things, was highly likely to trap Jack and Emmy on opposite sides of some serious magical barriers.

"*If* I lose, I agree that only the princess will remain asleep." She smiled sweetly, which almost disguised the glint in her eye. "But if your goatherd fails you and *I* win, you agreed to swear allegiance to the Good Fairies, Tarragon."

I had remembered that with perfect clarity, but it was still wince-inducing to hear it out loud. It's possible I'd been a bit rash when I agreed to these stakes. Marj had really, *really* irritated me that day. I was confident of winning—but if I didn't... I had been dodging swearing allegiance to the Good or the Evil Fairies for centuries.

I always thought both groups had far more in common than either one would admit. The Evil Fairies actively enjoyed wreaking havoc. The Good Fairies preached about helping people, but in practice tended to be oblivious, ineffective, and cause far more damage than they admitted to.

If I did join Marj's precious Good Fairies, I'd have to do things like meet a yearly quota of Good Deeds Performed for the Less Fortunate (with strict definitions of 'good deeds' and 'the less fortunate') and adopt entire family lines as godchildren and follow a whole lot of absurdly restrictive rules about appropriate interactions with humans (even more than the Rules the Fairy King and Queen already set down). It wasn't a simple matter of joining a club—it was swearing allegiance to an entire lifestyle and accepting a mountain of responsibilities and restrictions in the process.

Not to mention that I'd have to attend all of the Good Fairies' meetings. Weekly meetings. With Marj, and a dozen others just like her. The thought was enough to put me off food for a week.

"Even if I lose," I said, repressing a shudder, "I draw the line at sparkles."

The gleam in Marj's eyes was growing brighter and so were her sparkles. "I've always thought a little extra glimmer would do wonders for you. Maybe in shades of blue and purple—"

Not going to happen. "Oh look!" I said, casting a desperate glance around the courtyard for a distraction. I would have remarked on the beautiful packed earth floor if I had to, but thankfully, a better distraction was arriving. "It's your princess!"

A small procession was entering the courtyard. The fair Princess Rosaline wandered in with a few ladies-in-waiting and a few guards, apparently taking a shortcut through the less elegant part of the castle.

Everyone else in the area scrambled to get to their feet. Jack and Emmy, busy looking at each other, were behind the rest.

The princess had hair like spun gold reaching long and loose past her hips, pale skin, a perfectly symmetrical face and eyes the color of a summer sky. She was very beautiful, if you like that sort of thing. I didn't see how her looks could really be counted to her as virtue, though. I heard Turmeric magic them up at her christening.

"Your goatherd is staring at the princess," Marjoram pointed out, elbowing me at the same time.

It was true Jack was, but I refused to act bothered. Or to rub my side; Marj had a sharp elbow. "So? Everyone's staring at her." That was true too.

"Do you suppose he'd fall at her feet if she looked at him?"

I wasn't worried, thank you very much. Not worried at all. "Let's find out." Still invisible, I walked through the crowd, Marj drifting along behind me, until I reached the baby goat. She was sitting on the ground next to Jack, making it easy for me to lean over and suggest to her that now would be the best possible time to make a bid for attention.

The baby goat pawed at Jack's ankle and bleated, managing an impressively high volume for someone so small.

Jack turned crimson, and the ship in his aura hit suddenly rough seas. "Not *now*, Little One," he hissed. "Be quiet."

The kid ignored that direction entirely, and stubbornly butted her head against his leg, baaing all the louder. He picked her up, trying to quiet her, but she just stuck her head up above his restraining hands and bleated even more.

Marj murmured, "*So* uncouth."

I ignored her, watching heads turn in Jack's direction, while Emmy turned pink with repressed laughter. And as I had intended, the Princess noticed the commotion as well.

"Oh, what a darling lamb!" That spell about a lark's voice, 'musical with silvery, dulcet tones' was working fine. It was like listening to a flute talking, and about as easy to take seriously. "How old is he?" she asked, approaching Jack.

"She's a baby goat, actually," Jack corrected, blinked, looked suddenly mortified that he'd corrected her, and hastily added, "Your Highness. She's just a few weeks old."

"Does she have no mother?"

"Her mother died birthing her, so I'll keep her with me until she gets older," Jack explained, with a few fumbles, tacking on, "Your Highness," somewhat belatedly again. I tried to be reassured that he was at least still coherent and standing.

"Oh how *sad*!" That spell about an angelic disposition was apparently working too. "That's ever so nice of you to take care of her," Rosaline said, face glowing with approval.

Jack turned redder. "Oh, it's just...um..."

His job. It's just his job. That's clearly what he was trying to say.

"...thank you, Your Highness," was all he actually managed. At least he didn't fall over.

To distract myself from the anxious prickle running up my spine, I focused in on Rosaline, trying to read her aura. It was both obvious and inconclusive. Her aura gave an immediate impression as a big bouquet of flowers—except every flower had a signature of one of the fairies from her christening. The cluster of them all completely obscured whoever Rosaline was behind all those magical gifts.

The princess reached out to pat the Little One's head. "What is her name?"

Jack swallowed and managed a complete sentence. "She's just the Little One, Your Highness. We'll give her a better name when she gets bigger. Something more creative than the Big One."

So it wasn't the best joke, but points for trying. Emmy smiled.

"That would be a very silly name," Marj remarked to me, and I didn't bother trying to explain the comic intent. Though I did wonder how a woman who floated around in a cloud of sparkles could use the word 'silly' to describe anything else.

The princess just nodded gravely, and agreed, "No, that wouldn't be a good name. What about Fluffy or Cotton?" Her brow wrinkled in thought, which in no way detracted from her beauty. "Those would be better for sheep, wouldn't they? Perhaps Bess or Jane then. Those are nice names too." She extended the hand she'd used to pat the goat towards her nearest attendant, who promptly wiped it off with a handkerchief.

Seemed to me that a girl with twelve names herself ought to be able to come up with more creative names than those. Just a thought.

"I'll keep those in mind, Your Highness, thank you," was all Jack said out loud. Talking to the princess was not doing anything for the flapping sails in his aural ship.

With that, Princess Rosaline swept on and out of the courtyard. Jack watched her go, until she disappeared through a stone arch at the far side. "She's beautiful," he said, scratching the Little One's head without looking away from the emptied arch.

"Yes," Emmy said. She wasn't smiling anymore, and to be honest, neither was I.

"Is she as nice as she seems?" Jack asked.

"Of course," Emmy said, voice flat and aural banner gone limp. "The fairies know what they're doing when they make someone good and kind and charming."

"So we do," Marj said with a smug smirk, and asked me, "Still feeling as confident about our wager?"

With a worried twinge in my stomach, I had to admit I wasn't precisely as confident as I'd been before the princess walked onto the scene. To myself, I had to admit that. I didn't have to admit anything to Marj. I kept my back straight and voice firm, and just said, "I have faith in him."

"If you say so," she trilled. "And when you join the Good Fairies, I promise to be by your side every step of the way to help you learn the duties." Before I had time to do more than gag, she popped out in a shower of gold sparkles and little red hearts that I was positive she aimed at me deliberately.

I brushed hearts and sparkles out of my hair and sat down on the stoop next to Jack, who was sitting again with the Little One in his lap. Still invisible, I reached out to rub between the Little One's tiny nubs of horns.

"So what do you think?" I asked her. "Can I rely on your buddy Jack here?"

She bleated a noncommittal bleat.

"That's just how I feel."

Chapter Three

Three days after I chose Jack and Emmy for my wager, I sat on a windowsill in the very top of the highest tower in the castle, and watched Rosaline prick her finger on the point of a spinning wheel.

The princess lifted her hand from the spindle, a single drop of crimson blood on the tip of her index finger. She swayed, her eyes slid shut, and down she fell. She managed to land in an attractive position.

Echinacea had orchestrated the spindle in the appropriate place at the appropriate time, and the curse guaranteed that Rosaline would find it and touch it—so the devastation of the Waldisane cloth industry had all been for naught. The spell also guaranteed that I couldn't accomplish anything if I tried to interfere. So I only watched as fate took its course, as the flowers in Rosaline's aura curled up tightly, as the princess descended into a deep, deep sleep. I had wanted to see for myself, just to make sure it all went according to pattern. But now that it had happened, I kind of wished I hadn't come. Fate can be a grim business.

Rosaline's eyes had scarcely closed before Marj popped in, in a burst of gold sparkles that sprayed all over the room. She looked down at the princess and clasped her hands together. "*Oh*, it's happened!"

She needn't sound so delighted. I restrained myself to just saying, "Obviously."

"Now, we can't leave her here, of course—"

"We can't?" I said, brushing sparkles off my clothes.

Marj looked scandalized, eyes widening and sparkles taking on a positively offensive shade of pink. "Of course not! She has to look properly beautiful when the prince comes!"

"Oh." I scratched behind the point of one ear. "Right. Him."

And Marj went to work. She levitated Rosaline into the next room, where she conjured up a four-poster bed with silk sheets and velvet curtains. She arranged Rosaline on the satin quilt, and then really hit her stride with the details. Flowers. Extra pillows. Embroidery all over everything. Ribbons wherever there wasn't embroidery.

"You're shedding sparkles everywhere," I observed, trying not to step in them.

"They'll add an extra glow."

As if that was a positive. "Wouldn't it be easier to just put her in her bedroom?" I asked. "Where there was already a bed?" And save us both a lot of wasted time. Watching Marj decorate was not my idea of a good time.

"Don't be ridiculous, Tarragon, sleeping princesses must *always* be in the highest tower. This is How Things Are Done," Marj said primly, and added a pattern of bluebirds to the nearest pillow.

Right. How ridiculous of me. I consoled myself with the thought that really this was just a matter of picking my battles. So Marj overdid the decorations—but I had a more important fight to wage.

When Marj was finally satisfied with Rosaline's placement, she set off through the rest of the castle, intent on rendering everyone else just as unconscious as the princess. I followed after as she flew invisibly down the hall. The first people we came to were a pair of maids.

"Can't you walk faster?" the one in the lead asked her companion, balancing a loaded tea tray. "We're already late!"

And in another moment it was going to be too late to turn back. "You could just not do this," I told Marj. "Save yourself the embarrassment of losing, just refrain from putting anyone to sleep at all."

"You're being overconfident," Marj said, waved her wand and sent a spray of sparkles into the face of the slower-moving maid.

I wasn't being overconfident. I was just trying one last effort to avert the war through diplomacy. I hadn't really expected it to work.

"Sorry, I'm…coming," the second maid said, voice going vague halfway through the sentence. She slowed and stopped, a confused expression on her face.

"I *said*, hurry up!" the first girl snapped. "We need to…" She trailed off as Marj hit her with a splash of sparkles too.

Both girls yawned in near unison, legs folding as they slumped to the floor. Marj was already flitting off down the hall, so I cast a quick spell to keep the tea things locked into place on the tilting trays. The girls leaned against each other, sitting in the middle of the floor, eyes sliding closed and one girl hugging a teapot with one arm. I looked down at them and sighed—then stole a couple cinnamon cookies off the tray.

I bit into the first cookie as I turned to follow Marj again. I was just in time to see a guard come around a corner a ways down the hall, walking almost directly into Marj. He couldn't see her or me through our invisibility spells, but he did notice the sleeping maids. He got as far as, "Hey, what are you—" before Marj sent a wash of sparkles over him. He yawned, took two more steps towards the maids, and then fell right asleep standing up. He tilted sideways and luckily bumped against the wall before he could tip very far. He stayed there, leaning against the wood paneling, and began to snore.

I shook my head, and turned the corner to glide after Marj. I never flit; at my most expansive, I glide. I watched her hurl sparkles for three more hallways and several rooms. The whole thing made my skin crawl, and occasionally catching a slumping girl or rescuing falling items wasn't helping much.

"I feel like I'm watching you commit murder," I muttered, as she reached the large double doors leading to the throne room. Lots of people in there, and I didn't think I could handle watching that whole crowd slump over. Since I'd given up trying to argue her out of this, there wasn't much point in staying any longer. "I'm going to go find Jack."

"Well, if you really want to persist with this…"

"Yes, I *really* do." I had a point to prove to Marj, and proving her wrong would make up for a lot of years of arguments where I'd never been able to get through to her. And sure, I wanted to help all those sleeping maids and guards and even the aristocrats in the grand hall too.

Not that I was getting invested in them, or anything. Because I didn't do that, getting attached to people. I hadn't done that, not for five centuries.

None of that was anything I wanted to say to Marj. So I popped out.

I popped in again in the middle of a herd of goats.

I backed quickly away from a pair of horns, and fell backwards right over a second goat. I bounced back to my feet, automatically looking around to make sure no one had seen that. No one had, twice-over; I was invisible and no one was looking anyway. I was out in a meadow empty of anyone but the crowd of goats and Jack, asleep under a spreading tree nearby.

The goat I had fallen over bleated at me indignantly. "Oh, *maa* yourself, I didn't mean to fall over you," I said, climbing out of the sea of animals and brushing hair and grass off my clothes. Couldn't do much about the smell, unless I wanted to take the time for some magic, and I was too antsy to get on with things to bother with that.

The goats settled sulkily back into cropping the grass, and I walked over to Jack. He was sleeping on his back, the Little One curled up on his chest. I looked at him slantwise and confirmed that there had been no magic or sparkles involved in his sleep.

I kind of hated to wake him up. He was about to have a very bad day and I was about to seriously interfere with his love life. But at least I'd be raising his chances of a happy ending to higher than their current state of zero.

I glanced over my clothes, dark trousers and a loose brown shirt, the sort that would fit in with any not too well-to-do crowd of people. I conjured up a cloak to drape over it all, magicked up a beard, added a crooked staff for good measure, and decided that I looked enough like a shepherd to belong out in the fields.

I poked Jack in the ribs with the end of my staff, and said a cheerful, "Hello there."

Jack groaned and opened his eyes. "Hello." He looked up at me, eyes narrowing again but this time in suspicion. "Sorry, have we met?"

"No," I said, and leaned on my staff. "I'm a shepherd who's new to the area."

"If you're a shepherd," he said, moving the Little One off his chest and reaching for his staff beside him, "why don't you have any sheep?"

Sheep. Right. A slight flaw in my disguise. I had a lot on my mind, all right? "I'm between herds," I invented. "I've been planning to acquire one."

"Right," Jack said. And the next thing I knew, his staff was hooked around my ankle, and with a sharp tug I went sprawling every which direction.

It required all my willpower not to lash out instinctively with a spell, with the result that I was paying scant attention to my physical surroundings and knew only that the world was tumbling. When the land and the sky settled into their proper places again, I was flat on my back and Jack was standing over me, the end of his staff pressed firmly against my throat.

"You can 'acquire' a herd somewhere else," he said, expression hard. "Not here."

And I'd always liked to believe that I had a trustworthy face. Maybe the beard had been a bad idea. "No, no, that's not at all—you have completely misconstrued what I meant," I protested. Then I wondered if a goatherd would even know the word 'misconstrue.'

Apparently he did. "Maybe I misunderstood, maybe I didn't, but either way I'm sure *you* can understand why I'm not taking any chances."

"Yes, I completely and wholeheartedly understand," I said. I also appreciated that he had enough confidence to fight a potential threat—except that quality was useless to me if I couldn't get him off of this track and heading the direction I needed to win my wager. I raised my right hand. "I solemnly swear I am not interested in stealing your goats."

This was possibly a meaningless gesture, since my left hand wasn't on anything, but he accepted it anyway. He removed his staff, although his eyes were still suspicious.

I gingerly rose to my feet, rubbing my throat more for show than otherwise. I focused up my magical senses to check on his aura, see if I could get any insights on how to nudge him down the right path. All I gathered was that fighting potential goat-stealers apparently was good for his confidence, since that ship in his aura seemed intent on sailing right over me.

"Exciting country here," I said finally, with a cough. "Between you and your quick staff work and all that magic run amok back at the castle…"

"What magic?" he asked with gratifying speed.

At least we were onto the right topic. "Rumor has it that the princess pricked her finger. So they think."

"They *think*?" Jack said, eyebrows rising. "Doesn't anyone know? Didn't someone find her stretched across a spinning wheel?"

I would have liked to tell him he should immediately go off and find out, but I doubted he would take advice from me. Better to play this more subtly, give him enough information to make him want to go himself. "Well, if someone did, they can't tell anyone, can they?" I said, hooking my thumbs through my belt with a show of nonchalance. "Because of the thorns that have grown up all around the castle, so nobody can get in or out."

The thorns hadn't been up yet when I left, but I knew how Marj operated. Most people assume it's the evil fairies who put thorns up around the sleeping lovelies, but usually it's Marj and her friends who do it. Fairy Queen help us if any crass commoners bother the princess before the prince comes riding up.

"*What* thorns?" Jack demanded, and I was pleased to see his knuckles whiten where he gripped his staff. "And what do you mean…no one can get in or out? Did the curse hit everyone?"

I held onto my disinterested shepherd pose, and just shrugged. "It looks that way. Only nobody really knows, of course, because of the thorns."

"Right. Sure." Jack's gaze darted away from me, towards the castle that was out of sight beyond the hills, over to his goats, and back in the castle's direction. "I have to go to the castle. I have to—I have to go find—I just have to go." He scooped up the Little One.

Half the sails on the ship in his aura had gone slack when he heard of the trapped state of the castle's occupants, but now they were beginning to rally again. Still not a perfect set, but I liked the look of purpose. I would have liked it even better if I had been sure about what (or who?) he intended to go find. I pushed down thoughts of the far too many rules, responsibilities and sparkle-filled meetings that could be in my future, and told myself that *obviously* the word he hadn't quite said after 'find' was 'Emmy.'

With the Little One under one arm, Jack tried to herd his goats together. They didn't want to move in the morning, and they let that fact be known. They had thought they were settled in for the rest of the day to eat lots of tasty grass and did not take kindly to the altered plans. "Come on, get together. Hepzibah, don't bite Rafael! I don't care if you're upset about moving, we have to go to the castle."

"Interesting names for goats," I said.

"I have a creative cousin." I don't think Jack was paying attention to me. I don't think he was thinking either. I think he was just reacting. And that was fine. Rushing off to rescue his lady love was exactly what the situation called for. I folded my arms and thought with some smugness how good it would be to prove Marj wrong.

Jack finished getting all his goats in line, more or less, and struck off in the direction of the castle. I waited until they were out of sight, then turned invisible to catch up to him. I could have transported to the castle and waited for him there, but I wasn't taking chances on any interference stopping him en route.

It was a couple miles walk before the castle came into sight, but once it did, it was obvious even from a distance that the silhouette was wrong. The highest tower looked the same as ever, but it was sticking up out of a mass that was too shapeless to be roofs and stone walls. As we got closer, it resolved into the expected barrier of thorns. Jack plunged grimly on, finally coming to a halt a few dozen yards from the edge of the brambles, to stare at the endless array of spikes. The goats settled in and started eating the lawn. Jack eyed the thorns, and I took up my invisible position next to him to eye them too.

It had been a long time since I got near one of these gardens gone mad that Marj and her friends liked to fling about. They weren't merely thorns. Marj would never dream of magicking up something that ugly and unpleasant, so she'd made enchanted roses. Of course. Roses swarmed all over the outer wall of the castle and spread at least three hundred feet into the fields in a tangled mass that reached far above our heads. The blossoms were a vivid red and failed entirely to hide the sharp points of the hand-length thorns. I stared at those thorns and it all felt about as far from a party as a person could get. A breeze rustled the roses and my shoulders twitched too.

Jack and I weren't the only ones looking the overgrown hedge over. The castle was set in a parkland slightly apart from the nearest town, but close enough for everyone to quickly realize that something strange had happened. A crowd had gathered already, with more people streaming down the road this way.

"Have a relative inside?" a nearby voice asked, making Jack and me both jump. The voice belonged to a tall man with a sympathetic crinkle around his eyes and a dusting of flour on his shirt.

"No," Jack said, shaking his head. "I have…a friend inside. You?"

I really hoped he was just being discreet with that friend reference.

The baker's gaze was fixed on the wall of thorns. "My youngest son. He's a footman. Seemed like such a good opportunity…" His voice trailed away, and when he picked up again it was with a determined cheerfulness, all at odds with the worry blazing in front of my magical senses. "Of course, I told his mother there's no need to be alarmed. Said I'd come up here and see what was happening, just to set her mind at ease. Naturally someone will work out a way past all this mess. I mean, it's only thorn bushes."

"Right," Jack said, with a failing attempt to sound convinced, "just a matter of time."

That was true enough, except the time in question would be a century, if Marj had her way about it. That wasn't long for fairies, but for humans, it might as well be forever. I edged a step away from the baker, his worry pushing at me like a tangible force.

I could feel when the worry suddenly brightened a little, and I followed the baker's gaze to the cause of this new hope. A man with the build of a blacksmith was marching up to the wall of thorns, ax over one shoulder.

"Everyone stop troubling yourselves," the maybe-blacksmith called to the people gathered around, "all this needs is a good strong arm and some determination. They're just roses."

"They're *magic* roses," I heard Jack murmur, which was a very sensible comment.

The blacksmith swung his ax down and struck at a ropy branch of thorns. The wood split beneath the ax's sharp edge, one limb cracking free and falling at the blacksmith's feet. A ragged cheer went up from the onlookers, and I winced. I didn't manage to tone down my magic senses in time to avoid feeling the wave of disappointment that rippled through the crowd as the severed limb shivered and grew out a new branch, just as strong and thick as the original one.

The blacksmith gritted his teeth and hacked away at a second, a third and a fourth branch, but every single one grew back too fast for him to make any progress.

I was glad when Jack started walking along the perimeter of the thorns, goats trailing behind him. I hurried on after Jack, away from the struggling blacksmith and the worried baker.

Not that it was any better anywhere else around the castle. I nearly offered a crying woman a handkerchief before I remembered I was still invisible. I took advantage of the invisibility to trip one man, right after he told his companion, "The lack of response inside to any calls clearly indicates the curse has affected the entire castle, which is really a quite intriguing development in how the spell took effect." It was his tone of scholarly interest that bothered me, making him sound so devoid of any sympathy at all.

The worst one, though, was a little girl holding the hand of a man only a few years older than Jack. She looked up at her father with a glow of hope on her face and said, "Maybe a Good Fairy will come to rescue Mama and everyone else from the castle. That's what Good Fairies do, right?"

I stopped short to stare at her, stomach roiling. I remembered now, why I never came back after a christening went bad.

Jack had been gazing at the thorns as he walked, but he stopped now too, looking at the little girl with a tightness around his eyes. We both walked quickly away from there.

No Good Fairy was coming. The Good Fairy had already been, but she wasn't here now. Marj never stayed to see the reaction to her spells. There was only me, and what I could do was much more limited than casting a shower of sparkles over the castle and solving everything for everyone. It had better be enough.

I tried to shake off the worry eating at me, reminding myself that after all, I wasn't responsible for this situation, and I didn't believe in caring too much about anything anyway. It only sort of worked. "I hope you were the right choice," I told Jack, who couldn't hear me, and then I started casting a few discreet spells to facilitate my plan.

With a little magic here and there, pretty soon everyone but Jack had wandered out of the vicinity of the northeast corner of the castle. I cast one more spell to keep the area secluded, and then lifted my own invisibility.

"You're only going to get yourself poked that way," I remarked.

Jack, trying to pull a length of branch aside, didn't look up immediately. "I'm fine." Then he did look up, and jumped back so that he poked himself after all. "You're—wait, you're—very small."

I'd magicked myself down to a foot tall. People don't take you seriously as a magical being unless you look the part, and I'd much rather shrink than go for gossamer wings. Or sparkles. The pointed ears are worth something towards presenting a magical appearance, but not much. I'd also dismissed my beard and cloak, so hopefully he wouldn't recognize the 'shepherd' from the fields. Maybe my trustworthy face would do better here.

I raised an eyebrow at him. "You take magical roses calmly, but you're bothered by a man a foot tall?"

Probably my sudden appearance was as disconcerting as my size. In Waldisan and Perrelda both, people expected a certain amount of magic drifting around. Not as much as in Beaumont to the north, where magic was always more dramatic, but they did expect the occasional fairy floating through royal courts, every village had at least a passable herbwife, the coastal towns had periodic problems with serpents, and every decent-sized city was sure to house a magician or two.

"It's not the same." Jack shook his head, straightened up a little. "So…you're magical. Are you good or evil?"

"Good," I said promptly.

"Which is also what you'd tell me if you were evil," Jack pointed out, shrewdly if not very helpfully towards my goal of establishing trust.

"Well, yes, but I'm not evil. More importantly," I said, attempting to hurry on past that subject, "I'm here to help you get through those thorns."

His eyebrows didn't rise from their suspicious angle. "All right…maybe. What do you want in return?"

A fair question, considering how many traditions existed around that subject. If I joined the Good Fairies, I could think of at least six officially designated situations that would require me to ask for payment by firstborn child before I could interfere.

Fortunately, I was under no such obligation yet. Hopefully not ever. I crossed my arms and tried to smile in a trustworthy manner. "No charge at all. I'm just helping out of the goodness of my heart."

Jack stared at me for a long moment, doubt and hope warring on his face. Then he shook his head and turned back to the roses. "No, thanks."

My smile and arms dropped. *"What?"* How badly had I misjudged this? I had worried that I might have chosen a champion who would ultimately fail, but I had expected him to *try*. "Don't you even want to get in the castle?" I demanded.

"Of course I *want* to get in," Jack snapped, shoulders tight as he glared at the thorns. "But everyone knows that you can't get magical help for free. So whatever you're offering has to be a trick. I'll have to find another way."

I exhaled a careful breath. This was better than if he just didn't care, but not much. Especially since there was no other way in. And if he didn't get in, I'd have to forfeit to Marj. Time for a new strategy. "All right, you're right. I do want payment. After this is all over, you can pay me with a pound of—"

"Flesh?" he interrupted, eyes widening.

"No, *cheese!*" I protested, jabbing a finger towards the cluster of goats. "Goat cheese." What kind of stories had he been hearing? I'd had no idea the reputation of magical beings was quite this bad. "What would I do with a pound of flesh?"

"I don't know!" He frowned at me, looked at his goats. "Why do you want a pound of cheese?"

"I like cheese. Now do we have an agreement?"

He was still frowning, staring up at the high wall of thorns again. "Why do you want to help me?" he asked, voice small. "I'm just a goatherd."

"Yes, that's why. So—agreement?" There wasn't any time limit on how quickly I had to get him in there, but if he didn't agree soon my nerves were going to fray all to pieces.

I focused in on his aura again, saw that quite a lot of the sails in that ship were hanging slack with ropes twisted. But slowly a few adjusted, set a bit better, and slowly his shoulders straightened, and finally he said, "All right. I agree. I don't trust you, but I agree."

Fairy Queen be praised, we were back in business. I let out a long breath I hadn't noticed holding and said, "You won't regret this, I promise!"

I don't think he believed me, but he said, "So now what? Do you give me a magic sword?"

I blinked. "A what?"

"A magic sword. To cut the roses. The princes in the stories always—"

"Right, right, they do," I said. "But that's because they're mostly big lunks who don't know how to do anything but wave weapons around. I was thinking of a more non-violent approach. Don't fight if you'll be better served by talking." Slight paraphrase from a wandering adventurer I knew. It was his Rule #19—but that's a different story.

In this story, Jack was staring at me like I was crazy. "So you're saying I should...talk to the roses? Like using a magic password?"

"No, like explaining the situation."

"They're *roses*. They can't hear me!"

"That's what you think," I murmured, as the roses rustled above us.

His shoulders hunched. "They just moved. Even though it's not windy."

"They're magic, remember?"

He took a deep breath, and turned to face the roses. "So, I...would like to get through you. To the castle. Please. I'm not a prince and I don't have an enchanted sword and I'm just a goatherd and I just want to go in and look for Emmy. Can I do that?"

The roses shivered more vigorously. They weren't altogether happy with this, but *I* was delighted. Finally confirmation of just who inside the castle was uppermost on his mind. So maybe we'd started rocky, but prospects were looking up again.

"I can't tell if all that rustling means yes or no." Jack shifted from one foot to the other, forehead wrinkling. "The stories say Jacks are clever and all, but I'm really not, you see, so I don't know how to get past you. But I have to get in there. I have to find my...friend."

The rustling took on a mocking edge. I can't explain how something rustles mockingly, but if you had been there, you'd have heard it.

"I know it's not the right word," Jack muttered, "I guess she's my..." He hesitated, glanced at me. I crossed my arms and didn't say anything. There was only so much help I was allowed to give before I forfeited my wager. I could help him get into the castle, but I couldn't help him with the question of what Emmy was to him. Even though it should be *really* obvious and I *really* hoped he knew, or we were both in a lot of trouble.

Jack swallowed. "The stories...are always about princes and princesses. But couldn't a goatherd and a kitchen maid have true love too?"

The words seemed to echo and linger, and when they finally faded there was a suddenly noticeable silence. After a moment, the silence was replaced by a rustling of leaves and creaking of wood as the branches of thorns twisted and twined and rearranged. Slowly at first, then faster, they sorted and shifted and a shadowy, rose-lined tunnel formed before us.

"Does that mean yes?" Jack asked, staring at the tunnel. "Or was 'true love' the password after all?"

"Don't ask too many questions," I advised. "Just take advantage of the opportunity given you." And get on with this before he had time to change his mind again.

"Right." Jack peered down the length of the tunnel and visibly swallowed a nervous lump in his throat. "Well, come on then," he said with a fair degree of cheer to his goats. "Let's go."

The goats refused. Only the Little One had no objection. The others would not enter the rose tunnel for love, force, or pleading. I wanted to tear my hair—or possibly the goats' hair, whichever. I just wanted to get Jack into the tunnel so we could get on with this and get it settled, one way or the other.

"Can't you do something?" Jack demanded, trying to tug forward a goat who had set his heels into the grass.

"I don't think they'll listen to me either." Seriously. You ever try to argue with a goat? "But I can cast a spell," I added quickly. "So they'll be fine if you leave them."

He stopped glaring at his goats to glare at me. "I don't trust you, remember?"

"Then that limits how I can help, doesn't it?" I said through a clenched jaw. The way into the castle was *right there*. "So the question is, how much are you willing to risk?" Because the truth was, if he didn't care enough to risk more than a pound of cheese, I might as well forfeit now as lose later.

He looked at me, the tunnel, the goats, and back at the tunnel again. Then he picked up the Little One and told the other goats, "Stay here. Please." He turned resolutely towards the tunnel and plunged in.

I had really begun to wonder if he would. Though maybe it served me right; I had always said I liked common folk because they were practical and could think. I just hadn't anticipated how many practical concerns he'd raise.

I shook my head, threw a quick loop of protection around the goats, and hurried into the tunnel after Jack. I caught up before he'd gone a dozen yards.

Jack walked the first half with one hand on the Little One's head, taking one carefully measured step at a time. The tunnel was dark and narrow, with ropy, thorny branches on every side. I was small so I fit very well, but sometimes Jack had to duck to get through, and other times his shoulders brushed against the tunnel on either side. It wasn't hard to see what he was thinking about. If the tunnel should close…if the walls should push back together and the branches wind around him… The rustling of the roses didn't help. It had an ominous sound, the branches on one side seeming to call to the branches on the other side, longing to twine together again if only this foolish, insolent, audacious boy wasn't in their way.

It was beginning to unnerve even me, so I wasn't surprised when, halfway there, Jack's courage broke. He gave up walking and ran at full tilt until he threw himself breathless against the door to the castle. It swung open when he touched it and he half-stumbled and half-fell within.

The Little One bleated her disapproval. Personally, I'd been impressed that he'd walked as far as he had.

"Sorry," Jack told the Little One. "Are you all right?"

She bleated a grudging affirmative

"I'm fine too," I said, having glided after him.

"Sorry about that," Jack muttered without looking at me. "I expect a prince wouldn't've run."

"You haven't met many princes, have you?"

We had arrived in the front hall of the castle, a grand cavernous stone entryway. There were always four guards on duty here, and by what light entered through the branches over the windows we could see four red uniforms in approximately the right places. The men in them, however, were sitting on the ground, slumped back against the pillars where they normally stood at attention.

Jack ventured towards the nearest, and gingerly reached out to poke his shoulder.

The guard's head lolled to one side, and Jack leapt backwards. "He's dead, isn't he?"

Then the guard's mouth dropped open, and a loud snore emerged.

"He's *asleep*?"

"They all are," I said sourly. Marj was, after all, thorough. Under normal circumstances, a rule prevents fairies from casting spells on members of the armed forces, to keep us from interfering in wars. That should have excluded the guards from Marj's sparkling slumber—because when the King and Queen of the Fairies make a rule, you *don't* break it—but the situation of A Princess Slumbering For One Hundred Years, Necessitating a Full Complement of Castle Staff in Sympathetic Slumber constitutes an official and sanctioned exception to the rule. This came up more often than you might think.

Jack checked the rest of the guards too. They were all fast asleep, and no amount of prodding, shaking or shouting received any response. I wouldn't have bothered trying, but I let him go ahead.

"I guess that makes sense," Jack said finally. "The princess falls asleep and everyone else does too." His eyes widened. "So if I find Emmy…we'll just find her and then deal with it, right?"

"Right," I agreed. I knew how to deal with it. The obvious solution, of course. I just had to hope it would be obvious to him, since I wasn't allowed to tell him without forfeiting my wager. That didn't worry me much, though; he clearly knew his stories. He'd figure it out. "So, let's search," I said, rubbing my hands together. "Which direction do you want to go?"

Jack looked over his shoulder at me, from where he was still crouched in front of one sleeping guard. "Don't you have any advice? As a magical guide?"

Well, yes, I knew where he needed to go, but I couldn't *tell* him that. My job was to get him to the right place for my wager, without interfering so much that Marj could accuse me of cheating. "My advice is…to follow your instincts," I said, and tried the trustworthy smile again.

He stared at me for a moment, then shook his head. He stood, and scooped up the Little One, who had been wandering at liberty while he looked at the guards. "I'm Jack, by the way," he said as he turned towards the nearest door into the interior of the castle. "What's your name? Or can you tell me that?"

"No rule against that," I said, and floated up so I was about shoulder height on Jack. "My name's Tarragon, but you can call me Tarry." I extended a hand.

He shook it, carefully. "Nice to meet you, Tarry." Then he headed on into the castle. "Let's go find Emmy."

I floated after him, hoping that really was who we'd end up rescuing.

Chapter Four

For someone claiming to be all about goodness and light, Marj could make a castle seriously creepy. With branches snaking dozens of feet up over the outside walls, all the windows were obscured by leaves and thorns and crimson blossoms. What dim light got through had a reddish cast from filtering through the flowers. Add to that absolute silence, with no movement, no talking, no activity but slumbering bodies strewn everywhere, and even I found myself hunching my shoulders and vaguely expecting something to jump at me from the shadows. Even though I knew perfectly well Marj didn't go in for putting monsters in her enchanted castles.

On Jack's instinct, we set off for the kitchens. It seemed the logical place to start looking for a kitchen maid.

We walked through the courtyard, which was at least sunny and free of roses, apart from the ones hanging over the outer wall. It was still unnerving to pass slumbering chickens and sleeping dogs. We let them lie. Even the flies near the garbage heap had dropped down to the ground.

The kitchen made my shoulders hunch even higher at the overall wrongness of it. They had been preparing the midday meal when Marj came through in her storm of sparkles. Everyone was asleep over piles of chopped vegetables or leaning against the counters. The fire was reduced to glowing embers—it was asleep too. One girl had been cutting apples, and the flesh of the cut slices was still pale yellow, not brown or mushy. Still tasted good too. Everything had frozen precisely as it was in a single moment of time and remained so, unchanging and unaltered.

It was unnatural, disconcerting, and ultimately disappointing for Jack, because though he circled the entire kitchen and checked every sleeping girl, he finally had to admit that Emmy wasn't there. Which I already knew, but I thought I'd better let him look.

"So now what?" he asked of the room at large, sitting down on the edge of a table, next to where the cook had fallen asleep with her head on an empty plate.

The Little One, sitting on the ground next to him, bleated disapproval.

"I didn't say I was giving up," he told the baby goat, reaching down to pick her up and scratch between her ears. "I just said, now what?"

"You already *know* what," I said, floating up to the table. I lifted the cook's head and kicked the plate off to one side, then set her head down on the table again. She wasn't a bad old girl, really.

"Yeah," Jack admitted, "I was just sort of hoping I'd think of something easier. I'm going to have to search the whole castle, aren't I? If Emmy's not in the kitchen, she could be anywhere. Unless you could point me in the right direction?"

I put my nose in the air and assumed my most sage-like expression. "Search where your heart beckons, follow no pathways twice, fear not the uphill climb." Which was all good advice, if you looked at it from the right angle.

Jack sighed. "Sure, that's not cryptic at all. Can't you just tell me, turn left at the next intersection, go into the third room on the right and you'll find her?"

I *could*, and part of me really wanted to, but that wouldn't work if I wanted to win my bet. And I didn't want to spend future centuries as a Good Fairy, or leave the entire rest of this castle asleep. "If being a magical guide was that simple, anyone could do it."

Jack looked away and muttered, "Maybe it would all make sense to a prince."

"I really doubt it," I said, with perfect sincerity.

"Maybe." He pushed off the table. "If you haven't got anything better for directions, let's go search."

Searching was good. Searching would get him where I needed him. And if he thought he was searching aimlessly, I should be able to nudge him in the right direction. I nodded approval, picked up a plum as big as my head, and followed Jack out of the kitchen.

We explored the parts Jack knew first, a small section. I ate half my plum and made an absolute mess of my shirt before I gave up on it and let the Little One have the other half. By then we were heading on into the rest of the servants' area. Everywhere we went people had fallen asleep in the middle of their normal tasks. Jack passed the men with hardly a glance. He looked at the faces of the girls and then moved on.

I walked and floated and drifted along, looking at people sideways as we went by. You can find things out that way, if you're me. Some people I moved into a more comfortable position, or pulled the hem of a skirt to a more discreet height. Others I was not as kind to. I lowered a pot over the head of a big bully of a guardsman, and laced his boots together besides. Evening the balance a little, after Marj's senseless spell-casting. Not much, but a little.

Jack didn't pay a lot of attention to me, intent on his own search. "She's not here," he said at length, after we'd walked through all of the servants' quarter. "You didn't see her either, right?"

The Little One bleated a negative, and I confirmed it.

We continued into the rest of the castle. The part Marj and the nobility liked best.

"I feel like I'm not supposed to be here," Jack said, voice dropping to a whisper as he walked over plush red carpets and past richly embroidered tapestries.

"We're not. No one's supposed to be in an enchanted castle," I said. "Hence the thorns."

"Yeah, but I feel like I'm not supposed to be in this *part* of it." He reached out towards a lush velvet curtain, and then pulled his hand back before he actually touched it. "It makes me feel dirtier than usual."

"Yeah, Marj makes me feel that way sometimes." She did. She got this Look. Although it seems to me that a woman who leaves a trail of glitter everywhere she goes has no business looking down her nose at a little honest dirt.

"Who's Marj?"

"No one important," I said quickly, which would have bothered her immensely had she known. But I wasn't supposed to tell him certain information, and a discussion of Marj would skirt awfully close to some of those sensitive topics, so…and I didn't want to discuss how Marj's Looks made me feel anyway. I glanced down at my plum-stained shirt, and waved a hand to clean it up.

"On the bright side," I continued, "searching ought to be easier here. Most of the women have dresses that are too expensive for Emmy to be wearing. Narrows down the faces you have to look at." And even better, this was taking us in the direction *I* needed him to go.

"Yeah, that's true. Except I can't shake the feeling that one of them might suddenly get up and tell me I'm tracking mud on the floor."

We continued down the hall until we reached a set of enormous double doors, all covered over with carvings and gildings.

"That's the throne room through there, isn't it?" Jack said, staring up at them. Then his brow creased with worry. "How heavy are those doors?"

The royalty employed six footmen whose sole job in life was to open and close the doors to the throne room. They were all sprawled asleep in the hallway, so they weren't going to be helpful right now.

Maybe that was just as well. I hadn't wanted to watch this whole crowd get hit by Marj's spell, and I wasn't altogether sure I wanted to go in and see the results either. "We could go around."

Jack rubbed the back of his neck. "No…kitchen maids could easily be in the throne room, serving food or something. Maybe we could find another door, this can't be the only way in."

Hunting around for another door would just prolong this. So I waved one hand and the heavy double doors swung silently open. "I do have *some* use as a magical guide."

"Thanks," Jack said, and we ventured in.

The throne room had a high ceiling. The roses hadn't climbed as high as the uppermost windows, making this one of the better-lit rooms in the castle. It was full of elegant statues and soaring pillars and crowds and crowds of people in silk and lace, all stretched out or curled up on the red-carpeted floor.

"This is amazing," Jack breathed, staring around. "All these people...they're kind of intimidating crumpled asleep on the ground. What do you think they're like awake and standing?"

"Not as impressive as they seem."

Jack drifted towards the golden thrones at one end of the room.

"Lookit there," he whispered. "The king and queen of the whole country."

There they were in their velvet robes and their golden crowns, the king silver-haired and venerable, the queen blonde and tiny. The king was leaning his head on one hand and the queen was curled up in her throne with her head on her arm. Even asleep, I could still read their auras. The past sixteen years had not been kind. The queen's lily was brown and bruised, the king's oak tree riddled with cracks, branches bare and wintry. I winced and looked away, magically and physically, to look at Jack again.

Jack was staring at the royalty on their thrones.

I scrunched my eyebrows up. "You're not going to bow or anything, are you?"

"No." He rubbed the back of his neck. "I just...when I look at them, at all of them—" He waved a hand to encompass the room at large. "—it's so obvious that I'm not supposed to be here."

"We already said that, about the thorns—"

"No, I mean *I'm* not supposed to be here. If someone was going to get into a magic castle and try to overcome a curse, it's not supposed to be someone like me. It should be a prince, someone the king would approve of."

I was so used to arguing with Marj that commoners were every bit as good as royalty that my eye roll was automatic. "Kings and princes put their shirts on one arm at a time just like you do."

"No, they don't," Jack contradicted. "They've got attendants to put their shirts on for them. The servants talk about it."

That was...completely true. "Metaphorically speaking."

I still believed my fundamental point was right, but the derail had given me pause for thought. If I wanted to win my bet, it might be better if Jack *didn't* think too well of himself. That could easily lead him down the path I wanted, even if I had expected him to take that path for other reasons. So maybe I should agree with him, confirm that he wasn't as worthy as some imagined prince he thought should be here. Confirm that he wasn't supposed to figure as the hero in a certain kind of story, in the stories that were only ever about certain kinds of people.

Except...that wasn't true. A royal pedigree didn't make anybody fundamentally better than anyone else. And from what I could read of Jack, he was as worthy as anyone, even if he didn't know it. So it was probably against my own best interest, and even the best interest of all these slumbering people, but when I looked again at those sagging sails on that fine ship in Jack's aura, I couldn't help myself. "Now listen, I'm the magical guide, right? And I picked *you* to bring in here." I lifted my chin, swelled my chest with a deep breath. "You're here because you're supposed to be here, so enough with this 'a prince would be better' business. I never pick the wrong person to guide."

Possibly because I hadn't stepped up and been anyone's guide in centuries, but never mind that.

Still facing the thrones, Jack looked at me sideways. "Really?"

"*Really,*" I said, and would have clapped him on the shoulder but I was too short. Clapping someone on the calf just isn't the same thing.

All he did was nod, but his step was more assured as he walked on towards the door out of the throne room. I followed, hoping that telling him all that hadn't been a mistake. But if I could only win this wager by promoting Marj's view, then maybe I deserved to lose.

We hadn't set any time limit on our bet, and so far I had been willing enough to ramble along after Jack while he chose where he wanted to go. I knew I'd get him where I needed him eventually, and could afford to wander, even if the place itself was making me nervous. I *knew* it wasn't dangerous, so I could tell myself pretty convincingly not to bother about any irrational prickles.

But then, shortly after the throne room, we came on someone I recognized, and I had abruptly had enough of this whole business. We left the throne room by a back door, one used by servants, judging by the clothes of the people asleep in this hall. We passed two guards, three women Jack glanced at briefly, and then I saw him. Sitting asleep against one wall, legs straight out in front of him and arms folded. He was older than in my memory, hair cut a bit nicer and clothes definitely improved so apparently he'd done well for himself, but there was no question it was the farmer's son from Rosaline's christening.

I stopped in my tracks, staring at him. He smelled faintly of hay and horses, not a bad smell, so he must have talked to the Royal Horsemaster that day. He was wearing a wedding ring on one hand, and I wondered if his wife was asleep somewhere else in this blasted castle—or if she was outside, worrying about him. Even if she was in here, how about that farmer I figured he was the son of? Or a mother, or cousins, or friends—or even children, he could have a child visiting relatives or in town for school. No one's life existed completely inside these walls.

A clench of guilt and sadness twisted up my stomach. I had *warned* him. I had *told* him to get out of the castle when the princess turned sixteen.

"Aren't you coming?" Jack asked. He had walked on to the next crossing corridor, and stopped to look at me.

"Yeah," I said, still staring at the farmer's son. Then I shook myself, and hurried after Jack. "Turn left there."

"Really?" he said, understandably surprised since this was far more direct than I'd been so far. "Why?"

"Because you've been turning right a lot." Because left would get us to our destination, and I'd had enough.

"Sure," Jack said doubtfully, but turned left. Very soon after that, we came upon a flight of stone steps and I stopped again.

"Aren't you going to look up there?" I asked, nodding to the stairs.

Jack hardly glanced over. "I think those go up to that one tower, the tallest one. They don't use it much, so Emmy's probably not up there."

She wasn't, but if he didn't go up those stairs—either he'd find Emmy too soon and I'd lose by default, or we'd keep wandering around and around for a whole lot longer before we got back here anyway. Right now, either prospect made me want to physically shove him up the stairs.

I resisted. I needed to play this calm, or I was going to give him the wrong idea and lose anyway. "Probably not doesn't mean it's impossible. Don't you want to be thorough?"

He looked at me through narrowed eyes. "Is this what you meant about going uphill? Because frankly, for a magical guide, you haven't been much guidance so far."

I lifted my chin and sniffed. "I'm sorry if my services have not been up to the standards of guidance which I am sure that you, in your vast experience with magical guides and other similar adventures, have come to expect."

I might have boosted his confidence too much, since he didn't cave at that answer. "That doesn't actually tell me anything. So *do* you know something about the stairs or the tower?"

We could stand here arguing about it all day, but I could see a faster option. "Fine, go wherever you prefer," I said, and walked over to the Little One, sitting by Jack's feet, to scratch her head. And that made it easy to put a whisper in her ear that climbing stone stairs is heaps of fun, without Jack noticing I was doing it.

Only a moment after that, the Little One went scampering off up the stairs.

"It must be a sign!" I exclaimed, throwing my hands up in the air theatrically.

"Yeah, a sign that goat needs better discipline," Jack muttered, and went chasing up the stairs after her.

By the time we caught her, we'd gone up three flights.

"That was *very bad*," Jack informed her, picking her up and rapping her lightly on the nose. "I expect better of you."

She baaed unrepentantly.

"So we might as well keep going on up, right?" I said, with a waggle of eyebrows. If he said no, I might physically bar the way down.

Jack frowned with a touch of doubt in his eyes, but said, "Yeah, might as well." So on we went.

There wasn't much in the tower, and there was less and less the higher up we went. The dust increased as the furnishings decreased. I was surprised Jack didn't make noise about turning around, but from the way his jaw was set, I think he was determined now to go to the top, just on the principle of the thing. I certainly wasn't going to argue.

At the very top of the stairs, we found a small room with nothing in it but a spinning wheel. At the far side of the room was another doorway.

"That explains a few things, doesn't it?" Jack said, looking at the wheel but keeping a healthy distance away from it. "I wonder how it got here. Probably because of—that fairy. You know."

"Echinacea?"

He winced. "Don't say her name. Especially not *here*. You're liable to summon her."

"I know how to summon fairies, and saying her name like that isn't going to do it." What you really need is some fire and the right kind of herb. But don't tell anyone you heard it from me. The Fairy Queen doesn't like us to share it too freely.

"Still," Jack insisted. "It just seems like it's asking for trouble. Anyway, I bet she put it here somehow."

"She did. It's not difficult magic."

He nodded. "So if the spinning wheel is here…then where…?" He looked at the doorway into the next room.

I didn't say anything. Nothing seemed safe to say just then. I kept my mouth shut, dug my fingernails into my palms, and watched Jack.

He walked over to peer into the adjoining room, the Little One and I both trailing behind him. Though the room with the spinning wheel was dusty and unused, the next room was as rich and elegant as any we'd seen walking through the castle. I suspected Marj had put in even more pillows and decorations since I left. The large four poster bed stood at the center of the room, where Princess Rosaline lay sleeping, blond hair spilling across the pillows, hands neatly folded over her stomach. Naturally a shine of gold sparkles lay over the whole affair.

I'd brought the goatherd here, as per my agreement with Marj. Now everybody's fate, including mine, depended on what Jack was going to do about it.

Chapter Five

"It figures," Jack said, staring at the sleeping princess. "In the entire castle, she's the only one who managed to get into a bed."

I might've been amused if the moment hadn't been too important. Anyway, it was no credit to her since Marj got her there. I didn't comment, just leaned back against the doorframe, crossed my arms, and waited. And if my heart was beating harder than usual, I made sure it didn't show on my face.

"Well...now I've seen her, I suppose I might as well keep searching," Jack said after another moment.

I said "Hmm" because there was really nothing else I dared say. I wasn't going to risk Marj claiming that I influenced him in my favor, and I certainly wasn't going to risk influencing him in *her* favor either.

Jack was so utterly uninfluenced that he didn't move towards the exit. He went on looking at the princess. In fact, he was drifting slowly closer to the bed. Soon he was standing right next to it, looking down at the princess.

"She's beautiful, isn't she?" he said in a hushed voice. He reached out one hand to straighten a single tendril of golden hair that was not in need of straightening.

"Hmm," I repeated, fingers tightening where they gripped my crossed arms. The merits of the princess was not the direction I wanted his thoughts going. I wanted to go grab him by the ankle and haul him out—but that would definitely mean forfeiting.

"Supposing..." Jack said, "supposing someone who wasn't a prince kissed her? Would she wake up? The cook said something about that, that it doesn't have to be a prince."

A simple question with a simple answer, even if it wasn't one I liked giving. "All it takes is a kiss, from anyone."

He rubbed the back of his neck. "So I suppose...*I* could kiss her. Just to wake her up, I mean. Not to marry her, of course."

"You'd have to marry her," I said instantly. If he didn't know *that*—then it wasn't even a fair test of the principle. And it gave him too much freedom to choose wrong. "That's the rule. Whoever kisses her has to marry her."

"Oh. Well. In that case."

I waited to see if he was going to say again that he ought to go. He didn't say it. He also didn't do it.

After a long moment, he said, "You know, I suppose…I mean, if I wanted to, I could kiss her anyway."

I swallowed hard. He didn't *mean* it, he was just thinking out loud. I didn't really convince myself. The Little One bleated at him from her place on the floor by his feet. I quite agreed with her, but I couldn't risk saying so.

"I'm not saying I'm going to, I'm just saying I *could*. Wake her up and marry her. Whoever marries the princess gets the whole kingdom, and the crown, and the riches and… It's what everyone always wants, in the stories. To marry a princess and inherit a kingdom. And…I could do it. The prince isn't here, I'm the one who got into the cursed castle, *I* could do it."

Maybe I shouldn't have told him he was as good as a prince, even if it was true. I squinted at him, trying to read anything from his face, and then I used my magical eyes to squint at his aura too. I couldn't make any sense out of it right now, not any sense that would tell me how he was leaning. His metaphorical ship was all in a tangle, a sail here or there trying to catch a breeze but clearly with no determined course. Which is all just another way of saying he was trying to decide.

The Little One bleated again and pushed her head against his leg. He leaned down, scratched her head once, and kept talking.

"Any man would want to marry the princess if he could," he continued. I couldn't tell if he thought he was talking to the goat or to me. Either way, he was talking to himself. "She's so beautiful. And she's nice, too; she was nice when she talked to me in the courtyard. The fairies gave her all those gifts, so she's charming and graceful and talented...they made her just about perfect, really. She seemed perfect, that day in the courtyard."

The Little One bleated another time, and Jack fell silent.

Maybe I should have told him that all I could read of the princess was a big bouquet of flowers, nice for decoration but impossible to tell if there was anything else there. But maybe he wanted the decoration, in which case...I had chosen the wrong champion, and maybe even the wrong philosophy too. My stomach did an uncomfortable twist at the thought. But that was nonsense, I *knew* Marj was wrong. I had set out to shatter her worldview, and didn't like the idea at all of spotting cracks in mine.

Jack was silent for an even longer moment than any of the moments of silence that had come before and it was all I could do not to tap my foot with anxious impatience. Or grab him by the ankle after all and start pulling. I *hoped* this silence was coming at a strategic moment that was a good sign for my side, but it was impossible to tell if he was talking himself into or out of an idea.

"That wasn't true," Jack said finally. "She didn't exactly seem perfect. I think the fairies forgot to give her a sense of humor. Or creativity. And I don't know if she'd be interesting to talk to. Or understanding. She probably wouldn't understand at all about feeling like your whole life is just a small part of a much bigger story, or to wonder if there's any way to make your own part matter."

I held my breath. That sounded good, but he was still *standing* there. The sails in his ship were catching the wind again, not just one or two of them but more and more.

Jack bent down to pick up the baby goat, who rubbed her head against his chest. "Besides," he said, very faintly, probably more faintly than he expected me to be able to hear, "she's beautiful, but her eyes were just blue. Emmy's eyes are blue like the flowers out in the fields."

And that, *that* was what I'd been looking for. That was why I was right and Marj was wrong and the world was a beautiful place where love had nothing to do with royal titles or unearthly beauty or silly curses.

Jack smoothed back the Little One's ears, tucked her under one arm, and turned away from the bed. "Should we go?"

Yes was the clear answer, but I didn't want even a hint that I was the one making this decision. "That depends," I said carefully. "Is it your considered, deliberate and very much independent decision that you're *not* going to wake her up?"

He tilted his head slightly to stare at me. "Um...yes." He shrugged. "She probably is perfect, but I already found someone else who's more perfect for me."

Yes. I beamed at him—a smile, no sparkles—and flew across the room to vigorously shake his hand. "You're a good man, Jack. I knew you had it in you. I had faith all the time!" Well, most of the time. Mostly.

Jack blinked at me. "Thanks?"

"No, thank you. Really."

"You're welcome." He disentangled his hand and took a step backwards. "And I don't know what we're talking about, so I'm going to go look for Emmy now..."

"Good, good idea, excellent idea." I sent out a feeler spell around the castle. "If you want to find her, go straight down the stairs to the third floor and turn right, then right again at the first crossing."

Jack blinked. "If you can use magic to find her, why did we waste all this time wandering around?" he demanded. "Why didn't you say something useful back in the kitchen, instead of rambling about hills?"

Because I had to get him over to the princess first, but without making him think I was encouraging him to go to the princess and wake her up. "It's complicated. And why are you wasting time now talking to me? Go, go on, get." Go rescue his true love so I could make sure everyone else got rescued too. And make sure I wouldn't have to concede to Marj.

He squinted at me doubtfully, but headed for the door. As he thumped down the steps, I heard him say, "Magical beings are confusing, aren't they?"

The Little One bleated agreement.

As soon as he was out of sight, I grew myself to full-size and conjured up Marj.

She popped in with a cloud of sparkles and pink bubbles—as variety, I suppose. "Is it all over already?" she asked, then looked at the bed and visibly started. "But she's still asleep!"

"Right." I rocked back on my heels and grinned my smuggest. "Which means I won. The commoner rejected your magical princess in favor of his kitchen maid."

"He really chose not to kiss the princess?" Marj looked at me sharply. "Did you influence him?"

"Of course not. I wouldn't cheat on a wager." Mostly because it would mean forfeiting. "Don't you trust me?"

"Of course not." She flicked sparkles in my face.

"I wish you wouldn't do that," I said, and sneezed.

"Go on," she told me, "say again that you didn't cheat."

I sighed, causing the cloud of sparkles around my head to ripple. "I didn't cheat in any way on our wager."

The cloud stayed pink. If I'd been lying, it would have turned black and stuck to my face. The sticking wasn't strictly necessary, but Marj didn't like being lied to.

"Will you get rid of this now?" I asked, waving my hand through the cloud. Although really, I was too pleased by how this had turned out to be all that irritated even by a cloud of pink sparkles right now.

"Oh, yes..." Marj said, snapped her fingers, and out went the cloud. "It's very peculiar, though."

"Just admit it, Marj. They have true love too, without a royal title or a magic spell between them. Just like I've always insisted was possible." I would be bringing this up for decades. Centuries. Every time she started going on about the greater importance of anyone wearing a crown.

She didn't admit anything. Her expression grew distant, a sure sign that she was feeling around the castle, magically speaking. "He hasn't woken her up yet. Technically it's not over until he wakes up his little kitchen maid."

I knew she wouldn't give in easy, so this didn't dampen my spirits. "He's on his way to go do that, and then you'll have to admit it anyway. So, this?" I waved a hand. "This is just delaying the inevitable."

Marj crossed her arms, sparkles bright and defiant. "He could still change his mind."

I grinned at her. "You just can't accept the truth, can you? He's not going to change his mind."

"Let's make sure," she said, and popped out in a shower of gold.

I hadn't planned to follow Jack—but I wasn't going to let Marj interfere now. I popped out after her, sans the gold.

We both popped invisibly into the same corridor as Jack.

At the end of the long hallway, a cluster of serving women had fallen asleep with piles of linen in their laps, presumably in the process of moving laundry. Sitting below a rose-screened window was Emmy. She had a stack of sheets in her lap, with one hand resting on it and the other trailing on the floor. Her black hair was coming loose from its bun and curling in wisps around her face.

Jack stood near her, putting the Little One down as we arrived. The baby goat nudged Emmy's hand with her nose, seemed disappointed at the lack of response, and then went to investigate the other women nearby. Jack crouched down in front of Emmy and brushed a few strands of hair back from her cheek.

"Don't you feel a little voyeuristic?" I asked Marj, spell covering our voices too. "This really isn't any of our business."

"Of course it's our business," Marj contradicted, hands on her hips as she stared intently at Jack. "We have a wager riding on it."

"Still, it looks private," I said, resolutely turning my back.

Principle or not, I couldn't resist curiosity. I peeked over my shoulder in time to see Jack lean in and kiss Emmy. He pulled back and waited to see what would happen, face creased into anxious lines.

Emmy stirred, head turning. "Jack?"

Success. I elbowed Marj, making her float sideways a foot. "See? Isn't that romantic?"

Marj shook her head, apparently still stunned. "Just remarkable."

"It is not remarkable, it's only exactly what *I* keep telling you, and I want you to admit it!"

"Hush," Marj said, flapping her hand at me. "I want to hear what this supposed True Love couple of yours has to say to each other."

"You're still just delaying," I murmured.

Emmy's eyes fluttered and opened, and Jack, romantically if dopily, said, "You have beautiful eyes."

"That's sweet, Jack," she said, then blinked and seemed to come more awake. Enough to straighten up, look around and ask, "Why are you here? Why is everyone asleep in the middle of the hallway?"

"The princess pricked her finger," Jack explained, "and when she fell asleep, everyone else in the castle did too."

More or less. Somehow, one of these days, I had to make sure Marj got the proper blame for all of this. How she got by all this time without any damage to her reputation baffled me.

Emmy moved the sheets off her lap and let Jack help her to her feet. "That's a pleasant detail of the curse no one warned us about. Why are you and I awake?"

"I'm awake because I wasn't here when it happened," Jack said, "and you're awake because…um…"

"That part I remember," Emmy said, with a smile and a blush.

"Are you *satisfied*?" I demanded of Marj. "Are we finally done here? Will you finally just concede that I was right?"

She lifted her chin, drew herself up, bosom swelling with an indrawn breath—and before she could say anything, a roar sounded in the courtyard, so loud it seemed to shake the whole castle.

I glared at Marj. "If you're creating a distraction to avoid admitting—"

"Don't be silly, Tarry, that wasn't me." She smiled sweetly, just as an enormous dragon snout thrust through the window at the far end of the hall. "That was Echinacea."

Chapter Six

Echinacea glared balefully through the window, eyes a whirling purple, dark smoke trailing from her nostrils. She should have been able to see through Marj's and my invisibility spells, but she still focused her gaze on Jack and Emmy. For just a second they froze, staring back—then Jack grabbed Emmy's hand and they turned to run down the hallway, away from the dragon-filled window.

And there Echinacea found herself with a problem. Although she could get her snout in far enough to see, her entire head was too wide to get through the window without serious risk of getting stuck.

There was something comical about the way her eyes crossed, peering through the window. Or maybe I was just still feeling good from besting Marj. "If she wanted to get at people inside," I remarked, "she should have chosen a size small enough to actually get *in*."

Marj shrugged in a spray of sparkles. "She'll just transport them outside."

She'd barely said it before Jack and Emmy vanished in a flurry of black sparks. Echinacea withdrew nearly as quickly, leaving crushed roses in her wake.

Not good. Not comical. Potentially disastrous.

Without stopping to think, I sprinted for the window, scrambled over the stone sill, and leaped out into space. As soon as I was clear of the window frame I turned visible and changed shape.

Green scales formed all over my body, my face elongated into a snout, and wings popped up and unfurled from my shoulder blades. The whole experience was extremely itchy and turned my stomach for the first century or so, but I'd got over the nausea with practice and there was no time right now for a good scratching.

Spreading my wings, I circled once, squinting down at the courtyard as the breeze whipped past my face. Jack and Emmy were running for an archway at one end, while Echinacea reared back to strike. They weren't going to make it.

I drew my wings in and shot towards Echinacea. My dragonform was only twelve feet long, nose to tail, while she was a solid seventy feet. She might not even notice if I bit her, but I was harder to ignore flying straight at her face. "Bank your fire, woman!" I shouted as I dove towards her eyes, swerving aside at the last possible moment.

Echinacea shook her head, eyes narrowing into a glare. Then she reared back on her hindquarters to roar inarticulately at me and the sky, which was just fine since it gave Jack and Emmy a few extra seconds to reach, well, relative safety.

I circled Echinacea's head. Being smaller gave me the advantage of speed and agility. "This is really an overreaction. Take a deep breath," I advised. I'd had centuries to get used to Evil Fairies and their melodrama, so this all felt familiar and less worrying, now that the fury wasn't being aimed at the fragile humans.

Echinacea took a deep breath, sunlight shining on her black scales, then exhaled a burst of flame at me.

I dodged, but felt a flicker of heat along one wing. Closer than I'd like to admit. "That was rude."

"It was *rude* to disrupt my spell," she roared back at me, "and I'm going to flame alive the insolent boy who did it!"

I made another circle around her, managing to catch a view of Jack and Emmy. They'd reached the archway, but that really only helped a little. Normally it led to the rest of the world, but today it was blocked by thorns. Adding to the hazards, the two of them appeared to be struggling with each other.

I ducked another burst of flame from Echinacea, with slightly more safety margin this time, and dropped lower, close enough to hear Emmy say, "You are not going out there!"

"She wants to flame *me*, and if I stay here she'll flame both of us!"

Jack might be taking this hero thing a little far. I swooped down, landing between the enormous dragon and the two flammable humans just in time to hear Emmy say, "I forbid you to go get yourself killed!"

"Good advice," I approved, "you should listen to her, Jack."

He must've recognized my voice—it doesn't change much, regardless of shape—because after a few seconds he said, "Tarragon, is that you?"

"In the flesh." I twitched a wing. "More or less."

"Get out of my way," Echinacea ordered, smoke puffing from her nostrils.

I spread my wings in front of Jack and Emmy. "Absolutely not. I'm going to stop you from doing something I'll regret." I was hoping she wasn't too angry to remember that the Fairy Court has extremely strict rules about one fairy killing another. Yeah, she'd shot fire at me, but she'd been aiming to singe. She'd have to do a lot more damage to get past me now.

If she was too angry to care, we were all in trouble.

"Jack, why do you know the dragon?" Emmy asked, in the carefully controlled voice of someone who is trying to handle calmly a world that has stopped making sense.

"It's complicated," Jack said.

"I *said*, get out of my way!" Echinacea bellowed.

"I know, I heard you the first time," I said, pitching my voice calmly while I tried to judge from *her* voice whether she was furious enough to be reckless. "Half the country heard you. And I don't know what you're shrieking about anyway. If anyone's spell was disturbed, it was Marj's, not yours."

Echinacea probably didn't even hear me, considering she was rearing back and roaring at the heavens again. Again with the melodrama.

"I knew you should've given me an enchanted sword," Jack yelled over the roaring.

"What good would that do?" I asked. "You don't know how to use a sword."

"Wouldn't the enchanted part make up for that?"

"Not as much as people think."

I didn't like the timbre of Echinacea's roar. If anything she was getting more worked up, and if she decided to disregard the rules, I'd be hard-pressed to fight her magically, especially considering the firepower she had in this form. I needed a plan. Maybe I *should* bite her, maybe that would shock her enough to make her sit down and think.

I was still trying to decide whether I should go for the tail or for an ear when Marj finally put in an appearance. I'd bet she had spent the intervening three minutes fixing her hair. Now she came floating out of the window, every hair and every sparkle in place, and drifted down to the courtyard in a swirl of pink smoke. As if the place wasn't smoky enough from the giant flaming dragon.

"Now, now, my dear, do try to calm down," Marj cooed at Echinacea. "Let's just have a nice chat about all of this."

And wonder of wonders, the dragon actually swallowed her flames and sat down on her haunches, tail wrapping around her paws. She gulped a few times, and then turned a mournful expression towards Marj, scales wrinkling in distress. "It's just not *fair!*"

"Here we go," I muttered, and furled my wings, cautiously. I was never in my entire life relieved to see Marj, but I was relieved that Echinacea seemed willing to talk to her.

"No one has any consideration!" Echinacea moaned. "It's bad enough that everyone forgets to invite me to all the parties, or that I have to put up with the Good Fairies ruining my lovely revenge spells, but I at least expect some degree of severe inconvenience to be enacted against the royalty. Is that asking for so much? Evil Fairies have rights too. I know what the tradition is. The princess sleeps for a century. A mere few hours isn't enough." The dragon sniffed, and a gallon-sized tear dropped down to splash on the dusty ground. "I just want my rights."

"Of course you do," Marj agreed, reaching up to pat one of Echinacea's front feet. "Anyone can understand that."

Behind me I heard Emmy mutter, "I can't."

"But you see," Marj continued, "no one's violated your rights."

"I felt the surge of magic when the spell was broken. It was done by that—that—" She leaned down to peer at Jack. "Why, you're not even a prince. What are you?"

"I'm a goatherd," Jack said, chin raised defiantly. All right, so it *had* been the right decision to tell him he was as good as a prince. Even if it gave me a few bad moments.

"A *goatherd*?" Echinacea repeated, in a tone that made it clear she did not share my views on the relative merits of royalty and commoners. "That's even worse! A goatherd dared to wake up the princess?"

"But I didn't wake up the princess," Jack protested. "I was tempted—"

"You were what?" Emmy said.

"—but I didn't do it!"

"I felt the spell break and standing right next to you is—" Now Echinacea peered at Emmy. "My goodness, Turmeric must have lost her touch with beauty spells. You don't look like any princess I've ever seen."

Emmy frowned, pink spots appearing high on her cheeks. "I'm not the princess."

"The princess is still asleep," Marj explained. "She's just a kitchen maid."

I groaned. "Have you not learned anything, Marj? 'Just a kitchen maid'? Really?" I expected this from the Evil Fairies, but the Good Fairies could at least *pretend*.

Both fairies ignored me completely.

"A kitchen maid? How extraordinary." Echinacea tilted her head to one side and stared at Emmy as though she'd never seen a maid before. "So you, goatherd, you didn't wake up the princess?"

"I didn't," Jack confirmed, glaring at her.

"You woke up a kitchen maid instead."

"*Yes*," he said through gritted teeth.

"But why on earth would you do that?"

"Because I love her!"

Emmy looked up at him. "You do?"

Jack turned suddenly red. "That's...not exactly how I meant to tell you that."

She hugged him. "I love you too."

The Little One, who had climbed into Jack's shirt while the dragon was roaring, emitted a bleat of protest at being squished.

"Have I proven my point?" I asked Marj, and flapped my wings at her. "I think I've proven my point." There would be no allegiance to the Good Fairies in my future, and I was definitely *not* going to let this go until she conceded I had been right all along.

"Just remarkable," was all she said now, which was inadequate.

I glowered at her. "It's exactly what I always said—"

"So the princess is still asleep?" Echinacea interrupted.

Marj turned away from me to nod at Echinacea. "Yes, and likely to remain so."

Echinacea glowered down at us now, and her glower was more impressive than mine. Being a seventy-foot dragon gives a person a good glower. "For a hundred years. I demand that she sleep a full century. I expect serious inconvenience."

"You already *got* that," I pointed out. "The cloth industry in this country has gone all to pieces since they burned the spindles."

Echinacea snorted, a puff of black smoke rising into the air. "Mere economics. I want emotional suffering. I really don't think that's asking too much."

"You don't?" Emmy said, voice rising to an incredulous note.

Jack coughed. "Emmy, maybe we shouldn't get involved in this conversation any more than we have to." Which was sensible advice, if admittedly not terribly heroic. Ah well, one metaphorical sail at a time.

Echinacea turned her gaze on Emmy. "What did you say, kitchen maid?"

Emmy swallowed, but held her ground. "I don't see how you can consider it reasonable to put someone to sleep for a hundred years. It's not even Princess Rosaline's fault that you weren't invited to her christening."

I started to unfurl my wings again, just in case, but fortunately Echinacea threw her head back to laugh, not to roar—though even dragon laughter is thunderous. "You silly human girl; you clearly don't understand at all."

Emmy crossed her arms. "No. I don't."

"I'm an Evil Fairy," Echinacea explained. "Licensed and certified. This is what I *do*. I wreak havoc, I spread destruction, I destroy lives."

I held my breath, but she seemed to be done. Which was much better than if she'd started in to recite the entire Evil Fairy Code of Honor. It's long, and involves a lot of hyperbole.

"And that's supposed to be all right?" Emmy demanded.

Echinacea shrugged with a great rippling of scales. "It's a career."

"I'm a Good Fairy," Marj put in. "I do Nice things, spreading Light and Joy and Happiness everywhere I go."

I developed a sudden hacking cough at that moment.

"Oh stop it," Marj snapped, and flicked a burst of gold sparkles at me.

"What are you?" Jack asked me.

I twitched a wing, knocking sparkles off. "I'm a free agent."

Emmy was apparently still getting her head around the Evil Fairy business. "So you put the princess to sleep on the principle of things. Sort of. Because you're an Evil Fairy. But what about everyone else? Why do you have to make everyone else sleep too?"

Echinacea arched her neck out, whipping her tail across the courtyard. "That one's not mine. That's Marj's spell. I only require the princess to sleep. All the rest are quite irrelevant, so if we're sure the princess is sleeping, I have no further business here."

With a few flaps of her wings and a considerable windstorm, she rose up into the air.

"Oh, Echinacea, dear, are you still coming to Chervil's garden party next week?" Marj called after her.

"Naturally," Echinacea answered. "I wouldn't dream of missing it."

She flew higher, and then, when she was well above the castle and visible for miles around, she vanished in a burst of black smoke. *Seriously* overdramatic.

"You go to garden parties with her?" Emmy said, brow wrinkling.

Marj gave her a cool smile. "But of course. No one makes better scones than Echinacea. A garden party is never considered a superior one without them."

Emmy stared at Marj for a long moment.

"I think you had better let that one go," I advised. I didn't think I ought to mention that I went to those parties too. The Good and Evil Fairies weren't all or even a large percentage of fairies in total, but I still would have had to skip a *lot* of parties to avoid them. It rarely felt worth it.

Emmy shook her head, and finally said, "Right. Fine. You like her scones. Never mind that. About putting everyone else to sleep. If you're a good fairy, how can you do something so awful?"

Ah, innocence. She still believed you could actually make a moral argument with Marj on this subject.

The cool smile didn't even waver. "I'm not doing anything awful. *Evil* Fairies do awful things. *I* am simply being considerate of the princess. Surely you can see how dreadful it would be for her to wake up in a century and find everyone gone."

It was all so familiar and so ridiculous that I exhaled in a gusty sigh. So maybe a little part of me had hoped she'd be so moved by Jack and Emmy's love story that she'd immediately appreciate the value of the non-royal, recant of her former ridiculous ideas, and agree that it was far more important to not destroy the lives of the entire castle population. But I hadn't really expected that. I tried to be satisfied with the knowledge that I at least had ammunition now to hammer her with on the subject for centuries to come. Change can be slow among people who live for millennia.

Emmy took a deep breath. "I appreciate that it would be hard for the princess to wake alone. But this is hard for several hundred people. You weren't being very considerate of anyone else. Not of me."

"Or me," Jack said, reaching for Emmy's hand.

The Little One bleated her agreement too.

I knew how this *had* to turn out, per our wager. But that didn't mean I was going to stop Emmy from making her argument. Maybe Marj would even learn something. Doubtful, but maybe.

"I know the people who work here," Emmy continued. "They have friends, family, people who love them and depend on them, who live outside of the castle. Putting everyone to sleep for a century…no one who knows them will ever see them again, and by the time they wake up, everyone they know will be dead. You *have* to wake them up. Now."

Marj hesitated. "But the princess…"

"Perhaps one of you should have given her resilience and inner strength," Emmy said, staring Marj in the eye, "instead of beauty and dancing ability."

Chapter Seven

For a moment, Marj stared stubbornly back at Emmy. I turned my head to glare at her, taking shameless advantage of my current draconic form. She frowned at me, unintimidated—but capitulated anyway. "Oh *very well*. I suppose I can wake everyone up again."

Emmy's eyes widened, looking almost stunned at this turn of events. "Really? You mean it?"

"I'm a Good Fairy, dear," Marj said with her nose in the air. "We never lie."

She also had no choice. Because I *won*.

Emmy reached out and clasped Marj's hands, eyes bright. "Thank you!"

"Now, now, no need to get emotional," Marj said, pulling her hands free and turning her face away. She waved one hand through the air in a shower of gold sparkles. "Presto, etc. It's no great matter."

The gold sparks turned into pale yellow flecks of light and spread, drifting out in every direction around the castle. They soon filled the courtyard, more sparkles shimmering right through the walls to get inside.

Flies began buzzing again by the garbage heap. A confused rooster started to crow. People yawned and stretched and slowly got to their feet as the light flecks reached them. The roses, when touched by the magic, grew in reverse, heavy blooms shrinking to buds then disappearing entirely, branches collapsing down into themselves, tendrils snaking away in reverse, until nothing but a neat and decorative row of waist-high rose bushes circled the castle.

I reverted back to human form at the very first yawn. Most of these people waking up wouldn't be feeling friendly towards a dragon.

The castle went from utter silence to chaotic uproar in a matter of minutes. Everyone in the castle was waking up to wonder why they were asleep in such strange places, and everyone outside was rushing in to look for friends and family and find out what had happened. There were enough hugs and happy reunions happening to keep me grinning for a week.

A few people found themselves in odder positions than others. I heard an echoing bellow, and my grin broadened as I remembered the pot I'd dropped over one guard's head.

I lost Jack and Emmy in the swirl of people, but it was easy to find Marj, without even using any magic. I just followed the trail of pink sparkles, and found her basking in appreciation from a handful of people who realized she had woken them up, didn't realize she'd put them to sleep to begin with, and weren't too busy searching for people they cared about to pay attention to Marj.

"Oh, come off it," I drawled, crossing my arms. "This is ridiculous even for you."

She shot me a glare, and then waved her hands at the people around her. "Yes, you're welcome, of course; go about your business."

They scattered, and Marj and I walked on together.

"Are you going to stop complaining now?" Marj asked me. "Everyone but the princess is awake again."

"I was not complaining," I countered. "I was making valid and irrefutable arguments about the rights of humankind."

She just stared at me.

"Although I would be justified to complain that you pretended to be kind and generous, when the rules of our wager meant you *had* to wake everyone up."

She waved her hands dismissively; I dodged the resulting spray of sparkles. "Mere details," she said. "Besides, you didn't mention it at the time either."

"Yeah, well…" I shrugged. "I thought Emmy'd like to feel that she convinced you." It wasn't often a kitchen maid convinced a Good Fairy of *anything*. I hoped the story would spread. Encourage the kitchen maids of the world to speak up more often.

"She was very impassioned on the subject, wasn't she?" Marj said, tilting her head slightly and nose wrinkling in thought. "The whole affair really has been remarkable. Between the goatherd's loyalty to his kitchen maid love and the kitchen maid's plea for her friends…there is a depth to these commoners that I never imagined."

My eyebrows rose. "Marj, are you really admitting that I was right? That ordinary people are just as important and matter just as much as your precious royalty?" I felt recent events had provided proof on the subject, but I had expected her to wriggle around it somehow.

"Well, I wouldn't say that," Marj said, with my least favorite patronizing smile. "There's no need to go overboard. But I do think there may be certain special individuals…"

And there was the wriggling. "No, Marj, that's not it at all," I said, stomach sinking. "Saying that *certain* commoners are special is really the same worldview as saying only royals are special, just shifted a little. The whole point is—"

"Now don't start complaining again," she said, positively dripping sweetness in the words. "I think you should be quite happy. I'm seriously considering expanding my Good Doing to the non-royal. To a few, *special* non-royal people."

My sinking stomach plummeted. The intended message of all this had been to stop interfering—not to interfere more! "You really don't have to do that," I said faintly, trying to think how this had all gone wrong. I had clearly unleashed a plague, formerly infecting only the royalty, onto the rest of the world. "You could just…not do anything, have you thought of that?"

"Don't be ridiculous, Tarry," Marj said, eyes wide and sparkles bright. "The world needs me."

The world needed something, but it wasn't Marj and her cohort.

"And right now," she continued, clasping her hands together, "their Majesties need me to tell them about their daughter."

She bustled off and I trailed along after her, because I might as well see this through. And I kind of wanted to see how she'd explain recent events. The throne room was buzzing just like everywhere else, but it was a more high class buzzing in there. Marj swept right up to the thrones, the crowd parting before her. I mingled, discreetly. I wanted to see, but I didn't want to talk. I've never liked delivering bad news.

"Marjoram, my dear," the queen quavered, coming a few steps down from her throne to Marj, "whatever is going on? Everyone seems to have fallen asleep!"

"Yes, there was a spell to that effect, but it proved temporary," Marj said, which struck me as a very careful way to put it.

The queen clasped her hands together, knuckles white and eyes widening in mingled hope and fear. "Then…do you mean that the curse is over? That our daughter…?"

I winced, and looked away. Maybe I should have stayed in the courtyard.

"Alas, I must deliver sad news to you." Marj assumed her tragic mode, head to the side, hands folded, mouth pulled down. I swear she practices it. "It is my deepest regret to inform you that your beloved daughter has pricked her finger and fallen into an enchanted sleep."

The king came down from his throne too, and put an arm around his wife. "But we all awoke from our enchanted sleep. Surely Rosaline—"

"Curses are very complicated," Marj said, expression fixed. "And sadly, Rosaline has fallen under the curse and will not awake for a hundred years."

A ripple of exclamations and dismay ran through the room. The queen gave one pained cry then turned to hide her face against her husband's shoulder, her own shoulders shaking. I didn't read their auras. I didn't want to see.

The court was all in a flurry around me, and I kept my head down and kicked at the base of the pillar I was standing near. I wished we could just send someone up to kiss Rosaline and wake her now—but that would bring Echinacea back. She'd probably kill the princess and flame half the court besides. So really it was better this way.

Only, 'better' wasn't always the same thing as 'good.'

And maybe, if everyone wasn't so stuck on tradition, if Marj and the other Good Fairies ever really tried to help, to counter the Evil Fairies…but one battle at a time.

The queen lifted her head again after a few minutes, and said, "I want to see my daughter."

"Of course," Marj said instantly. "I've put her on such a nice bed. Let me show you."

So Marj led the king and queen off to see their sleeping princess, and I slipped out. It wasn't like I was going to do anything here, and why hang around with the people in mourning when I could go find someone more cheerful?

On a hunch, I went out through the same door Jack and I had used earlier in the day. The hallway beyond, with its scattering of sleepers, had cleared of people. I followed it along to the first door back out into the courtyard, and from there I didn't have to look far before I spotted the farmer's son again. He had a six-year-old boy clinging to his leg and excitedly chattering about a dragon, while a woman was holding onto his arm, smiling through tear stains and telling him how worried she'd been. So *that* was all right.

Grin restored, I went to look for Jack and Emmy. They were in another part of the courtyard, sitting on a step and far too absorbed in each other to pay any attention to all the hubbub going on around them.

"Mind if I join you?" I asked.

Jack looked up with a grin of his own. "Hello, Tarragon. You're full-sized now."

"Maybe I was full-sized before," I countered, "if a foot tall is my normal size, and now I'm grown to gigantic proportions."

He shook his head. "I'm not going to argue about that. Or about anything, considering how much I owe you right now."

"Don't mention it. Just let me have that pound of cheese," I said as I sat down, moving the baby goat to the side to make room. I scratched the Little One's head, and pulled a plum out of my jacket pocket with my other hand. Some of those waking servants had left trays or baskets of food behind when they went looking for friends or answers. "Besides, I scored a point on Marj. For that, I may owe you one. You too, Emmy, you told her off beautifully." It wasn't their fault Marj was charging off in the wrong direction. And it really had given me more ammunition in arguments with her. Even if she hadn't come around on the philosophy the way I had hoped.

"Thank you, I think," Emmy said. "You're the smaller dragon, right? We've never exactly been introduced."

"Strange, that's true," I reflected, polishing the plum against my sleeve. "I was the smaller dragon, yes. The name is Tarragon, at your service."

"Emmaline Lang, and it's a pleasure to meet you." She tipped her head to one side thoughtfully. "Tarragon…that explains it then."

"Explains what?" Jack asked.

"The way he turned into a dragon. Tarragon can also be called dragon-herb."

I blinked in surprise, swallowed a mouthful of plum and asked, "How did you know that?"

"I *do* work in a kitchen."

"So you do," I agreed. "Yet another advantage of kitchen maids over princesses. Never yet met a princess who knew anything about my name." I'd always been kind of proud of it, too.

"I think kitchen maids have plenty of advantages," Jack remarked, putting his hand on her shoulder.

She turned towards him. "I rather like goatherds myself."

"Don't mind us," I murmured, offering a piece of plum to the Little One.

I don't think they would have. But all of a sudden Jack exclaimed, "*Goatherds*. My goats! I left them outside of the roses!"

"They're fine," I said lazily, "I cast a spell, remember?"

"Yeah, but still." He got up to his feet, grabbed Emmy's hand and started towards the nearest gate.

I picked up the Little One, pulled another plum out of a pocket, and followed them, at an easy stroll but still keeping up. There's a trick to it. Once we reached the outer wall of the castle, Jack paused in the last archway.

"I'm trying to remember where I left them," he said, head turning as he made a scan of the surroundings. "Everything looks different now without the roses. Where did we come in? Wasn't it towards the north?"

"The northeast," I contributed.

"Yeah, thanks, the northeast..." He trailed off, looking at me. "Say. Magical guide and all, any guidance to offer here?"

"Now that you ask." I concentrated a moment, and then nodded. "Head right."

We found the goats within a few minutes. I was perfectly capable of being a useful magical guide, when I tried properly and didn't have my hands tied by the rules of a wager. The goats hadn't wandered at all, and were standing around near the castle walls, placidly chomping on Marj's shrunken rosebushes. I felt like encouraging them to carry on. Jack tended more towards alarm.

"Hey, don't eat those," he ordered, letting go of Emmy's hand so that he could push his goats away from the roses. "Those are magical roses and there's no telling what they'll do to you." He got the goats away and turned around, only to discover that, while his back was turned, the Little One had tried an experimental nibble. I may or may not have encouraged her. Jack groaned. "Not you *too*."

Emmy was giggling. I don't giggle, but I shared the sentiment, and probably looked it.

"You two are no help," Jack complained.

"What can I say?" I said with a shrug. "I'm not a certified Good Fairy. It's part of my charm."

Chapter Eight

I kept an eye on the Waldisane castle and its inhabitants over the next few weeks and months. I wasn't *obligated* to the way Marj was (it was so good not being a Good Fairy), but I kept an eye out anyway. Just out of curiosity, just to see how it all turned out.

I didn't get close, though. Marj kept popping here and there, shedding sparkles and drinking tea and setting up a tower in the woods to hold the sleeping princess and growing roses around it, and I definitely didn't want to get tangled up in all of that. Or to see Marj, period.

Besides, the king and queen were mourning their daughter, and that was far too depressing a situation for me to want to get near.

Everything was far more cheerful out in the fields. I popped there every so often to see how Jack and Emmy were faring—which was very well. And that was very good for me too. I had standing policy for five centuries of not getting too attached to anyone, which meant I rarely checked back in on people after crossing paths at a party or christening, but I had a vested interest this time. After all, if Jack and Emmy's romance fell to pieces, what would become of my new evidence to convince Marj that commoners could have True Love?

Eventually the day came when my path crossed with Marj's again, and I didn't dodge quickly enough. It was at a fairy party, but not hosted by a Good Fairy so the sparkle count was manageable. Besides, the scones were amazing. I had a splendid time, until Marj cornered me halfway through the afternoon, feeling that she must fill me in on every detail of the delightful tower she had built for Rosaline.

I nodded a lot and ate three scones—orange flavored, with raisons.

Finally, after describing the careful thought put into each and every pillow on Rosaline's bed, she asked idly, "So whatever became of those commoners you were so fond of?"

I gritted my teeth. I *wanted* to answer this question, and she still managed to ask it in a way that got my hackles up. "You mean Jack and Emmy? The ones who proved that you don't have to be a royal to have true love?"

"If that was their names," she said idly. "So they are still in love?"

"*Yes*, they're still in love," I said, and bit viciously into a fourth scone.

She studied the fingernails of one hand, and with a wave of her other hand turned them lavender, with little red heart patterns. "You really think it'll persist much longer?"

She was far too good at needling me. It was a talent of hers I did not appreciate. "Yes, of course it's going to persist. Just as lasting and permanent and a good sight more real than those nonsensical royal relationships you like to magic along. They're getting married next month and I'm sure that—"

"*Married?*" She looked up from her nails, and her sparkles took on a brighter shade of pink. "But that means a wedding! Why wasn't I informed? I adore weddings!"

She also adored shedding sparkles and hearts and conjuring up doves and roses and…you have no idea how awful it could get. Truly.

"Small wedding," I said quickly, waving my hands in a deprecating gesture. "Very small. Just a small little tiny affair, nothing noteworthy—"

"But I must attend!" She clasped her hands together, looking odd since only one had lavender nails. "It would be so quaint and delightful."

"Out of country too," I rambled on, "Jack's from Perrelda, next kingdom over to the west, you know, they're planning to move there anyway, and besides, he said his family would never forgive him if he didn't have his wedding back there, so it's not even a local wedding, and—"

"And why in the cosmos should that matter? I can transport there as easily as anywhere else."

True, it didn't matter in the slightest. I was just clutching at straws, and I was ready to reach for some desperate ones. "But they're not royalty or anything, and I know how you feel about commoners, so surely you don't really want to—"

"I have been considering what you said on that subject," she said, voice growing firm.

"Um." I swallowed. "You have?"

"Yes." She nodded decisively. "I have decided to explore the greater options for Doing Good outside of the realm of royalty. At least among special individuals."

I had definitely unleashed a plague. "But you don't need to do anything good to Jack and Emmy's wedding. Really."

"We'll see," she said with an airy wave of one hand. "I just want to attend. Help a little with the decorations."

Fairy Queen preserve us. Marj had no real concept of what 'a little' actually meant. 'Restraint' and 'subtlety' were also words she was unfamiliar with.

I tried. Honestly. I did my best to convince her to keep her nose and her wings out of the whole business, but Marj can be awfully stubborn when she fixes on something. It runs in the family.

Eventually I gave up arguing and excused myself to go warn Jack and Emmy of the approaching doom.

I did a quick orienting spell, then popped into the field where Jack was grazing his goats. Emmy was there too, visiting on her afternoon off from the castle. I told myself that was a positive; tell them both at once and get it over with.

I had opted for being a foot tall again. My dragon form would have been more defensible, but I thought I would look more pitiful if I was small.

"Hello, Tarry, you've shrunk again today," Jack greeted me as I trudged up the hillside they were sitting on, and Emmy chimed in with a cheery, "Hello, Tarry."

I sat down cross-legged on the grass at the top and heaved a deep, deep sigh, dredged up from the very depthmost depths of my being. "I'm sorry. I'm so sorry. I'm so, so, so, so sorry."

"What did you do?" Jack asked, eyes narrowing in suspicion.

"It can't be that bad," Emmy said.

"Maybe it is. What did you do?"

"Promise you won't hate me?"

"It really can't be that bad."

"What did you *do*?"

"Promise you at least won't hate me for very long?"

"Tarragon, I swear, what did you—"

"We promise," Emmy interrupted. "Now what happened?"

I sighed one of those depthmost sighs again. "I kind of sort of accidentally let slip to Marj that you're getting married next month. She wants to come."

Jack frowned. "Marj. Is she the one with all the…" He trailed off, fluttering his hands in the air.

"That's the one. With all the…" I fluttered my hands too. "That's Marj."

"I think it's nice," Emmy commented. "I mean, I was upset with her about putting everyone to sleep, of course, but she did wake them all up again in the end. It's nice that she wants to come to our wedding."

"You're insane," I informed her. "She wants to help *decorate*."

"See? That's sweet," Emmy said, clasping her hands around one knee. "I think it's sweet."

I groaned. "It's not sweet. It's sparkly. And dove-strewn. And completely horrible."

She shook her head. "You're overreacting. Weddings are supposed to be dove-strewn. I'm sure that whatever Marj has in mind will be lovely."

I shot an appealing look at Jack, hoping for an ally. He didn't exactly rise to that role, just shrugging. "I mean, if Emmy's happy about it…"

Well. At least they weren't angry with me. That was something. "Fine. It's up to you." Masses of doves never killed anyone. Although, if Marj got the wrong idea into her head, death was not actually beyond the realm of possibilities for this situation. "But I absolutely have to draw the line, if she tries to offer you a gift, any gift at all, *refuse*. Tell her you're not interested, you don't want it, just don't take it." I kept running through the possibilities and felt my head spinning. "Why don't you just elope? It's not too late, you could go today!"

Emmy laughed. "I'm sure everything will be fine."

If they weren't going to listen to friendly advice, what could I do? "All right, have your dove-strewn wedding next month. But *no gifts* from Marj." I beckoned the Little One—bigger by now—who settled down behind me, so I could lean back against her. "And don't forget I advised you to elope instead."

"We can't elope," Jack said. "I already wrote to my cousin Catherine to tell her we're coming. Catherine and Uncle Jacob are expecting us to have the wedding at their inn."

"Is it a really low-class, common inn?" I asked hopefully.

Jack lifted his chin, looking offended. "The Nightingale is a perfectly respectable inn. It's been in the family for forty years, and Catherine and Uncle Jacob do a very good job running it."

"Oh. I was hoping Marj might be scared off by an inn, if it was disheveled enough."

Maybe it was my glum expression that convinced Jack not to be insulted after all. "Cheer up, Tarry. It's a nice inn and they're nice family and they'd be very disappointed if we eloped. Besides," he continued, with a slight laugh, "I didn't actually tell Catherine that we're getting married at her inn. I told her I was getting married, and *she* told *me* that it would be at The Nightingale. Once Catherine decides something, it happens."

"A very strong-willed woman?" I suggested.

"Definitely. But in a good way," he added quickly. "Like when we were kids, she always decided what game we'd play. Only, that was because everyone else was standing around saying, 'I don't know, what do *you* want to do,' and Catherine would actually say something. Things get done when she's around."

"Which I suppose makes the wedding, and the doves, inevitable." I metaphorically threw up my hands, and literally nudged the Little One to shift into a more comfortable position for leaning. "So, after the wedding," I resumed. "Future plans?"

Jack reached out to pick up Emmy's hand from where it rested on the grass. "You know we were planning to stay in Perrelda. It's a good country, the family's there, and I always figured I'd settle there when…well, when I decided to settle somewhere."

"And I don't have any family near here anyway," Emmy said, "so it makes sense to go back there. And there's fields and a castle there, the same as here."

"I can still take care of the goats, settle in one place and expand the herd."

"I can work in a new castle…for a year or two, anyway," Emmy said, cheeks turning slightly pink.

"A year or two?" I repeated

"You know, until—well, eventually we'll…"

I blinked. "Oh, you mean until you're—oh that's nice, that's sweet. Can I come to the christening?"

Emmy giggled. "Of course."

"Don't you think you're rushing this?" Jack protested.

"Hey, can I give a christening gift?" I asked, eyes lighting up. I'd always secretly wanted to, but the royalty has this way of looking at me funny that dampens my enthusiasm. "I could come up with such a good christening gift. None of these musical dulcet voices, you know, I could do so much better than that. Much more creative. More practical, too. Maybe the ability to talk to horses. Or to fly, that's a good one."

"I really think you're rushing this," Jack muttered, glaring down at the grass.

"And I swear I won't slip to Marj about this one, absolutely not. No Good Fairies or Evil Fairies, they're both disasters at christenings. I'm practically the only fairy safe to invite. Ooh, I know, I could give a christening gift to be impervious to magic spells, just in case Marj manages to turn up, and wants to give the poor kid an angelic disposition!"

"Can we try to focus on the wedding first?" Jack asked, with an almost plaintive note in his voice. "Before we jump to the next event?"

"Right. Of course. The wedding." My mood and expression soured. "With all the doves."

"I think doves are lovely," Emmy said.

"Yeah, in moderation. Marj doesn't believe in moderation." I sighed. "Feathers everywhere."

And sure enough, when the day arrived, there were feathers. Everywhere.

Chapter Nine

I arrived at The Nightingale for Jack and Emmy's wedding a couple hours before the ceremony, expecting to be early. I found plenty of preparation still going on, but I was too late for a final attempt to stop Marj before she started decorating. She was already fully mobilized when I strolled in the door.

I could see at a glance why the place hadn't scared Marj away. Nothing fancy, but the floors were polished wood, plenty of light came in through the front windows, the fireplace didn't smoke and there was a level of overall cleanliness I would have approved of, if I hadn't hoped to frighten Marj away with a little wholesome dust.

To *my* eye, as I stood by the door, the decorations looked complete. All the tables had been pushed off to the side, and chairs were lined up in rows at the center of the room. A carpet rolled out for an aisle, with an arch covered in blue loops of cloth at the end. All very lovely, very simple. Which meant Marj had barely got started.

Even as I approached her, she waved a hand and sent a shower of gold sparkles over the archway.

"Hello, Marj," I said, sticking my hands in my pockets. "I see you came to decorate."

"I told you I wouldn't miss it! And in a couple more hours, it should be perfect."

The things she could do in a couple of hours were alarming. "Are you really sure you have time for all of this in your busy schedule?"

"Oh yes, I blocked the whole day off!" she said, smiling widely at me.

Great. So much for tactic one. Next attempt. "All the same, maybe you shouldn't waste your considerable decorating talents on such a small event," I said, and tried to smile winningly.

"I consider it a challenge," Marj said, and snapped her fingers. A ding sounded through the room, and a dove popped into existence in mid-air between Marj and me.

"Well, maybe, but—" I broke off, taking a hasty step back as another dove materialized a few inches from my face, accompanied by its own dinging. "You did that deliberately!"

"I don't know what you're talking about, Tarry," Marj trilled, turning away to face the back wall. She raised both hands above her head, and tendrils of roses swarmed up over the wall. Meanwhile the dinging went on, more doves appearing every few seconds.

I retired in defeat, retreating back to the counter running along one long wall. Having something at my back made me feel I was less likely to be attacked by doves, or tripped over by The Nightingale's staff, and I could still watch Marj. Maybe I'd spot an opportunity to damp down some of the nonsense. After all, it was my fault she was here.

I had barely taken up my new post in time to get out of the path of a young woman hurrying out of the kitchen. "I thought I heard the clock," she said, glanced around at the dozen people moving through the room carrying boxes and trays, and then looked at me. Probably because I was the only one not moving. "It can't be twelve already?"

Luckily, I have a good sense of time. "No, it's only a little past ten. The ringing noise is—"

Right on cue, another ding and another dove arrived in a flurry of feathers.

She blinked at the nearest dove, then her gaze swept around the room to take in the considerable flock that had already formed. "That's…a lot of doves." She grimaced, pulling her long chestnut braid over one shoulder. "A vast multitude of doves."

"Agreed." At least I wasn't the only one with some perspective here. "But don't bother telling her. She won't listen." I might not be able to stop Marj from spraying sparkles all over the room, but I could at least head off a confrontation that would not possibly end well for any humans involved.

"I assumed that," the young woman said, and her face lightened into a smile. "Besides, I make a policy of never arguing with anyone who can turn me into a frog."

I liked the glint of humor in her brown eyes, and grinned back. "Probably wouldn't be a frog. They're too slimy. More likely she'd turn you into a kitten."

"A kitten?" she repeated, nose wrinkling in a way it hadn't when talking about frogs.

I tried a little magical reading, and picked up an impression of a garden, suggesting a more complex personality than if I'd read a single flower or a bouquet. But it didn't explain at all why she wouldn't like kittens. "It's her usual choice," I said. "Especially pink kittens."

Her irritated expression smoothed out again, face relaxing, and all she said was a light, "How charming. So how do you know what the Good Fairy would do?"

I could have told her my background, except people don't always want to have a cheerful conversation after they find out that you can turn them into a frog—or a kitten. My hair hid my ears so I could pass for human. I just said, "We're acquainted."

She nodded. "I'm Catherine, by the way." Her gaze drifted out to where Marj was now decorating each chair with a dusting of pink and gold sparkles, and her nose wrinkled again. "I don't suppose you know if the Good Fairy will take her doves and sparkles and roses with her when she leaves my inn?"

I recognized her name, although Jack's cousin was younger than I'd expected. From her face I guessed she wasn't more than nineteen, but even standing still, she projected an air of confident self-assurance that I would have expected in someone older.

"She'll probably remove some of the decorations, but I regret to say there will likely be sweeping up to do," I admitted. I studied Catherine's aura closer. Something about it didn't seem quite right, not with my impression of her from Jack's description or, now that I was looking closer, with the aura itself.

"I suppose we can always serve dove pie for supper if we have to," she remarked. "So you're a friend of Jack and Emmy's?"

Paying attention to her aura, I wasn't paying attention to what she said. She had a very carefully arranged garden, all neat rows and trimmed shrubs, but it was…flat. It was entirely too flat.

"You *are* a friend of Jack and Emmy's, right?" she prompted. "Because if you were looking for a room—"

"Oh! No—I mean, yes, I'm a friend of theirs," I said quickly. That wasn't a garden I was looking at. It was a fresco of a garden, painted on a wall. "I'm Tarry, I met them in Waldisan." I stared harder, magically-speaking. She really did have a garden in her aura, but it was tucked away behind the painted wall…

"Did you work at the castle with Emmy?"

"Uh…no." I tried to refocus my attention on the conversation. I had rarely seen someone with such a complicated aura. What was she asking? Where I had met them, right. "I…" I should have had a story ready, if I didn't want to tell her the truth.

I hadn't given that enough thought. I didn't often meet the same people twice, and now I was confronted with the problem of not knowing what Jack or Emmy might have already told her, or what she would tell them later that could get awkward.

I was still weighing alternative responses, and seriously considering using magic to facilitate a distraction, when the problem was solved for me. Catherine's gaze darted out to the room and she called, "Sam, don't bump into that—"

There was a clatter of falling chairs and a series of thuds, as one of The Nightingale's staff sprawled amongst two over-turned chairs and a basket's-worth of rolling, bouncing walnuts.

"Who let him carry that?" Catherine muttered, leaving the counter to chase walnuts.

Whoever was responsible, I was grateful. I followed Catherine, scooping up several walnuts that had rolled in my direction.

"Sorry, Catherine," the fallen Sam said, clambering out of the tangle of chairs and gathering up nuts. He was a thin man, his red shirt his most striking feature. "They're all right, just a little…" He frowned, squinting at one walnut he was holding up. "…sparkly."

In a shimmer of gold, the chairs suddenly righted themselves, setting back in place with a screech of wooden legs against the floor. Sam scrambled backwards and nearly knocked over another chair. I snapped a quick spell to keep that chair in place, then looked up in time to see Marj sniff disdainfully and turn away, apparently feeling the situation was beneath her comment. I glared at her back, right between the fluttering wings. All right, so Sam was clumsy, but I still had my magical senses on alert, and he had a nice aura, like a puppy. One with very big paws.

Out of the corner of my eye, I noticed Catherine glaring at Marj too. Then she shook her head, and turned back to Sam with a smile. "No harm done. Brush the sparkles off, then take them out to the courtyard," she said, handing him a handkerchief pulled from her apron pocket.

"I'll help," I said immediately, not eager to return to the former topic of conversation. I pulled a handkerchief out of the air, realizing too late that that was not a good idea for discretion. I glanced quickly around, but no one seemed to have noticed.

Catherine dropped a handful of walnuts into Sam's basket, then rose to her feet. "Thanks, Tarry. And Sam, try not to trip over anything else, all right?"

"I always *try*," he said with an unabashed grin.

She smiled back for just a moment, then was off to deal with someone who had a question about a pie.

I helped Sam dust sparkles off the walnuts, and safely deliver them out to the long wooden table laid in the courtyard. I liked the prospects for the post-wedding meal. But snacking before the ceremony would probably be frowned upon, so I went back inside to avoid temptation. Besides, I still wanted to keep an eye on how much damage Marj caused.

She had added banners and trailing ribbons in every conceivable place, gold sparkles glimmered all over everything, and while the doves had eventually stopped appearing, dozens were milling about the room. Marj herself was busy adding gold patterns on the petals of her roses.

I casually leaned against the sill of an open window, where a dove was sitting cooing to itself—and casually shifted an elbow to knock the dove out into the yard. It fluttered to the ground and kept cooing. I checked on Marj. No reaction. I reached down, picked up two more doves, and tossed them out the window too.

I was liberating my seventh dove when I realized that someone in the courtyard had noticed. A tall man with dark curly hair, carrying a basket of bread, was watching me as he walked towards the inn door. He grinned when our gazes met, so I grinned back and threw the dove out into the air. It flapped off to join its fellows.

I paused in my dove-tossing to watch the man with the bread as he came into the room. Magically speaking, he looked like a forest, with young trees that were growing fast, and occasional blocks of stone scattered between the trees. Another unusual aura.

Inside, the chaos in the room had grown as the ceremony got closer—one reason I'd been able to hide my dove disposal from Marj—and Catherine was the eye of the storm that all the hubbub circled around. The forest man with his bread cut right through the swirl to approach her.

"The baker just delivered a dozen loaves, Cat," he told her. "Should they go to the kitchen to be cut up or can they just be put out in the courtyard?"

"Just put them out, Anthony, it's simpler," was all she said, and her tone was ordinary enough too. But all the colors on the fresco in her aura suddenly turned brighter, and one of the trees in her garden went into flower as she looked up at him. "And don't call me Cat," she added, giving me a sudden theory about her kitten problem.

"Sorry." Instead of turning back towards the courtyard, Anthony glanced around and asked, "Do weddings always involve this many doves?"

I glanced around too, and sad to say, I hadn't made much of a dent.

Catherine smiled—and she gave Anthony a different smile than everyone else. "Not usually."

"That's a relief," he said, a few flowers springing up in his aural forest as he looked at her smile. "I was about to suggest eloping."

"A few doves would scare you off from a wedding?"

I took a quick glance at Marj, but she wasn't paying attention to the two of them. I would definitely *not* let slip to her about another wedding, and not inflict another couple with too many doves and several gallons of sparkles.

"A few doves?" Anthony repeated. "No. An entire flock, maybe."

"My, how committed you are," she said, voice too teasing to really be severe.

He set the basket of bread down on the counter, put both hands on her waist, and kissed her forehead. "You know I'd marry you even if it involved hundreds of doves."

She set her hands on his shoulders, leaned in and kissed him lightly on the lips. "You'd better." For a moment they looked at each other, unmoving in the midst of the busy room, branches from his forest reaching out to intermingle with the flowering tree on the far side of her wall.

Even after centuries, I had never got tired of seeing people in love. It's one of my favorite things about humans, and one of the reasons I went to so many weddings.

I sent another dove to join its friends outside, glanced back at Catherine and Anthony in time to see her step back and say, "I have a million things to do still—and that bread needs to go to the courtyard."

"Whatever you want, Cat." He picked up the basket, and headed for the door.

"And don't call me that."

"Yes, dear," he said over his shoulder, with an utterly unrepentant grin.

Despite the million things left to do, Catherine watched until Anthony disappeared out the door.

I watched her watching him, and contrived to wander casually that direction as I gathered up a couple more doves. When I was close,

I asked her, "Got something against cats?" I'd always liked cats myself. I knew a talking cat who was great fun at a party.

Catherine looked at me blankly for a second, but only a second, before she made the connection. "Not really, no. I have something against nicknames. They're too…cute. And a cat is only a jump from a kitten, and kittens are silly, useless and frivolous."

"And you're none of those?"

"Not in the slightest." As if to emphasize the point, she walked away to the kitchen to make sure everything was going smoothly at that end.

I tucked a dove under each arm and strolled outside to the courtyard, where the sparkle count was lower, the chaos was about the same, and Jack was pacing.

I shooed my doves off, then leaned against the nearest wall and watched him stride up and down. "You look nervous." There was a tumultuous breeze blowing through his aura, although he seemed to have sails set to weather it, suggesting there wasn't anything too wrong there.

"I'm not nervous." Jack considered. "I might be nervous. I'm kind of nervous. Is it normal to be nervous?"

"Yes." From my vast experience on this subject, commoners tend to be more anxious before weddings than royalty do. It's usually more of a business transaction for royalty, whatever Marj may say about it.

"Should I be nervous?"

About making a vow regarding the rest of his life, and doing it in front of all his friends and family? You wouldn't catch me making a promise like that. The rest of your life is much longer when you're a fairy. I said, "No," anyway, because telling him to be worried wouldn't help.

"But I think I *am* nervous."

"Look at it this way: you already faced down a seventy-foot dragon." I clapped him on the shoulder. "Compared to that, this should be nothing."

He cocked his head for a moment, thinking, then grimaced. "It doesn't feel that way. What if I say the wrong thing?"

"Say 'yes,' and the rest will take care of itself."

I don't think he believed me. All the same, he didn't look like he was actually going to faint or be sick, and that was better than some grooms I'd seen.

When the ceremony was five minutes away, I slipped back inside to find a seat. The gleam of sparkles made me wince; it was as if half the room had been turned into gold. At least Marj finally seemed to be done. She was sitting in the front row dabbing at her eyes with a handkerchief—which seemed excessive, when nothing had even happened yet.

I like the front row too, but I chose the opposite side of the aisle from Marj. Seats were filling up, but there was space by a venerable-looking gentleman with gray hair, who looked pleasant and like he'd be a good buffer between myself and Marj. I dusted sparkles off the seat and sat down.

"Hello," I said. "Friend of the bride or the groom?"

"I suppose the groom," he answered, "considering he's my nephew."

Ah. This must be Uncle Jacob. "May I compliment you on your very fine inn?"

His expression grew warm, and we were off on a conversation about his inn, which swiftly became about his daughter too.

"I don't mind admitting she practically runs the place," he said. I wanted to chalk some of that willingness to confide up to my trustworthy face. I was sure I really did have one, the initial reaction of a certain goatherd aside.

"Must be a lot for her to do," I observed. I'd spent plenty of time wandering in and out of inns to know something of how they worked.

"She and Anthony manage it between them," Uncle Jacob continued. "He only began working here last summer, but none of us can remember how we kept the inn functioning before him. I do what I can, but Catherine really hasn't let me have proper control of anything since I was ill last winter. Even though I'm not nearly as infirm as she thinks I am."

"And you're not as well as *you* think you are either," Catherine countered, coming up just on cue. She kissed her father's cheek and sat down on his opposite side, just moments before the ceremony began.

Jack still looked nervous right until Emmy stepped through the door in a sweeping dress with blue flowers in her air. And then I'm pretty sure he forgot the rest of us were there, and even forgot about the doves and the sparkles.

So maybe he wasn't rich and powerful and endowed with fairy-given talents, and he didn't know how to use a sword. But the expression on his face as he looked at Emmy…well, any prince with any sense at all should have envied him.

The sparkles didn't blind anyone and nobody tripped over the multitude of doves I hadn't managed to push out, so I sat back, set aside my general annoyance with Marj, and just enjoyed the ceremony. No curse cropped up at the last moment to interfere and true love (because that's what it *was* and I *would* convince Marj eventually) ruled the day.

After the ceremony finished, everyone streamed out to The Nightingale's courtyard, which swiftly filled with people and food and a lot of confused doves wandering through. I had just piled up a plate from the banquet table and was looking for a seat when Marj came fluttering up to me.

"When do you think would be an appropriate time to bestow gifts?"

I dropped my plate. It flipped in midair and hit the ground, narrowly missing a dove scuttling by. "*No gifts,*" I told her, stomach flipping too. "Absolutely no gifts, Marj, I really have to insist on that."

She pursed her lips. "How utterly nonsensical. Everyone gives gifts at weddings."

"Everyone's gifts are not like your gifts," I muttered. I took a quick look around to make sure no one was looking, and cast a take-no-notice spell to be sure. Then I levitated my supper back into the air, cast a shower of magic over it to take care of any dirt and/or bruising from impact, magicked the plate up beneath the food and, when the whole thing was reassembled, took it in my hands again. "Your gifts are…unique."

"Exactly," Marj said, hands on hips. "Unique and special and I'd hate to deprive them. Do you think they'd like an enchanted castle?"

Enchanted castles tended to eat people alive; literally and figuratively were both possibilities. Besides, a castle of any sort was completely inappropriate for Jack and Emmy. "No," I said, and bit into a fruit tart. "I don't think they'd like that."

"What if I made the goats talk? And speak wisdom couplets, perhaps."

Wisdom couplets. Really now. "Absolutely not." They could never eat those goats after that.

"I could give Emmy a dress that shone like the—"

"Marj, *no*. No gifts. None."

She frowned at me, sparkles growing to an offensive brightness. "But why ever not?"

"Because…I have right of prior claim," I said, scrambling about and seizing on that as an excuse. "I claimed them as my champions. In our wager. If anyone's going to give them magical gifts, it's me. No one else."

Marj's frown didn't entirely disappear at this, but the sparkles dimmed and she said, "Well, yes. I suppose. I'd hate to tread on your toes."

Which was a laugh, since Marj treaded on everyone's toes, *all the time*, even though she usually went around a foot off the ground. But I wasn't going to contradict her. "Right," I said with a vigorous nod. "No toe treading."

"So what are you giving them?" Marj asked.

"A set of dishes that will never crack or break, and that nothing sticks to."

Her look of dissatisfaction deepened into definite disapproval. "But that's not exciting at all."

"It's a good sight more useful than a dress that shines like the sun," I said around the last mouthful of my tart. "Those things blind people, and they never wash well."

She rolled her eyes. "Oh, honestly. You are so prosaic."

"All the time. Can I go sit down and eat now?"

"I'm not stopping you."

No, but she had a thoughtful expression that was worrying me. "You're not thinking about magical gifts, are you?"

"Not for your little friends, no. But I do want to pursue the possibilities of Doing Good among the common people. If not here, there must be other opportunities."

Of all the ideas for her to actually stick to. I tried to repress a shudder. "Fine, you think *long* and hard about that. Take your time and let me know when you have an idea." Maybe I'd be able to head her off before she put anything into action.

Marj smiled sweetly. "Oh, I already have an idea. Did you hear there's going to be a ball at the castle in a few months?"

That didn't sound so bad. How much trouble could she cause interfering with a royal dance? I picked up a chicken wing from my plate. "No, that's news to me."

"Mm-hmm." The smile and sparkles brightened. "Prince Roderick is looking for a bride. They're inviting all the eligible young women in the kingdom."

That was a nice line but it had to be factually inaccurate. Perrelda was too big a country for them to literally invite every girl. Probably all the local ones, though. "I love dances like that."

"Oh, I *know*. They're so romantic."

I snorted. "Forget that. There's nothing romantic about choosing a bride based on her dancing ability. I love it that they always invite all the women, but never think to invite all the men. Creates a serious imbalance, meaning there's plenty of girls to dance with."

She rolled her eyes again, gold and pink sparkles picking up a silver edge of annoyance. "You're impossible."

"No, I just know how to have a good time. So why do you care about this dance?"

Her eyes gleamed with calculation. "I'm sure there must be some deserving common girl who needs my help to attend."

Clearly, of all the people with problems in the world, some girl who wants to go to a party is really the most in need. "Why do you always have to meddle?" I groaned, but to tell the truth, it was mostly for form. Mostly I felt relieved, because Marj may have actually hit on something harmless. Maybe I *hadn't* unleashed a disastrous force of nature on the common folk, if she could get this new idea out of her system just by arranging a dance invitation.

"I thought you would be happy that I'm helping a commoner," she snapped.

"I'd be happier if you'd just stop messing about with people's lives at all."

"You really are impossible," she huffed, and flounced off.

I went happily back to my chicken. With any luck, Marj would be too miffed to speak to me for the rest of the evening.

It took two days to get all the sparkles out of my hair, but the party was worth it. I went to the buffet table six times, and the dancing lasted past midnight. The commoners really did put on the best parties.

Although I expected I'd go to that ball the prince was putting on too. After all, the demographics were so promising.

Book Two: Cinderella's Substitute

She had fled as soon as it struck twelve, and in such haste, that she had dropped one of her little glass slippers… The king's son caused it to be proclaimed by sound of trumpet that he would marry her whose foot would exactly match with this slipper. They began by trying it on the Princesses, then on the Duchesses, and so on…The gentleman who had been entrusted with the slipper…had been ordered to try [it] on all girls without exception.

Charles Perrault

I dropped back into The Nightingale often over the months after Jack and Emmy's wedding. I rarely became a repeat visitor anywhere, but this was my kind of place—good food, friendly people and pleasantly informal. Marj would have hated it, if she had spent more time there than a brief wedding ceremony. And I had to keep an eye on Jack and Emmy, to make sure my True Love couple and arguing point with Marj stayed in love and happy.

That was a nice convenient excuse, anyway.

Deep down, I suppose I knew I kept coming back because the friendly acceptance from people who already knew me was hard to resist. Usually I drifted in and out of parties and made new friends every evening but never kept them past the final dance. And usually that was good, that was what I wanted. At least, that was easier.

But it wasn't really the same, and just by visiting Jack and Emmy a few times and going to their wedding, I'd started to drift into a different relationship. I'd started to become part of a circle, and that was something that hadn't happened in five centuries.

Five-hundred and twelve years, to be precise.

Every time I went to The Nightingale, I told myself I'd better not come too many times more. I had to cut ties eventually, I didn't stay involved with anyone for long. It always ends badly, eventually. But a few months, that was harmless enough. Nothing wrong with coming just for now. At least until Prince Roderick held that royal ball Marj had been so keen on. I had to keep an eye on that too, just in case she managed to wreak real havoc after all, and The Nightingale was as good a place as any to pick up news.

"It's still a whole week until the big event, but the entire castle is already in a flurry preparing," Emmy bemoaned on one afternoon. She had found a position as an undermaid in the kitchens of the Perreldan royal castle, giving her inside knowledge I was eager to learn.

"But it's flurried because you're making all that fantastic food," I pointed out, leaning forward where I sat at the long table in The Nightingale's kitchen. "Tell me more about the food."

She waved her hands expressively. "There's swans and peacocks and entire pigs and mountains of bread and racks of lamb and endless, endless things that need chopping and stirring and boiling and so on and so on."

"And on your day off you come to help me make bread?" Catherine said, punching a roll of dough on the counter in front of her.

Emmy shrugged, lifting flour-covered hands. "It's different. You don't yell at everyone every two minutes the way the head cook does."

She didn't need to tell to get results. The kitchen at The Nightingale was the friendliest room at the inn, and you only gained admission by doing something useful. Anthony, Jack and I had all been pressed into service to peel the mound of turnips at the center of the table. Sam had escaped only because he was deep into balancing the budget at the far end.

"Tell me about the desserts, Emmy," I said, trying to bring the conversation back to more important matters. "I want to know what to expect when I go to this ball."

"How did you get an invitation?" Anthony asked, negotiating a careful ribbon of turnip peel.

I shrugged expansively. "I have connections." It was true I had connections, but not true I had an invitation. I was just going without one. You can do that, when you're a fairy. I couldn't explain that, since I was still keeping the pointed ears and magical abilities discreet. "I wouldn't want to miss a party like this. Besides the food, all those girls can't dance with the prince all the time."

"If you're going, maybe I'll see you there," Catherine remarked, setting her dough onto a tray.

My knife slipped a half-inch and broke the continuous ribbon of my peel. "Wait, *you're* going?"

"Why not?" she asked, raising her eyebrows. "You know Marion, our upstairs maid? She and I are both going, with some of our friends."

"I thought they were only inviting women who are eligible," I said. "Because of that whole choose-a-bride business." The idea of Catherine being eager to win the eye of the prince just seemed all at odds with everything I knew about her. It was unsettling me.

She just shrugged. "Anthony and I aren't married yet, so technically I am eligible. And I always enjoy the castle's parties."

I frowned at my turnip. "Yeah, all right, but why would you want to go to a dance where the point is for the prince to pick out a bride from the attendees?"

Catherine laughed at that. "But that's not the point, Tarry. You've been listening to the palace's stories. They want everyone to believe that every girl in this country is simply fainting with delight over the prospect of marrying the handsome Prince Roderick."

"That implies unfortunate ideas about the rest of the men in the country, doesn't it?" Emmy commented.

"It does," Anthony said, pausing with a new turnip in hand. "I never considered that angle. That's rather disturbing, actually."

"But it's not true anyway," Catherine said, closing the oven door behind her loaf of bread. She reached for a dish towel to wipe her hands. "Plenty of girls toy with the idea of marrying the prince, but for most of them, it's much more important that it will be a good party with excellent food, and all their friends are going. That's why I'm going."

And that was a reason for attending a party that I could understand. Even so, I had been to this type of ball before, and I was none too sure that everyone had the same attitude as Catherine. Maybe most of the girls realized they were unlikely to capture the prince, but I'd also bet most were secretly hoping.

Even if Catherine had a very rational viewpoint about the whole thing, I was surprised by the lack of objection from another quarter. I glanced at Anthony. "So you really don't mind that she's going to a dance where the prince is choosing a bride?"

He looked up from his turnip with a grin. "You say that like you expect me to forbid it."

"We can guess how effective that would be," Jack murmured.

Catherine flicked Jack with the end of her dish towel. "If it really bothers him, I won't go." She turned and looked expectantly at Anthony. "So?"

"It depends." Anthony set his knife down, folded his hands and regarded her with mock gravity. "Do you have any intention whatsoever of falling in love with the prince?"

Catherine smiled sweetly. "None at all."

Anthony picked up his knife again. "Then I'm not bothered."

"But then again," Catherine drawled, eyes glinting wickedly, "these things do have a way of happening unexpectedly."

Anthony looked across the table at me. "As long as you're going, how's about you make sure she doesn't dance with the prince?"

I shook my head. "What makes you think I have that kind of power?"

"Oh, I *see*," Catherine said, "so I'm allowed to go, but I'm forbidden to dance with His Royal Highness?" Her hands were on her hips in disapproval, but her eyes were merry. And, for that matter, her aura was merry too when I checked it, with sun shining and flowers blooming in that garden she had behind her wall.

Anthony reached out one arm, caught her around the waist and pulled her down onto his lap. "You can dance with anyone you want. As long as you come back home to me."

"Always," she said, placed her hands on his shoulders, and lightly kissed him. "Now let me up, I have two more loaves of bread to prepare."

"That's my romantic Cat," Anthony said with a laugh, releasing her.

"And don't call me that," she said, throwing the dish towel at him.

"Sorry," Anthony said, catching the cloth in one hand. "You know, if you *do* marry the prince, I expect you to at least name your firstborn child after me."

"Naturally," Catherine agreed. "If it's a boy," she added, and dodged the towel Anthony threw back at her. They both appeared to turn their attention away from each other at that point...but to my magical eyes, the trees in each of their auras were still leaning towards the other.

I grinned down at my turnips. I did like being around happy people who were in love, and having those people inhabit an inn with a steady stream of good food was not an inconsequential bonus. I knew it would be time to move on soon, because I always moved on, but I was enjoying it while it lasted.

The castle kitchens remained flurried for the rest of the week, as did the rest of the castle. The reports on the food got better every time I talked to Emmy, and by the time the evening of the party arrived, I had a numbered list in my head of over two dozen dishes I was determined to taste.

I arrived outside the castle gates with a take-no-notice spell firmly in place, and joined the winding line of people going up the front steps and into the castle. The footmen failed to notice that I didn't present an invitation, and I just strolled on into the ballroom among the crowds of lace and satin and twinkling jewels.

The ballroom was one of those marble and gilt affairs, with soaring pillars and enough room to hold, if not every woman in the country, still a pretty good selection. Also a banquet table stretching all along one lengthy wall, heaped high with roasted meat and stacked tarts, pies and cakes and all manner of delicacies. I headed that direction.

And that's where Catherine found me, midway through the evening. "I knew you'd be over here," she said with evident satisfaction, as we both stood with our plates near the roasted duck.

"You're clearly insightful," I said, raising my knife in salute.

"Not really," she laughed, "you're just obvious on this subject."

On food, yes. On other subjects, less so. "I happen to appreciate the finer things in life, like stuffed swan. Have you tried the stuffed swan?"

"I haven't," she said. "This is my first pass at the table."

It was my seventh, but who counts? "Let me give you the grand tour," I said, and did.

Catherine was wearing a green dress that was blessedly free of sparkles or excess bows, and had her hair pinned up instead of in its usual single braid. She looked both elegant and normal, which can be a difficult combination to pull off. Believe me, quite a few of those girls had gone altogether overboard trying to dress themselves up to catch the prince. If I was him I'd have been frightened, but princes usually don't mind having hundreds of girls throw themselves at their feet, literally or figuratively.

Me, I thought Catherine had the right idea on it. Never mind the prince, and enjoy the party. And the refreshments.

"And there at the end," I concluded the tour of the table, "they have roasted goat, but don't tell Jack."

"I don't think Jack minds, although he does get concerned that his goats would be alarmed by talk like that."

"Perfectly reasonable concern. Let's find somewhere to eat."

We found a free space at one of the dining tables along a second wall, and as we ate we discussed the dance and the dancers and the music. We were nearly finished with our food when I finally asked the obvious question: "So, have you danced with the prince?"

Her eyebrows lowered, but not far enough to be really alarming. "Why, are you planning to report to Anthony?"

I grinned. "I doubt he's expecting me to. Just curious."

"Well, I haven't. No one has." She waved her hand in the direction of the local royalty. "Almost no one. Haven't you noticed? He's been dancing with that one girl all night."

"I wasn't paying attention." I try not to pay too much attention to princes. I peered through the passing figures in the crowd, trying to catch sight of him now.

"You're the only one who wasn't. Didn't you see the way half of the women are glaring?"

"Sure, but I figured it was just a general feeling of being slighted." Invite ten times as many women as men to a party involving coupled dancing, and you can't possibly avoid a large percentage feeling snubbed. Simple math. The girls' feelings had clearly not been uppermost in mind when the royalty planned the dance; they just wanted to trot as many girls as possible past His Royal Highness, so he could choose one out of the herd.

Other dancers finally parted enough that I could see Prince Roderick and his partner. They were almost at the other end of the hall, and all I could see of the girl was her blonde hair and her pink dress, sparkling in the light from the chandeliers.

Maybe it was the sparkles that stopped me from trying to look closer. For just a minute, I thought of Marj, of her plans to help a deserving girl go to the dance…but sparkles were strangely popular; there were other women who sparked a bit when the light hit them. Any one of them could be the girl Marj had decided to help. I hadn't heard anything more about her plans; with any luck, whatever girl it was would have a perfectly nice evening and then go home again. No problems, no dire consequences, nothing for me to worry about.

Still, the sparkles made my spine prickle. I didn't want to sit there and contemplate them anymore. That's probably why I pushed aside my plate—it was empty anyway—and asked Catherine if she'd like to dance.

Catherine hesitated. "I should try to find Marion and the other girls I came with. I lost track of them a few dance sets ago, just before I decided I was too hungry to hunt through the crowd for them without getting something to eat first."

I assumed an expression of sorrow. "I feel rejected. And you're missing out too; you're never going to meet a better dancer than me." I wasn't kidding on that last part. I had centuries of experiences attending dances and parties and forest revels, although the dance steps had changed a little over the decades.

She laughed, taking my dismay no more seriously than I'd intended her to. "All right, Tarry, maybe a dance or two."

It was three before we actually got down to the business of finding Catherine's friends, which I discreetly facilitated with a little magic. I had met Marion, so I could find her again. Once we were all together, introductions went around and we reached a consensus that it was too warm inside. So I somehow ended up out in the garden with four charming girls—not that I'm complaining.

With a shortage of benches outside, Catherine and I both perched on the edge of a fountain. While the other girls chatted about the prince and what few men were present, and complained about that particular shortage, Catherine pulled her shoes off, remarking, "My feet are killing me. I should've known these new shoes were a bad idea, but my old dance shoes have a hole in the toe."

"Are they too tight?" I hazarded, because I had to say something. It was very much a guess, considering I hadn't personally had sore feet in five hundred years. Fairies don't walk that much, not even ones like me who don't hover.

"Just the opposite," Catherine said, dropping one shoe and then another with a soft thud onto the pavement beside the fountain. "Too big. My usual cobbler was so busy with extra demands for the dance that I had to go to a new one, and I don't think he believed his own measurements about how small my feet are."

I looked down at her feet. "They are small." They were. And that was about as far as I could have taken that conversation, because there's just not much that I can say about shoes or feet. Or that I would want to say. Luckily, we were interrupted at that moment by the ringing of the enormous clock in the grand hall.

At the first toll, there was an exclamation from a corner of the gardens screened by a cluster of trees. "Oh, it's *midnight*! I lost track of the time. I have to go!"

A man's voice answered. "But wait, you can't just leave *me*."

I shook my head. Leaving at midnight? The party would go on until two at least, leaving plenty more time for more trips to the buffet.

Or more dances, if that's what you like. But the girl in the garden apparently didn't like anything enough to stay longer. She emerged from the trees and ran across the lawn, stumbled once but kept going.

"Isn't that the girl who was dancing with the prince?" Catherine said as we watched. "I recognize the sparkles on the dress."

"Here he comes too," I observed, and tried not to notice that an oddly early exit from a woman wearing a sparkly dress *could* mean Marj was involved after all...but it wasn't proof, you know. People could do odd things without Marj being behind it.

Prince Roderick came running out of the trees a few bells after the sparkly girl. I recognized him by his red jacket, all done up with elaborate gold braid. You'd think an able-bodied young man would be able to catch a girl wearing heels and an ankle-length dress, but no. By the time the twelfth toll tolled, she had disappeared down the walk, off the castle grounds and out of sight.

He was yelling "wait," but she didn't come back. I could've flicked magic here or there, but if she didn't want to stay, it wasn't my business to interfere. *I* don't manipulate the love lives of the royalty.

"I wonder what happened there," Catherine mused, hands clasped around one knee. "You don't usually hear about girls running away from princes."

"Maybe she didn't like him," I said with a shrug. "Not all princes are charming."

"Maybe," Catherine acknowledged, "but she sounded regretful when she said it was midnight."

Prince Roderick had stopped on the lawn, close to where the girl had stumbled. He bent down to pick something up, and I cast a minor spell to sharpen my eyesight so I could see what it was.

It turned out to be a shoe, made of glass. I felt a new respect for the girl involved—first for walking at all in glass shoes, and then for continuing to run in only one. And I also felt an increase in the qualms I was trying to ignore, because giving a girl shoes made out of glass was exactly the kind of thing that would seem like a good idea to Marj.

Or she could just be a wealthy girl with eccentric taste in footwear. That was entirely possible too.

The prince slowly walked back into the castle, gazing at the shoe in his hand.

"I wonder what they're going to do about finding him a bride now," Catherine said, as Prince Roderick disappeared inside. "The one he would have picked just ran off, and after ignoring everyone else all night, he can't go choose one of them now. It wouldn't look right."

I tapped my fingertips together. "Yes, and we must always be mindful of how things look. They'll probably launch a grand search for the girl who ran away. That's what they usually do. I wonder if she wants to be found."

"They *usually* do that?" Catherine said, laughter lurking in her eyes. "You've been through this before?"

I must have been more worried than I wanted to admit, because I shouldn't have said that. "I've heard stories," I said with a vague wave of one hand. Actually I'd seen it all before, but admitting that would reveal my origins. Humans have short life spans and usually only see the adventures of two, maybe three generations of royalty. We fairies who live longer and travel farther are more fortunate—or less so—to see much more royalty go by, and things like this come up more often than you'd think. Not the precise details, necessarily, but princes hunting for lost damsels was pretty usual.

Catherine didn't ask about those stories I'd heard, and I quickly suggested heading back inside for another trip past the food, to avoid giving her more time to think about it.

Tragically, I only had time for one more plate before the party broke up early. The end of the ball occurred directly after the royal herald announced that Prince Roderick's choosing of a bride would be unavoidably and regrettably delayed due to unforeseeable and unpreventable circumstances, etc., etc.

Clearly they'd try to hunt down the girl with the glass slipper, and I just hoped she didn't have a fairy backing her. Not that it would *necessarily* be a bad thing if Marj helped some girl marry a prince, except…it was Marj. It would surely go wrong somehow if she was involved.

I would have felt better if the royalty had decided that, seeing as the girl ran away, maybe they should just take a hint and drop the idea. But that's how I saw it, and I'm not a prince. They see the world differently.

Catherine and her friends left the ball in a shared carriage, and I walked a short distance away from the castle before I popped out. Just before I left, I cast a quick alert spell. If anything crucial developed regarding fleeing damsels and glass shoes, I'd know about it. I couldn't exactly define what crisis might come out of this, but I wanted to know what happened. Just in case.

Chapter Eleven

Prince Roderick couldn't have been too desperate to find his missing girl. For two days, my magical alert didn't ding at all. I wavered between hoping this meant they were dropping the idea after all, and worrying that delay just meant a more elaborate disaster was building.

Finally, when I was about to go to a festival in Giramm, my magic senses told me there were new developments with the Perreldan prince. My spell couldn't tell me what, but I did know where—the main square of Ryvideau, center of the capital city and not far from The Nightingale. I consoled myself with the thought that Girammese cuisine tended to be bland anyway and, turning invisible as a precaution, transported off to the square. I needed to find out whether I should worry or not, and maybe if all was well I'd make it to the festival only a little late.

The main square was a nice big one with shops on four sides and a couple fountains. I could see the castle looming on the hill up above, but could barely see the flagstones of the square for the crowd gathered. Had to be hundreds of people, who presumably had heard by more conventional means that there was news to be had. Trumpet fanfares were drawing ever more people in.

I maneuvered through the crowd, a dicey business while invisible. Although at least the place was packed enough that people could always blame any jostling on the visible crowd around them. I had to wave a little magic about when people just wouldn't move, but finally got myself into a position leaning up against a lightpost where I could see the royal herald. He was a thin man of indeterminate height perched on horseback, with very heavy gold braid on his shoulders.

The four guards accompanying the herald broke off their incessant and excessive trumpeting, and the herald launched into his announcement—with a long round of "hear ye, hear ye's" and so on. I rolled my eyes, and was thoroughly regretting the lack of refreshments for the occasion by the time he finally got to the heart of the matter.

"The royal family is hereby making it known to all the people of the kingdom that, due to His Most Royal Highness Prince Charles Henry Albert Roderick Michael Irwin Norman Gillian the Third's chosen bride's tragic and mysterious disappearance from the middle of the royal ball held two days past, leaving only this glass slipper behind her, the royal family has resolved that every girl who attended the ball shall try on this slipper, and the crown prince shall marry whatsoever maiden the shoe fits."

I watched to see if he'd have to take a deep breath after that absurdly long sentence, but if so, he hid it well. I hadn't realized Prince Roderick went by his fourth name. Shows how much I care about royalty's names. As for the rest of the announcement, well, it about figured. I had expected a hunt for the missing girl.

Behind the herald, one of the guards tucked his trumpet under one arm and held up the glass slipper on a pillow, while a buzz ran through the square—a largely female buzz, I noted.

I crossed my arms and leaned back against my lamppost with a more relaxed feeling. This seemed pretty harmless. Stupid, but harmless. So they wasted a lot of time trying a shoe on a lot of girls, so what? The girls would probably have fun with it and, barring glass shards, nobody was going to get hurt. Maybe they'd find the right girl (though surely there had to be more reasonable ways to locate someone?) and maybe not, but like I said, I didn't care much about the royalty's romances.

I also didn't especially care to watch crowds of girls fall over themselves trying to get a shoe on, so I was ready to pop out to that festival. Just before I could, a goat came nosing up to me, seeing right through my invisibility spell and butting its head against my leg.

"Shoo," I said with a wave of one hand, and the goat bleated at me reproachfully. That's when I realized I actually knew this goat. "Oh, hello, Little One. I suppose Jack still hasn't come up with another name for you?"

She *maa*ed a negatory.

"I thought not," I remarked, and then looked around to see if I could spot Jack. Considering that he had several other goats surrounding him, it wasn't hard. I phased visible carefully. There's a method that doesn't make people wonder how you've suddenly appeared. With the Little One at my heels, I worked my way across the square towards Jack. I gave a careful berth to the crowd of girls surrounding the royal herald.

"Happen to lose a goat?" I asked Jack when we were close.

He turned around just as the Little One bumped up against his legs. "*There* you are," he said to her, then looked up and saw me. "Hey, Tarry. What are you doing here?"

"Came to hear the royal announcement," I said, jerking a thumb back towards the herald. "You too?"

"No, just here by chance. I was on my way back to The Nightingale to stable the goats for the night."

"Want company on the walk?" I could have gone on to that festival…but now I was thinking I might quite like to wander by The Nightingale instead. It was almost time for supper.

"Glad to have it," Jack said, and we fell into step walking out of the square and down the relevant street. "Catherine mentioned she saw you at the ball."

"I like a good party. And the food was wonderful." I sighed, feeling hungrier at the memory. "Do you think Emmy knows the recipe for the stuffed swan?"

He laughed. "She might."

At The Nightingale, we went in through the back door directly into the kitchen, ducking under the wisteria blooming above the doorway. The kitchen was in its usual hubbub, with preparations for the evening meal well underway. Jack and I found places to sit where we wouldn't be tripped over, and joined the general bustle of conversation. Prince Roderick and his decree was one topic of conversation, but the weather, the guests, the menu for supper, and the plans for the next month were topics too.

"So where's Anthony today?" I asked, stealing a piece of mushroom that Catherine was chopping.

"He's out of town," she said, without interrupting the steady rhythm of her knife. "He usually is this time of month, on the trip to Alphoson Port for supplies."

Marion was cutting onions next to Catherine, and elbowed her good-naturedly. "But he might be back tonight, something Catherine is *distinctly* aware of. She's in a much better mood today than she was yesterday."

"Yesterday I was tired from staying up too late dancing," Catherine countered. "And today I am well-rested, the inn has no vacancies, supper might actually be on time for a change and—"

"And Anthony might be back tonight," Marion concluded with a smile.

Catherine was smiling too, if fighting it.

I was doing mental calculations. It was at least a two-day trip, one way, between Ryvideau, where we were, and Alphoson, where the port was. If Anthony was due back tonight he had to have been gone for several days at least, which meant... "So he was out of town while you were off dancing at the ball? That's a remarkably unsuspicious young man you have."

"He just trusts me, that's all," Catherine said, and that ended the discussion. It might not have been the end, except that we were interrupted by a sudden explosion of apples.

I didn't even have to look to know that would be Sam, tripping over the threshold with a boxful.

"Are you all right, Sam?" Catherine asked, bending down for an apple that had rolled near her feet.

"I'm fine," he said, rising to a crouch to gather up fruit. "There's all kinds of excitement going on out in the street. Royal heralds and everything. They're going door to door."

"They must be bringing that silly shoe around," I said, picking up three apples and trying a few spins of juggling.

"Probably," Sam agreed. "They'll be here soon; they were only a couple buildings down."

At that news, several people very nearly stepped on Sam as they went rushing out the doorway.

"Clearly supper's going to be late after all," Catherine observed, but she went outside too, if with less urgency.

I tucked two apples into my jacket and, taking a bite from the third, strolled after the crowd, batting a cluster of wisteria out of the way as I stepped across the threshold. I hadn't planned to hang around to watch the show, but if the show came to me…besides, nobody was going to get supper until after this shoe business was settled.

By the time the heralds, the soldiers, and the various attendants rode into the yard, everyone was outside. The herald read off the same proclamation from the square, they showed off the glass shoe, and then the herald asked if any women belonging to this household had attended the ball.

"We did," Marion said, stepping forward from the cluster of people. "Catherine and me."

Catherine sighed but came forward too. Almost instantly, the herald's chief attendant had a stool in place and was proffering the shoe. They were already getting good at this. I leaned back against the wall and took another bite out of my apple. I wondered what method they were using to cover the town and make sure they had every house; checking streets off on a map, maybe?

Marion went first, perching on the stool and undoing her left boot. The attendant struggled to slide the glass slipper onto her foot, but couldn't get it over her heel.

"Oh well," Marion said with a shrug. "I guess I don't get to marry the prince."

Now that was an attitude I liked. I could just imagine all the ways this spectacle could get really awful if girls got too intent on trying to get that slipper on, or too distraught when they couldn't.

The herald's attendant dusted off the slipper while Marion re-laced her boot. When she was standing again, the herald looked down at Catherine from his horse. "Your turn now, miss."

Catherine didn't move, except to shake her head. "I'm not the one you're looking for. You can just go on to the next house."

Lines creased the herald's face as his expression turned deeply troubled. "My orders are to try the shoe on every maiden who attended the ball. You did attend the ball?"

"Yes, but it's not my shoe. So there's no point in my trying."

Seemed to me that was just good sense and I approved—but I didn't even have to peer hard at the herald's aura to know he wouldn't. He had that kind of look to him. "If you attended the ball, you need to try on the glass shoe," the herald insisted. "My orders say it must be every girl."

I crunched into my second apple. I'd bet the herald and Marj would get on beautifully.

"But that's pointless," Catherine protested, arms crossed. "I'm telling you that I'm not the one you want. Trying on the shoe would just be a waste of everyone's time."

"Like this conversation?" the herald's attendant suggested. That got him a glare from the herald, but it also brought Catherine up short.

"All right!" She raised her hands in surrender. "If that's the only way to make you go away so we can get back to cooking supper, I'll try your slipper on." She sat down on the stool and yanked one shoe off.

The attendant stepped up with the glass slipper and crouched down to try it on her foot. The slipper went on easily, Catherine's toes sliding to the end of the shoe and the back slipping neatly over her heel. There was a moment of surprised silence in the yard—until I coughed on a chunk of apple that had abruptly stuck in my throat.

Worry was crawling up my spine again. All right, so the silly thing fit her, but when they said the prince would marry whoever the shoe fit, they couldn't really mean...no, of course they couldn't. It was just a fanciful way of putting it. Proclamations are always fanciful.

"You're the girl," the attendant said, sounding awed.

"*No*, I'm not," Catherine said, rolling her eyes. "I already told you, it's not my shoe. It's just a coincidence that it fits. It probably fits hundreds of girls and I'm just the first one." She reached down to take the glass slipper off.

All the trumpets started blowing again, making me jump. After this was settled, after we all went back inside and had supper, I needed to go find somewhere nice and relaxing. I was getting altogether too wound up, and over nothing but a mistake.

"What's that for?" Catherine demanded.

"Announcing that we have found the girl we were searching for," the herald explained, dismounting from his horse and taking her arm. He took it graciously, true, but took it firmly as well.

Catherine stared at him blankly as chaos erupted in the yard. Everyone from The Nightingale seemed to be talking at once. At the sound of the trumpets, more curious onlookers had come in from the streets, and, within what felt like seconds and wasn't really much longer, a considerable crowd had formed.

I kept my back against the wall, bit into my apple again and kept watching. This *could* turn out to be funny. Sure, the herald was interpreting his proclamation literally, but that didn't mean they would at the castle. So either the herald was going to have a crisis immediately because Catherine was not going to stand for this nonsense, or he was going to have a crisis an hour later when he tried to present the wrong girl to the prince. Either way, anybody that stuck on protocol and literal orders deserved a crisis.

"But I *told* you, I'm not the right one," Catherine protested. "You want the girl the prince danced with, the one who owns the shoe. That isn't me."

"My orders don't say anything about finding the owner of the shoe," the herald maintained, a piece of idiocy that made me feel even more that he had that crisis coming to him.

"But that's what they imply!" Catherine said, yanking her arm away from the herald's grip.

"All they say is to find the girl the shoe fits. And it fits you."

Sure enough, further objections made no impact, whether they were made by Catherine or by anyone else. Very swiftly the herald and his men got Catherine onto the back of a horse and rode away for the castle. Which clearly meant someone back at the castle was going to have to sort this out, and I heartily hoped the sorting would mean firing the herald. And that it wouldn't mean any bigger problems for anyone than that. It wasn't like they'd actually insist on Catherine marrying—no, that was just irrational. Even the royalty weren't that crazy.

It took longer to shoo the crowd out of the yard than it had taken for them to come in, and a much more somber group finally trooped back into the kitchen. Getting supper out had been entirely forgotten, and I couldn't help a wistful look at the stew left simmering by the fire.

"I don't like this," Catherine's father muttered, which seemed to express the feelings of everyone, judging by expressions.

"Maybe you'd better sit down, Uncle," Jack said, reaching out to take his arm.

Mr. Williams waved off aid—but sat down. "I *don't* like this."

Jack looked at his uncle for a moment with a worried frown, then abruptly turned to me. "Can't you do something about this?"

My stomach twinged uncomfortably. Partially because my identity as a fairy was plainly about to come out, and partially because I didn't like the expectant way he was looking at me. I didn't know that Marj was involved here, meaning I didn't know if I was responsible at all, and I didn't want him looking to me to fix things. And anyway, there was no *real* reason to think anything was *really* wrong.

I tried for a casual shrug. "Maybe. But I don't see what you'd want me to do."

Jack's eyebrows lowered. "I'd want you to get Catherine back somehow," he said, teeth gritted.

"I'm sure she's fine," I said with a great show of cheer, "and she'll be back as soon as someone with a brain realizes she's the wrong girl. So there's no reason to be worried." I hoped they'd believe me. *I* tried to believe me. "Besides, this'll make a great story someday!"

No one else seemed swayed by the story opportunities, and Mr. Williams was looking at me sharply. "Why does Jack think you'd be able to do something? What can you do?"

I glanced around, and realized everyone was staring at me. I sighed. No, definitely wouldn't be able to dodge this one. "I suppose there's not much point in trying to hide it anymore." I swept one hand through the air, leaving a trail of blue smoke behind it. "I'm sort of what you might call magical."

"He's a fairy," Jack contributed.

I'm sure I looked chagrined. "Thanks, Jack." And here it came.

Marion first. "But you're not—"

"—female, I know. We aren't all."

Mr. Williams next. "I thought fairies always had—"

"—wings, I know. They're just an affectation; if we want to, we can fly without them."

Sam last. "But don't fairies always…" He waved a hand through the air, narrowly missing hitting a bottle on the table next to him.

"Sparkle. I know." I grimaced. "I hate sparkles. Are we done grilling me on whether or not I'm a suitable fairy?"

"Sorry, Tarry," Jack said, and went too swiftly on to, "But can't you do something?"

I shook my head. "There's nothing to do. Catherine's not the one they want, we know that and she knows that and they're going to figure it out quickly. It's not like she's been kidnapped. It's just a misunderstanding." With a little effort, I could still see the amusing side. "You know, if they were *trying* to get the wrong girl, they couldn't do better than this. With some other girl, the prince's biggest problem would be breaking the news that he's not marrying her. Catherine, on the other hand, will probably throw something at him."

"He may be right about that," Jack allowed, but didn't sound convinced.

"Of course I'm right," I said, with all the wonderful confidence of false cheer and utter ignorance.

Chapter Twelve

The morning after the Great Glass Slipper Confusion, I popped back into The Nightingale's kitchen, only to find it strangely empty. I wandered out into the common room, and found the staff gathered around one of the tables. Not a cheerful face in the lot. Add to that the fact that Jack was there, at a time when he should have been out with the goats, and it didn't take a person of my considerable intelligence to realize something was wrong.

"All right. Why the grim looks?" I asked, pulling out a chair and sitting down. Even though I was pretty sure I knew, just by who wasn't here.

"Catherine's not back," Marion answered, gaze on the handkerchief she was fiddling with.

"She's not back *yet*," Jack said, a hopeful sentence except that he was frowning. "The castle sent a messenger this morning to tell us not to worry."

"That's all the message said?" I asked, folding my hands tightly on the table. A 'don't worry' message *worried* me. "Nothing more helpful?"

"That was all," Jack confirmed. "Anthony nearly took a swing at the messenger."

I had already noticed that Anthony wasn't in the circle either. "Is he back?"

"He got in late last night," Jack said. "He wanted to go straight to the castle then, but Emmy convinced him that there was no point, because no one gets in there at night when the gates are closed. He went with her this morning. Just after almost hitting His Highness' messenger."

Despite the twisting of my stomach, I couldn't help a grin at that thought. "Why didn't he do it?" Royal messengers tend to be irritatingly satisfied with themselves.

"He didn't because we stopped him," Marion said, crumpling her handkerchief in one hand. "We don't need him getting tossed in the dungeons for attacking a royal messenger."

Mr. Williams was drumming his fingers uneasily on the table. "I still think I should have gone to the castle with Anthony."

"That's not necessary," Jack said instantly, on top of Marion's, "Someone has to keep business running here."

Mr. Williams frowned, but nodded.

"They have to realize they made a mistake," I said, but knew even as I was saying it that it didn't ring as convincingly today as it had yesterday.

"And when do you think that's going to happen?" Jack snapped. He glanced at Catherine's father, and swallowed whatever else he had in mind.

I spread my hands. "I don't know. But I can go find out. How about I just pop off to the castle and find Catherine and see what's going on? Would that make everyone feel better?" And that wasn't committing to anything, or taking on any responsibility for the situation, it was just…information-gathering.

The consensus was that yes, information-gathering would be welcome. So I popped out of The Nightingale, and popped back in again in a castle hallway. A very elegant hallway—lots of silk tapestries. I had aimed for Catherine's general whereabouts, and now I did a quick orienting to make sure I was in front of the right door. I concluded I was, and knocked.

The response was prompt. "If you're here to explain *again* why I have to stay here, I swear I'll throw something."

Definitely the right door, and I felt relieved by the amount of defiance in her voice. "I was hoping you'd explain it to me."

There was a moment's silence. Then the door opened and Catherine looked at me with eyes widening in surprise. "Tarry? What are you doing here?"

"I was sort of in the neighborhood," I said, strolling in.

They'd given her a good room. I was willing to give them points for that. We were in a sitting room with big puffy couches, a carved wooden breakfast table and silk draperies over the windows. I could see a big bed through a doorway into the next room.

They'd also given her a new dress and someone had been fussing with her hair. I was less willing to give them any kind of points for that. In a silk dress and with her hair pinned up, Catherine looked practically royal and there was something disturbing about that. She would have looked better with flour on her hands.

Her aura was more reassuring when I checked it. All looked nearly normal with her wall and garden. The fresco on the wall was in muted colors, but the garden behind was still bright. A surface-level upset was remarkably good, for the circumstances.

"How did you get into the castle?" Catherine asked, shutting the door behind me.

No good reason to hide the truth anymore. "I popped in."

A puzzled crease appeared in her forehead. "You…what?"

"Popped. You know." I waved a hand through the air, disappeared from where I was, and reappeared two feet to the left. "Popped."

She didn't faint. "Oh. That explains how you know Marjoram."

"It does explain that," I agreed, feeling a little relieved by the calm reaction. "You're handling this news well."

She laughed, but there was something wild in the laugh. "Don't take this the wrong way, but at the moment your magical qualities are something of a minor issue."

"Understandable." Breakfast was set up on the table near the window, complete with silver dishes and lace doilies. The table was set for one, but big enough to seat six, and held enough food for all those six. It's a royalty thing. I sat down and began buttering a biscuit. "Want to tell me what's been going on over breakfast?"

She crossed her arms and stared out the window. "I'm not hungry."

I had noticed the food looked untouched. "All right, just tell me what's going on," I said, reaching for the honey. Having found Catherine unharmed and argumentative, I felt much better already. No tragedies here, just a misunderstanding.

She sighed, and dropped into the opposite chair. "Nothing's going on. That's the problem. That ridiculous glass slipper actually fit me, they started blowing those bloody trumpets, and before I hardly knew what was happening, I was here. And then—nothing. The prince was too *busy* to see me last night. If I was the right girl, I'd be insulted."

I wished I could say it was shocking, except it wasn't. It was rude, but not a surprise. I just nodded sympathetically.

"Prince Roderick should know I'm the wrong girl, but he hasn't been by, and no one else will believe me. And in the meantime...I'm here." Catherine picked up a spoon, turned it restlessly over in her hands. "I'm not locked in, but there's guards and courtiers and ladies-in-waiting and I don't have a chance of getting out the door without someone stopping me. I already tried once." She looked at me, a sudden idea lighting her eyes. "Though if I had a friend to magically transport me out..."

"They'd just track you down at the inn again," I pointed out.

"I know, but..."

"It would just prolong the mess in the end."

"I know, but..." Catherine sighed, dropped the spoon and put her chin on her hand. "I know. But how is everyone at home?"

Worried. "Concerned," I said diplomatically. "But fine. Holding up. I think your father wants to storm the castle, but everyone is working to keep him at home."

"Good, that's good." She reached up, I think an automatic gesture to push hair out of her eyes. Finding her hair was all pinned back, she let her hand drop and picked up a roll instead. "Did they get supper out on time yesterday?"

"No one mentioned it," I said, hiding a smile at this so very Catherine of questions.

"It was probably late." She tore the roll in half. "This would have to happen when we're all filled up, too. I need to get home. Can't you do something?"

There it was again. People find out you have magic, and they want you to solve all their problems. Not that I wasn't willing to help, but I didn't like this idea that suddenly everyone was *depending* on me.

"Sure," I said, "as soon as we figure out the best thing to do." Which sort of put the responsibility back towards her, taking me off the task of finding a solution.

"You could feed the prince to a dragon," Catherine muttered, tearing bits of roll to shreds. "Do you know any?"

"Yes, but princes give them indigestion."

The day before, that would've gotten me a laugh. Today, barely a wan smile. "Then how about you find the prince, so he can confirm that I'm the wrong girl?"

"That I should be able to do." I cast my awareness out around the castle, looking for that distinctive ooze of princeliness. It was easy—Roderick had it in spades, and he wasn't even very far away. "Good news. Prince Roderick is coming this way."

"Really?" Catherine said, dropping her mutilated roll. "What did you do, summon him?"

Technically, non-magical beings can't be 'summoned' in the strict sense of the word. And I hadn't compelled him to come either, considering I can't actually compel anyone to do anything. The Fairy Court has rules about these things. "Just blind chance. He was on his way here anyway."

"It took him long enough to think about it." She rose to her feet, smoothing her dress. "Thank you for the warning."

"Any time," I said, and reached for a third biscuit.

"Ah, Tarry? I don't suppose you ought to be here when he arrives," Catherine said, voice apologetic. "It would be difficult to explain."

Oh, right. Protocol and stuff. "Now that you mention it," I acknowledged, and stood up to go, perfectly ready to wash my hands of the business. This was all going to be fine. Catherine would talk to Roderick, and the whole matter would be solved without needing any involvement from me.

"Or you could turn invisible and stay around," Catherine said quickly. "In case there's trouble."

I hesitated. It was so tempting to just wave and go on, find somewhere much more cheerful and less fraught and not come back here until the crisis was resolved. But…suppose she really needed my help? And suppose Marj really had been responsible for that stupid glass shoe, making *me* responsible for starting this whole chain of events?

"Yeah. I can do that," I said, picked up another biscuit, and faded out, biscuit and all.

Prince Roderick walked through the door scant moments later. He looked like everything a prince was supposed to be. Tall and handsome and young. He was wearing a multitude of gold braid and a rapturous expression that looked as carefully designed as the braid. The expression dissolved away into petulance as soon as he saw Catherine.

"But you're not the right girl," he complained before she'd even completed a curtsy.

"That's what I've been telling everyone," Catherine said with a triumphant smile, and the flowers on her fresco blossomed into brighter shades. I settled back into my chair, feeling a weight lift off my shoulders. There it was, the answer to the whole problem.

Roderick turned to the smaller man with him. "Leonard, she's not the right one."

I glanced where Roderick did. I'd hardly noticed the other man when he had walked in, and hadn't noticed him at all when I'd been magically searching the castle, though he'd probably been with the prince then too. Princes cast big shadows.

"How unfortunate, Your Highness," he said smoothly. "I can't imagine how such a mistake could have occurred. Clearly we should not have trusted the herald to handle such a delicate matter."

The prince sighed deeply. "Why is everyone always wasting my time like this?"

A grin lit my face. Maybe I'd get to see Catherine throw something at the prince after all.

Catherine's smile vanished. "Wasting *your* time?" Her hands clenched into fists at her sides. "You came in half a minute ago. I've been stuck here since yesterday, because you couldn't be bothered to come see if I was the right girl or not."

Roderick blinked, apparently surprised. "I was busy," he said, with calm assurance that this would explain everything. "I was out hunting."

For just a moment she hesitated, expression softening as though she meant to give him the benefit of the doubt. "And you didn't get a message?" she guessed.

"I got a message. But I was hunting."

Me, I was too familiar with princes to be surprised. I just rolled my eyes, crammed the last of the biscuit in my mouth, and picked up a muffin. Blueberry, it looked like.

Catherine sat down, heavily. "Your hunting was more important than coming to see the woman you love? I mean, I'm not her, but you didn't know that before you came in here."

"I didn't give you permission to sit in my presence," the prince noted.

"So arrest me," she said, reaching for a biscuit.

"I suppose that isn't necessary," he decided, and sat down in one of the other chairs—luckily, not mine. "And I don't love the girl I was dancing with. I just think she's pretty." He looked at Catherine with a more thoughtful glint in his eyes. "You're pretty too."

My mouthful of muffin stuck a little as I swallowed. That was just a compliment, right? It wasn't implying anything…right?

Apparently Catherine heard the same undercurrent I was trying not to hear. She put the biscuit down again. "I'm going home."

"Pretty in a different sort of way. She was kind of more…" He frowned. "Less solid."

I scratched behind an ear. I was all about metaphors for people's characters, but it was hard to know what that was getting at. The girl from the ball had been silly, maybe?

With metaphors on my mind, I adjusted my magical senses to get a look at the prince's aura—and winced. His aura shone, and not in a nice way. It was all light bouncing off of very polished mirrors, and once I managed to look past the light the view didn't get better. Naturally there were reflections upon reflections of Roderick, repeating all over his aura. It made a nice royal oak tree aura look like an absolute winner by comparison.

Catherine was glaring at the one real Roderick she could see. "I don't even know what that means, but I don't actually care because it doesn't matter. Because I'm going home."

"It may not be that simple," the small man with the prince said. Leonard, that was his name. He sat down in the chair at the prince's right. I tried to get a look at Leonard's aura, but Roderick's was so overpowering that I had spots in my magical eyes.

"The difficulty," Leonard continued, "is that we have already announced that we found the prince's bride."

"So un-announce it," Catherine said, picking up her biscuit again to tear it viciously in half.

"We could do that," Roderick said with a nod, and I found myself nodding too. That was good, that would just settle all this.

"I don't think we could do that," Leonard said.

"Maybe not," Roderick amended.

"It is imperative that the common people respect the royalty," Leonard said, steepling long-fingered hands. "Announcing that we have found a bride, and then announcing that we have not will only lead to ridicule. I am the royal family's chief adviser, and it is my job to prevent such misimpressions."

"He's very good at it," the prince commented.

Finished with my muffin, I picked up a triangular piece of toast and started nervously munching on a corner. So maybe this wouldn't be resolved *immediately*, but it was just a negotiation, it was still going to wind up in the right place in the end.

Catherine stared at both of them, pieces of biscuit seemingly forgotten in her hands. "You're suggesting that I marry the prince to save the royal family from a little embarrassment? That's absurd. I won't do it."

Leonard cleared his throat. "There is no such thing as *a little* embarrassment when one is a member of the royal family. These things are immensely serious. On ridicule are revolutions made. I am not merely suggesting you marry His Highness. I am strongly advising it."

Leonard's expression, even his tone, were utterly inoffensive, utterly non-threatening, and yet there was something underneath it all that gave me a prickle. Not the same prickle that Marj's sparkles gave me, but one that was equally unpleasant. I tried again to look at his aura, but it all seemed misty and indistinct. Drat Roderick and his mirrors.

"Find some other way to prevent a revolution," Catherine snapped, dropping the biscuit and balling her hands into fists again on the table. "I'm not marrying him."

"Anyone would think you didn't want to marry me," Prince Roderick said with a gleaming smile and such serene confidence that I abandoned my aura hunting to stare at him instead. Sure he was self-absorbed, but *really*?

"I don't want to marry you," Catherine said flatly.

Roderick's smile turned puzzled. "But all young women want to marry me."

"*I* don't. I can't. I'm already promised to marry someone else."

"But you came to the ball, didn't you?" Leonard said, voice soft. "Clearly you considered yourself eligible."

There was that point again. Leonard apparently was working from the traditional expectation about why girls attended the royal ball. Figured.

I was surprised when Catherine dropped her gaze. "Technically…I mean, I'm not married yet…but that doesn't exactly mean…the point is, I *am* promised to be married. So that's it then."

I swallowed the last of the toast and slowly reached for another muffin. She'd ended strong but I wondered about the confusion. She'd seemed so confident about her reasons for attending—but maybe the teasing had bothered her more than she let on? Or maybe she was regretting it, now that it was causing problems. Hard to say. Catherine had such a nice wall in her aura that sometimes I forgot it *was* a wall, that at the end of the day the pleasant exterior was still hiding deeper things.

The prince, who'd probably never had an introspective thought in his life, ignored Catherine's uncertainty and moved right ahead with his questioning. "So there's this engagement, but what sort of man are you promised to?" he asked, leaning over the table. "You know, rich man, poor man, beggar man, thief?"

I thought that sounded familiar from some old rhyme, but did he actually divide the world up that way? More likely he divided the world up as himself, and everyone else.

Catherine blinked. "Ah…poor man, I guess. But hard-working," she added hastily, rallying again. "Good prospects. And really this is none of your business and I don't know why we're even *talking* about—"

"But he's not inheriting a title?" Roderick persisted. "Not commanding armies or anything like that?"

Catherine's expression was fighting between anger and confusion. "No, of course not, that's ridiculous."

The prince folded his arms in evident satisfaction. "Not a problem, then. Break the engagement. There's not much he can do about it, if he hasn't got an army. We could even find him someone else to marry. We have lots of serving girls."

I coughed on my toast at that one. Lucky thing my spell covered sounds too.

Catherine's hands were still clenched into fists, and her knuckles were turning white. "That is the most *absurd*—can't you understand, I agreed to marry him because I *want* to marry him!"

"Of course you did when you agreed to the engagement," Prince Roderick said. "But now you have a better prospect."

Catherine's eyebrows rose and her eyes all but flashed fire. "And what makes you so sure you're a better prospect?"

He shrugged. "I'm the crown prince. I'm the best possible prospect."

Catherine gaped at him for a moment. Then her mouth closed, she leaned back in her chair and shook her head. "You know, you're really not charming. I always heard that princes were supposed to be charming."

I snorted. That was the kind of rumor Marj and her ilk liked to spread around.

Roderick's eyes narrowed into disapproval. "I think I resent that. Leonard, am I charming?"

Leonard, who had practically faded out of my notice for the last two minutes, was very swift to say, "Of course, Your Highness."

It was at that moment that something pinged in the corner of my awareness. My awareness has a wider spread than humans' awarenesses do. I was, at the moment, at least vaguely conscious of the entire castle. Down one flight and a few hallways over, something was going on. As unsettling as the conversation was here, I was happy to turn somewhere else. I mentally zeroed in to pick up the details.

Once I had them, I modified my invisibility spell and waved a hand to get Catherine's attention. "Don't react to me; they can't see or hear me right now. You need to go downstairs. There's a disturbance you ought to get involved in. Down one flight, turn left."

A tiny wrinkle formed between her eyebrows—her only visible reaction. It was enough to convey that she wasn't sure about this. "Listen, just trust me," I insisted. "There isn't much time. Go. Make up an excuse. Say you need air or something."

Catherine sighed breathily. "This is all so emotional," she said faintly, directly on top of a comment Prince Roderick was making—not an important comment. "I think I need to step out for just a minute." She got up and moved towards the door without waiting for anyone to respond.

"I didn't give you permission to leave my presence," Roderick protested. "Leonard, I didn't give her permission."

"No, Your Highness. Most shocking."

Catherine didn't stop, and the prince took two steps after her. He didn't take more than that, because I cast a quick spell. I was hoping this situation would help lead to a resolution for the larger problems, and I didn't need the prince interfering.

Roderick nearly toppled forward, but caught himself. "My feet are stuck to the floor," he said, staring down at them. "What on earth has the maid in charge of cleaning this floor been *doing*?"

"Stuck, Your Highness?" Leonard said, bending down to look at the royal feet.

I snatched up one muffin then hurried out after Catherine. There was about to be a scene that I didn't really belong in, but I wanted to be there, to be sure that it went as it should.

Chapter Thirteen

I followed Catherine invisibly, downstairs and down the hallway to the left, to the scene of the disturbance. Specifically, a young man was arguing with a group of guards.

"I told you twice already, I came in through the kitchens, and I need to see someone. I'm not planning to assassinate any royalty!"

Judging by the crossed arms and glowers, the guards were not pleased by this explanation.

Catherine, on the other hand, felt differently. "Anthony!" she cried. She pushed right past the surprised guards and threw her arms around Anthony, knocking him back a step before he steadied himself.

He put his arms around her, tightly. "Hello, Catherine."

From my invisible position farther back down the hall, I could see his face, and I could tell I wasn't the only one who thought she didn't look right in that dress they had her in. On the other hand, it was elegant enough that the guards apparently decided they better not try to haul her or the man she was hugging off to the dungeon. At least, that's how I interpreted the glances being exchanged. That was good, since it saved me having to throw any spells around to prevent the disturbance elevating into a full-on conflict. The guards even backed off a few steps, although they kept glowering.

I took up a position leaning against a wall where I could see the guards, in case they changed their minds, and bit into my muffin. A little heavy on the walnuts, but I liked the cinnamon.

"It's so good to see someone *sane*," Catherine said into Anthony's shoulder. "They're all completely mad around here."

Did that mean I didn't qualify as sane? She had seen *me* recently. I considered being offended, and might have been if I hadn't also been feeling vaguely guilty about her predicament. Even though I *didn't* know that I was responsible. That argument was wearing thin, though.

While I wrestled with conflicting feelings, Anthony suggested, "So I suppose anyone sane would do just as well?" His voice was light enough, but something more serious was lurking underneath. I was still magically attuned and I could tell the birds in his aural forest had set up a chorus on seeing Catherine, like usual, but the song was muted.

She smiled up at him, and whispered, "Not as well as you."

A wider smile lit his face. "It's good to see you too, Cat."

She leaned up and kissed his cheek. "I missed you, Anthony."

That's all she said. It worried me, and judging by the wrinkle in his forehead, I think it worried him too. She hadn't told him not to call her Cat. That had to mean something.

As if picking up my thought wave (impossible), he said, "Everyone's been worried; what's going on?"

She shook her head. "You wouldn't believe me if I told you." She cast a glance back down the hall and sighed. "And here it comes." She took a step back from Anthony, but also took hold of his hand.

I checked over my shoulder in the same direction she'd looked. Here it came indeed. Prince Roderick and his pale friend, Leonard. How had he got loose from the floor so quickly? I'd cast that spell in a hurry, practically while running out the door, so maybe I hadn't cast it very precisely.

The prince struck a regal pose, shoulders back and head raised (I swear I've seen it etiquette books), and announced, "This really doesn't seem like appropriate behavior for the woman who may be marrying the crown prince."

I winced. This was clearly going to get more awkward before it got better.

Anthony's eyebrows shot up. "The woman who *what*?" Sure, that had been the point of carrying off the girl who the glass slipper fit, but obviously Anthony had not been prepared to find the prince embracing the idea too.

Catherine gave his hand a tug. "Anthony, darling, remember I said they're all completely mad around here?"

At this moment, Roderick demonstrated what was, for him, an absolutely astounding depth of insight. "You called him 'darling.' This must be the poor man without any armies."

If Anthony's eyebrows could have gone higher, they would have.

"That's not how I said that," Catherine muttered. "I didn't even *say* that exactly." She glared at the prince. "Are you at all familiar with the concept of tact?"

Roderick's nose raised another inch. "I don't need to be tactful to commoners. I'm the crown prince. And I have diplomats to be tactful for me."

Catherine rolled her eyes. "I suppose I should have expected that response."

This was true. I had. I was also tempted to bounce the remainder of my muffin off the back of Roderick's head, but it would probably just cause more complications in the end.

Anthony was still grappling with the most imperative point. "What do you mean she might *marry* you?" he demanded.

"It's possible I misspoke," Roderick said, head at a thoughtful tilt. "It would be more accurate to say she's almost definitely marrying me."

And I was presented with a suddenly clear picture of what Anthony must have looked like when he almost hit the royal messenger. Before any violence unfolded, Leonard smoothly put in, "Perhaps this is a conversation which would be better carried out in seclusion and with some discretion." He cast a nod towards the cluster of guards, who were watching the goings-on with what looked like the same keen depth of interest I possessed.

"I'm sure you're right, Leonard," Roderick agreed.

And somehow Roderick, Leonard, Catherine and Anthony all ended up going back to the room they'd given Catherine. I followed, still invisible to everyone but her.

Upstairs, everyone seated themselves around the breakfast table. Catherine sat first, Anthony quickly took possession of the chair next to her, and Roderick and Leonard sat on the table's opposite side. I took the vacant chair nearest the food. I'd about demolished the baked goods, so I picked up a plum from the fruit basket.

With any luck, actually presenting Catherine's fiancé to the idiot prince was finally going to get through his cloud of self-absorption enough to convince him she wasn't going to marry him. And then we could all go home in time for dinner at The Nightingale.

Which was *their* home, I mean. Not my home. Obviously.

Anyway, that had been my hope, when I sent Catherine to get Anthony. It's harder to brush aside someone when he's actually sitting there. I hoped.

Leonard opened the discussion by asking Anthony his name.

"Anthony Maurier," he answered, voice clipped and expression guarded.

"Maurier. Sounds foreign," Roderick commented.

"It was, several generations ago. My ancestors fled Beaumont in the north when the monsters got bad. Can we talk about something more important than my family history?"

Leonard swiftly picked that one up. He explained again about the importance of avoiding embarrassment to the royal family by admitting that they had carried away the wrong girl, and incorrectly announced that they had the right girl. Anthony found this to be no more vital a concern than Catherine had. I ate two plums while he argued the point, but Leonard was still unwilling to budge. Not promising at all, and I was getting worried again. Why did they have to be so intent on this idea?

Since I couldn't ask, I was pleased when Anthony voiced a similar question. "What's really baffling," Anthony said to Prince Roderick, "is why you want to marry her."

Catherine was not so pleased. She turned her head to look at Anthony. "That's baffling to you?"

Anthony grimaced. "I didn't mean...that is, I know why *I* want to marry you, but he just met you today."

Roderick shrugged broadly, gold braid on his shoulders winking in the light. "I can't see what that has to do with anything."

"You wouldn't," Catherine muttered. She was clearly coming to understand what she could expect from His Most Royal Highness.

Anthony was still flailing in that area. "You're talking about spending your life with someone, and you don't think maybe you should have known her longer?"

Roderick smiled in the most patronizing of ways. "But I'm not talking about spending my life with her. I'm talking about marrying her. There are occasional state functions and ceremonies, of course, formal dinners, and naturally I'll need her to produce an heir or two, but apart from that we wouldn't have much to do with each other."

I glowered at Roderick and chomped into another plum. This, right here, this was why I did not bother involving myself in royal romances.

"If it makes so little difference who you marry," Catherine snapped, "why can't you pick someone else?"

Leonard shook his head. "Regrettably, enough details and rumors have escaped regarding your identity that choosing another girl could become complicated."

"Then what about the girl from the ball?" Catherine asked. "I thought His Highness here wanted to marry *her*."

"She was very pretty," Roderick said, gaze drifting into the distance.

I wondered if Roderick knew anything else about her. Why couldn't they keep looking for her? Do it in secret, if they didn't want to admit their mistake. Although it could be hard to secretly try a glass slipper on every girl in the kingdom, if Roderick really *didn't* know anything else about her.

"And finding the young woman by means of a slipper made a romantic story to keep the common folk happy," Leonard said, folding his hands on the table. "That has been accomplished. Some word may escape that this is not the same girl, but we will find a way to address that. After all, the shoe did fit her, and that's what really counts. Few people have any idea what the original girl looked like, so we should be able to quell rumors that she's the wrong one."

"But the original girl?" Catherine persisted. "Aren't you in love with her?"

Roderick shrugged. "Easy come, easy go. That's how these matters are."

"Not to me," Anthony said shortly.

The prince sighed. "Clearly you're upset. What can I do to make you happy?"

"You can *not* marry Catherine," Anthony snapped.

Roderick's eyes squinted in a puzzled expression. "You mean her, right?" he asked, with a gesture towards Catherine.

"What do you mean I—yes, of course," Anthony said.

Comprehension flashed across Catherine's face. "He's never asked me my name."

"I have people to remember names for me," Roderick said with a wave of one hand. "Now as for not marrying…her, Leonard has already explained why it's necessary. So asking me not to just isn't a practical idea. What if I paid you instead? Say, a thousand gold pieces?"

So not charming. I wished I could just turn him into a frog and end this whole business, but the Fairy Court wouldn't allow it. Fairies can only turn princes into frogs under specific sanctioned circumstances.

Anthony's mouth opened and shut. He shook his head and tried again. "I don't want—you can't just—that doesn't…" He gave up. "You're right," he told Catherine. "They're all mad."

Her smile was wan. "Completely."

"I think I resent that," the prince observed. "I'm being generous here. I could just throw you in the dungeon, but I'm trying to be considerate. Lately I've been accused of not being charming enough."

Catherine twitched, with a noise halfway to a laugh, and I groaned and bit into my plum again. Could I possibly formulate a situation that would allow me to turn him into a frog? Probably not. It would be easier if he had two younger brothers; that opened all sorts of possibilities, but no, Roderick was the only one.

Anthony folded his arms and stared back at the prince. "You can't just throw me in your dungeon. What would the charge be?"

"Irritating me." And I swear Roderick said it with a straight face.

Anthony shook his head; I'm not sure if it was in denial or disbelief. Maybe both. "That's not a criminal offense."

"It's not?" Roderick said. "It should be. Do something about that," he directed Leonard.

For the first time, Leonard was not instantaneous with a response. He was staring at the basket of plums—only two left now—sitting on the table. About to reach for another one, I withdrew my hand. Had he noticed the six that had disappeared since we'd all sat down?

"Leonard?" Roderick said. "About irritating me?"

Leonard looked up. "Of course, Your Highness. I'll look into it."

Maybe I was being paranoid.

"Obviously this conversation is not going anywhere meaningful," Leonard continued, I assume in prelude to something else, but Catherine broke in on him.

"It's not going anywhere at all, because it's already at a conclusion. I'm not marrying the prince, find someone else, I'm going *home.*"

"I don't think we can permit that at this juncture," Leonard said, face perfectly smooth.

Catherine's shoulders went tense. So did Anthony's. Mine were all right, but my stomach was sinking, and not under the weight of plums and pastries.

"Are you saying I'm a prisoner?" Catherine asked, voice carefully even.

"Let's not put it so indelicately," Leonard said, tapping his fingers lightly on the table. "Let us say that it is of the utmost necessity that we continue our present conversation into the future, which, under current conditions, mandates that you remain within the castle at this juncture." He got that whole sentence out without even a blink.

"So I'm a prisoner," Catherine said, and flicked a glance in my direction.

I could guess at what she was thinking. Since she was the only one who could hear me, I commented on her thought. "I could transport you out, but if you go home they'll know where to find you. Say the word if you want, but I don't think it'll help much."

The corner of her mouth quirked downward, but she also shook her head a little. I kept my magic to myself. Which was just as well because…I was willing to help but I still didn't like the idea that it was up to me to fix this. Especially not when I had no idea how to do it.

"As we don't seem to be making progress, I suggest we adjourn this discussion for the moment," Leonard resumed. "His Highness and I have many other pressing matters, and have already devoted an undue amount of time to this one. We will give you time to consider our offer, and will return to this subject at a later point."

He stood to go. Roderick did too. Anthony didn't move, and for that matter, neither did I. But the royal representatives couldn't see *me*.

"You will accompany us out, of course," Leonard said, staring down at Anthony.

Anthony leaned back in his chair. "I don't have any other pressing matters."

"That is irrelevant. We cannot allow the two of you to remain here unchaperoned. We have the purity of the royal blood lines to consider, after all."

Catherine's cheeks turned red, and Anthony growled "you can't be serious" through his teeth. I wondered if they really were. If Leonard was just being a pain, all right then. But if he was serious about *this*, that meant troubling things about how serious he was about Catherine marrying Roderick.

"When it comes to the good of the royal family, I am always serious," Leonard said serenely, which didn't actually tell me much. "You will accompany us out."

"Then I'm going too," Catherine said, rising to her feet. "I'm going down to the kitchens to see a friend. That's not out of the castle, so you ought to be happy about it. And Anthony's going to walk me there, and then he's going to go home to tell them I'm fine."

"I can't tell them you're fine," Anthony objected. "You're not fine. And I'm not going anywhere."

"I *am* fine. You're going, and then you're coming back."

"And if I can't get in again?" Anthony said, with a suspicious glance towards Leonard.

Catherine looked at me. "I'll get him in. Definitely," I promised. That at least was something I could easily help with, without even feeling unduly invested or likely to have it all blow up at me eventually. How nice to have *one* course of action that felt that way.

"You'll get back in," Catherine said. "Trust me. Now is everyone satisfied?"

"Doesn't bother me," Roderick said with a shrug.

Leonard tapped his fingertips together. "Perhaps with a guard en route to the kitchens."

"One that's at a discreet distance," Catherine countered.

"I believe that would be acceptable," Leonard said.

I don't think it was completely acceptable to anyone (except Roderick), but it was sufficiently acceptable to everyone that we pursued the plan. Leonard and His Most Royal Highness headed out on whatever they had to do, and Catherine and Anthony went to the kitchens, with that guard at a discreet distance. I picked up the last two plums and followed them, strolling along next to the guard, also discreet. Or seemingly—my ears are much more effective than the guard's, so I could still hear everything they were talking about anyway.

Yeah, maybe I shouldn't have been eavesdropping, but Catherine was supposed to be so good at plans and if she had an idea she was sharing with Anthony, I wanted to hear it. It would take a weight off my mind if she'd contrive to rescue herself from this whole stupid situation.

And how could I resist eavesdropping when the very first question Anthony asked was, "Do you have a plan?"

"Not beyond the next hour," Catherine admitted. "I might be able to come up with something within that next hour, though."

"That's not exactly reassuring, Cat."

No, it really wasn't, and my shoulders sagged. I was more reassured when she responded absently with, "Don't call me that." It couldn't be too bad, if she was still saying that. "There's someone I need to talk to…but maybe I better explain about that when there isn't a guard around."

Not so reassuring, assuming she meant me. Maybe she meant Emmy.

"All right," Anthony said, casting a glare back towards the guard. "I suppose I could always challenge the prince to a duel."

"No, you couldn't. He'd kill you."

Anthony hunched his shoulders. "Thank you for that vote of confidence."

I wracked my brains for the rules about interfering with duels.

"Oh honestly, darling, be practical," Catherine said, putting a hand on his arm. "You know it's true."

I was pretty sure I remembered the (inconvenient) rules, but was hoping to think of a loophole.

"What, because he's a prince? And princes are good at everything, and win at everything, and are better than everyone else at everything they do, and—"

"And they're trained to use swords from childhood."

Anthony was silent for a long moment. "Well, yes. There's that. I'm not completely unfamiliar with combat, though. I was in the army once."

"For a week."

"Ten days," he countered.

"Close enough."

I gave up hunting for ways around the rules. There was no loophole that was going to let me help him overcome that level of imbalance in skill.

Catherine tucked her arm through Anthony's, leaning against him as they walked. "If there was a competition that involved balancing a budget and keeping six guests with fifteen different demands happy all at once, while making sure clumsy clerks don't spill apples everywhere, I am sure you would win. Easily. But unfortunately, duels are usually fought with swords. Which you've never really learned how to use."

"Yes, well. I don't suppose having right and all that on my side counts for much?"

"Not when people are waving sharp objects around." Catherine mustered up a smile, lifting her chin. "Maybe we don't even need a plan. They can't force me to marry him—"

"I have a bad feeling," Anthony muttered.

Me too. My gut didn't like this at all, and after a half dozen baked goods and as many plums, it wasn't hunger confusing the issue.

"They can't, and sooner or later they'll have to accept that I'm not going to agree, and then they'll have to deal with it."

"That's what worries me," Anthony said. "How they'll deal with it."

Catherine bumped her shoulder against his. "They'll send me home. We're not barbarians."

Anthony sighed. "I sincerely hope you're right."

We were all arriving at the kitchens by now, though the guard and I were still farther back than Anthony and Catherine. They stopped before the big double doorway and I halted a dozen paces away.

"I'll talk to Emmy for a while. At least she's rational," Catherine said. "You go home and tell them what's going on."

Anthony rubbed the back of his neck. "I really think I ought to stay here."

"*Trust me*," she said, putting her hands on his shoulders. "Go home, tell them what's happening, and then come back."

"All right. Fine." Then he put his hands on her hips, pulled her against him and kissed her.

I couldn't resist focusing my magical eyes to watch the branches of their respective auras intertwine. Plus I do believe she swayed a little around the knees.

"Are you trying to prove something?" she whispered.

"Yes." Anthony shot another glare at the guard and kissed her again, quickly this time. "See you soon, Cat."

"Very soon," she agreed. "And don't call me that."

He smiled, if faintly. "Yes, dear." Then he turned and headed for the nearest route out of the castle.

Catherine went into the kitchens and I followed along behind, managing to duck through the door while it was still swinging. People get nervous when doors are pushed open by invisible hands.

Although from the general hubbub of the kitchen, they might not have even noticed. A few dozen staff rushed about, pots simmered, knives flashed and the whole place made The Nightingale's kitchen look downright peaceful.

Catherine smoothed her hands over her silk skirts and marched up to a woman who seemed to be giving directions. "Excuse me, I'm looking for my friend Emmy."

The cook looked at her face with a surly expression, then her gaze scanned down to take in the elegance of Catherine's dress. Her expression modified to be…well, slightly less surly. "Down at the far end," she said, nodding her head in the relevant direction.

"Thank you," Catherine said, and proceeded down the length of the kitchen with her head high.

I followed, but got delayed by the necessity of dodging flurries of people rushing about. All I needed was to be bumped into while I was invisible. People get much more upset about that than they do about mysteriously opening doors.

By the time I caught up, Catherine had found Emmy slicing a considerable pile of onions. There was a flurried round of greetings and exclamations and questions and half-explanations that I wasn't paying close attention to, because I was occupied carefully phasing myself visible again. By the time I was done with that, Catherine had picked up another knife and joined Emmy in her slicing.

"You don't have to do that," Emmy protested.

"It makes me feel more normal," Catherine said, neatly splitting an onion in half with one strike. "And I can pretend it's Prince Roderick's head."

"Can I have an onion? I'd like to pretend that too," I said, strolling up closer.

"Hello, Tarry," Emmy said with a smile. "Jack was hoping you'd turn up this morning. Did he ask you to come here?"

"I sort of volunteered." I conjured up a knife, selected an onion and gave it a good whack. "Hey, that *is* satisfying." Though it would have been nice if she'd been chopping something I could snack on. Raw yellow onions…no, thanks.

"We need to talk," Catherine said to me in low tones. "Where can we do it?"

Apparently she had meant me earlier. I had known it really but I wished I had more answers for her. "Here's fine. Just give me a minute to cast a take-no-notice spell."

"A what kind of spell?" she asked.

"Take-no-notice. Does what it says." I shrugged. "People can see us and hear us, but as long as we don't do anything too shocking, they won't notice what we do, won't listen to our conversation, and if they happen to hear or see anything, they won't think about it or remember it. It's convenient."

"A convenient way out of this mess would be even better," Catherine said, lips tight. "Can you do anything to help?"

Great. A nice, open-ended, 'please fix my life' request. "Depends what help you need." I whacked another onion. "If you need any. Maybe they'll realize you're not going to agree, and that will be the end." And there would be no need for me to get tangled up in this.

"I wish I was as sure of that as I want Anthony to think I am." Catherine frowned down at the onions in front of her. "They seem strangely insistent on my marrying the prince. I don't know why, but they are, and that worries me."

"Maybe the prince fell in love with you," Emmy suggested with a slight smile.

Catherine rolled her eyes. "Not likely. That idiot with the gold brocade has no more depth of feeling than a…than an onion. Less. Onions at least have layers."

"So why does he say he wants to marry you?" Emmy asked, sweeping chopped onions aside with her knife and reaching for another.

"Sparing the crown embarrassment from admitting their mistake," Catherine answered.

I shrugged. "It could be true. Royalty tends to be unable to laugh at themselves, or to let anyone else laugh at them."

"Seems to me," Emmy remarked, "that if the prince marries you, some people are going to realize you're not the one he danced with at the ball, so that's a problem for them. Admitting you're the wrong one and searching for the right girl would be a bigger problem, maybe. But what if they already had the right girl? Surely switching girls wouldn't be a bigger problem than explaining you to begin with."

"Hey, that makes sense," I said, tapping my knife point against the counter. This could be the solution. This could be a way I could actually help without getting all committed and involved. "There wouldn't be a problem if they just had the right girl to replace you with."

"But they're not *looking* for her," Catherine said, and gave a section of onion a vicious chop.

Right, because their only method couldn't be done secretly. That didn't mean it was the only method possible. "But maybe we could find her for them," I said triumphantly. "I have an idea about that." It wasn't an idea I loved—but it was an idea.

"Can you pick up a scent from that shoe the prince has?" Emmy asked.

"I am not a tracking dog," I said, lifting my chin. "I don't follow scents. I follow auras. By now, so many people have handled that shoe and tried it on that I'd never be able to pick up anything." The only thing I might learn was the person who had originally made it. But I had a strong suspicion on that subject anyway.

Catherine's lips pinched together. "So what *can* you do?"

"I know someone who might know the girl we need, so I'll go talk to that someone and see what I can find out." I hated to think of Marj as the best chance at a solution—but it would even be worth visiting her house to get all this cleared up before it spiraled into even bigger crises. And to find out how justified my guilty sense of responsibility actually was, once and for all.

Catherine's expression didn't relax. "You know someone who might know something. That's your best plan?"

"If it doesn't work, we'll think of something else," I said with a wide and hopefully encouraging smile.

"You're awfully calm about it," she muttered.

Yeah, because I was faking it. I shrugged. "Getting upset won't help." And even if she was annoyed with me for not being upset, people get even more agitated when a fairy *does* get upset. It's like it knocks their entire worldview out of balance or something. Yet another reason I tried not to get too mixed up in the affairs of humanity. I don't want to be responsible for anyone's worldview if I can avoid it, thanks. "Anyway, I just think—"

I was interrupted by an exclamation from Catherine. She lifted her hand, a scarlet line blooming on one fingertip. "My knife slipped."

I conjured up a handkerchief and handed it to her.

She wrapped it around her finger. "It's nothing, really, it's small. I swear, something about this place...I've chopped thousands of vegetables, I never cut myself."

Emmy was watching her closely, eyebrows drawing together. "Are you all right, Catherine?"

"I'm fine." Catherine kept her gaze on the handkerchief she was tying. "I said it's just a small cut. It's barely bleeding."

"No, I mean...are *you* all right?"

"I'm *fine*."

"It's all right if you're afraid," Emmy said softly.

My shoulders twitched and I tried to keep my gaze on my onions. I didn't *like* emotional displays, not of this kind of emotion. They were so uncomfortable.

"I'm not afraid," Catherine said, picking up her knife again and chopping an onion in half. "I'm irritated. And apprehensive. And I don't appreciate the royalty interfering in my life because I like it the way it is, and I want to marry Anthony and run The Nightingale, and if they insist on my marrying the prince…" She swallowed. "Well, I just won't, that's all." She set the knife down again and rubbed the back of her hand across her eyes, which were starting to look moist. "Sorry. It's…the onions, you know. Bothering my eyes."

I didn't mention that I'd cast a spell to neutralize the effect of the onions when we'd started chopping. "Want another handkerchief?"

"No, I'm fine. But thank you." She summoned up a smile. "Thank you for all of it, for offering to help. Because this really isn't your concern at all."

Somehow, her saying it didn't make me feel it. "I like helping a friend when I can." That was true enough. Also, it's *completely* different than adopting an entire royal family unto the 17th generation, which is how Marj operates. "And you and Anthony are nice kids, and I like to help nice kids out of messes." When I could. When an opportunity presented itself that didn't mean things like long-term commitment. This one…was already getting beyond the kind of thing I really felt comfortable doing.

"Kids?" she repeated with one eyebrow raised.

I managed a grin. "I look close to you in age, but you'd be surprised how old I am. It's the magicalness. Anyway, I also like to stick it to arrogant royalty, and I might get a good chance at that here."

I didn't want to mention my other reason. If my suspicions were right about the origins of that shoe, then this was my fault. For setting Marj on this 'help a commoner' business to begin with, leading us all to here. That, however, remained to be seen.

And with another promise that we'd come up with something else if this didn't work, I reluctantly went to go see.

Chapter Fourteen

Marj was at home. Marj's home involves endless piles of flowers and pillows and silk curtains and pink furry things. And sparkles, of course. Don't even ask about the sparkles. She somehow managed to combine the aesthetic of a very small, overcrowded parlor, with the walls and floorplan of the most enormous, sprawling of palaces. All in all, it's a place I try not to go, barring the temptation of unusually great scones, or the necessity of duty.

In the present case, it was the latter and my hopes for scones were low. I popped into Marj's entryway, squinted against the pink sparkliness of it all, and took the most direct path to follow my magic orienting towards Marj. I wound up at a closed door, knocked, and was slightly disappointed to hear her call back, "Come in!"

I had held onto a sneaking hope she might tell me to go away. I hadn't had any hope that she wasn't actually home, since I could sense her aura as soon as I came into the building. Marj's aura was particularly piercing, whether I was trying to see it or not. It felt a lot like a tea kettle, whistling shrilly as though it was about to explode, probably in an extremely sparkly cloud of steam. I admit personal feelings may influence my impression.

With no excuse for escaping, I pushed the door open, winced against the overpowering blast of flowery perfume, and stepped into Marj's boudoir. Which seemed to sort of combine a bedroom and a parlor. I think. Sadly, it did not include the functions of a kitchen, a breakfast nook, or a dining room.

I moved a pink kitten off of the nearest chair—wondering as I did if it had been something else before becoming a pink kitten, and if so, had it been a sentient something else—brushed sparkles off and sat down. The chair was spindly and covered with ruffles, but it took my weight. "Hello, Marj. I need a word."

Marj was sitting in front of an immense mirror, which had a frame of spiraling, carved decorations that seemed to be trying too hard. She had powder puffs and lipstick and I don't pretend to know what else hovering in the air around her head. "I really don't have time right now, Tarry, there is *so much* going on."

Fine, I didn't want to spend a long time here anyway. "Right to the point then. About Prince Roderick's ball. Did you help a girl go?" And had she ruined everything in the process?

"I did," she said, her reflection beaming at me. "Aren't you pleased? I helped a commoner."

"I might be pleased. I'm not sure yet." I tightened my fingers on the seat of the chair. "Does any of that so much going on involve the girl you helped?"

Her eyes shifted to the side, a sure sign she was checking something magically. After a moment she shook her head. "No, nothing happening with her. No one's brought the shoe around yet."

I barely stifled a groan. I had suspected this, maybe even known it deep down, but it still gave me a sinking feeling to hear it confirmed. "The glass shoe?"

She laughed. Marj's laugh sounds like bells. She spent decades practicing to get it that way. "Yes, of course, silly, what other shoe?"

Yes, there couldn't be any other important shoe in the entire kingdom. If the glass shoe came from Marj, then Catherine's problem was my fault for pushing Marj in this direction. "Have you been paying any attention at all?" I asked, leaning forward, chair creaking. It was *more* Marj's fault though. "There are big problems with that situation. Your girl ran out on the prince, and left her shoe behind—"

"And they're obviously being a bit slow about finding her, aren't they?" Marj remarked, arching her eyebrows as a bit of coal leaped in to outline them. "But I'm sure they will eventually. It'll be such a lovely wedding."

I gritted my teeth. "But the point is that they're not looking for her!"

That finally penetrated her cloud of cosmetics. She waved aside a powder puff to turn her head and stare at me. "What do you mean they're not looking? How utterly absurd. They have the shoe, don't they? They're supposed to try it on every girl in the kingdom until they find the one it fits."

Of course Marj would see that as a logical course of action. "Yes, they got that idea, but—"

"So they're just being slow about carrying it out?" She turned back to her mirror. "Oh, that's no great problem. Really, Tarry, I wouldn't have expected you to be anxious about it. Although it is sweet of you."

Sometimes talking to Marj is, well, impossible. She only hears the parts she wants to hear. I rubbed my temples, tried again. "I don't think you exactly understand here, Marj, they're not carrying that shoe around because—"

"They thought of the idea, though, that's the main point; now they just need to act on it." Marj waved away her hovering items of make-up to study her reflection. "Be a dear and encourage them to start trying the shoe on girls. It won't take them long to find the right one, seeing as she lives in the capital city; they ought to get to her early."

Miraculous. Possibly useful information! "Where does she live?" I demanded. "Where in the capital city?"

"Oh, in this cute little house; it's surprisingly nice, for one of those small places. Quite poor, but cute." Marj stood up from her chair. "Now you tell them to start hunting. I'd go myself, but like I said, there's just so much going on today. You wouldn't believe it! One of my other projects is coming to a head, and I really must attend to it. There's this beautiful girl and a Beast and—well, it's really all quite complex."

"Marj, would you just tell me—"

"I really don't have a moment, I must be flying." She cast a shower of sparkles over herself and fluffed out her wings. "And I really can't be bothered for the rest of the day; there's that matter with the Beast, and then there's this garden party I simply must attend. The societal implications will be absolutely dramatic if I don't. Anyway, you take care of that glass slipper business. I know I can depend on you, with that fondness you have for helping common people." She smiled sweetly, said, "Tootles," and popped out in a shower of sparks.

I tried to pop after her, but magically and metaphorically slammed into a wall. She'd blocked me. When a fairy doesn't want to be followed, we aren't followed.

I bounced off the metaphorical wall, landed back sitting in Marj's boudoir and sighed. If kittens could sigh, I think the pink kitten would have sighed too.

I was already fairly deep into this, and I knew now I was only going to get in deeper. This whole business was ultimately my fault, and much as I wanted to shove responsibility for dealing with it back onto Marj, she clearly wasn't going to do anything useful.

Which meant it was on me to fix it, before it reached the level of actually ruining lives and making me responsible for, potentially, generations to come.

I returned to the castle, and found Catherine walking back towards the room she'd been assigned. "Did you find out where that girl is?" she asked the very moment I fell into step next to her.

Nothing like easing into this with a little small talk and friendly banter. I frowned at my feet, noticing as I did that I had sparkles stuck to my shoes. "Not exactly."

"Oh." It was a single syllable that spoke volumes of disappointment.

I tried to tamp down the guilt twisting my stomach, and to put a good face on it. "I found out about her glass slipper. My crazy cousin Marjoram made it for her. And I can't talk to Marj right now, but I'll get more information from her when I can. In the meantime, I did narrow it down. I found out she lives in Ryvideau."

"Thousands of people live here," Catherine said, tone not lightening an iota. Even her steps seemed heavy as we descended a carpeted staircase.

"Not that many thousands," I persisted, trying to scrape my shoes against the edge of the steps, leaving bits of sparkles behind. "And even less of them are young blonde girls who went to the ball."

She rubbed her forehead. "But there's enough who *are*."

"It's still a starting point." This news was utterly failing to cheer her up—and it didn't help that I knew as well as she did that the idea of hunting down the right girl based on being blond and living in Ryvideau was a very long shot.

I wished I had got a look at the girl's aura when she was running away from the prince. Then I might have gone strolling through town looking at auras and found her, but without knowing what to look for, I could walk right past her. She might be giving off strong emanations of longing for the prince to find her, but after that stunt with the glass slipper, half the girls in town would be dreaming of the prince right now too. Bizarre as that seemed, when I thought about Roderick.

But speaking of Roderick...maybe we could find this girl if we could find out more about her. "We need to know more, right? So why don't we ask for more information from the only other person who we know for sure has met this girl?"

"Who?"

"His Most Royal Highness Prince Charles Henry etc., etc., commonly going by Roderick."

Catherine tipped her head to one side, eyebrows rising. "Oh yes. Why didn't we think of him sooner?"

I grinned, and it wasn't even very forced. "Because it's hard to imagine him being helpful about anything?"

"True enough," she said with a nod. "It's not such a bad idea, though. I guess we may as well try."

I put on a severe expression to cover up my worry and tried to sound stern. "You could at least *pretend* to feel hopeful about this."

She only shrugged. "Sorry, Tarry. I guess I'm feeling discouraged at the moment."

And that's what worried me. Discouragement wasn't normal for Catherine. I took a quick peek at her aura, and that stone wall was looking very high. I looked away, magically speaking, and suggested, "Try pretending. Maybe you'll start to believe it."

"I'll try." She shook her head, and straightened her shoulders. "If we're going to do this, let's go ahead and do it. Can you find out where the prince is?"

I took a moment to orient. "Yes. Follow me."

We found him in what looked like a den. Lots of wood paneling and animal heads on the walls. Roderick was eating a roast chicken at a table in the center of the room, and he was alone.

"Oh, hello," he said when we came in the room. "You have my permission to enter."

We had already entered, but never mind that.

"Hello, Your Highness," Catherine said, crossing the room to sit down across the table from him. "We need to talk to you about something."

"I didn't give you permission to sit." When she just stared at him, after a moment he added, "Of course, you may if you wish."

I rolled my eyes and sat down in the second chair. It was all hard wood and straight lines and not any more comfortable than Marj's chairs, but at least I didn't worry that this one would splinter under me.

Roderick was regarding me with a quizzical expression. "And who are you?" he asked.

"Tarragon. Pleased to meet you." I stuck out a hand, which he ignored.

"No, I don't care what your *name* is," he said with a shake of his head. "I want to know why you're here."

I hesitated. Besides being mildly offended, if not surprised, I realized that I had once again failed to plan a cover story. I was *used* to explaining away my presence at parties, but different situations called for different answers and I hadn't had to think about this for centuries.

"He's a friend of mine," Catherine said, while I was still muddling towards an answer.

And because it was Roderick, apparently that was enough. "Ah, naturally. Any friend of…" He waved his hand in Catherine's general direction.

She sighed, sounding resigned. "You forgot my name, didn't you?"

"Is there a reason I should remember it?" he asked, eyebrows raised and eyes wide and innocent, as though he was genuinely interested in finding out if such a reason might exist. Too bad Roderick wasn't working alone in all this; I could have just magically whisked Catherine away and he'd be hopeless at ever finding her again.

"Considering I'm not going to marry you, I suppose not." Catherine folded her hands in front of her, back straightening. "We wanted to talk to you about the girl you danced with at the ball."

"She was very pretty," he said immediately, and I gritted my teeth. It was like the man only had one script where that girl was concerned, and the refrain was getting old.

"Yes, you said that already," Catherine said, irritation making its way into her voice. "We want to find her so that you can marry her instead of me. What was her name?"

"I don't know."

I kind of wanted to smack my forehead, but resisted. Or to smack Roderick's forehead. Either one, because I should have seen that coming.

"You danced with her *all evening*," Catherine protested. "Why didn't she tell you her name?"

"I suppose because I didn't ask her."

I was still heroically resisting violence, but for a moment, I really thought Catherine was going to throw something at him. Maybe the chicken. To my private disappointment, she just sighed again instead. "Of course you didn't."

"I don't see why you care that I don't ask people for their names," Roderick complained. "No one ever asks me for *my* name."

"That's because you're the crown prince," I pointed out. "Everyone already knows your name."

He smiled. "Yes, isn't it nice?" Then his gaze drifted downwards. "I didn't give you permission to eat that."

I had unthinkingly reached for a chicken wing sitting on the platter on the table. "Oh. Sorry." I put it down again, but Roderick waved his hand.

"Well, I'm not going to eat it *now*. After you touched it."

I almost argued with him (I have very clean hands, thank you) but if he was going to let me have it... I picked up the wing and took a bite.

Next to me, Catherine cleared her throat pointedly. "Can you tell us anything about what the girl looked like?"

"She was pretty."

Now *my* fingers were itching to throw the chicken at him. Or maybe the wing I was holding. Except it had really nice sauce on it and...anyway. "You *said* that. Anything else?"

Roderick went into deep thought, which was obviously difficult for him. When he emerged, it was to announce, "She was blonde."

"We knew that already too," I muttered, and took the second chicken wing off Roderick's platter. Hazard pay.

"Did she say something that might tell you where she lives?" Catherine asked, leaning forward in her chair. "Where she could be found?"

"I don't think so."

Her hands clenched in her lap. "What did you even talk about all evening?"

Roderick considered. "Me, mostly."

Catherine's hands relaxed and she slumped back in her chair. "I was right before. This is hopeless, and there was no reason to believe you'd be any use at all."

"I think I resent that," Roderick objected.

Before he could carry on and decide for certain, the door opened and Leonard entered, silently. He bowed to Roderick, nodded to Catherine, and looked at me.

"Tarry," I said, folding my arms. "Friend of Catherine's."

He nodded. "I see. And Miss Catherine, have you had a change of heart regarding your marital plans?" His voice was very polite.

Catherine lifted her chin and leveled a steady gaze at him. "No. I have not."

He smiled. It didn't look nice. "What a pity. I believe it would be best if you and I had a private word on the subject, then. Your Highness, surely you have other matters to attend to?"

"All right, Leonard," Prince Roderick said, and got to his feet. I might have wondered that he took directions so easily, but it all fit his general pattern. He didn't seem likely to get seriously bothered by anything.

Leonard looked at me again. "And you…"

"I'm not going anywhere," I said, then glanced at Catherine. "Am I going anywhere?"

"No," she said, gaze on Leonard and jaw tight.

I nodded. "I'm not going anywhere." Part of me wanted very much to be anywhere else, because this couldn't possibly be pleasant. But I was in this now, so I had better see it through.

Leonard nodded as well. "If you insist."

Prince Roderick exited, and Leonard took his chair at the table. "Now, Catherine, you're being rather stubborn on this subject, you know."

"Of course I am," she said, arms crossed and chin still raised. "It's *rather* important to me."

"I understand perfectly," he said. "But I don't think you quite understand what may happen if you continue to refuse."

An uneasy feeling crawled up my spine. He was so polite, voice so mild, and yet I did not *like* that last sentence. I stared at the remains of the chicken on the table in front of Leonard, and felt no urge to steal any more of it to snack on.

"Your precious royals will be embarrassed," Catherine snapped. "They'll survive."

"That wasn't the consequence I was thinking of." Leonard tapped his fingertips together. "I was thinking of that dear little inn of yours."

Oh, this was not going a good direction. I locked my hands together in my lap, resisting a reckless urge to slap him with a curse or two.

Catherine's eyes narrowed. "What about my inn?"

"There are so many rules and regulations and taxes and so on that apply to businesses such as an inn."

"We don't break any laws, and we pay taxes—"

"I've no doubt you do, but if someone were to take a careful look at a place like that, I am sure that every establishment is, well, not quite perfect. There's always another rule, another tax, and enough of that sort of thing could be simply crippling to a nice business like yours." He smiled, still so polite. "If you catch my drift."

"Yes. I think I do," Catherine whispered.

"This doesn't mean you have to do anything," I interrupted, knuckles white by now. I don't like bullies. I don't like bullies at all. "He can't force you to—"

"Tarry, please don't."

"And then there's your...friend. Anthony." Leonard was still smiling. "He was in the army once, wasn't he?"

"Briefly," Catherine said in a guarded tone. "What does that have to do with anything?"

"Wouldn't it be a shame if someone were to discover that his release papers weren't exactly in order? If it was necessary for him to return? It can be quite dangerous on the border with the Magic Lands to the north, you know. All those interesting monsters that come down out of the mountains. Quite dangerous indeed, especially with the right word to the right camp commander."

If I turned him into a toad—but would it even help? He couldn't be acting alone, this was all government and politics and those things are tangled and multi-headed and...and also, there are *rules*. I was starting to feel sick to my stomach, but I hadn't forgotten there were rules.

Catherine had gone pale. "You can't. You couldn't. I won't *let* you."

"You can try to prevent me," Leonard agreed, voice soft. "You know what you need to do."

Catherine's eyes shifted to me. Stomach twisting, I slowly and regretfully shook my head. A flaming dragon is something that a few spells can usually handle. What Leonard had in mind, those weren't threats that I had a ready spell on hand to fight. Which didn't mean I wouldn't try to do something, the churning disgust and guilt in my stomach guaranteed I would try to do *something*. But I didn't have an answer ready that I could hand to her.

She looked away again, not before I caught the expression in her eyes. Or rather, saw that there wasn't any. Her brown eyes had gone absolutely dead.

There was no more animation in her voice than in her eyes. "I believe I will be accepting His Highness' proposal of marriage then."

Chapter Fifteen

Leonard went on for a while about how splendid Catherine's decision regarding marriage to His Royal Highness was. I ignored most of the details, while trying to marshal up a plan of attack. Bureaucracy is so much more complicated to fight than a dragon. Dragons just have flame, teeth and claws. Bureaucrats have legal regulations and fine print. Fairy law tied my hands, making it even harder to figure out what I could do about the human laws that were entangling Catherine. I didn't get very far on a plan, if you can define 'not very far' as 'nowhere at all.'

Catherine said very little. I could see the flowers in her aural garden shrinking down into buds and pulling back into the branches, while the leaves furled up tightly. It was like some kind of warped spring operating in reverse.

Eventually, Leonard concluded for the moment, and suggested that Catherine return to her room. He also suggested that I not go with her. There was, after all, the purity of the royal blood lines to consider. I could have protested how absurd that was, but it didn't seem worth the effort. I nodded agreeably, and walked away. Then, once Catherine was alone, I popped back into her room.

"Hello again," I said, offering my best smile because I didn't have much else to offer. "I can go if you want me to."

She was sitting at the table again, now cleared of its breakfast array, and just shook her head. "It doesn't matter."

I usually like to be greeted with more enthusiasm than that, but under the circumstances, I couldn't blame her. I sat down at the table too. "There still might be a way out of this," I said, painfully aware that optimism which had rung hollow an hour ago was now cavernous in its emptiness.

She shot me a look. Not even that. Half a look. "Care to cast a spell to make the prince and his flunky fall asleep for a hundred years? That might solve it."

I shifted uncomfortably in my chair. I had thought of that idea too. "I'm not actually allowed to do that," I said, words heavy on my tongue. "There are rules."

"I thought the fairy Jack and Emmy ran afoul of did that."

"She did. Well, Echinacea cast a spell to kill the princess, and then Marj changed it and put everyone to sleep. But they were personally involved. Echinacea was snubbed when they didn't invite her to the christening, and Marj was Rosaline's godmother, which gave her plenty of connection—that meant they were allowed to use Significant Spells. I'm not directly involved here; the prince isn't trying to do anything to me, which limits what I'm allowed to do to him." I was rambling, and also gesturing somewhat extensively. Both are nervous tics. I stopped.

Catherine just nodded, and rested her chin on her hand. "I had a feeling the answer would be something like that. That's a truly stupid rule, by the way."

I shrugged. "Oh, I don't know, the principle behind it's not so bad. It's supposed to keep us from getting involved where we shouldn't. Not that it doesn't allow an awful lot of fairies to poke their wings into other people's business anyway. There are others too, like how we can't interfere with members of the military. Supposed to keep us out of wars and…and so on." Rambling again. Maybe if I sat on my hands…

"So the conclusion is that there's nothing we can do, and it would be best to just accept the inevitable."

And right before my metaphorical eyes, I saw another row of stones form on the top of her aural wall, building it up higher and stronger and harder to breach. Not even a fresco on these stones, just gray rock.

I looked away, physically and metaphorically, leaned back in my chair and stared at the ceiling. "So you're going to marry the prince. You think you can live with that?"

She was silent for long enough that I had to peek at her, to see that she was staring at her hands in her lap. "Honestly?" she said finally. "I'm not sure I can live with it. But the alternative is that The Nightingale closes, my father loses his business, my friends lose their jobs, we all lose our home, and Anthony goes off to be killed by monsters. And I know that I *can't* live with any of that."

I really wished that some of those people, maybe all of them, were here right now to argue about this with her. Maybe she'd listen to them. But unfortunately, there was just me. It was too many voices to be speaking for, as if all of them were leaning on my shoulders at once. "They'd all tell you not to marry him anyway," I said, a slightly cowardly attempt to shift responsibility onto those not present.

"I know," she said, with a smile that didn't lighten the sadness in her eyes. "Which is all the more reason why I should."

It was brave and heartrending and made the entire situation seem all the more *stupid* by comparison. Grand noble sacrifices made by good people to help other good people they cared about ought to at least have a decent reason for needing to be done. Not a stupid whim of Marj or an idiot prince. "If we could just find the original girl...if the royalty just wasn't being so stubborn over that business about marrying whoever the shoe fits..."

"But they are," she said flatly.

"Yes, and I wish I knew why, because I still don't understand why they're so set on it." A thought occurred to me. "You know, what I just said, that wasn't right. It's not the *royalty* that's set on it, it seems more to be—"

And before I finished that sentence, I was fatally distracted by a sudden blinking alarm on the edge of my magical awareness.

"Seems to be what?" Catherine asked.

I focused in on the flashing alarm. "Wait, I'm picking up something. Anthony's trying to get back into the castle, but the guards don't like the idea. I'll go get him." Because this was *good*, this was someone who was going to have a vastly better chance of arguing with or cheering up Catherine than I was having, so I'd go get him and...

Then I noticed she'd gone a shade paler. I was already on my feet, but I stopped short of going anywhere. "That is," I said uneasily, "if you want me to." And I didn't know what I'd do if she said no.

Luckily, she clasped her hands together in her lap and nodded a single, careful nod. "If you would, please. Better to get this over with. And I'd rather he didn't hear the news somewhere else first."

Because he was going to take it so well hearing it from her. Still, get them together, get them talking, maybe things would get better?

"Right then," I agreed, and raised my hand to transport myself out.

"And I don't want to tell him why," Catherine said.

I stopped mid-gesture. "Wait now, what?"

"I don't want to tell him," she repeated. Her gaze was steady but her knuckles were turning white where her hands interlaced. "He'll feel guilty and he'll try to talk me out of it, and...I don't want to tell him why I'm marrying the prince. It would be easier for him if he thinks I'm doing this willingly. It'll be easier for him to...move on." If I didn't have magical hearing, I'm not sure I even would have heard the last two words.

"Because you *want* him to do that?" I said, stomach sinking. If she was already talking like that, she was even more resigned to this than I'd thought.

"I don't want this to ruin his life too."

"I think it's too late for that," I pointed out.

"Any more than it already has, then."

I shook my head. "It's up to you, of course, but—"

"Please don't try to change my mind," she said, gaze on her hands.

I didn't try. It wouldn't do any good. I just popped out to the perimeter of the castle. I chose my spot carefully—around the corner from where Anthony was arguing with the guards, but behind a guard shack out of sight of anyone, so no one would get upset when I appeared. I strolled over to the disturbance at the gate.

When I was close, I remarked, "You know, Anthony, you have an impressive talent for getting into arguments with royal guards."

Anthony turned towards me, his glower diminishing slightly but his shoulders staying just as tense. "Jack told me you might be here." He looked at the guards, who were all glowering back, took a step closer and leaned in to ask, "Are you the reason Catherine was convinced it would be all right if I left?"

"I am. Walk with me." I waved a farewell to the guards, who did not wave back or even blink, and started down the road away from the castle.

"That's the wrong direction," Anthony pointed out, without moving.

"We just need to get out of sight," I said, and gestured for him to follow.

He did, his expression grudging. Curiosity lurked in his eyes too, suggesting Jack had also told him other things. "So you really are a…"

"Yes."

"I always thought fairies were…"

I heaved a sigh. "Everyone does. But I'm not. More importantly, I can get you back into the castle."

"How's Catherine?"

Catherine was not something I wanted to discuss. I'd rather not talk at all, really, because it was going to be very hard to talk to Anthony about anything right now, until I wasn't the keeper of information he needed to hear. "Better ask her that. Come on this way."

Rosaline's castle in Waldisan was in a nice flat field, but Roderick had his castle up on a hilltop—not that either of them made any decisions about that. One road led down from Roderick's castle to the capital city clustered around the base, but we didn't need to go all the way down. A few buildings stood here and there along the road, guard posts and such like that, and I led the way behind one of them. That blocked us from the sight of the guards at the castle, and then an easy wave of my hand transported us both inside to Catherine's room.

"You could have warned me," Anthony said, shaking his head.

"Sorry." Sometimes I forget other people aren't used to sudden dematerializing, especially when I have other things on my mind.

Catherine had moved to the window, and was standing with her back to the room. Now that I was seeing them both at once, the contrast between hers and Anthony's auras was enough to make me wince. Her garden had gone altogether into the deepest winter, while his forest was still full of green leaves and sunshine.

"Hello, Cat," Anthony said, face lightening in a smile and aural birds setting up a song as he looked at her. "Everyone's all right at home. Is there any news here?"

Catherine turned around, face set into an expression too blank to be natural. "Yes, actually. I told the prince I'm going to marry him."

I flinched. Nothing like getting into delicate matters gradually, or giving me a chance to escape the scene before the explosions happened. On the other hand, maybe a second voice would lend some weight while he talked her out of this? He was going to be much more effective than I was, but maybe I could help.

Anthony's expression didn't change, but the metaphorical birds stopped singing and his voice sounded careful as he said, "All right. So you have a plan that starts with making the prince believe you're going to marry him. What's the next part?"

The man really had an impressive level of optimism. I didn't know whether that should make me worried or hopeful. I sidled over to sit down at the breakfast table again; even with no food on it, I felt more comfortable sitting at a table.

Catherine's hands were clenched into fists within the folds of her skirt. "There isn't any plan, and there isn't any next part. I'm going to marry Prince Roderick."

"That's really not funny."

"I'm not joking. I told the prince I'm going to marry him, and I am. I thought about it and there are certain advantages."

Not telling him the truth was one thing, but did she really have to convince him she *wanted* to do this? This conversation needed to hurry up and get to the part where he talked her out of it, where my hanging around might accomplish something. I cleared my throat. "I still think we should talk about alternatives so—"

"*Certain advantages*?" Anthony said over me. "What did they *do* to you?"

And after that they were going back and forth so quickly, I couldn't get a word in for several lines.

Catherine shook her head. "They didn't do anything; I just—"

"I leave for two hours, and I come back to *this*?" It was still spring in his forest, but a gale was now blowing. "What happened? What did they bribe you with?"

Her chin went up. "You really believe I'd take a bribe?"

He didn't pursue the idea. "Did they threaten you? Is that it?"

"No, they didn't threaten me." If there was an extra emphasis on the 'me,' Anthony apparently didn't catch it.

"Then what happened? Because this doesn't make any kind of sense, Cat."

"Don't call me that," she whispered.

Anthony groaned, which gave me enough of a pause to say, "I really think we should all just sit down and talk about this." I tapped my hands against the table, just by emphasis. "We may decide this isn't the best course and—"

"*We* aren't deciding anything," Catherine interrupted, "*I* decided and I'm not going to change my mind. I'm marrying the prince and there's nothing else to say."

"Nothing else to say?" Anthony repeated. "Really? Do you love him?"

And that had more weight than anything I might have said in a year of arguing. The question settled into the middle of the room, so heavy it practically had its own aura.

"That's not the point," Catherine said faintly, a non-answer that didn't shift the question at all.

"No? Really?" He stepped closer to her, looked down into her face. "Well then…do you love me?"

I held my breath. If this didn't work, I doubted anything else would. And I didn't know how to fix this after that.

She looked away, and the trees in her aural garden shrank back too. "That's not really the point either."

"Of course it's the point." He reached out, took her hands. "It's the only point that matters, because I love you and five minutes ago I believed that you loved me, so you can't just go off and marry some idiotic prince."

"You don't understand," Catherine said, pulling her hands away. "You don't know what's going on, you don't know anything about this, you don't know anything about me—"

"Don't say that," Anthony interrupted, catching her hand again between both of his. "Because I *do* know you." His voice softened. "I know you love running The Nightingale. I know you'd do anything for the people you care about. And I know that you want to seem strong and independent and capable all the time, and that you don't think cute names fit that picture...so you *tell* me not to call you Cat, but I always thought that somewhere deep down you liked it."

One corner of her mouth turned up in a very small smile. "I thought I had you fooled with that last one."

He smiled, just a little, too. "I don't know what's going on today, but don't tell me that I don't know *you*."

I let out a breath I'd been holding for three minutes, because I could see the atmosphere in the room lightening. He was still holding her hand, his branches were reaching over her wall, a few leaves were starting to tentatively unfurl in her garden, and it was all going to be all right. We could all sit down, and talk about other ideas, and come up with a plan and...and...and those leaves tightened up again and another row of stones slammed onto the top of her wall and she pulled her hand away.

"But it doesn't make any difference," she whispered, "it doesn't change anything."

His face went white and his trees snatched backwards and it was clear enough to both my mental and literal eyes that she had just shattered him. And I think she knew it too but was too stubborn to admit she could see it.

I, on the other hand, had had enough with the direction this conversation had been going. "Do you still think this is the easier way, Catherine?" I asked. "Because I really think you should just tell him the truth." And maybe then he wouldn't back away and stop fighting, as he was plainly about to do.

Anthony's head snapped around to look at me. "What truth? What do you mean?"

"Tarry!" Catherine protested.

"*Cat.*"

"Anthony—"

"Leonard," I said unhappily, as a new presence appeared on my awareness. And a heartbeat later there was a knock at the door.

"Ignore that," Anthony said shortly. "Cat, tell me what's going on."

She just shook her head, and went to open the door.

Leonard strolled in, so calm by comparison to everyone in the room that it was disconcerting, and surveyed us with a cool look. "You keep interesting company," he said to Catherine.

"Don't worry," I said, and waved a hand at Anthony. "We were chaperoning each other." Light words to mask a coil of frustration. Of all the people we didn't need to see right now, just when maybe Catherine was about to give Anthony all the weapons he needed to fight this, and maybe he would have come up with an argument that maybe would have made her change her mind…and maybe we could have got to a place where my messing about with Marj wouldn't ruin both their lives.

"I didn't expect you to get back into the castle," Leonard commented to Anthony. "How did you manage it?"

"Never mind that," he snapped. "What have you done to Catherine?"

"I take it she mentioned that she has decided to marry His Royal Highness."

"Yes," Anthony said, with all the warmth and enthusiasm of a glacier. "She mentioned it."

Leonard smiled. I was growing to hate his smiles. "I think it was quite a wise decision."

"You would," Anthony muttered.

Catherine made another attempt at placating him. "Anthony, please, if you would just try to accept this it would be much easier."

"I don't want this to be easier," he said, turning to glare at her. "I want it to be impossible so you won't do it!"

"You are obviously upset," Leonard said, sitting down at the table, far enough from me that I didn't feel too strong an urge to move away. "Perhaps it would be better if you were not here, where you can upset Catherine as well. I believe you were in the army once?"

My stomach sank with the terrible suspicion that that was not in fact the change of topic it appeared to be. Catherine's eyes widened, likely with the same thought.

Only Anthony looked confused. "Briefly. So?"

"Are you aware of the consequences of desertion?"

Anthony's brow creased as the confusion grew. "I didn't desert. I volunteered and was in the army for ten days, before everyone agreed on a discharge because I wasn't the right sort for the military. Not everyone is."

Leonard was smiling again. "So you say. But discharge papers can be faked."

Anthony's confusion didn't lift. "What are you…?"

Leonard's voice was soft, and smooth as silk. "Would you rather be hanged as a deserter, or return to the army?"

"No, you can't," burst from Catherine. "You said if I—" She broke off, shooting a half-guilty glance at Anthony.

She didn't break off in time, not for keeping him in the dark. "He said if you…" Anthony may not have been right for the military, but he wasn't stupid. We could all see him putting it together.

"I said a great deal about what would happen if you did not agree to marry the prince," Leonard acknowledged. "I didn't say anything about what would happen if you did."

I dug my fingernails into my palms. Somehow, some way, some day, I was going to turn that man into a toad. It might take a long time to figure out how to twist around the Fairy Court's rules, but I was going to do it.

If Anthony had needed any more clarification—I don't think he did—that was it. He stared at Catherine. "*That's* why you agreed to marry the prince?"

"Don't tell me it's not worth it, Anthony."

"It's *not worth it*, Cat!"

She threw up her hands. "This is why I didn't want to tell you! I knew you'd try to talk me out of it, and that you'd get this…anguished look you have right now—"

"I wasn't anguished before?"

"Now you're guilty-anguished; it's worse."

"It doesn't feel worse."

"It makes *me* feel worse!"

"Obviously," Leonard cut in, "you are having a negative influence on Catherine's state of mind. It would be better, therefore, if you were not here. And we can always use more men on the border with Beaumont. Think of it as patriotic."

I couldn't turn him into a toad unless he threatened me personally, but there had to be something. A loophole, somewhere. Maybe if I just up and kicked him, that would get him to threaten me—but then the Fairy Queen would say I provoked him and…something, there had to be *something*.

"This doesn't even make sense," Catherine protested. "If you carry out the threat regardless of what I do, why should I marry the prince? I'll change my mind about it, refuse to cooperate. Then what would you do?"

"I'd reconsider that if I were you," Leonard said, voice ever so polite and helpful. "Some areas of the border are more dangerous than others. Some camp commanders are more apt to, how shall I put this, *lose* men than others. And of course, we wouldn't want anything dreadful to happen to your precious inn either."

Catherine's momentary resolve crumbled. "All right," she whispered. "I'll marry him."

Anthony's aural forest shuddered, caught in an earthquake indicating a far deeper pain than the earlier gale. "Cat, please…"

"Don't call me that."

And at that, Anthony actually smiled. I didn't, and he wouldn't have either, if he had been able to see the frosty coldness that had settled over her garden.

Catherine didn't smile back. "No, I mean, really don't. Not when I've agreed to…not when I'm going to…" Her eyes were bright and wet, but she blinked once, took a deep breath and held onto her composure. "Just don't," she whispered.

I was going to have to adopt both their family lines for the next seven generations. That was the only way I'd be able to redeem this level of disaster.

Anthony stared at Catherine for a long, painful moment, then turned to Leonard. "All right," he said flatly. "When do I join up?"

Leonard folded his hands together—and smiled. "Very conveniently, there's a new group leaving for the border in an hour. They're gathering in the courtyard now."

It was very convenient. So convenient that I felt sure Leonard had arranged matters somehow. Groups set off for the border pretty regularly, but maybe he'd moved this one's departure up or something.

Anthony just nodded, expression blank. "Perfect."

"If there's anything you need to do before you leave, you had better take care of it quickly," Leonard advised.

Anthony's smile this time was more ghost than genuine. "Only one thing anyway."

He was only a few steps away from Catherine. He crossed the distance in a moment, pulled her into his arms and kissed her. Her hands lifted, hovered for a heartbeat, then slowly settled onto his shoulders, slowly slipped around him.

Anthony drew back just an inch, still holding her tightly. "I love you," he said, voice rough. "I don't care who you agreed to marry, I still love you, Cat."

Leonard cleared his throat. "I suggest you bear in mind that you are speaking to the future consort of His Royal Highness."

Anthony released Catherine, who sank down onto the nearby windowseat, and he looked Leonard dead in the eye. "Go to Hell," he said, and walked out without looking back.

Chapter Sixteen

Leonard left soon after Anthony, and insisted that I leave too. I did—
and to be honest, it was a relief. I walked out of Catherine's room, and
transported away from the castle, even away from the country. I went
to an orange grove on the western coast of another continent entirely,
because it was far away, it was one of my favorite places, it had a high
concentration of magical energy which is always steadying—and just
now, some green, growing trees felt steadying too.

I dropped onto the grass below a tree, rolled onto my back to
look up at the leaves, and took a deep breath.

Tragedies happened all the time. I knew that. Everyone knew
that. People got sick, people died, someone fell under a curse or their
business failed or the crops didn't grow or a dragon flamed a village.
Or two people in love had circumstances conspire against them so that
they couldn't be together. That was life, that was what happened, every
day.

It's just, knowing that is very different from watching it play out.
This was why I had spent five centuries going to parties; always
christenings, never funerals. I had gotten tangled up in other people's
problems before, and it had sent me running in search of festivals and
revelry for centuries since. Sure, I helped someone out when I stumbled
over an opportunity, but I didn't stay in any place long enough to see
the tragedies.

Yet here I was, watching a tragedy happen again. It was even
worse when it was happening to two people I liked, who wouldn't be in
this mess if I hadn't lost my temper and made a bet with Marj. I could
tell myself I'd been trying to teach her a valuable lesson, and maybe
that was part of it—but too much of it had been my own pride. With
that basis, maybe it was only natural that she had learned exactly the
wrong lesson.

It would have been comfortable to blame the whole mess on
Marj. That would have absolved me of responsibility and let me just

wash my hands of the whole business and move on. Find another inn with a warm kitchen and good conversation.

I stared up at the green leaves of the orange trees, sunlight filtering through so that they seemed to glow from within, and thought about the cold, bare winter branches of Catherine's aural garden, about the root-shaking shudder that had gone through Anthony's forest. And about all the times I had ranted that Marj didn't respect the common people, that she didn't regard them as having any value as individuals and wouldn't admit their lives mattered.

I sighed, sat up, and cast a quick spell to get grass stains off my clothes. Another spell snapped a few short branches off the tree above me and dropped them down into my hand. I waved a hand over the leafy branches and brought them out into blossoms even though the season was wrong. Then I got to my feet and transported back to the castle in Perrelda. I might not have an answer to avert this particular tragedy, but I could see it through. And maybe I could mitigate the damage, if only a little.

I transported into Catherine's sitting room, and when I didn't see her there, I looked through the doorway to the bedroom. She was lying across the bed, face-down with her head in her arms. If her shoulders had been shaking I would have backed away…but they weren't, so I knocked on the door frame.

"Catherine? I might be able to help…"

"Go away," she said without lifting her head, voice muffled.

I carefully put on my most optimistic expression, and projected the same tone into my voice as I walked into the room. "Not until you at least listen to my idea."

"I don't *care*. It doesn't matter now. It's too late. They're sending Anthony to the border, and I'm marrying the prince, and they'll just make everything even worse than it already is if I refuse." She groaned. "As if it isn't bad enough." She rolled over and stared at the canopy above the bed, while I stared at the frost on her aural garden. "Anthony is bad at fighting. He's wonderful at running The Nightingale but—and the inn, Anthony and I basically run everything. I don't know how

Father will ever…it probably won't even make any difference, my marrying the prince, because they won't be able to keep the inn going and Anthony's going to be killed by some monster coming out of the mountains anyway and *it's all my fault.*"

That last was so much like what had been echoing in my head that it made me start guiltily. "It's not your fault, Catherine. All you did was go to a dance."

"Yes, exactly, I ruined everyone's life because I wanted to go to a stupid party! If I hadn't gone, if I hadn't tried the shoe on…"

"If the prince hadn't had the ball to begin with," I countered, sitting on the edge of the bed. "If Marj hadn't decided to help a girl go to the ball and made a glass shoe for her." I swallowed, and rubbed the back of my neck. "If I hadn't encouraged Marj to start paying attention to people who aren't royal. That's…really where this whole thing started, I was trying to prove a point to Marj."

Catherine sat up on the bed and looked at me for a moment, brown eyes searching. My whole spine went stiff fighting the urge to look away. Finally she shook her head. "It's not your fault, Tarry. You couldn't know it was going to turn out like this."

I let out a breath. "Well. I'll agree to that if you'll agree that it's not your fault either." I wouldn't actually believe that it wasn't my fault, but I was willing to say it.

"Agreed," she said, probably lying too, with a half smile that didn't reach her eyes.

I offered my handful of orange blossoms as a peace offering and suggested, "We could say that it's Roderick's fault."

"Let's say that." She took the blossoms, ran her fingertips along the waxy white blooms. "But it won't really matter whose fault it is," she said in a low voice. "It won't make it seem any better, if The Nightingale has to close or if…if Anthony is…"

"He'll be all right, Catherine. I promise." I took a deep breath. "Because I'll go with him. Join the army too." Because I was resolved now, I was going to see this through. Whatever that took.

Her expression didn't lighten, and she kept her gaze on the blossoms. "I thought you aren't allowed to interfere with soldiers."

"No," I conceded, "but if a monster comes charging out of the mountains, I can interfere with *it*." The rules were far less strict when dealing with, say, a hippogryph compared to a human. Too bad Prince Roderick and his nasty friend weren't basilisks. I could've dealt with them if they were.

She finally looked up, eyes wide and vulnerable and shoulders tight. "That would...that would help, that would really...are you sure? I mean, I didn't think fairies did that sort of thing, committing to something like this."

I shrugged broadly. "Haven't you heard? I'm an unusual fairy." And I grinned to hide the twist of guilt in my stomach, and hoped she couldn't hear the unspoken lie. Because the truth was, historically, I had committed to far less than the average Good or Evil Fairy.

"Thank you," she said softly, "for helping Anthony. It means the world to me."

And that just made the guilt even worse. "I still think we'll find a way to help you too," I said quickly. "That girl the shoe belongs to, I haven't given up on finding her. I can't get anything out of Marj right now, but in a little while—if you just push for a long engagement to the prince—nothing's really settled yet, so..."

"We'll see," she said, but while those were positive enough words, there was nothing in her voice to suggest any hope at all.

"Right, we will," I said, just as though she'd spoken with great enthusiasm. "Chin high and don't give up. And right now, I'd better go join the army before they start marching." And before I got to the point where I couldn't pretend to be cheerful anymore.

She just nodded and I stood up to go. Then I turned back, one hand on the bedpost. "Hey, Cat?"

She looked up, face a little too carefully blank.

"We'll both be coming back," I said. "I promise."

She looked down again—but she nodded, and I couldn't reasonably ask for more at that moment.

I walked out of the room, and once I had a closed door between us I leaned back against the wall to concentrate on taking some good steadying breaths and fight the urge to go running back to my orange grove. I didn't *like* tragedies.

After a few deep breaths, I sent my magical senses questing out to find Anthony, and then followed the signal through the maze of corridors. I got into a couple dead-ends, but I found my way eventually to the courtyard where the new recruits were forming up.

High stone castle walls loomed over the inner courtyard, and men were all but overflowing it. A couple of men in uniform were apparently directing the whole business, though it was hard to discern from the results that anyone was directing it at all. Twenty men—some carrying weapons, some not, most carrying bags but not all, none of them in uniform—milled about on the packed earth. I think Anthony was the only one who wasn't talking, and most of them were shouting.

I stood in the last doorway leading onto the courtyard, hidden in the shadows. I conjured up a sword and a pack for myself, and then cast a quick spell so no one would realize that they were supposed to have twenty men, not twenty-one. That was a minor enough spell that I could get it past the ban on magic use on the military. The Fairy Queen wouldn't like even that, if she found out, but the result was small enough that it should go unnoticed.

That settled, I sidled into the group. I had to dodge one man who was hurrying by, and I was nearly impaled by a few elbows, but eventually I made it over to Anthony. No one else was trying to talk to him. They couldn't see the cold stillness of his aural forest, with nary a leaf moving, but everyone could see his hunched shoulders, crossed arms and scowl.

I thought about the cheerful man who'd strolled into The Nightingale with a basket of bread just before Jack and Emmy's wedding. The comparison was painful.

I did my best to muster up a merry outward appearance. It didn't look as though it would be any easier here than it had been with Catherine. "Hello there."

He barely flicked me a glance and his expression didn't change. "What are you doing here?"

I put one hand through the strap of my bag over my shoulder, and slouched a bit, in what I hoped was a tough-looking way. "I decided to join the army."

His eyes narrowed. "I don't need your help. I'll be fine."

"Hey, I just decided I'd like to go fight a few monsters." I raised my fists, threw a shadow punch. "Might be fun, eh?"

He just stared at me, and I don't think the false good cheer fooled him at all. It certainly wasn't contagious. "Why are you here? Go do something useful. Go help Catherine."

I gave up the cheerful attitude, squared my shoulders and said, "I'm helping Catherine by helping you, so she doesn't have to worry about you. So you can help her by letting me help you."

"I *don't* need your help," Anthony said, and settled back into his scowl. "But I also don't care enough to argue with you."

"I'll take what I can get." It was at least nominal permission to do what small amount I could to help this situation, and that would have to do for now.

So we both stood there, silent in the midst of the hubbub, until eventually the two uniformed men felt that we were ready to go. I have no idea what criteria they used to judge that. More yelling got everyone into a line, if a rather straggled one, and off we marched.

We didn't get any great fanfare or sending off. People from Perrelda had been setting off for the border with Beaumont for nearly a century. The mere fact of someone going produced no great excitement, so the amount of fuss made depended on who was going. It looked to me like this group was essentially the scrapings of society—mostly people who didn't have anywhere else to go. Mind you, I *like* the scrapings of society, but I'm sure there wasn't a single one in the group that Marj would have considered 'special' enough for her attention.

The line straggled even more once we were out of the castle. I strolled along next to Anthony in silence on the road down the hill, down the side road that took us around the edge of Ryvideau and out of the city, and on for another mile in open country. Finally I couldn't take the weight of not talking anymore and said, "At least it's not raining."

"I don't want to talk," Anthony said without looking at me or breaking stride. "Not about the weather, not about the future, not about my thoughts on anything or your thoughts on anything, and definitely not about balls, shoes, or royalty."

"Does that leave anything to talk about?"

"If it does, I don't want to talk about that either."

"Right." I let a moment pass before commenting, "It's going to be a long walk, then." When he didn't respond to that, I ventured, "How long a walk is it, anyway?"

"Three days," he said, put his head down and trudged on.

"Right." I carefully cast a spell to keep my feet from getting sore. Fairies don't walk much.

It was a long day. Even though we didn't start walking until early afternoon, it was still a long day. Within an hour I thoroughly regretted not planning instead to meet Anthony once he got to the border—but now that I was here, it felt like cowardice to back out. And if the humans could do this, surely I could too.

It was just...so *boring* traveling by foot. And so slow. And it gave me so much time to think. To think about all the people I had known over so many centuries, and to wonder. I had always liked to just imagine that everyone I danced with at a party or had a nice conversation with over a banquet table had gone on to lead a long and happy life.

But I had very rarely gone back to check. Because while it might be true for some, maybe even most, I had never wanted to know about the ones whose lives had turned out differently.

Chapter Seventeen

Our second day of marching towards the border began altogether too early if you ask me. We'd camped in a big empty field, and it was still misty in the early dawn light when we were all ordered to wake up, pack up and get ready to move out. The only consolation was the loaves of bread being handed out from the back of a cart that had trailed us on the march.

It was less consolation when they only let me have one loaf. I took it and wandered back to where Anthony was rolling up his blankets. "Good morning," I said around a mouthful of crust.

All I got in response was a very perfunctory nod.

I sighed, sat down cross-legged on the damp grass and rested my chin in one hand. "Tell me the truth. Is it me?" I didn't usually hang around with unfriendly people. I didn't know how to handle this.

"What?" Anthony said, looking up, then shook his head. "No, I just have a lot on my mind. Thinking about…back at the castle."

Yeah, that made sense. But it was reassuring to hear anyway. It was hard enough committing to help someone through a rough situation, without having to deal with that someone not liking me.

Anthony fastened up his blanket roll with a rope, and added, "I was also thinking about the dream I was having. There was a hippogryph in it."

My eyebrows rose. "Sounds unpleasant," I said, and bit into my bread again.

He glanced up again, this time with a half-smile. "Not really. It was chasing Roderick."

I was so relieved to see even a slight smile that I grinned back. "Maybe we can tame one after it comes out of the mountains and send it to eat the prince."

"We should do that." Then even the half-smile faded. "I don't suppose you know if anything is happening at the castle?"

The castle probably wasn't even awake yet. At least, not anyone outside of the lowest-level servants. But who ever said worry was logical? Out loud, I just said, "I left spells that would tell me if anything important happens. No news so far."

"All right," he said, and then there was a silence as he finished gathering up his belongings and I studied his aura. Still all cold and still, but not frost-covered like Catherine's. As if they were both deeply pained, but she had given up while he was still waiting for things to get better again.

"Do you suppose she'll really go through with it?" Anthony asked suddenly, without looking at me. "Marry him, I mean?"

I couldn't answer a question like that! "I...don't know. You know her much better than I do." I wanted to just leave that there and change the subject, but it didn't feel right. It would have been cowardly. So I asked, "What do you think?"

He rubbed the back of his neck. "I don't know either." He squinted up at the pale blue morning sky. "Catherine will do anything to help people she loves, so that part makes sense. But it's not like her to give in without more of a fight, so...I don't know."

I had been bothered by her despair, but it had been hard to separate how much of that was my own discomfort versus something genuinely off about her. Now that he was saying this, it made me worry more. "It did seem strange, that she wasn't fighting harder about this."

"I can't work out what it means, though." Some of the leaves in his forest curled into themselves in a very alarming way and I didn't want to hear what his next thought was going to be.

Quickly I said, "Maybe it's just—"

"Unless it means," he continued right over me, "that there really are certain advantages of a prince compared to an aspiring innkeeper, so she..."

"It doesn't mean *that!*" Keep on that line and he was going to get all frost-covered, and I couldn't handle despair from him too. "That much I'm *sure* of. If you could see her aura when she looks at you, you'd be sure too."

"Her what?" Anthony asked with a puzzled expression, and not as much reassurance as I would have liked.

"Aura. It's a fairy thing." And I spent the rest of the time until we got marching again trying to explain auras. I didn't describe Catherine's, that's too private, but I tried to get the general concept through. A discussion of auras was so much less emotionally fraught than a discussion about who was marrying whom and why.

Once we were trudging along the road again, it seemed most natural to keep talking. At least, I definitely wasn't going to ask Anthony if he wanted to be silent again today, and he didn't bring it up.

So we walked along the dirt road winding between green fields as the sunlight grew brighter, the line of soldiers straggling out over several hundred yards, and I said, "Tell me where you're from. Why you didn't stay in the army before. How you ended up at The Nightingale."

He hitched the pack on his back a little higher. "You want my life story?"

"That'll do for a start." Lots of walking ahead, and I'd much rather think about his life than about mine.

"Well. I suppose to begin at the beginning…" he said slowly, and I was so relieved he was willing to pursue the topic that I could have floated. "I should begin in Alphoson Port. That's where my family's from, at least since my great-grandfather left Beaumont. We've done pretty well since then. I'm more or less alone and poor at the moment, but I'm originally from a large and wealthy family."

Some people might have said that in a way that made me think they were trying to impress other people, people like Marj, but Anthony just presented it like it was a fact. "I might've guessed that," I said. There had been a flash or too suggesting he was well-educated, at least. "Very large and wealthy?"

He shrugged. "My father was a successful merchant, so somewhat wealthy. And large enough. I have two brothers and three sisters. Our mother died when we were still young and my father never quite…" He shrugged again, his gaze on the horizon as we walked on.

"Well, we looked after each other, mostly, my brothers and sisters and me. But life was pretty good, growing up. Simple, anyway. We knew where we fit and what we were supposed to do, and we just followed along that path, going to school and going to parties and all of that."

That sounded like a pretty nice life to me, even if his telling of it was a little formal. "Good parties?" I asked hopefully.

"Yeah, I guess so. Some of them." No smile on that, and no enthusiasm either. Not the important part of the story, apparently. "If I ever thought about it, which I didn't much, I guess I expected to become a merchant like my father. I always had a good head for numbers and for dealing with people and it probably would have worked out all right. Maybe that's what I'd be doing now, if my father hadn't lost most of his money three years ago."

A pause, as Anthony kicked a stone out of the path and I processed that last sentence. I had not expected something like that, and he'd just dropped it there. What was I supposed to say? Sorry to hear it? That seemed meaningless.

Before I came up with anything better, Anthony resumed with, "Father had a bad string of luck with his business. A few ships he'd invested in heavily were lost at sea, and in the end almost everything had to be sold to pay the creditors." He kicked another stone, watched it fly off through the grass alongside the road. "The house, the carriages, the horses, even most of Mother's jewelry."

My unease was growing. This was not the cheerful story I had been expecting. I reached back into my pack, pulled out the extra loaf I'd smuggled away from the breakfast cart, and bit into the end. He'd been happy just a week ago, so he must have come out of the shadows somewhere. I tried to bide my time and kept listening.

"By the time all the debts were paid, all that was left was a cottage near Cyudry, a little village up north. We'd never even been there; I think it was left to my mother by her godmother. Anyway, we didn't have much choice at this point but to move up there.

"George and Connor, my brothers, they took it all right." Anthony scratched behind one ear. "I guess I took it all right too. I mean, we'd never any of us been very attached to high society anyway, and it was sort of an adventure.

"My two older sisters were much more upset about it all. Miranda and Noreen really cared about fine society and fine clothes and all the rest of it. And there was a bad bit at the end in the city..." He sighed, looking down at his feet. "They both had suitors flocking around them when we had money, but as soon as the money was gone, the suitors disappeared too. They acted indignant about it, claimed they didn't really like any of them anyway...but it must have hurt." For a moment he was silent, and I guessed he was remembering more recent events.

This was less uncomfortable than spending the day not talking, but not by much. I munched nervously at my bread, hoped he'd start talking again without me needing to say anything.

He did, shaking his head and picking up the former topic again. "Miranda and Noreen are like that. Proud, but mostly they're determined not to let anything show. They complain plenty about anything they don't like, but they won't talk about how they're really feeling about anything."

I wondered what their auras would look like. Walls, maybe, and I doubted they'd have frescoes as nice as Catherine's. It didn't sound as though they had learned the art of balancing careful defenses with a friendly appearance. It reminded me too about the blocks of stone I had noticed in Anthony's aural forest, the ones that might have been a wall once but had since changed. Had he had a girl in Alphoson Port? Or if not that, what else had made him put up a wall?

He didn't volunteer any story like that, still talking about his older sisters. "They didn't let anyone see what they really felt about leaving the city, but they complained to the skies about the travel conditions and the food and the small, drafty cottage once we reached it. Beauty at least handled it all more quietly."

That prompted me to finally interrupt. "Wait. Beauty?"

He gave a slight laugh. "Sorry, I forget sometimes how odd that must sound to people hearing it for the first time. Beauty's my youngest sister."

"And that's her name?"

"Not originally. Originally it was Jeanne Marie. But she was a pretty little girl and she picked up the nickname, and by the time she should have outgrown it, we'd all gotten used to it. At least it fits her; she's very beautiful." He shoved his hands into his pockets, gaze turned away from me towards several crows in the field alongside us. "That's probably part of why she's everyone's favorite."

The words were too deliberately casual, and they gave me a new guess about that wall he might have had. "She can't be *everyone's* favorite."

"Most people." He watched the crows flap upwards, to soar off circling into the sky. "Beauty has always been Father's favorite, and he's never hidden it very well. It was...not pleasant to grow up with but I was always—George and Connor and I, we did all right, we had teachers and friends and each other and—it was all right."

Well, maybe, but judging from the way his hands appeared to be clenched in fists, still shoved in his pockets, it wasn't *all* all right.

"It always bothered Miranda and Noreen the most; maybe they felt like they were in the most direct competition with her. I don't know. I don't blame them for resenting it, but I never thought they were right when they were nasty to Beauty about it. It was Father's fault, not hers. Besides, Beauty's so..." He hesitated a long moment, and with a frown concluded, "...nice."

I raised an eyebrow. "I swear you say that like it's a fault."

"No, of course it's not, but..." His forehead scrunched up in wrinkles. "Beauty never complains. She never gets mad or even irritated. She's good-tempered and sweet-natured absolutely all of the time. I used to try to provoke her when we were both kids. I wasn't trying to be mean, I just wanted her to show *something* that wasn't perfectly good. And I could never get her to fight back." His voice dropped a little. "I know it sounds like a ridiculous complaint, but it could get surprisingly hard to live with."

I thought about some of the Good Fairies I knew, who were so very, very sweet. "Actually, that makes a lot of sense."

Anthony glanced at me like he was surprised—but I didn't want to talk about Good Fairies. I was glad when he didn't ask and just nodded, his shoulders straightening like he felt better on the subject. "Anyway," he continued, "we moved up north to the country. And Miranda and Noreen were right about the cottage being drafty, but it wasn't that bad. It was small, and we were all crowded on top of each other, and pushing a plow will never be my favorite way to spend the day, but we got by. We worked a lot harder than we had in the city, but I think we had more fun too. And then about a year and a half ago, everything went strange." He glanced at me again. "*You* might not think it's strange."

"I have seen much strangeness," I acknowledged.

"Father took a trip back to Alphoson. He thought he could get some money back from one of his investments, but it didn't work out that way. It was all complicated with fees and taxes." He waved a hand, dismissing the details. "That's not the important part. On the trip back, he rode through the forest, lost his way, and stumbled across a huge stone castle. We'd been living on the edge of that forest for over a year, and never even heard a rumor about a castle. But there it was, apparently abandoned."

"Was it enchanted?" I asked. They're always enchanted.

"How did you guess?" he said, clearly a rhetorical question.

"Wait, don't tell me; it turned out to belong to a great and terrible Beast, right?"

"See, I knew it might not seem as strange to you."

"I've heard similar stories." And I knew that the Good Fairies favor certain scenarios. Find a Beast in a castle and there's a fairy back of it somewhere. I could already figure where this was going. "Did the Beast fly into a rage about something?"

"Yes." Anthony shoved his hands back into his pockets, jaw set. "Father tried to pick a rose in the garden because Beauty had asked him to bring her one. The Beast appeared across the lawn, this enormous creature with a lion's mane who walked on two legs. He started ranting and roaring and threatened to murder Father. Over a *flower*. I mean, that's insane, right? He only let Father go on the condition that he promise to bring one of his daughters back to the castle in a month.

"So Father came home, told us the whole story, and vowed he'd go back by himself. But Beauty insisted on going instead." He sighed, mouth twisting. "She never gets angry and she won't argue, but she can be incredibly stubborn in her own way. George and Connor and I, we would've tried to fight the Beast—they're better at fighting than I am so maybe we would've accomplished something—but Beauty wouldn't hear of that either. So after a month, Beauty and Father rode into the forest, and Father came back alone. And we haven't heard a word from Beauty since."

He studied the ground beneath his feet for several steps, though I doubt he was seeing it. "Miranda and Noreen think she's dead. I like to think, maybe not."

"Not all Beasts are horrible," I offered. At least this was a problem I felt more comfortable commenting on. "I've met pleasant ones. And I've seen stories like this that turned out happily in the end." Marj would say that obviously that's how it was *supposed* to turn out...but I didn't want to mention her utter disregard for the times it didn't come right, when someone didn't prove pure enough of heart or whatever. Disappointing a Good Fairy usually meant serious enchantment. Or death.

Since I left it with the encouraging comment, Anthony's expression lightened a little. "Thanks. I like to hope. That's about all any of us can do. George, Connor and I rode into the forest once to look for the castle, the day after Father and Beauty went in. We beat around among the trees all day and we couldn't find anything. One trip was enough for Connor and me. We were never going to find it until that Beast decided he wanted us to."

"Enchanted castles tend to be like that."

"George rode in a few more times, but even he was convinced eventually. Which means there isn't really anything to do except hope."

He was talking about hope, with his gaze on the horizon, but I was feeling if anything more depressed. Business reversals, a preferential father and a missing sister…definitely not the cheerful life story I had been expecting. When would we get to that part? "So how did you end up at The Nightingale, after all of that?" I asked. There had to be good stories *there*.

I was not encouraged when Anthony grimaced. "This doesn't always sound good to everyone, but my brothers and me, we left home about a month after Beauty disappeared. A month was long enough to convince us that it didn't make much difference to our father if we stayed or not. He was never the same after he rode back from the forest, but none of us were the one he wanted. He only wanted Beauty, and it didn't matter to him if *we* were there or not. That's no life, hovering around a heartbroken father who doesn't care that you're there. The Beast sent money back with Father so we had some options. We hired someone we knew from the village to look after the farm, Miranda and Noreen were looking after Father, and we set off into the world.

"George and Connor wanted to join the army. I didn't have another plan, so I went with them. Which was not a bad decision, but, well—I had already suspected, and I very quickly confirmed, that I don't have any natural aptitude for fighting, and I don't have enough interest to learn it."

I had listened to enough men brag at parties about their wonderful fighting prowess that I was surprised to hear the opposite. "That doesn't bother you?"

"No, not really." He shrugged. "Maybe it comes of having two older brothers who *are* good at fighting. I always had to do something different, just to stay out of their shadows. And it's not that I *couldn't* have stayed in the military—I can take orders and camp and march and all of that, and I'm sure if I tried long enough I'd get at least decent at swinging a sword around. But I didn't want to, and there are so many other things a person can do instead.

"So it only took ten days for me to figure out that joining up wasn't really what I wanted to do. I don't suppose it's always all that easy to get out of the army, but by then George was already great friends with the camp commander—George is like that—so we talked to him and, after volunteering originally, I un-volunteered and we all wished each other the best. It was all very amicable and legal and legitimate and it *wasn't* deserting."

"Hey, *I* believe you," I said, raising my hands.

"Yeah." He glared at the line of soldiers trudging ahead of us for a moment before continuing. "So I still didn't have much of a plan, but now I was on my own. I just knocked around for a few weeks. Picked up odd jobs here and there, earned enough in one town to go on to the next town. Somewhere in there, I decided to visit the capital. I figured as long I was wandering, I might as well wander somewhere that might be worth seeing.

"I reached Ryvideau on a market day. Throngs of people everywhere, all kinds of business going on. I probably could have found twelve people willing to hire me for something within an hour. But somehow, I walked into The Nightingale." His voice softened. "And that changed everything."

"Just like that?" I prompted. He couldn't fall silent now, just when there were signs of the story taking a turn towards the cheerful.

"Sure, just like that. I met Catherine." He smiled then, and I realized that, if Catherine had a smile just for Anthony, Anthony had one just for her too. "They were busy at The Nightingale too. Hordes of people had come to town for the market, plenty of them wanted somewhere to stay, people were running everywhere, and flying through the middle of it all was Catherine. Her hair was coming out of its braid, she'd been in and out of the kitchen and had a smudge of flour on one cheek, and I thought she was the most beautiful girl I'd ever seen.

"I was still staring when she stopped and asked me if I was looking for a room or a meal. I got some sentence out about a job. I was thinking of chopping wood maybe. She gave me this long look, pointed at Sam behind the front counter, and told me to help him. Then she disappeared back into the kitchen. So I went over to the front counter, where it didn't take me long to realize that Sam is, well, not exactly the most capable individual."

I remembered the dramatic spilling of the walnuts at Jack and Emmy's wedding, and a handful of other similar incidents involving Sam. "He does seem rather…"

"He is. But when you work at The Nightingale, it doesn't take long to become family. So Sam stays. Besides, he's very popular with the guests; they find his haplessness endearing. And he's really good with the budget too. He says numbers are the only things he can balance."

I had to smile at that, less for the joke than for Anthony's quick and apparently unconscious defense of the clumsy Sam. He was right about it being like a family.

Or so I had gathered about families. Mostly from observation.

"Anyway, he's not good at supervising anything," Anthony said, "so it didn't take long that first day before I was telling him what to do. And I found out I was good at it. Keeping track of which guests wanted what, sending water up to one and extra blankets to another, taking names of people looking for rooms, giving directions to one about where the main square is and calming down another and…it was twelve problems all at once, people whirling all over the place, and I was good at keeping on top of it. Practically the next thing I knew, the entire afternoon had gone by and I was sitting down to supper in the kitchen with the staff, with Catherine sitting next to me.

"I'd seen her go past a few times during the afternoon, but I would've sworn she hadn't even looked at me. I hadn't learned yet that Catherine can keep track of twenty things at once without appearing to try. She must have noticed something during the afternoon because she asked me if I was looking for permanent work. I hadn't been—but I decided maybe I was now.

"So I said yes, and she said yes, and I was surprised it was that simple. I should've known looking at her, but somehow I was still surprised that she had that kind of authority. I guess I never pictured a young woman running an inn. I said something about that and I'm lucky she wasn't offended. Instead she shook my hand, told me her name was Catherine Williams and that she was related to the owner.

"I made an assumption on that and said I'd be glad to meet her husband. I wouldn't have been glad at all, and I was surprised myself at how glad I *wouldn't* have been. She looked puzzled and I said..." He grinned suddenly. "I very awkwardly and ridiculously said, 'I mean Mr. Williams,' and she smiled and told me that the only Mr. Williams she knew was her father. And *I* said I was glad. That time I was, too. I probably sounded like I was flirting with her, which I didn't exactly mean to...then. But it did all go from there."

"That's lovely." *Those* were the stories I liked, stories about people meeting and falling in love and finding out what they wanted to do with their lives and being happy. And somewhere along the way, dismantling their walls and putting down new roots. "That's a good story."

He smiled, looking more at ease than he'd been for at least two days. "It's a good life. I love Catherine and I like running an inn, and ...it was *good*, better than life had ever been." The smile faded away, and the bleakness came back into his face. "Until along came a glass slipper and a prince and..." He dragged a hand past his eyes. "And I don't want to talk about that."

No argument here. Until we had good news on that front, I didn't want to talk about that either. "What do you want to talk about instead?"

"You heard my life story. So tell me yours. Tell me about fairies."

So much for not thinking about *my* life. On the other hand, both my life and fairies as topics covered a lot of ground. "Fairies are a broad subject. Like if I asked you to tell me about humans. What do you want to know about us?"

"I don't know," he said, and kicked another stone off the path. "You heard how I ended up here—how did *you* end up here? What does a fairy spend his time doing anyway?"

There we were back on my life again. I really would have liked to divert the conversation off of me, focus just on that second question in a general way and discuss, say, the sillier things Marj and her friends did. But it didn't seem exactly fair to do that, after he'd told me his story. I tried to think how I could be honest without being...*too* honest.

"Remember you said you just wandered for a while?" I said finally. "That's sort of what I do. I travel. Visit new places, meet new people. I've been just about everywhere, but if you wait long enough between visits, the places change, so they're sort of new. And the people change even faster." Especially when you don't ever go looking for the same people twice. "I go to a lot of parties and mostly just see where the winds take me."

"No work, no responsibilities—sounds like fun."

"Well, *I* like it," I said with great and possibly overdone heartiness.

He was staring at the road winding into the distance. "I don't know, though. Does it ever feel kind of aimless?"

I scratched behind the point of one ear, which did nothing about the uncomfortable itch the question gave me. "...not often."

"It's just, when I was traveling," Anthony said, "I enjoyed it but it also felt kind of rootless."

I blinked. I hadn't described his aura to him, but he was clearly a self-aware young man.

"I don't know, maybe it was just me," he went on. "But don't you ever wish you had more of a purpose?"

"I could have one. If I wanted to. Any time." I could hear my voice rising and I took a deep breath, despite the tightening in my chest. "I could stay in one place for twenty years, if I wanted to." Not that I had. Not for a long time. I had stayed a hundred years in one place once…but it had been five centuries since I had stayed anywhere for even twenty days, let alone years. I didn't mention that, just hurrying along to say, "Twenty years isn't even all that long, for me, I could stay longer. If I ever wanted to."

"Twenty years isn't that long?" Anthony said, in the voice of one who was barely over twenty himself. "How old are you?"

An easier topic. "I don't really know; I lost count somewhere after a thousand."

He stopped walking. "A thousand *years*?"

I halted a step after him. "Fairies live a long time. I've been told I don't look a day over eight-hundred," I said with my cheekiest grin.

"Try twenty-five," he muttered. "So fairies live a *very* long time. Tell me something else about fairies. Do you have royalty?"

"Yes. Just one court for all the fairies, and even though I can pass as human, you'd never make that mistake with the King and Queen. And incidentally, they put on very good parties. I remember one time the Lord Chamberlain drank so much nectar he started seeing pink elephants…"

And from there out we managed to steer mostly clear of any weighty discussion about his life or mine, making the entire conversation far less fraught. And making it a much better day of marching than the previous day had been.

Chapter Eighteen

Centuries of living, and few things stretched on longer than our third day walking to the army camp. It wasn't an unpleasant day, except that by then I felt like we had been walking *forever*. By the time we arrived in the late afternoon, I think I would have been delighted no matter what the army camp looked like.

And it did require that kind of emotional investment to feel that way about it. The camp was an untidy collection of tents in rows, with a small handful of more permanent wooden cabins—but not much more permanent. All of it was tucked into a hollow between two hills. Perreldan soldiers had been holding the border with Beaumont for a century, but we were obviously not in one of the outposts that had been standing for decades.

"Miserable looking spot," Anthony observed, as we stood on the last rise before descending into the small valley.

So someone wasn't in the right mindset. Just the opposite, in fact. "You'd have something bad to say about the Elysian Fields right now."

He didn't deny it, said, "It's still a miserable spot," and stumped off down the trail.

Yeah, well, it probably was, but it *had* to be more interesting than continuing along the dusty road. Besides, if our biggest problem turned out to be that the camp was less than aesthetically pleasing, we'd be doing very well.

Magic ran fairly freely in every country in this part of the world; Marj and I were proof of that. But the trouble in Beaumont was that magic didn't merely run. It ran amok.

Beaumont had always been more impressively magical than its neighbors, with a much higher concentration of centaurs and unicorns, besides more troublesome creatures like manticores and hippogryphs. Up until a hundred years ago or so, they were reasonably well-behaved. Beaumont's human royal family had long-standing treaties with some species, alliances with others, and an army to keep anything hostile under control. But then the last of the royal line disappeared a century back, no one managed to take over, and the whole system fell to pieces. No one enforced the treaties, the army fragmented without any government to direct or pay it, and any creatures with an inclination to create havoc saw this as a golden opportunity. The Fairy Court didn't consider this under their jurisdiction, and no one else wanted to get involved either.

Perrelda and Waldisan shared Beaumont's southern border, Waldisan further to the east. I could remember the panic that swept through when monsters started coming down out of the mountains and, instead of wanting to have a chat, they were thinking about a snack—of the human kind.

It put a real halt to the parties for a few years, while something resembling actual warfare went on at the border. Then the humans built walls, got organized about defending them, and after those first few years most of the monsters decided they could stay busy enough fighting with humans and each other inside the wall, rather than go fight with the human armies outside. The monster problem had been contained for decades, though it could still get hot around the border at times; some years were worse than others. Recently they'd had a bad run of hippogryphs.

Going to the border was not normally the death sentence Catherine viewed it as. Of course, someone going to the border with royal hostility hovering over him could be in more danger. But that's why I was here.

We trooped into the camp, and there was a pleasant little speech from the camp commander about how we were doing our patriotic duty, etc., etc. It might have been pleasanter if it hadn't been painfully obvious from his bored tone that he'd recited the same speech dozens of times. After that, we were directed to go collect tents for ourselves and other supplies from the appropriate buildings in the camp, and were dismissed. I could've conjured up whatever I needed, but that would have attracted attention.

Anthony and I walked down the main avenue—if you could give it that much dignity. We passed individuals and clusters of men on either side, the earlier inhabitants of the camp, talking or training or playing dice games. In a group of the last, one man stirred as we went by.

"Hey, Anthony!" he shouted, stepping away from his dice-playing friends.

Anthony looked over, and broke into the a broad smile. "Hey, you old rogue! How many monsters have you killed?"

"Dozens, of course, dozens."

They went through a round of back-slapping and shoulder-punching. That gave me a chance to look at our new-found friend. He was six-five easily and very broad too; I'd've bet on him against most (though not all) of the monsters I'd met. I guessed he was a few years older than Anthony. He had curly dark hair that strongly resembled Anthony's, and I did a quick magical check to confirm what the resemblance made me suspect. I could've found out his name magically too, but there was an easier way to learn that.

When there was a pause in the back-slapping, I stepped up with one hand out. "Hello. George or Connor, I assume."

He laughed, and nearly shook my hand off.

"Sorry, Tarry, this is my big brother George," Anthony said, throwing another punch at his brother's shoulder. "George, my friend Tarry."

There was more hand-shaking and a few statements along the lines of "any friend of Anthony's" which was all right by me, because if this one had felt hostile, I would've needed magical defense. Could've gotten dicey, since I wasn't allowed to cast a spell on him. I wasn't worried though. He had a nice aura, a big friendly bear who was never going to fathom why other people found him intimidating.

"Is Connor here too?" Anthony asked, once the introductions were done.

"No, last I heard he's in another camp farther west a ways. But what're you doing here, Tony-boy?" George asked. "I thought we all decided that you weren't for the army and that the army wasn't for you."

I half-expected Anthony to descend into gloom again, but he held onto his grin. "Someone has to keep track of you, right?"

"Right, right, sure. But I thought you were off running an inn."

That time the grin faded. "The situation got…complicated."

"But at least there's nice weather!" I said at random, in a desperate and utterly pointless effort to change the subject before this got…well, complicated.

George didn't even look at me, and didn't pick up his brother's mood swing either. Apparently not a sensitive sort. "What happened?" He elbowed Anthony. "The innkeeper's daughter throw you over?"

"No, she did not *throw me over*."

A person with all the emotional sensitivity of a rock still would have picked up *that* mood swing. "All right, Tony-boy, all right," George said, easily and soothingly. "I believe you, she's devoted, you're destined to be together, I believe it."

Anthony looked at the ground, scuffed one foot in the dirt. "Yeah. I believed it too."

I winced. It would have been so much easier, talking about the weather.

"So why *aren't* you together?" George asked, still grinning. "I'd expect you to prefer to be with her than with me. She's probably prettier."

"Much," Anthony agreed, with a smile that didn't reach his eyes. "It's all kind of a long story."

And that was my cue to let him explain, while I betook myself to do something more useful than interjecting unneeded comments. Which would also let me avoid hearing the whole depressing tale again. "How's about you tell the long story while I go look up a friend?" I said, with just enough of a twitch around the eyes that Anthony caught what I had in mind.

He agreed, I bade them both farewell, and I strolled off in search of a secluded spot from which I could pop myself back to Roderick's castle. It's a *much* more convenient way to travel than walking.

I had gone back and forth to the capital several times already in the past three days, which had provided some distraction from the endless trudge, even if it hadn't been cheering at all. I had visited the castle, of course, and also spent some time wandering Ryvideau's streets by night, in the hope I could magically pick up a sense of the girl who owned the glass slipper. That plan had so far failed utterly. I didn't really know what I was looking for, and after that stunt hauling the shoe around, so many girls were dreaming about Roderick that it was nauseating.

It wasn't much better at the castle, where they were making wedding plans. Considering that a royal wedding takes months to organize, that still gave us some time to deal with the situation, a point I was trying to both hold onto myself and mention as often as possible. Catherine was spending her days with the resident ladies-in-waiting, minor female nobility and suchlike (and had judged them all "nice enough but rather useless"). There were a few ripples going on because Catherine wasn't the girl Roderick had danced with at the ball; the royalty were trying to smooth these down and, wherever I saw a chance, I tried to hearten them up. Too early to tell which way public opinion would ultimately break on the subject.

This trip, I found Catherine alone in her room, eating an early supper. Or rather, pushing it around on a plate.

I settled into the opposite chair. "I have good news today. We finally reached the army camp."

"That's not good news," Catherine said, spearing a piece of turnip, lifting it up and then staring at it instead of eating it.

"I know." Considering the monster hazards went up significantly now, it was possibly bad news. But I didn't like delivering bad news, so I was determined to brazen through and emphasize the good. "But the *good* news is that we bumped into Anthony's brother George. He's stationed at the same camp."

"That's better news," she acknowledged, setting the turnip down again. "That might help Anthony."

Not quite the enthusiasm I had hoped for. I folded my arms, tried to smile. "Sure, of course. He cheered up on seeing him." Unlike Catherine on hearing about it.

"That's nice," she said, staring at her plate.

I found myself staring at the plate too. The turnip had come out of a fish pie, and I was pretty sure I could smell figs in there too. "Are you going to eat that?"

"No," she said, and pushed it across the table at me. "I'm not hungry."

I'm always hungry. Or at least, I'm always open to the idea of eating. "So," I said around a fig, "it is nice. About Anthony and George." Even if her response had been wildly inadequate. "And now we just need to sort out what we're going to do about you."

She rested her chin on her hand and closed her eyes for a moment. "We're not going to do anything about me. There's nothing to do. I'm going to marry the prince, and find some way to live with that."

We'd had this conversation. More than once. I took a quick glance at her aura, saw a lot of frost, and looked away again. "Now listen, Marj is sure to decide to speak to me again soon, we'll locate that girl from the ball and then—"

"And then what? It's *too late*. It won't make any difference now."

I slumped down in my chair with a sigh. How could I fix this if she wouldn't even believe that it could be fixed?

The sigh was echoed on the other side of the table. "I know you're trying to help, Tarry, but trying to believe things can still change just makes it more painful. And much harder to accept the inevitable."

"You're not married yet," I protested, stabbing at a turnip with more force than the poor vegetable really deserved. "Nothing's inevitable yet. Promise you won't give up until it is, all right?"

Her gaze lowered, chin still on her hand. "I promise to try."

Not as much as I wanted, but apparently the best I would get. It can't be said that the rest of my conversation with Catherine improved, and when I couldn't handle it anymore I popped back to find Anthony and George again. I magically located them sitting on the floor of a tent I assumed was George's, popped in nearby, and then entered the tent by conventional means.

I hadn't even finished folding myself into a seated position before Anthony was asking if there was news.

The news was that Catherine was alarmingly depressed. I wasn't going to tell him that. "Nothing much, no," I said, noticing as I did that George was staring at me. "Problem?"

"You really don't sparkle," he said, head tipped thoughtfully to one side.

I looked at Anthony. "I take it you mentioned my origins."

"Hope you don't mind."

I shrugged. I don't know that I would have chosen to have my fairy-ness mentioned, but it had probably been inevitable. "Nah, it's all in the family, after all. Are you wondering why I don't have wings too?" I asked George.

"Well…"

"Never mind that, it can wait," Anthony interrupted. "How's Catherine?"

Which was really just asking more directly what he'd already been asking when he asked about any news. I still didn't want to tell him anything. "She's good," I lied. "Quiet."

Even that was apparently saying too much, because a worried crease appeared between his eyebrows. "Quiet isn't good. Cat's never quiet."

"If she's never quiet, how do you know if it's good or bad?" I pointed out.

"Because it's not normal. And that's not good." He drummed his fingers against his leg. "I should have found some way to keep from leaving. Are you sure you can't—"

"For the fourteenth time, I'm sure," I said with a huff of a sigh. "I couldn't magically transport you from one end of this tent to the other, let alone all the way back to the castle." Actually, distance didn't make much difference for me when it came to magical transportation, but I thought it might get the idea home to him. I couldn't transport him anywhere, not while he was in the military, not without severe consequences.

"I know, I know," Anthony said. "I just wish there was something I could *do*."

"You could kill a hippogryph," George suggested.

Anthony turned his head to stare at his brother. "No, I probably couldn't, and even if I could, how will that help the situation?"

"It won't," George acknowledged. "But it might make you feel better. Nothing like a good fight to work out bad feelings."

I could've hugged the big bear. It was just so nice to have someone hopeful around.

Anthony, on the other hand, rolled his eyes. "I don't think that's going to make me feel better."

"It always makes *me* feel better."

Anthony looked at me, and nodded at George. "That's George for you. Nothing ever bothers him."

"I don't see how sitting around glaring helps you," George continued, and clapped his brother on the shoulder. "It's a rotten deal all around, Tony-boy, but life is what it is, and you'd better just live with it."

Anthony leaned back on his hands, and looked up at the ceiling of the tent. "I feel like I should be angry with you for saying that, but somehow I can't work up to it."

Great. Now Catherine and Anthony were *both* being depressed and unresponsive. It made me want to smack Marj with a stupid glass slipper. Roderick too.

"You could save your aggression for the hippogryphs," George suggested, seemingly untroubled by Anthony's nonresponse. "You ought to have a good chance at them. You're in my unit, and we're on dawn patrol this week. That's when the hippogryphs are out."

Anthony and I looked at each other, and I could see from the suspicious narrowing of his eyes that we were having the same thought.

"George, would you say that dawn patrol is the most dangerous?" I asked.

He considered that. "It's not as though people die every day, but comparatively, I suppose so. Why?"

Anthony was at the same conclusion. "You think the royalty set me up."

"I think they might have," I said. We were, after all, expecting something of this sort. "But what have you got to worry about? They calculated without me. And without this bear here; I'd bet on him against hippogryphs." I don't know that I'd bet a *lot*—hippogryphs can be nasty—but I was in 'cheer up the humans' mode, and emphasizing our sterling abilities against monsters was an optimistic direction to go.

The bear was looking puzzled. "Why do you think the royalty set you up?"

"Because they want to get rid of me," Anthony said, voice careful, "and putting me in the sightline of hippogryphs is a good way."

"Sure, sure, I understand that," George said, waving a big hand, "but it seemed to me, from what you said, it wasn't so much the prince who wanted to get rid of you. It was that adviser person."

"Leonard," Anthony said, a puzzled frown coming over his face. "George is right, it was Leonard; but we never talk about Leonard. Why don't we ever talk about Leonard?"

Now he had me confused. "What do you mean we don't talk about him? Don't we?"

"No, we don't. We talk about sending hippogryphs after Roderick, or we talk about what the royalty might be doing, but we don't talk about Leonard."

"He's an unpleasant subject?" I hazarded.

"But so's Roderick and we—"

The rest of Anthony's sentence was drowned in three blasts from a trumpet somewhere in the camp.

George was on his feet before the last blast had died away. "That means supper. Let's go."

George was a large man standing in a small tent. We were between him and the exit, so getting out of the tent just then was a matter of self-preservation. Besides, I never objected to hastening after something to eat. Out of the tent, George charged off, I assumed in the direction of the food, and Anthony and I followed in his wake, joining the streams of men all headed the same way. It was a jostling, crowded walk that did not facilitate conversation. We eventually found ourselves in a line outside of a large tent that, based on smells, had to be the mess hall.

"Is George always that enthusiastic about food?" I asked.

"Generally," Anthony answered.

"I knew there was a reason I had a good feeling about him. I haven't met the rest of your family, but I like this one, Tony-boy," I concluded with my most innocent of expressions.

The corners of his mouth pulled down in a pained look. "Don't start calling me that. George does it, but that's, well, that's how George is."

"Was that how Jeanne became Beauty?"

"Pretty much. That one stuck, though, and lucky for me, 'Tony-boy' so far has not, so don't start calling me it."

"Now do you *really* not want me to call you that, or is this a case where secretly you—"

"We're not talking about that." His tone was even more of a warning than the words. "And no, really don't call me that."

Well, that had been stupid of me. Like he'd want to be reminded of that. Something that used to be so cheerful but now… I folded my hands behind my back. "Like you say, Anthony."

He nodded, staring moodily at the tent ahead of us, I think just because that's what happened to be in his line of sight. "George and his stupid nicknames," he muttered. "I don't want to think about nicknames. Let's talk about something more cheerful. Like hippogryphs."

Hippogryphs, half eagle, half horse and all lethal, are not generally considered a cheerful topic. But that's what we talked about.

Somehow we never got back on the subject of Leonard.

Chapter Nineteen

Six days after arriving in the army camp, we encountered our first hippogryph. For five days before that, we—meaning me and Anthony and George—went out on dawn patrol, which involved wandering up and down around the wall with other men, most of them sleepy. We spent the rest of our time in the camp, where they made us drill sometimes but not too often, and the food was not great, but plentiful.

I popped back and forth between the castle and the camp at regular intervals, for all the good it did. All I could report to Catherine was that Anthony was so far unharmed by monsters, and all I wanted to report to Anthony was that Catherine was still quiet and unmarried. I didn't report to Anthony or anyone else just how much Catherine's quiet acceptance was worrying me.

I popped into The Nightingale to see Jack and Emmy and everyone else a few times too. Mr. Andrews was more capable than his daughter thought he was, but she wasn't entirely wrong. The inn really had depended on Catherine and Anthony; the rest of the staff were managing in the short-term, but where there used to be controlled chaos, there was an increasing amount that was becoming uncontrolled.

On our sixth morning, we rolled out as usual and marched back and forth for a couple of miles along the wall with our unit of thirty men. After a cursory pass, our commanding officer split us up into ten groups of three and sent us off in different directions to beat about among the pine trees within a mile or so of the wall. George, being great friends with the commander, had orchestrated it so our group of three consisted of him, Anthony and me. That was all right by me; I could use magic in front of a larger group, but it would be so much more convenient not to.

We strolled off through the pines, probably more relaxed than we should have been. George and I were relaxed, at least. Anthony had been in a perpetual bad mood for six days, and was currently expressing it by thwacking at pine branches as he strode along.

"You're going to dull the edge of your sword that way," George commented helpfully.

"So?" Anthony said, and smacked another branch. "I'll go back to camp and sharpen it. I don't have anything better to do."

"Yeah, but what did the forest ever do to you?" I asked, with a nod at the trail of pine needles he was leaving in his wake.

Anthony scowled, but shoved his sword back into its scabbard. "How much longer are we supposed to wander around out here?"

"What's your rush?" George asked, inhaling deeply of the pine air. "I think it's nice out here."

I was happy enough to get into the forest too. It had advantages on the crowded, noisy camp. I liked a crowded party, but I wasn't used to so many people around for so long. "It is nice, until the monsters come out of the bushes," I said. "Though if a monster does show up, at least you can thwack at a hippogryph with a clear conscience."

Judging by the glare he shot me, Anthony didn't see that as much of a consolation. We tramped around for a few minutes more, and George had just decided we ought to turn back, when the quiet of the forest was shattered by a long, painfully drawn-out screech. It scraped up my spine and sent my shoulders to my ears, while all the little background noises of birds and small animals went suddenly silent.

"What was that?" Anthony demanded, gaze darting around the trees.

"You ever hear an eagle screech?" I asked, casting magical sensors out. In the thick forest, I had a better shot at finding the sound's origin that way than by using my eyes.

"No," Anthony said. "Was that an eagle?"

"No, I'm reasonably sure that was a hippogryph." Which was not a reason to be alarmed. I hoped.

"I think it's that way," George said, drawing his sword and facing north.

"Are we even going to consider the possibility of retreat?" Anthony asked, though as he said it he was drawing his sword and turning towards the sound too.

"You ever try to outrun a horse?" I asked him, just as my magic set off a mental clamor of alarms. There it was, a hippogryph, a few hundred yards away. I took a deep breath. No problem. This was why I was here.

"Could you stop with the hypotheticals?" Anthony snapped.

"Hippogryphs can run like horses and fly like eagles," I said. "Retreating, probably not a good idea."

As if to punctuate the words, another screech tore through the forest, mixing with the clamor my magic was making and making me dizzy with the combination. I didn't need magic to know that the hippogryph was getting closer.

I shut off the alarms, and wished I could shut off the twist of nerves in my stomach as easily. I could *handle* this. Nothing was going to go wrong. Although it couldn't hurt to be more defensible physically… I sprouted shining green scales as I did a rapid morph into dragon form.

"I didn't know you could do that," George said, blinking twice and staring up at me.

"It's useful sometimes," I said, stretching my wings and wishing I had time for a proper scratch—but too late, as the hippogryph crashed through the trees and into view.

It had the head and wings of an eagle and the body of a horse, which meant a combination of red eyes, sharp curved beak and lashing hooves. It was considerably bigger than an eagle, a horse, or my expectations: sixteen feet, easily, from beak to rump. I wished, not for the first time, that my dragonform was larger than twelve feet long. And several feet of that was tail.

The hippogryph reared up on its hind legs, forelegs striking out, gray feathered wings outspread, and screeched again. I roared back at it. I like to think that I have an intimidating roar as a dragon.

The hippogryph didn't even hesitate. It screeched once more and charged. I threw caution and strategy to the wind and met it. We closed in a tangle of scales and feathers and bruising hooves pummeling at me. Luckily my scales were tough and while the hooves hurt some, the wildly battering wings were actually more bothersome. I arched my neck and snapped at the feathers. By the time the hippogryph got upright again, I had my jaws latched onto one wing. It put great effort into trying to shake me off, which didn't work, but did fling me around.

I flapped my own wings, trying for some leverage, and did my best to order, "Do something," through a mouthful of feathers.

"Do you have a strategy for these monsters?" Anthony yelled to George.

"There's always been a bunch more people around before," George yelled back. "And they're usually not this big."

"That's not encouraging!"

"Hurry up," I growled, flopping as the hippogryph flapped. I scrabbled with my paws, aiming for the horse body but not connecting with any force.

"I don't know anything about eagles, but I know something about horses," Anthony said, moving around to the hippogryph's rear. "You get the front end."

"Right."

The hippogryph reared another time, and when it came down again Anthony threw himself across its back. I was certain Catherine would not have approved of this at all, and would have expected me to prevent it, but by now I was so rattled from being shaken around that I couldn't have come up with a spell to save my life—which was unfortunate, since I might have needed a spell for exactly that. Fairies don't die easily, but it can happen.

But we were lucky this day. With me hanging off one wing, and Anthony clinging to its broad horse's back, the hippogryph was hampered enough and distracted enough that George was able to get in close with his sword. One solid strike severed the eagle head from the body. The hippogryph jerked a few more times, spasmodically, before crumpling dead to the ground.

Anthony rolled off the dead hippogryph, sprawling on his back on the forest floor. "I don't ever want to do that ever again."

I detached from the wing, shuffled back a few paces, and spat out a mouthful of feathers. "That thing tasted *awful*."

"Wasn't that great?" George was practically bouncing, swinging his bloody sword around in his exuberance. "I've never heard of three people taking down a hippogryph this size before!"

"Two people and a dragon," I corrected, nosing over my scales to check for any damage. I'd be feeling bruises for a while, but nothing serious.

"Close enough. We made a great team, don't you think? We could make a career of this!"

Anthony sat up, and stared at his brother through narrowed eyes. "Why would we want to do that?"

George beamed at him. "Because we're good at it!"

"I'm good at running an inn too, and I'll take an inn over a screeching, rearing, red-eyed, be-feathered, completely lethal hippogryph any day." Anthony got to his feet, brushing dirt, pine needles and feathers off of his clothes. "The guests at The Nightingale don't bite your head off if supper's running late. Not literally, anyway."

Crisis past, I turned back into my human form, with a shiver of disappearing scales. It didn't help get the taste out of my mouth. In fact…feeling a scratching inside my cheek, I reached into my mouth and pulled out a bit of feather. I gazed at it ruefully. "Great. I'll probably be picking feathers out of my teeth for days." Sure, I was relieved that we'd all survived too—but it really was a *nasty* taste. Like cheese gone bad. And rolled in mud.

George, meanwhile, was waxing on about the possibilities that existed for a group of really good hippogryph-slayers. Finally, Anthony interrupted him to ask what we should do about this one we'd just slain.

George considered it, head cocked as he stared at the dead monster. "Oh. Well, I don't suppose we could carry it." He looked at me. "Could you transport it?"

"I could, but how do you plan to explain it?" The truth would reveal a whole lot more than I was comfortable announcing to the army camp. That group was not predisposed to be friendly to anyone with magic.

"Good point." George picked up the head, grasping it by the top feathers. "We could just bring this back."

"Charming," Anthony said, nose wrinkling as he looked at the bleeding eagle head.

"We can mount it on something," George said, and slung an arm—the one not carrying the head—around his brother's shoulders. "Now come on, Tony-boy. You were really good at that! And wasn't it exciting? Got some aggression out, right?"

"Exciting? Try terrifying, George. Throwing myself at a monster is not something I want to spend my time doing."

"Just a little exciting?"

Anthony glowered at him, and kept it up for a good ten seconds before finally dissolving into a grin. "Well…maybe a *little* exciting."

"See!" George said, and nearly pulled Anthony off his feet with a one-armed hug. "I knew there was a fighter lurking inside you somewhere. Just needed the right incentive to bring him out."

"That's really not what this means, George," Anthony protested, as they began walking back in the direction of the camp.

I fell into step with them, tongue worrying at a bit of feather caught between two molars. I gave it up for the moment, so that I could tell Anthony, "You know, you're not as bad at fighting as you think you are."

He shook his head. "That wasn't fighting, not the part I did. That was more like trying to catch a horse."

"You always were modest, Tony-boy," George said. "Come on— be proud. *I'm* proud of you."

"Never mind me; you two did the hard parts," Anthony said, still grinning. "You wrestling with the hippogryph and you swinging the sword around and—"

Halfway through the sentence, George and Anthony disappeared. I went another two steps before I stopped; it was that sudden. I turned around to look where they had been, as though maybe I'd missed them somehow. Nothing, no sign, no indication, footprints up to a certain spot and then nothing, the hippogryph head lying dropped on the ground next to the termination of the footprints. I stared at the final prints, shoulders rising back up around my ears and stomach twisting up into knots again. This could be even worse than a hippogryph.

How could I explain to Catherine that I had *misplaced* Anthony?

I tried to visualize that conversation, and my shoulders got even tighter. Definitely worse than a hippogryph.

I had to find him. Both of them. And since I had options for doing that it was *too soon* to panic.

I took a deep breath, weighed options. Then I circled where they'd last stood, waving my palm over the place. I was rewarded with a flare of sparks—pink. I also got a distinct sense of—well, of a tea kettle about to explode.

It was as good as a signature. Whatever had happened (likely a transportation spell), my dear cousin Marjoram was behind it.

What Marj could possibly want with Anthony and George was beyond me. Not to mention how she'd magically transported two members of the military without any apparent consequences—or any sign that there would be consequences coming. The King and Queen of the Fairies don't always realize immediately when a rule is broken, so there could be delayed wrath…but a spell that breaks a rule looks different from one that doesn't, and this one was clean. Which was impossible.

Though the 'how' was a more baffling question, the 'why' was more urgent.

I checked first to see if Marj was still blocking me—she was. Since she had been every time I checked over the last few days, this was no surprise. I took another deep breath, and sent my senses out in search of Anthony instead. I'd spent enough time around him that it was easy to do.

I let that breath out in a rush as Anthony pinged on the edge of my magic. Marj wasn't blocking me from following *him*.

Which meant we were in business.

Book Three: Beauty's Brother

There was once a very rich merchant, who had six children, three sons, and three daughters…

She saw at her feet one of the loveliest Princes that eye ever beheld, who returned her thanks for having put an end to the charm, under which he had so long resembled a Beast…Beauty was overjoyed to find in the great hall her father and his whole family, whom the beautiful lady, that appeared to her in her dream, had conveyed thither.

Jeanne Marie Le Prince de Beaumont

When I popped in again, I was bracing myself for anything, including a flaming dragon—or worse, Marj. A quick glance, however, showed no sign of anyone else with magic, only a half-dozen humans nearby, so I relaxed a little. I'd landed in what appeared to be the entrance hall of an impressive castle, all gold pillars and marble floors. Carved arms holding elaborate candelabra lined the walls of the large circular room—though considering it was daylight, the lit candles seemed a tad unnecessary. An enormous staircase swept down from above.

The cluster of people present stood at the foot of the stairs. None of them noticed me, all involved in talking to each other, voices both excited and alarmed. My gaze cut through the crowd to go first to Anthony and George, and I relaxed a little more. I was in the right place, and so far they hadn't been harmed, including being turned into kittens.

I glanced over the rest of the cluster. There was also a third young man, taller than Anthony, less broad than George, and with the same curly dark hair as both. Had to be Connor, the third brother. Next to him were two women of a similar age, both attractive but with a certain coldness to their features. The last member of the group was significantly older, with white hair and a frail air. It didn't take a genius or any magical ability to figure out what I was looking at—Anthony's entire family, or close to it. My bet was that the two women were Miranda and Noreen, which left Beauty still missing. I was about to use my magic to make sure, when I heard my name called.

I swung my attention back to Anthony, who had turned my direction. "What's going on?" he asked, with a touch of relief in his eyes.

There it was again, the expectation that the fairy must have all the answers, and could solve the problems too. And all right, I did have some answers but...that wasn't the point. I walked closer, tried to project a casual air. "I don't know exactly. Just that Marjoram's somehow behind it all."

His mouth twisted into a grimace. "How can you tell? I haven't seen any doves."

That would have been a joke, if he had sounded less bitter. "She sort of left her signature on the spell that carried you and George off," I explained. "She'll probably be showing up here."

Anthony's expression set into even grimmer lines. "Good. I want to talk to her about a glass shoe."

I suddenly regretted telling him anything. "Oh…no, I think you'd better not talk to Marj." Not when his face looked the way it had when he wanted to take a swing at the castle guards. That conversation was sure to end in kittenhood. "Why not let me talk to her? I know how to deal with her so—"

"Because that's solved things so far?" he snapped.

Which shut me up rather.

Being a generally nice person, he looked apologetic almost immediately. "Sorry. I shouldn't have—"

"No, it was true," I said, and scuffed my foot along the marble floor. "So how'd the rest of the family get here?" I asked, because I didn't want to talk about my recent non-accomplishments with regard to Catherine's problems.

"Apparently they were all transported here too," Anthony said, both of us turning to look at the others again.

They had gone on talking during our exchange. Considering the circumstances, I suppose I didn't seem all that interesting by comparison.

"I'm sure this is the Beast's castle," Anthony's father was saying. "I remember this hall. It was darker then, but it's the same hall." He looked around the room, eyes wide with hope. "Maybe Beauty is here. I've missed her so."

Miranda—I looked sideways and magically confirmed it was Miranda—looked grieved, eyes hooded and lips tight. "You just saw her yesterday."

"He did?" all three brothers said in near-unison.

Mr. Maurier nodded, beaming happily. "She visited for a week."

"It turns out the Beast is a nice one," Noreen said. Her voice was more resigned than pleased.

I think Anthony noticed that too. "That's good news, isn't it?" he said.

"Of course," Noreen said, sounding surprised that he had asked, but then she sighed. "Things always have a way of working out for Beauty, don't they?"

I squinted mentally, to look at Noreen's aura. I felt rather resigned too, to see a tall, utterly unwelcoming wall, marked and cracked in places as though it had been damaged in rough storms. No fresco like Catherine's, and if there was anything nice hiding on the other side of it, the wall was too big and thick and hard for me to see. I looked at Miranda, standing next to her sister, and saw a similar aura; her wall was if anything even more entrenched, stretching up high and also digging down into the earth with something like stone roots.

Small wonder Anthony had said his sisters never showed their true feelings. With walls that strong, I wondered if *they* even knew what they were hiding anymore.

I was about to take a look at the third brother when a flourish of trumpets interrupted both me and the continuing conversation among the family Maurier.

Up at the top of the stairs, a veritable herd of servants in red livery came streaming out. They descended the steps to line up by the banisters on either side. The trumpeter stayed at the top, blowing a few more notes of fanfare. Then he tucked his trumpet under his arm and announced, "Presenting his most Royal and Illustrious Majesty, the powerful and honored sovereign, liege lord of…"

And so on, and so on, and I stopped listening to look past the trumpeter at the two people just coming into view at the top of the stairs. He was at least as handsome as Roderick, though darker and with longer hair. She was dazzlingly beautiful, with shining mahogany hair, flawless features, and Anthony's blue eyes. Magically speaking, she was a rose garden, while he was a lion.

I should have looked closer at his aura. I meant to. But the trumpeter actually got to the name of the country, and in the way that certain words catch your attention, that name drove every other thought right out of my head. Beaumont. This was the king of Beaumont, the country that had been in anarchy since its last monarch disappeared a hundred years ago.

I stared at the king as he and the woman descended the stairs, pieces coming together to form a picture I didn't like at all.

I think everyone else was staring at the woman. She was definitely Beauty, based on the way the formal descent dissolved into a tumultuous, emotional huddle as soon as she got to the bottom of the stairs.

I thought I heard Miranda or Noreen mutter, "It figures, doesn't it," but I could have been wrong. I could have imagined it in the chaos of family greetings and exclamations and embraces.

I hung back, still turning over possibilities, and also mindful of not intruding myself where I didn't belong. While I was hanging back, a cooing voice behind my right shoulder trilled, "Isn't it *touching?*"

I knew who that was on the instant. If she'd been a man I would have collared her, but you can't exactly collar a plump woman in a fluffy pink dress. I just wheeled to face her. "Marj, I need to talk to you." About a lot of things, but first things first. "About that glass slipper—"

"Oh, not now, Tarry," she said, flapping her hands at me and spraying gold sparkles everywhere. "Don't you have any sense of the moment?"

"A sense of urgency is what I have," I said through gritted teeth, "and about Roderick's ball—"

"Not *now*." She turned right away from me and evaded my hand reaching out to grab her arm, without even appearing to try. She strode up to the family group, without any concern for not intruding, and clapped her hands a few times for attention. Then she launched into a sugary speech about what a marvelous person Beauty was, for having seen the value in the ugly Beast, who it turned out had been suffering under a dreadful enchantment and was really a handsome king. (Big surprise, that. Though maybe it would be more surprising if you hadn't been through this situation a few times.)

I crossed my arms and tapped my foot and waited. She was not getting away this time.

She was also not worrying about conciseness, or excess use of synonyms. It was a very long and *very* sugary speech, full of words like affable, charming, sweet-tempered, humble, patient, generous, courageous, compassionate, judicious, virtuous...you get the idea. I only had to listen to it for a few minutes, and that was enough for me to easily understand how, if speeches like this followed Beauty around through her whole life, being related to her could be a hard road. Even if it was all true. Maybe especially if it was all true.

I still wanted to get to my primary business (Catherine), but couldn't pass up the opportunity to address my secondary business when Marj started talking about His Majesty King Cesar's enchantment.

I interrupted to ask, "How long were you a Beast?"

Cesar gave me a long stare, as though he was wondering who I was. I was not in the mood to explain my lack of sparkles, so I just stared back while Marj twittered vaguely in the background, until he finally said, "I lost track somewhat after the first few decades, but I think it was around a hundred years."

Well, that fit, didn't it? "And how exactly did you become a Beast to begin with?"

"I was enchanted by a wicked fairy," he said, eyebrows drawing down and brow darkening.

I turned towards Marj, raised one eyebrow and *looked* at her. "A wicked fairy. Really."

Marj shrugged with an extra flounce—and looked away.

"Don't tell me," I drawled. "This fairy wanted to teach you a lesson, right?"

Cesar's darkened brow was joined by a scowl. "How did you know?"

"Instinct." I shook my head with a great show of sadness. "What a *terribly* wicked thing to do, turning you into a Beast and letting your country descend into chaos for a hundred years." I tsked disapprovingly.

"Back to the point," Marj said tightly, cleared her throat, and returned to her 'bestowing gifts on the masses' voice. "Beauty, for your virtue and perceptive heart, you have been greatly rewarded." And then she turned her gaze on Miranda and Noreen. "But you two ladies…"

I knew that voice too, and it distracted me right out of my general annoyance with Marj into a more immediate alarm. It was her 'I'm just so disappointed in you' voice, and it never boded well. "Marj, what are you about to do?" I hissed.

She ignored me completely, apart from talking louder. "I can see the malice in your hearts, and I am very much afraid that you must be Taught a Lesson."

Worse and worse. Mine wasn't the only voice raised in protest this time.

Marj ignored all of us. With a benevolent expression, a gracious wave of her hand, and a shower of lavender sparkles, she turned Noreen and Miranda into statues.

Unlike some magicians I've seen, Marj's statue transformations are instant. Noreen and Miranda froze into position with near-identical expressions of shock and alarm, and were cold hard granite practically before my stomach finished plummeting.

I always knew Marj did things like this, and yes, even their brother had said these two could be nasty sometimes—but that didn't make it any more comfortable to watch.

Of course an uproar of voices rose from the rest of the family, and in the confusion I heard Anthony protest, "I thought you were supposed to be a *good* fairy!"

"I *am* a Good Fairy," Marj said, benevolent expression still firmly in place. "I am not to blame for your sisters' transformations;

that was necessary because of the jealousy in their hearts." She folded her hands together in front of her and smiled sweetly. "When they repent of their faults, they will return to their original state."

"Oh wonderful!" Anthony snapped. "I'm sure turning someone into a statue will cure them of jealousy!"

"Precisely," Marj agreed, without a trace of sarcasm. "And in the meantime, they will stand as statues at the entrance to the castle as their punishment."

I noticed suddenly that all those liveried servants, even the trumpeter, had disappeared. Not magically, they'd just beat a hasty retreat while everyone was distracted. And considering someone was throwing magic around to turn people into statues, they were probably smart.

Part of me wanted to flee too, the part that still wanted to wash my hands of this whole mess and go forget it all at some party a country or two away. But I ignored that part, which was easier to do while I was good and angry with Marj.

Besides, the rest of Anthony's family wasn't retreating either.

"This seems like it's going too far," George began, voice mild but forehead furrowed, "so hadn't you better—"

"Not another word," Marj said, punctuating the statement with a shower of gold sparks. "I have taken entirely necessary steps and you are not to worry yourselves any further on the subject."

"Doesn't that seem unlikely, considering they're our sisters?" Connor said, voice quiet and serious. I finally looked at his aura, and found a grove of oak trees. Not entirely unlike Anthony's aura, except that Connor's was steadier, old-growth trees with thick trunks and spreading branches.

None of the objections made any impression on Marj. Not Anthony's passion or George's concern or Connor's solemn statement. I hoped Beauty might get farther, when she said, "This does seem a bit harsh."

But Marj only smiled sweetly and said, "Now, Beauty, that's just your kind and generous heart. And with your unselfish heart, I know you will make a wonderful queen." She clasped her hands together. "I'm going to transport you all to His Majesty's kingdom, where I'm sure you'll be *very* happy."

His Majesty's kingdom was Beaumont, which had been a byword for anarchy, chaos and disaster for a solid century. And Marj was just going to send everybody there? I tried to get around the edge of the crowd of people to reach Marj again. Maybe I *could* collar her. Somehow I had to make her actually listen to me and stop unrolling horror upon horror.

I wasn't the only one with new objections. "Wait," Anthony said quickly, "wait a minute, I can't go off to another country. I have commitments here so—"

"Perhaps it's time to think of your family commitments," Marj said, voice ever so kind.

I winced, while Anthony stared at her. "Well, yes, but—"

"Good. All settled, then." Marj clapped her hands, setting off a puff of sparks.

To the humans, I imagine it just looked like the room shimmered a bit. I was distracted by the head-spinning rush of magic as the entire castle, with all inhabitants, moved a hundred miles northeast. I swayed, clenched my eyes shut and took a deep breath. She could have given me a moment's notice. When the world had settled and I opened my eyes again, the view out the windows had changed, the forest gone, replaced by long sweeping lawns.

"And here we are," Marj said happily. "Wasn't that painless?" Since that question was clearly aimed at me, it proved she was not as oblivious to my glare as she was pretending.

Most of the humans were staring towards the windows, but Beauty stepped forward to clasp Marj's hands and say, "Thank you so much for everything."

"My great pleasure, dear," Marj said with a benevolent smile. "Now I've got to be flitting so—"

Not before she talked to me! I started moving forward again, ready to physically lay hold of her if necessary.

"*Wait* a minute," Anthony interrupted Marj's chatter, "I never agreed to come to—"

Marj turned towards him, benevolent smile vanishing, and gold sparks flashing suddenly, dangerously bright. "There is always space for another statue in the gardens." It was all the more unsettling because her voice stayed sweet. "Would you care to join your sisters?"

One of Anthony's feet edged backward, but he didn't actually retreat. "Um…no. But I don't think you understand…"

I didn't think he understood how dangerous Marj's expression had grown. This situation was bad enough, and I didn't want it getting even worse. By now I was close enough to lay a hand on her shoulder. "Marj, it's time we had a discussion."

"Not now, Tarry," she said, trying to shrug me off, "I told you I have to—"

"Yes, *now*." I snapped the fingers of my free hand and transported us both outside the castle, into the garden I'd seen through the windows. It was one of those painfully controlled gardens, all box hedges and round rose bushes, with never a leaf out of place. The flowers were nice, though.

I'd landed us in a wide intersection of several paths, and now I squared off facing Marj. "You're running rampant over people I like, and I don't appreciate it."

She batted her eyelashes once, slowly. "I thought you *wanted* me to become more involved with the common folk. "

"This is not what I had in mind!" I yelled, hands clenching into fists.

"Although a girl with the natural grace, charm and—well, beauty of Beauty can hardly be considered *common*—"

"Don't start waxing on about her again," I groaned, "I can't stand it."

Marj steamed right on ahead. "I'm sure the family must be distantly royal in some way; that was my conclusion when I originally arranged for her to encounter the Beast. Although today has demonstrated that the royal blood is showing itself more strongly in Beauty than in *some* members of her family."

"That doesn't give you the right to run rough-shod over them!" My philosophy caught up to my initial outrage and I quickly added, "And that whole royal business is ridiculous anyway."

"Oh really, Tarry," she said with a dismissive shrug, "just because I'm encouraging family members to spend time together…"

I had to consciously uncurl my hands. I took a deep breath and aimed for a calm tone. "That is not what you are doing. You are not encouraging. You are insisting. You are manipulating everyone's lives when you have no right to do that. And speaking of manipulation—you turned the king of Beaumont into a Beast for a hundred years? It never occurred to you that maybe he was actually *doing* something as king?"

"He needed to learn a lesson in humility," she said primly. "He wasn't a good king."

The sheer disregard for consequences was utterly maddening. "And anarchy went so well as an alternative? This country's been a disaster zone of magical mayhem for a century. Why didn't you consider any of that?"

"That was not my concern," Marj said, and stared at me through half-lowered eyelids. "Nor do I see how it's your concern. It certainly hasn't been for the last century."

That…was uncomfortably true. I had known about Beaumont, but I hadn't done anything about it. I changed the subject. "Fine, never mind the politics. I'm *concerned* about that idiotic glass slipper of yours, which they still haven't gotten onto the right foot, not that you've been paying enough attention to notice."

For the first time, she actually deigned to look bothered, eyes widening. "I thought you were taking care of that! How difficult can it be to direct the prince and his men and the slipper to the little cottage with the triple oaks, just off the main square, and try the shoe on a girl named Ella? Really, how hard is that?"

I didn't know whether to hug her or shove her into a rose bush. "That's bloody impossible when you don't give me that kind of information, Marj!" But now I had it, now I could *do* something.

She shook her head. "Nonsense. I must have mentioned it."

"No, you did not mention it. But you did now, that's good, now I'll be able to get Catherine out of a mess."

"Who?"

I opened my mouth, closed it again. Did I really want to get into this with Marj? "Never mind. Next point, Anthony's mess, how did you even get him here to begin with? George and Connor too, they're all in the military, so how'd you use magic on them?"

"Are they in the military?" she asked. "I didn't notice."

I folded my arms and went back to glaring at her. "Right. Because you weren't paying attention to what they were doing, you just snatched them away from it."

She tapped one finger against her chin. "It really is rather inexplicable."

"Your inability to pay any attention to what other people are doing?" I snapped. "I've always found that inexplicable."

She sniffed at me. "Now you're just being rude. You know I meant how I transported them here. I wish I could remember the details of the spell, but it was so long ago that I cast it."

Sometimes I suspected Marj of being either very stupid, or very smart and using apparent stupidity for the sole purpose of frustrating me. "Yeah, that spell was a whole ten minutes ago."

"No, no, I cast the spell originally over a year ago," she said, flapping a hand and not allaying my suspicions to any significant degree. "Bringing Beauty's family here was scheduled to happen automatically when she broke the spell over the Beast. It's all quite the standard procedure, you know, in this sort of situation."

The fact that a standard procedure even existed was mind-boggling—or would have been, if I hadn't seen this enough times to get over the boggling centuries ago. And in this particular case, it did offer an explanation. "They weren't in the military a year ago. And then after you brought them here, they sort of weren't in the military anymore. So it's a loophole." There are at least as many loopholes in magic as there are spells, maybe more. I hadn't known this one existed, and possibly no one had. It's not the kind of thing that comes up often. "So that's how you got them here. Now about letting them go again—"

Marj's sparkles glowed a brighter pink. "I am absolutely firm on that decision. Beauty wants her family around her, and that settles the matter."

My jaw clenched. "That's very nice for Beauty, but the rest of them—"

"My decision is made," she said, and clapped her hands again.

If I'd had two seconds of warning, even one second—but she caught me by surprise. By the time I realized what she was doing, I wasn't looking at Marj and the box hedges anymore. I was standing out in the woods, sent back to the former location of the Beast's castle.

"Oh come on, Marj, who's being rude now?" I complained to the empty air. "Banishment? Really?" I should have expected it, of course. Worrying about other people is *distracting*.

I tried to pop back, smacked straight into a magical wall, and went absolutely nowhere.

I had been focusing on Marj, and it wasn't all that surprising to find out that I was still blocked from following her. I shifted my focus to Anthony and tried to pop after him.

Still nothing, and now my stomach gave a twist of worry.

I needed a new strategy. Rather than going anywhere, I concentrated on sensing Marj's spells. I could feel her magic wrapping around Cesar's castle in Beaumont, like a sparkly, strangling cloud. Very little checking confirmed that the news was not good. She had me completely blocked from popping anywhere near the castle.

While I was looking at that spell, I noticed another one in operation too. I couldn't pop in, and Anthony wouldn't be able to walk out, whenever he decided to try that—soon, I expected.

Problems. Big problems, all around.

Although it did occur to me...if I wanted to just wash my hands of the whole thing, this could be my excuse. I was *banished*, what more could I do?

Except, of course, I could go talk to Catherine. I could try to solve her problem, now that Marj had finally given me useful information. At least, I could solve Catherine's *old* problem. Her new problem was that her fiancé was trapped in a castle in Beaumont.

That thought made me sigh in sheer exhausted frustration. It wasn't *fair*. You barely get even close to solving one problem, and up pops another. It was like trying to drink a waterfall dry; it never stopped.

But as long as I was standing here in the middle of the deluge, well, for now I'd go help to get her out of this stupid engagement to stupid Prince Roderick. And then?

I sighed, rubbed my temples, and admitted to myself what really I already knew.

After we dealt with Roderick, I'd see how I could help her help Anthony, banishment or no.

Sure, part of me did still want to run from the whole sorry mess. But if I did that—then I'd always know that things had gone bad here, very bad, and I hadn't done anything about it. So maybe I couldn't fix this, but I could at least *not* ignore it. I could see it through, make whatever effort I could to get Catherine and Anthony and their families the happy endings they should have. Even if it meant getting very water-logged in the process.

Chapter Twenty-One

"At least Anthony's with his family now," Catherine said, and went on eating her breakfast.

I was flabbergasted, amazed and astonished. I had magically transported to Roderick's castle (no sparkly walls getting in my way there), found Catherine in her room, and launched into the latest update. I had started, at her choice, with the good news, that we'd be able to find the original girl from the ball now. To say she took that calmly was putting it mildly. All she'd said was that she didn't think it would make much difference by now. I had set my perplexity at that aside to move onto the bad news, the news about Anthony, and the perplexity was only multiplying.

I stared at her calm face, and had to swallow twice before I could say, "My insane fairy cousin abducts Anthony and traps him in a castle in Beaumont, and you have no reaction? You're not at all upset?"

She didn't even look up from stirring her porridge. "It's not as though I can do anything about it."

"That's not the point!" I protested, rising from my chair at the table. "Don't you *want* to do something? About Anthony, and about yourself? You don't want to marry Roderick, so why aren't you trying to do something?" *I* was determined to do something, why by the Fairy Queen wasn't she?

"But there's nothing to do, and it doesn't make any difference what I want," she explained, and I swear she did it with a distinctly sugary smile. "I've decided the best course is to accept life as it is. Fighting against it doesn't do any good, and only makes everything harder. Now do you want some porridge? There's plenty here."

For once, I had no appetite. I was past astonished and beyond flabbergasted. We had left amazed behind as well. "What is *wrong* with you?"

"Nothing's wrong with me, Tarry."

"No…no, I'm not sure about that." When I'd asked the question, it had been more or less rhetorical. But what if something really *was* wrong? She had been strangely quiet for days, but I had shied away from thinking about it too much, too guilty and uncomfortable to face whatever it might mean.

I took a deep breath, nerving myself up to take a closer look at her aura. I'd been shying away from that too. I'd glanced in a haphazard way, but hadn't really *looked*. The wall was too high, the garden behind it too wintry, the whole picture too depressing. I focused now, magically staring past the wall to peer at the garden. It was still all snow and ice and…and my stomach flipped as I saw something I hadn't paid enough attention to notice before. The trees and flowers in Catherine's garden weren't just pulled back into a passive but healthy winter slumber. Under that coat of ice, they were wilting and drooping and dying.

I sank back into my chair, staring aghast at her. This was so much worse than I had thought. This level of collapse, I couldn't believe it was all caused just by the prospect of marrying Roderick, unpleasant though he was. Something else had to be going on. "What happened? What have you not told me?" What clues had I not picked up, because I didn't want to see them?

She raised her eyebrows, but it was in only the mildest of curiosity. "You know everything that's happened, Tarry. There's nothing new." That blank expression, that calm voice, were even more disturbing contrasted with the shattering state of her aura.

I surged up to my feet again, paced back and forth before the table, trying to think. "Did someone hurt you? Is Roderick threatening you or The Nightingale or someone else?

"Of course not," she said, lifting a spoonful of porridge. "Roderick has never threatened anything."

That pulled me up short. That was literally true, the threats hadn't come from Roderick. But I hadn't really meant Roderick, I had meant Leonard, so why had I said Roderick?

A teasing wisp of memory came back to me, Anthony starting a conversation we'd never finished. He had asked a question that we'd never answered. I asked the same question out loud now. "Why don't we ever talk about Leonard?"

I don't think Catherine shared the sense of momentousness that I was feeling, considering the way she shrugged and glanced out the window. "I suppose he's just the kind of person people take no notice of."

It was like a thunderbolt. I stared at her. "Wait. Say that again."

A single eyebrow rose this time. "He's the kind of person people don't notice."

"No, that's not what you said. You said people *take no notice* of him."

It was like a fog lifting. I hadn't picked up on Leonard magically the first time he and Roderick had approached Catherine's room. I had never gotten a proper read on Leonard's aura, and had never really tried. Roderick had somehow gotten out of my spell to stick his feet to the floor, and Leonard had been there at the time. We all spent much more time talking about Roderick than about Leonard, even though Leonard, when a person thought about it, was the one who was really running affairs.

But a person didn't think about it, ever. Except for half a thought here or a trace of an idea there, none of us ever paid any attention to Leonard, or to the fact that we didn't pay any attention to him. Now, finally, when I was looking at it, the conclusion seemed astonishingly obvious. "We never talk about Leonard because he's using a take-no-notice spell. Or a variation on one."

Catherine looked at me doubtfully. "You think Leonard's a fairy?"

"No, that's impossible; I'd know if he was a fairy. There's no way to hide it from another fairy." I was pacing again, trying to puzzle out the rest of this. "But he could be something else. A magician, maybe. Probably a magician, they could cast a spell similar to mine."

Catherine leaned her head on one hand. "Well, perhaps he is a magician. So?"

"So? *So*? That's all you have to say?" Which brought me right back to the original question, the unfathomable way Catherine was behaving. Only now I was pretty sure I knew who was responsible. What had Leonard done to her?

Catherine sighed. "I don't know what it is you want me to say or do."

"You're supposed to fight! You're supposed to care, to make decisions, to want to act. You're supposed to show some willpower, or to—" I stopped pacing. "*Willpower.*"

That was it, the key to the whole ridiculous situation.

It even explained Roderick's constant failure to form an opinion and his automatic deference to Leonard's views.

Leonard was using magic to drain wills.

I knew about a spell for it. Completely forbidden, of course, utterly against the rules. The Fairy Court looked very severely on anyone caught using it, fairy or not. But they don't monitor magicians as closely as they monitor fairies, and if a magician could hide it, then he could do it, could draw magical power for himself by stealing the will of someone else. The stronger the will, the more power to gain. And now it all made sense why Leonard had been insistent about Roderick marrying Catherine. He had wanted to ensure a queen with a strong will.

Catherine waved her hand in front of my eyes. "Tarry? What about willpower?"

I blinked. "Nothing. Never mind." I seized her wrist and pulled her towards the door. "Come on. We're going to go have a talk with Leonard."

I had to concentrate hard to find him in the castle. I walked around as I concentrated, because sometimes a different place helps. Knowing about a 'take no notice' type spell is the first and most important step to seeing through it, but it still required effort. Once I finally found him, I stopped walking and transported Catherine and myself to a hallway nearby.

Catherine rubbed a hand across her eyes. "That feels strange."

Some corner of my mind noted, regretfully, that she really should have been upset with me for not warning her.

I didn't bother knocking. The door Leonard was behind was locked, but that's never a problem if you're me. One quick spell and I shoved the door open, pulling Catherine in with me. Leonard was sitting in front of a desk covered in papers. He glanced up with only the faintest signs of interest when we entered.

"Is there something I can do for you?" he asked.

I saw no point in beating around the bush. Maybe a bold offensive would make him back down. "Yes, there is. You can stop draining Catherine's will."

"Stop doing what?" Catherine said, with not nearly the level of interest or outrage she should have shown.

Leonard raised one eyebrow. "Interesting theory. What inspired it?"

"Right, like I'll just go away because you pretend you don't know what I'm talking about. Not going to happen." I crossed my arms and gave him a double-barreled glare. "What is going to happen is that you will lift your spell on Catherine, and then you're heading for the edges of the map before I let the Royal Court in on what you've been doing."

He smiled without showing any teeth. "I hardly think the royal family of Perrelda will believe your word over mine regarding this insane idea you're having."

If that's the level he thought we were playing on, then I held all the cards. "Maybe not," I agreed. And smiled. "But I had the Fairy Court in mind, and *they* will believe my word over yours."

His eyes widened, so briefly I could almost believe I had imagined it, before his usual calm returned. "The Fairy Court. Really."

I snapped the fingers of both hands, setting off twin plumes of dark blue smoke. "Yes. Really." The Fairy Court was a good threat, a force no one wanted to reckon with. It would have been even better if I hadn't been half-bluffing by invoking them. I could take this to them, and they'd believe me, and they'd probably do something…but even as a fairy, I didn't really want to reckon with the Court either, if I could possibly avoid it. You never know how something like that will turn out.

"How interesting." He stood up and came around his desk, peering at me closer. "I thought there was something peculiar about you when we first met. You certainly don't have any of the usual signs of a fairy."

"I'm unusual."

"Ironic, really," Leonard continued. "One reason I opposed Roderick's original choice of a bride was that I saw she had magical support."

"She's not the only one." I folded my arms again, did my best to look imposing. "Now that we've established my magical credentials, are you feeling like surrendering?"

"No," he said, voice almost regretful. "I'm not."

With a quick motion of his right hand, he launched a spout of flame in my direction. I threw up my left hand, palm out, creating a shield against the flames. With my right, I threw a shield over Catherine as well, as a precaution. Under normal circumstances, I would have looked for help from her, but the circumstances were not normal. She had dropped into a chair, looking over the back to stare at us, without any sign of plans to do more.

I belatedly realized that I should not have brought her at all, and blamed the lapse on that take-no-notice spell. Even knowing about it, it still affected impressions, and I had so hoped he'd just back down, lift his spell on Catherine and scurry off. So much for that happy possibility.

I also hadn't realized how powerful Leonard was. My shield was holding his fire back, but it was taking more effort than I liked to think about.

Obviously I wasn't going to tell him that, though. "You honestly think fighting a fairy is a good idea?"

"Oh, I honestly do," Leonard said, smiling again. "I have quite a nice set-up here, one I could keep going for many years still. I don't intend to let one unusual fairy ruin it for me."

Fire was still pouring from his right palm, and I could see him raising his left for another spell. To forestall that, I conjured a ball of flame in my own free hand and threw it towards him. He made a sign with his left hand and deflected my flame with a quick shield. I tossed a second and third fireball in quick succession, and he had a shield up to catch every one.

Just as I was throwing Fire Ball Number Four at him, the door opened, and Prince Roderick stuck his head in. "There you are, Leonard; I was looking for you." He glanced over the scene. "Is this a bad time?"

"We're a little busy." Palm hot and needing a new idea, I tried conjuring up arrows to pelt at Leonard. He deflected the first several, then started sending them in sharp curves so they came back towards me. Worse than useless. I hurriedly waved them all out of existence before they hit.

I didn't like how fast Leonard could cast his spells. I had powerful magic, but I didn't have much experience using it like this. Parlor tricks were more in my line than battle magic. Maybe a defensive strategy was best. Let him wear himself out with fancy spells and outlast him.

"I'll just wait," Roderick said, and strolled over to stand near Catherine. Conveniently, that put him inside my shield—not that his welfare was my highest concern. "I say, Leonard, I didn't know you could do magic. That's interesting."

"How long have you been draining *his* will?" I asked.

"Years," Leonard said, grinning. This smile had teeth, and it was even less pleasant than his others.

"It shows."

"Pity he's found out now about my magical abilities." Leonard waved his left hand almost lazily through the air, and every small, hard object in the room rose a few inches. "I'll try to wipe his memory later, but I might have to just kill him. How inconvenient."

A chill ran down my spine. I had already known this was serious, but for him to talk about murder so casually…

Roderick only laughed. "You know you don't mean that, Leonard."

All those small, hard objects—a few bits of statuary, a couple paperweights, and an entire chess set—came pelting towards me. I turned them into feathers just before they hit.

Leonard's eyes narrowed, and I tensed for the next attack.

Instead, what came next was Catherine's voice. "Tarry?" she said, voice wavering. "I feel…funny…"

I risked a glance in her direction. She had one hand pressed to her temple and she swayed unsteadily in her chair. My gaze flashed back to Leonard. "What are you doing?" I demanded, face hot and not from his flames. "How did you get to her past my shield?"

"It's obviously no good against a spell already in effect." He had his left hand outstretched, palm up, in Catherine's direction. "I find myself in need of more energy. And she has such a great deal of will."

It was working. I was still blocking his flames with one hand, and my palm was burning hotter as his power increased. I couldn't afford a defensive strategy anymore, I didn't have another plan—frantically, I threw another ball of flame at him. He waved it aside, reached out towards Catherine again, and closed his hand into a fist.

"*Oh.*" She shuddered and her eyes slid shut, just before she toppled to one side.

Roderick, in proper princely fashion, caught her. He looked down at her face, her cheek against his shoulder. "Um…miss?"

I was angry and afraid and this felt like the last straw. "You forgot her name again?" I yelled.

"Are you still on about that?" Roderick complained.

"Catherine! It's *Catherine!*"

"It won't be anything soon," Leonard drawled. "I could drain someone's will for years without affecting her physical health." He raised his fist in a quick motion, and Catherine jerked convulsively. "Or I can affect it. Very quickly."

"Stop it," I growled, trying to keep one eye on Catherine and the other on Leonard, to keep up my own shields while throwing magical power into blocking his attack on Catherine, to come up with some kind of *solution*...

Leonard was smiling again. "I won't stop if you keep fighting. Are you feeling like surrendering?"

I hesitated.

He raised his fist higher, above shoulder-height now. Catherine shuddered again, and fell back against Roderick.

"All right!" I lifted my free hand over my head. "I surrender."

Still smiling. "I want your word that you will not oppose me. You're obviously not an Evil Fairy, defending fair maiden and all that, and Good Fairies never break their word."

"Yes, fine, I promise, you have my word." He extinguished his flames, and I lowered my shield. "Now stop hurting Catherine!"

His smile only grew. He lowered his hands, and turned them both palm out.

Catherine moaned, a sound that choked off abruptly. A blizzard was blowing through her aura, and I couldn't even see the garden through the snow.

"She just stopped breathing," Roderick announced.

"What are you doing?" I demanded, heart hammering. "I surrendered!"

"She knows too much now," Leonard said, voice serene. "I told you what would happen if you didn't surrender. I didn't say anything about what would happen if you—"

"Yes, yes, I get it!" I snapped, and dropped my head, hair falling forward over my eyes.

"Aren't you going to do something?" Roderick asked.

"I gave my word," I muttered, shoulders slouching. "You do something."

"What can *I* do?"

That was pretty much the response I had expected from him.

With my hair hiding my eyes, I watched Leonard. He had his head back, his chin up and his eyes closed, a rapturous expression on his face as he drew in Catherine's energy.

I waited. One heartbeat. A second. A third...

And then I flung every bit of magic at him that I could. No spell, no planned attack, just pure raw magical energy crashing at him, at a moment when he was wide open to receiving it.

He twitched once, eyes flying open. "What are you—no, you gave your word—"

"Good Fairies always keep their word. But I'm not a Good Fairy." I grinned. "Means I can lie."

I kept pouring magic at him. I wasn't sure just what it would do, but I knew it wouldn't be good for him.

He shrieked once, there was a sudden flash, and when it had faded Leonard had collapsed into a heap on the floor.

I let my shoulders relax, turned away from the incapacitated magician, and turned towards Catherine. She hadn't moved, slumped against Roderick.

"She's still not breathing," Roderick said, looking down at her.

My shoulders tensed right up again, my own breath coming in fast hitches and uneven starts. How long had she not been breathing? A minute? Two? Leonard's spell was broken, she should be fine now. She should be waking up.

I dropped down to my knees next to her, hunting for a spell that would help. There was no obvious one, because willpower-draining spells almost never happened. "Catherine? Wake up!" I raised my hands to cast general healing magic over her, my fingers glowing green, light spreading across her face. I didn't know if it would be enough, didn't know what else to try. When you avoid battle magic, you don't learn healing magic either. "You have to wake up, because

Anthony's never going to forgive me if you don't. *I'll* never forgive me if you don't." Had I waited a few seconds too long? "Catherine? *Cat*!"

She suddenly inhaled, a gasp as much as a breath, and coughed on the exhale. "Don't call me that," she groaned.

Nothing she could have said would have delighted me more. "Cat! You're back!" I sank back onto my heels, grinning at her, put a last push into the healing spell then let it fade out.

Her eyes opened, and she grimaced. "Really don't call me that." She shifted, squinted up at Roderick. "What are you—let go of me."

"You could thank me for catching you," he pointed out.

"Thank you," she said, pushing away from him. She swayed as she rose, and I got to my feet in time to catch her arm. She shook her head, but didn't push me off. "I'm fine. Or I will be in a minute."

I knew this was partially bravado, but there was truth in it too. Snow was melting away in her aura much faster than it ever did in life, and green leaves were already unfurling all over her garden.

"What happened?" Catherine asked, pressing her palm against one temple.

"Leonard overdosed on magical energy and burned himself out," I said.

"Is he dead?"

"No. But don't worry, I'll deal with him."

I set Catherine back in her chair, and then turned to Leonard again. With my physical eyes, I could see that he was unconscious but breathing, and with my magical eyes I finally took a good look at his aura.

It was a labyrinth, a maze of passages and turns and walls, a masterpiece of hiding and manipulation. I peered into a passage and then hurriedly looked away. One glimpse told me that I didn't want to see the things hiding behind Leonard's walls. But at least I was reassured by the scorched state of his aura, by the black cinders and soot. He had burned out his ability to do magic for years to come, maybe forever.

And now that his defenses were down, I could cast other spells. Fairies are allowed to cast all sorts of spells on magicians who've directly threatened them.

So I turned him into a toad. His skin changed first, going all warty and brown. His body began to shrink, eyes migrating out to the sides, lips disappearing and mouth widening. The shrinking sped up, even as his fingers elongated and torso swelled. A few seconds more, and Leonard the Toad sprawled across the stone floor.

I let out a sigh. "That was immensely satisfying."

"I wonder how we'll run the country without him," Roderick remarked. "But I suppose Mother and Father will work out something."

I had almost forgotten that Roderick must have parents around somewhere. Sometimes Kings and Queens are like that—they fade into the background and you only know they're there because there can't be a crown prince without a king farther up.

Catherine shot Roderick a glare. "You're impossible. And by the way, I'm not marrying you."

He blinked. "You're not? Why not?"

"I was only marrying you to begin with because Leonard was threatening people I care about."

"He was? I didn't know that." Roderick frowned, puzzled. "Why would anyone need to be threatened into marrying *me*?"

"So not charming," Catherine muttered. "I'm not marrying you, partially because you're a conceited, insufferable bore, but mostly because I want to marry Anthony." She smoothed her hands over her lap, back straightening, and looked at me. "Speaking of whom, can we turn your cousin Marjoram into a toad?"

"Regrettably, no. Fairies aren't allowed to turn each other into small slimy animals. Or even small fluffy ones." I braced myself for a desperate appeal, or a new round of despondency over this new crisis. I was resolved to see this through, but exactly what that meant...

But Catherine just nodded briskly and said, "All right, so we'll think of something else. There must be some way to get Anthony away from her."

"Now wait, what about me?" Roderick interjected, arms folded and chin raised petulantly. "I have to marry someone, and you're the best choice since they've already started the arrangements. They're nearly finished writing the invitations!"

I still couldn't turn Roderick into a toad—but without Leonard, Roderick didn't seem even a quarter as dangerous anyway. Maybe I'd finally get to see Catherine throw something at him after all.

Catherine stared at him, and said slowly and clearly, "I don't want to marry you."

He shook his head. "That's just foolishness. You'll get over it."

"No. I won't."

Roderick drew himself up to his full height. He was a proper handsome prince, so that was a solid six feet, plus an inch or two. "I insist that you marry me." The authoritative effect was rather spoiled by the pleased expression which flashed across his face an instant later. "I don't remember ever insisting on anything before. I think I like it."

Apparently Catherine wasn't the only one reclaiming some lost willpower, now that Leonard's influence was removed.

Catherine was still sitting down, putting her much lower than Roderick, but she had a far more intimidating glare. "You can insist, but I refuse and you can't force me to marry you."

"No, I probably can't," he admitted. "But I could make lots of trouble trying. Why don't you just give in instead?"

"Or I could just turn you into a toad," I suggested. I couldn't actually. I'd get into trouble. But Roderick didn't know that.

The prince tugged on his collar. "You wouldn't do that." He sounded gratifyingly uncertain.

"This is just wasting time," Catherine said. "You don't really want to marry *me*, you just want to marry someone. Right?"

He thought about it. I think it required effort. "Yes. I suppose so. Someone pretty, of course." He glanced at me, a nervous peek, then back to Catherine. "And you really are the most convenient one. Since you're already here and it's all arranged and everything."

"But what if," she pressed on, "you could marry the girl from the ball? The one who actually owned the glass slipper?"

"Oh yes, I liked her. She was very pretty." He shot a pointed look at Catherine. "And she appreciated my finer qualities."

I couldn't help wondering what those were. His magnificent talent at filling out a formal jacket?

Catherine let that go by without a comment. "If we find the girl from the ball, will you marry her and let me get on with my life?"

"Do you know, I think that would do nicely," Roderick decided. "But how are you going to find her?"

Catherine looked at me. "Tarry, didn't you say…"

A problem I could actually solve! "House off the main square, three oaks," I said eagerly. "I have it on the most reliable of sources."

"Good. So we'll go find the girl for Roderick to marry, that gets him out of the way—"

"I don't think that's a polite way to put it," Roderick said.

"—and then we'll work out how we're going to rescue Anthony."

She was being so confident, so assertive, so *Catherine*, that I could feel a considerable smile stretching across my face. "Have I told you that I'm really glad you're back?"

"Thank you for helping me get back," Catherine said, smiling too. She rose to her feet. "Now if you'd just take us to where that girl is, we can start sorting everything out."

"On the other hand," I mused, "I got to give directions once in a while, while you were enchanted. So there were some advantages."

"Tarry!"

"Just kidding. Before we track down Roderick's true love, there's one minor point to take care of." I picked up Leonard the Toad by one hindleg. He kicked, starting to wake up. Must have been an unpleasant waking. I opened the window, and dropped him into the garden outside. "There's a nice pond to the north," I advised him, which was more generous than he deserved, then turned back to Catherine and Roderick.

I raised one hand for a spell. "Now let's go find the girl who owns the glass slipper."

Chapter Twenty-Two

Since I'd never seen the house we were visiting, it was safer to pop somewhere I was familiar with nearby. The main square was one possibility, but suddenly appearing there, with the crown prince in tow no less, would have created considerable disturbance. I transported Catherine, myself and Roderick to the front yard of The Nightingale instead. Catherine wanted to see her father anyway.

Unfortunately, we came out of thin air just as Sam was walking across the yard carrying a basket of eggs. The result was utterly predictable.

"Hello, Sam," Catherine said, stepped over the smashed eggs, and hugged him. "It's so good to see you! Is Father inside?"

With great effort, Sam managed, "Yes. I think so. Yes."

"Good!" Catherine headed off into the inn. She really must have been happy, to not even comment on the eggs. And the place really was falling apart without her, if no one had stopped Sam from carrying eggs to begin with.

We wouldn't be going anywhere for at least a few minutes, so I figured I could do a small good deed while waiting. Sam's eyes got even bigger when I levitated the nearest smashed egg and magically put it back together.

Roderick, meanwhile, was pacing. "Don't you think we're rushing this whole thing?"

I rolled my eyes, and gave a magical nudge to separate a floating yellow blob into its original two yolks. "Considering your inability to learn a girl's name has already wreaked havoc with everyone's life for more than a week, no. I don't think we're rushing."

"But I don't even have the glass slipper," he complained, pushing his hands into his jacket pockets.

"Why do you need it? Won't you recognize the girl?"

He stared at me like *I* was the daft one. "That isn't the point."

I sighed, paused with three partially repaired eggs hovering in front of me, and waved a hand at him. The glass slipper appeared in his hand; he fumbled but, with princely reflexes, held onto it.

"Don't drop it," I advised.

"And furthermore," he continued, "I can't possibly do this without heralds and a dozen guards in attendance, and I need my trumpeter, and I don't think I'm dressed appropriately, and I really ought to have my black stallion, and also—"

"All right, all right, *all right*. Just give me a minute." I finished with the eggs, picked up the dropped basket, and shooed all the floating eggs into it. I put it into the still-staring Sam's arms, turned him around, and gave him a light push towards the inn. "There you are. Off you go to the kitchen. Walk slowly."

An uncertain "thank you" trailed behind him.

And then I turned back to Roderick. "I'll transport everyone here, but you have to explain it to them."

He nodded. "Agreed."

I drew the line at magicking his clothes—I don't do wardrobes, outside of emergencies—but I brought his guards and trumpeter and so on. They were more than a little confused and it took time to explain, but it was still faster than getting them the human way. We had it all worked out by the time Catherine emerged from the inn, one arm around her father's shoulders and eyes suspiciously red—though I'm sure she would have denied that to her last breath.

The rest of the staff came out behind Catherine, and I noticed Jack and Emmy among them. Under normal circumstances, neither of them would have been here at this time, but they'd been helping out in Catherine and Anthony's absence. Two more people whose lives had been disrupted by Roderick's faulty memory.

With slightly more hubbub and hassle, we finally got moving. Naturally Roderick led the way on his black horse. I conjured up a horse for Catherine too; technically she was engaged to the prince still, and proper ceremony, etc. etc. So she rode next to him, which was convenient since she actually knew the way to a house with three oaks.

Neat rows of heralds and guards spread out walking behind them. I fell in with that group. Behind the last guard came the entire population of The Nightingale, and we swiftly picked up additional numbers from curious passersby.

It was, I admit, an impressive display. It would have been more impressive if it had lasted for more than two minutes. Up one street to the square, left down another street, where everyone came to a halt in front of a small cottage with a cluster of oaks looming up behind it.

"I wish I could remember who lives here," Catherine said as she dismounted. She looked over her shoulder to find me. "Did you learn the girl's name?"

I stepped through a few rows of guards to stand next to her. "Marj said it was Ella. You know her?"

Catherine's eyes had widened. "Yes. Yes, I do. But I never would have guessed…"

While we spoke, Roderick marched up the flagstone walk in his most princely fashion, glass slipper under one arm, and rapped smartly against the wooden door. The occupants were clearly waiting for the knock—they couldn't have missed our arrival—and the door whisked open instantly. The woman behind it was of middle years, not exactly ugly but looking like she tried much too hard at not being ugly. Behind her crowded two girls around Catherine's age, pretty, but also looking like they put too much effort into it. Too many flounces, too heavy make-up, hair twisted into too elaborate of styles. They might have been prettier if they'd tried less.

All three dropped very deep curtsies, the young ones stifling giggles.

Roderick bowed neatly, then gestured to his herald, who read off the proclamation about the glass slipper again.

With the proclamation as cover noise, I asked Catherine, "Which one is Ella?"

"None of them. Ella's the third sister. Stepsister to these two, actually, and that's her stepmother." She smiled slightly. "So you and I and probably Roderick all know that neither of those girls is the right one, but what do you want to bet we go through the nonsense of having them try on the glass slipper anyway?"

"I don't take losing bets."

We were both right. Even though it was pointless, apparently ceremony and protocol had to be followed. The herald produced a seat, and with grand flourishes Roderick tried the shoe on each of the stepsisters. Not surprisingly, both had feet too big for the slipper.

"Do you have another daughter?" Roderick asked the stepmother.

Her expression was much too innocent to be believable. "Oh no, no one. Just my two lovely girls. Are you sure they mightn't try the slipper again?"

"Don't be ridiculous," Catherine said, stepping forward, hands on her hips. "Where's Ella?"

"Ella who?" the stepmother asked in an unnaturally high voice.

Catherine just rolled her eyes. "I'll try the kitchen." She pushed past the stepsisters, and disappeared inside.

"Lovely weather lately, isn't it?" Roderick remarked conversationally, as we all waited.

"I really think my daughters ought to try that slipper on again. Don't you think so, girls?"

They thought so. Before we were actually subjected to that, Catherine reemerged, one hand around the wrist of another girl.

I scratched behind one ear and studied this new girl with the sudden worry that Marj had given me the wrong directions after all. I couldn't see any resemblance to that sparkly pink girl at the dance. This girl's clothes were badly patched, she had a handkerchief tied over her hair, and there were smudges of soot on her face. If she was the right one, Marj had clearly gone to an extreme about finding a non-princess to help.

Although there was no reason extremism from Marj should surprise me.

I caught a flash of doubt for a second on Roderick's face too, before he hid it away again with proper charming princeliness. Who would have guessed he really could turn that on when he wanted to? He gestured Ella to the seat, and gallantly tried the glass slipper on one dirty foot.

The shoe fit her just as easily as it had fit Catherine. I heard a communal intake of breath from the crowd, and I let out a sigh of relief.

Just to clinch the thing, Ella reached into the pocket of her tattered skirt and drew out the match to the glass shoe. She slipped that one on as well, and an instant later a shower of pink sparkles spread over her. When the sparkles cleared, the soot was gone and the tattered dress had transformed into an elegant, shining pink one.

"You really are the pretty girl from the ball," Roderick exclaimed.

"I knew you'd come find me," she said, smiling sweetly at him.

And that was all the attention I paid to that little scene, because I had recognized those sparkles. I didn't even need magic to find the source; a quick glance around and I spotted Marj hovering near the edge of the crowd. I pushed through a line of guards to reach her.

She gazed at Ella and Roderick with hands clasped, her eyes shining in her best "isn't it all so romantic" look.

I didn't care in the slightest. "Marj, I really need to—"

She snapped one hand up, palm out. "I'm not speaking to you."

"*Marj*—"

A shield flashed up between us. I poked it with one finger. There was a crackle of sparks—pink ones, of course. I poked once, twice, threefourfivesixseveneight.

No useful results. The only result at all was that Marj glared at me, waved her hands, and vanished from sight. I could tell in a vague way that she was still present, but when I couldn't tell anything more than vaguely, I wasn't going to get far with a conversation.

I glared at the spot Marj had vacated. Of course it would be too much to ask that we might talk to Marj, get her to see reason about Anthony, and solve everyone's problems in one afternoon. The world just wasn't that considerate.

Shoulders slouching, I turned back to the focus of everyone else's attention. I don't think any of them, not even Catherine, had noticed my brief interaction with Marj. It had taken only a matter of seconds, they were all distracted looking the other direction, and with the pink sparkles going on around Ella, Marj was blending into the surroundings much more than she usually did.

I drifted back into the crowd, drifted back next to Catherine. I didn't bother telling her about Marj. It wouldn't help anything. Instead, I asked, "Do you know Ella well?"

Catherine shrugged. "Not very well. A little. I did offer her a job at The Nightingale once."

"Really?" Catherine was so protective of her inn, I was surprised she'd make a job offer to a girl she only knew slightly. Although she'd made an offer quickly enough to Anthony—so maybe it was really that I was surprised she didn't know better someone she was willing to offer a job to.

"Mm-hmm. Everyone in the neighborhood knows that her family doesn't treat her well. Not the kind of thing that you report to the City Guard, but they make her do all the work around the house and—well, you could see her clothes. We needed a new upstairs maid about a year ago, so I asked her if she was interested. It doesn't pay a lot but it was also room and board, and better than her situation here." Catherine shook her head, and her lip curled into a disgusted expression. "She said she didn't think her stepmother would approve."

I raised an eyebrow. "But wasn't that the whole point? To get out so her stepmother's approval wouldn't matter?"

"Exactly! But I couldn't seem to get that idea through to her, that it was a step she could take to become independent and change her life for the better." Catherine folded her arms, staring at Ella. "She told me that when it was time for her life to change, Fate would step in, and she'd wait until then."

I looked at Roderick speculatively. "I suppose it happened." Or maybe Marj was playing the role of Fate here. Neither Marj nor Roderick was someone I'd want to leave *my* fate up to.

"I suppose," Catherine said. "But I'd rather make my life for myself than wait until it's made for me. There's no telling what it will be made into, if you don't take any hand in the making."

And that attitude was why I'd rather help a Catherine than help an Ella, any day of the week.

I wondered if Leonard had known more about the owner of the glass slipper than the rest of us. With his magic, it was possible. That could be another reason he'd been in favor of Catherine, over Ella, as a bride for Roderick. It didn't sound like Ella would have had much will for him to drain.

At the center of the crowd, Roderick was still gushing about how pretty Ella was, and she was still gushing about how sure she'd been that he would come find her. Which might have been touching (maybe) if I didn't know he wasn't the right one to thank for that. After a minute or so more gushing, Roderick, still playing the perfect prince, very romantically swept her into his arms and kissed her.

There were sighs and exclamations and scattered applause among the crowd in response.

I glanced at Catherine, and surprised a wistful expression. "Surely you're not feeling jealous now."

She jumped. "What? No, of course not. Not really. Not exactly. Well…" She sighed. "Maybe sort of."

"Please don't tell me you've suddenly decided that you want Roderick after all." After all this trouble to get her out of an engagement, if I had to get her back *into* it…not to mention explore the possibility that Leonard's magic had seriously unbalanced her mind.

"*No*," she said with a shudder. "Don't give me nightmares, no, I *do not* want Roderick. It's just…" Her glance drifted back towards Ella and the prince. "Let's say I'm jealous of the situation she's in, not of who she's in it with." The wistfulness lasted just a moment longer, and then she shook herself. "But standing here moping about it won't help any. I don't think Roderick is going to pay attention to us anymore. Let's go home and figure out how we can get into that castle in Beaumont and rescue Anthony."

We held council of war around the table in The Nightingale's kitchen, with Catherine's father, Jack, Emmy, and the rest of the staff. Like Anthony had said, the staff at The Nightingale was a family, and everyone wanted to be part of the discussion on how to rescue their missing member. After an hour of wrangling, we arrived at a plan. A plan I would have felt better about if we hadn't reached it mostly by ruling out all other possibilities.

The fastest way to get to Cesar's castle in Beaumont would be to transport directly by magic, but that was out due to Marj's spell. I could only transport if I knew where I was transporting to, or who I was transporting near. I didn't know anyone or anyplace in Beaumont outside of the castle, and the castle was blocked. The closest I was sure I could get anyone was the border. From there, we'd need a new form of transportation.

Catherine's initial idea was that I could fly her to the castle in dragonform, but the truth was that I just wasn't a big enough dragon, especially not trying to carry her over mountains. I might barely be able to do it, but the effort would leave me virtually defenseless should we encounter anything winged and nasty up there. Beaumont had an uncomfortably high number of flying monsters. Hippogryphs were just one of too many examples.

That put us on horseback, and since I could turn lizards into horses if necessary, that was a perfectly viable option. Beaumont had plenty of monsters at ground-level too, but I felt better about the odds of fighting from the ground. I didn't feel perfect about those odds, but I felt *better*. That left the remaining problems on the human side.

Catherine's father did not approve of any of this. "I still think this journey is too dangerous, Catherine. Beaumont is still in anarchy, overrun by monsters. You shouldn't risk it."

"Father, we've been over this already." We had. Twice. "I told you, I have to do this."

He frowned at her, arms tightly crossed. "You just escaped from one dangerous situation. I don't like the idea that you're throwing yourself immediately into another."

I was slightly gratified to see I wasn't the only one who felt the crises were coming altogether too close together, in an exhaustingly unfair sort of way.

We had filled in Catherine's family and the rest of the staff on recent events, without mentioning just how very seriously in danger she'd been towards the end of that fight with Leonard; it wasn't something she wanted her father to hear. Since I didn't want to get blamed, that was fine with me. They still knew the situation had been bad enough.

"Couldn't Tarragon go on his own?" Mr. Williams asked.

Catherine's hands were white-knuckled where they curled on the table. "Father, *no*. I need to go. If Tarry goes alone and it goes badly, Marjoram will find new ways to keep him out. Which could make a second trip even harder, if not impossible. So we can't afford to be cautious; we have to try everything right at once."

That *everything* we might try was uncomfortably vague. Once I was there, I might find a way around Marj's spell to free Anthony, but I had no guarantee that a way even existed. I also should be able to splash enough magic around at the castle to make Marj come to us, opening the door for an argument with her, but I *really* hoped that wouldn't be necessary. The idea that the future could depend on changing Marj's mind made me queasy. Not too queasy to stop eating, but still.

I swallowed a mouthful from the loaf of bread I'd been working through (the third loaf, actually), and contributed, "If it comes down to talking to Marj, Catherine's much more likely to accomplish anything than I am. Marj and I have been arguing for centuries. I don't usually get far." Catherine's force of personality was a good point in our favor, and I'd take any reassurance.

All of this was, in the end, long odds, and I was pretty sure Catherine knew it too. That was really why she was insistent on going. She wanted to be with Anthony, and since he was in Beaumont she had to go to Beaumont, whatever the results turned out to be. She hadn't said that out loud; it would have made it sound as though she wasn't coming back, and I could see how she wouldn't want to say that to her father.

The arguments we did offer didn't make Mr. Williams happy about the idea, but he finally gave a reluctant nod.

"So that settles it then," I said. "Catherine and I are going, by horseback."

Jack cleared his throat. "I'm coming too."

"That's not necessary," I protested. I felt bad enough taking one fragile human into a dangerous country. I didn't want to risk someone else too.

"This is going to take several days, right? Do you know anything about camping?" Jack challenged me.

Not really, no. Picked up a bit in the army, but not much. "I can conjure up an entire house if I need to," I countered.

"Which would attract attention, and waste all the magic energy you'll need to deal with whatever monsters you attract," Jack countered in turn.

I hesitated. That was unfortunately reasonable. "Yeah. Well." I wanted to appreciate all this new confidence he'd gained since the day we were facing down a magical thorn hedge, but it wasn't so convenient when he was going to confidently argue with me.

"I don't know much about fighting monsters or breaking curses," Jack said, voice firm, "but traveling and camping are things I know how to do, and you'll need help with that part too."

"And I'm going too," Emmy announced.

Jack turned his head to stare at her, immediately on the other side of this argument. "Now wait a minute, that's a completely different proposition!"

"If you're going, I'm going," Emmy said, mouth set in a stubborn line. "I can help cook."

"*I* can cook," Catherine said.

"I can help," Emmy repeated. "And besides, you don't know what you're going to get into once you're there. You might find that you need a couple more people in your corner."

I conceded the argument at that point, and Catherine gave in on the subject too, after a while longer. Jack took the longest to finally agree to Emmy coming.

"Anyway," Emmy said, once the question was settled, "more people ought to make it less dangerous, right? A larger group would scare off a few monsters."

"Probably right," I acknowledged. It was one reason I was willing to agree; at least I might be taking them into less danger. "Four's a good number. Large enough to keep some minor threats at bay, but not big enough to attract too many major monsters."

"About those *major monsters*," Mr. Williams began.

Oops. "Which we probably won't meet," I said hastily. "Extremely unlikely that we'll encounter them. No reason they should notice us. And if they do, hey, that's why there's a fairy along. No problem." I grinned as unconcernedly as I could, and chomped into my bread again.

I hoped there would be no problem, anyway. I knew now that bodily wrestling with a hippogryph was probably not the best way to handle that situation, and I had confidence that I could throw shields up and launch flames at any monsters; most monsters wouldn't think as fast or as creatively as Leonard.

Truthfully, I would have had more confidence that we could defeat a monster if anyone in our proposed party had known anything about fighting, but I didn't mention that. Jack did know something about fighting with a staff, which could be useful for any monsters smaller than, say, a goat.

We talked on about details and plans and further logistics, until we started to think about preparing supper. By 'we,' I mostly mean me (I was hungry) and Catherine, who felt it was suppertime. She was just getting me intrigued by a discussion about a baked egg and cheese dish when there was a knock at the door.

"I'll get it," Sam said, and left the kitchen for the main room.

Marion shot a glance after him. "Look out for the—"

There was a yelp and a thud, swiftly followed by a voice saying, "Sorry. I'm all right."

Marion sighed. "We rearranged the tables last week and he keeps bumping into the chair nearest the kitchen."

Mostly intent still on the egg and cheese prospects, I only half-listened to the sound of footsteps continuing to the door, and the door opening.

"Hello, welcome to The Nightingale," Sam said. "Is there something we can do for you?"

"I think so," a new voice responded, and my attention snapped fully to the proceedings in the main room. It was a new voice to this conversation, but not, unfortunately, new to me. "I'm looking for…well, she has brown hair. I think she lives here. Only she was at the castle until recently."

"You mean Catherine?"

"That's the one! I'm looking for Catherine."

Catherine had her head in her hands. "Don't tell me. It can't be. I refuse to believe it."

"Maybe I can divert him," I said, rising to my feet. "I'll tell him you left the country."

But even as I spoke, I also heard Sam saying, "She's back this way," and two pairs of footsteps came towards the kitchen.

I shot a querying look at Catherine, who looked at me through her fingers and said, "He'll just keep searching for me here, so let's face him down and have done with it."

It was nice, seeing her back to normal. I sat down again, and a moment later Sam entered the kitchen, followed by a man wearing a cloak with the hood pulled up over his head.

He pushed the hood back almost at once, turning towards Catherine. "There you are. I was looking for you."

She looked up at him and frowned. It was a frown that would have made me leave. He didn't even seem to notice it. "Why are you here, Roderick?"

"Roderick?" Marion repeated, voice wavering up to a higher register than usual. "*Prince* Roderick?"

She was halfway through a curtsy when he waved his hand at her. "No, no, don't. I'm here incognito."

Marion wobbled upright again, and started patting at her hair distractedly.

Roderick dropped into a chair at the table. "I wanted to talk to you," he told Catherine, then glanced at me. "You too. Probably."

Catherine folded her arms and stared at him. "You forgot my name again."

Roderick grimaced, running a hand through his hair. "Do you *have* to keep sticking on that point? I admit names are useful when trying to find someone, but I found you anyway, so what's the problem?"

Right. Because names don't matter for anything else. Some princes, I swear.

"Why aren't you with…" Catherine's eyes narrowed. "The girl with the glass slipper. Do you remember *her* name?"

Roderick shrugged. "I'll learn it eventually."

"Ella. It's Ella."

"Right. I'll learn it. I'll need to know it for the wedding ceremony, but there's plenty of time until then. Anyway, never mind about that right now." He leaned forward with a conspiratorial air. "You're going to go rescue your friend. Right?"

I was slightly impressed that he had remembered our business at all. For Roderick, that was deeply considerate.

Judging by Catherine's glare, she felt differently. "You mean *Anthony*?"

"Sure, if you say so," Roderick agreed. "So I heard you two talking about getting him away from someone in Beaumont. You're going to go try to do that, aren't you?"

"From my cousin Marjoram," I said, purely on principle because I didn't really care if he remembered Marj's name, "and yes, we are. What about it?"

"I've decided I'm coming with you," Roderick said, and smiled.

No one else smiled back.

"You're joking, right?" Catherine said into the surprised silence.

"I want an adventure, and you have one," Roderick said. "There's mountains and monsters and it's all very dangerous and exciting and I want to go. It's what princes do."

Mr. Williams cleared his throat. "How dangerous?"

Catherine groaned. "Father, we'll be fine. *Without* His Royal Highness."

Roderick leaned back in his chair, somehow managing to sit smugly. "I'm probably crazy, but I have this strange feeling you don't want me to come."

"You *are* crazy, and it's not a strange feeling at all," Catherine snapped. "I don't want you to come."

His eyebrows rose. "Why not?"

"We don't like you," I said. I pride myself on my diplomacy, but clearly Roderick required a verbal bash over the head to get anything through to him.

"You don't? That's odd." He looked thoughtful for a moment, then shrugged. "Oh well. I still think I should come with you."

Fairy Queen help me, I hadn't bashed hard enough.

Catherine rubbed one temple. "We don't want you to come, so why don't you just go home?"

Roderick shook his head. "No, I can't do that. There's going to be all kinds of fuss about weddings and dresses and nonsense like that going on at home. That girl with the slipper—"

"*Ella*," at least four of us said in unison.

"—right, on the carriage ride back to the castle all she wanted to talk about was shoes and dresses. She'll get the whole castle blathering about that too, all the girls will be fluttering around discussing weddings instead of me, and it won't be any fun at home for months. I'd rather go with you." He raised his chin, probably going for regal but coming off arrogant. "Besides, you need me."

Maybe verbal bashing was too subtle, maybe I needed to actually hit him with something. A very big stick, maybe.

Catherine was glaring again. "I don't ever need you for anything."

"What do you know about traveling through mountains?" Roderick asked.

"I know a little," I said, which was more or less true. I'd been in mountains, over mountains, under mountains…I hadn't actually ridden on horseback with a group of humans through the mountains, though.

Roderick nodded smartly. "I've done extensive hunting in the Fallaron Mountains. I know all about traveling through mountains. And I'm excellent at fighting monsters."

It suddenly occurred to me that princes did, in fact, learn how to fight. And Roderick had been out hunting the day his herald carried off Catherine, so that fit. And hadn't I heard a story somewhere about Prince Roderick and a hippogryph hunt?

All right, so he was an idiot, but if he was an idiot who knew how to fight hippogryphs…

Mr. Williams was already convinced. "If having him go with you would reduce the risk, then he should go. Maybe he could bring some soldiers. A company or two."

"No, no good," I objected. "That many people would just attract attention. It'd bring more monsters onto us."

"I'll go alone," Roderick declared, and somehow conveyed a heroic pose while sitting down. "It would be more exciting that way. Companies of soldiers can be so disciplined sometimes."

Catherine didn't budge. "You're not going with us, alone or otherwise, and—"

"Wait a minute, Catherine," I interrupted, "maybe he should come."

"*Tarry!*"

"No, I mean it." I never would have guessed I'd wind up on Roderick's side in an argument against Catherine, but here we were.

"Roderick, you know how to fight monsters? Like hippogryphs and ogres?"

Roderick smiled winningly, in his best princely fashion. "Absolutely. I've taken down five hippogryphs, single-handedly."

This was probably exaggeration, but I also doubted that Roderick was smart enough to think of making it up from nothing. "I think we should take him. He might be able to help, and the most important thing is that this works." And that the fragile humans not get eaten by monsters while on my watch. Roderick wouldn't be my first choice for support—just off the top of my head, there was a wandering adventurer I'd met recently who would have been much pleasanter company—but Roderick was what we had to work with.

Catherine stared at me for a long moment, brow furrowed. Finally she said, "All right. I agree he can come on one condition." She turned to Roderick. "What's my name?"

There was a long pause. And I really wanted to bring someone who knew how to fight hippogryphs, and really didn't want everyone to get killed. She wasn't looking at me, so I mouthed her name to him.

"Catherine!" he said triumphantly.

Her gaze whipped around to me, eyes suspicious. I tried to look back, lost my nerve and took a nervous bite of more bread. She shook her head, and muttered, "I was sure you wouldn't get it. But fine, you can come."

"Excellent!" Roderick said, beamed, and did the colossally stupid thing of adding, "You know, you could be more grateful about me helping you."

If he'd been closer, I would have kicked him.

"If I thought for a moment that *helping me* mattered to you, I would be," Catherine said, rising to her feet. "I'm starting supper. It's going to be late again, I'm sure."

Chapter Twenty-Three

To my and Catherine's mutual if differently-inspired dismay, supper was in fact late again. That still didn't prevent us from getting out at dawn the following morning. Roderick turned up at daybreak in the yard of The Nightingale with his horse, an extravagant black stallion named Midnight. He was just the sort of horse a prince would ride. For the rest of us, I transformed lizards into horses. They didn't have the bloodlines of Roderick's charger, but they did have good dispositions. Lizards, as a rule, tend to be calm creatures.

After a fair amount of flurry and hubbub and last minute shouts of advice from those staying behind, I transported myself, Catherine, Jack, Emmy, Roderick, the horses, the supplies and all, to the border with Beaumont. I landed us just on the far side of the wall, the nearest point to Cesar's castle that I could get an accurate fix on. It wasn't all that close, meaning we had several days of riding before us.

Within an hour, no one was speaking to Roderick. That was wasted effort, considering he rode on blissfully unaware that he was being shunned.

Catherine rode in the lead near the beginning, but gave up the place—reluctantly—to Roderick once we got into the mountains proper. We quickly fell into a pattern: Roderick in the lead, Catherine and I a bit behind him, Jack and Emmy together bringing up the end, leading an extra horse carrying supplies.

Catherine was quiet most of the morning. That wasn't a good sign, but at least this time I was reasonably sure she was just preoccupied, not having her will drained by an evil magician. Around midday, she started asking me questions about Beaumont.

"My information's a century out of date, remember," I warned. "I haven't been here since the king was removed and everything went wild. It was a nice country back then, mostly villages and farms. I went to some good weddings put on by local farmers. They used to make this traditional roast pig with seventeen herbs and—"

"What about the magic?" Catherine interrupted, fingers tight on her reins. "And all these monsters everyone keeps warning us about. Where were they then?"

I swallowed, and shook myself out of my memories of juicy slices of ham dripping with fat and seasoned with…never mind. The magic. "Beaumont always had more dramatic magic than in other countries. It has to do with, oh, cosmic converges of magical forces, and also with simpler things like where communities happened to settle a thousand years ago. Point is, the monsters used to be more like local color than actual dangers. But then when the king disappeared, all the interspecies treaties dissolved, and matters got…out of hand." I hadn't been in Beaumont, but I'd heard about what had happened. It had been practically the only topic of conversation at parties for a few depressing years. "Thousands of humans fled near the beginning."

She nodded. "Like Anthony's family, a few generations ago."

"Exactly." I scratched behind the point of one ear. "I suppose some people still leave as refugees now, but you don't hear much about that anymore."

"We've had a few travelers come through The Nightingale," Catherine said, gaze on the horizon. "Beaumont sounds like it's still a terrible place to live. Anyone who's staying can't leave."

I shifted uncomfortably in my saddle. "Yeah, well, I suppose. So you already know about the country?"

"Just rumors. I thought you might have been there."

"No," I said, and stared at my horse's ears. "Not in a long time." Because I didn't go to terrible places to live. Who would choose to do that?

"How long do you think it'll take to get to the castle?" Catherine asked.

I was hazy on that. "I've never traveled the distance like this before, and I don't know the state of the roads or what problems we might run into before we get out of the mountains, or even *after* we get out of the mountains—"

She interrupted me with, "Give me a rough estimate."

I knew she wasn't going to like this. "Four days. Maybe five. Roughly."

She didn't comment, but the guilty twist in my stomach made me all too aware of her frown.

"Not soon enough?" I asked.

"The only thing that would be soon enough would be immediate." The frown softened, but her expression stayed worried. "I just…it wouldn't be so bad if I knew what was going on. I could live with a five-day trip if I knew everything was all right. If I knew that the crazy Good Fairy hadn't decided to expand her statue collection."

"I'm fairly sure I'd know about that if it happened," I said, trying to offer what I could. "I spent days with Anthony recently and I'm fairly sure I'd pick up on something that dramatic happening to him."

Catherine was not the type to take comfort easily. "Fairly sure? How sure is fairly sure?"

If I had had time to set up the right warning spells, I could have been more certain, but Marj had banished me too quickly. "Maybe eighty percent."

She sighed. "I guess that'll have to do for now."

I could think of no further reassurance, so we just rode on in silence.

On that first day of riding through the mountains, we saw two dragons, one hippogryph, and what might have been a roc but could have been a gryphon. All were flying overhead in the far distance (hence my uncertainty regarding the roc-or-gryphon) and none took notice of us. That was at least in part because I had cast a take-no-notice spell, although on a group as large as we were, such a spell is chancy at best. Plus it tends to be much less effective on magical beasts than on humans.

While watching for monsters and ignoring Roderick, I also mulled over my conversation with Catherine. First it was just in that way that things making me feel guilty inevitably repeat again and again in my mind—but eventually I got onto more productive mulling, and by the time the shadows grew long and Roderick announced we should look for a campsite, I had an idea. I wasn't even fairly sure it would work, but it might.

I reined in my horse and waved at Catherine to do the same, then told the others, "Why don't you ride on and find somewhere to camp? I want to try a spell to find out about what's ahead. We'll catch up."

"Do you think it's a good idea to split up?" Jack asked.

"I have lots of warning spells set up. If anything happens to you, I'll know about it right away and transport there."

"All right," Jack said, shot Roderick a look, and lowered his voice to say, "But why do we have to get stuck with him?"

"Oh come on, Jack," Emmy said, "it won't be that bad."

Jack shook his head but followed Emmy, both behind Roderick who had ridden right along without us.

The trail here was wide, with plenty of room to dismount. I slid down from my horse, and cast a quick spell to make sure neither of our horses wandered off.

"So what are we doing exactly?" Catherine asked, following me a few paces away from the horses. "And why did you want them to ride ahead while you found out about the trail?"

"It's not the trail we're finding out about. I was thinking of farther ahead than that." I crouched down and smoothed a space in the dust. "I've got this idea, and if it works, we're going to be invading Anthony's privacy. I thought we'd be better off doing that without a crowd."

She kneeled down next to me quickly at that news. "What are you going to do?"

"I don't know if this is going to work," I cautioned, slightly alarmed by her eagerness. If I couldn't make this happen for her, I was going to feel even worse. "Marj's spell might interfere."

She nodded tightly and asked, "What are you trying to do?"

"If it works, we can at least see what's going on at the castle. Now shh, let me concentrate."

She bit her lip, didn't say anything else, and I focused on my spell. I magically reached out towards my sense of Anthony—I could still feel him, somewhere behind the haze of Marj's magic, but it was all blurry and vague. I sharpened my focus, pushed past what felt like gauzy swathes of sparkles, wrapped around in endless layers. When I had as good a read as I could on Anthony, I brought in the second part of my spell. All I could know by sensing Anthony was that he was still alive, and I was after more than that.

As the power of the spell grew, the smooth patch on the ground in front of us began to glow. I fed it more power, batted back at the strangling gauze trying to slide into my way. Another push of magical energy, the glow flashed and transformed into images, like looking through a window onto a scene miles away.

Most of my focus was on a magical level, but I heard Catherine inhale sharply.

The scene showed a cluster of people sitting around a table, spread with the remnants of supper. Anthony was in the center of the picture, poking with a knife at a mostly full plate. George, sitting on Anthony's right, had a full plate too, but from the way he was going through it—quickly—he was probably on a second round. Connor was sitting at the table too, an empty plate pushed aside to make room for a stack of papers he was looking over. A few more empty plates indicated previous diners had already gone. The only other person still at the table was Beauty, peeling an orange and looking critically at Anthony.

"We can hear and see," I told Catherine, "but it doesn't work both ways; they're not aware of us."

Catherine nodded, leaning in closer.

We were plainly joining a conversation that was already in progress. "Really, Anthony," Beauty was saying, "can't you at least try to be happy here?"

Anthony stabbed a carrot. "No, I cannot 'try to be happy here.' Doing that would imply that I'm *staying* here. I don't accept that."

Streamers of sparkles battered at my spell, trying to block me out again. It took most of my concentration to keep the connection open, so

I didn't have much mental space to think about what I was seeing as it went by.

"Sometimes we all have to accept situations we don't like," Beauty said, eyes wide with sympathy and smile sweet.

"That is true," George remarked around a mouthful of goose.

Anthony ignored George, and scowled at Beauty. "Don't preach platitudes at me. And sometimes not accepting a situation is the only way it ends up changing."

"That's true too," George said, reaching for another piece of bread.

"Why do you feel so sure it would be best to change anything?" Beauty asked, head tilting. "Is it so horrible here?"

"She has a point; it's really not horrible here," George agreed.

Anthony shook the carrot off his knife, glaring at his plate as though it was what was bothering him. "It doesn't matter whether it's horrible here; I don't have a choice about being here. *That's* what's horrible."

"That's hard to argue with," George acknowledged.

"But if you made half an effort to be content here," Beauty said, "maybe you'd find that this is what you'd choose anyway."

"Though now that she mentions it—"

"Will you just stay out of it, George?" Anthony snapped.

George looked wounded. "I just think that you both have good points."

"You're not helping anything by saying so."

"Yes, George, I think you'd better let us talk," Beauty said, voice gentle.

George sighed and muttered, "I get no respect. The oldest one, and I get no respect." He looked mournfully at his plate for a moment longer, then shrugged and returned to eating.

Beauty and Anthony returned to their discussion. "Could you try to understand this?" Anthony said. "Please? It doesn't make *any* *difference* whether it's nice here. The point is that this isn't my life.

This is your life, and I don't want to live your life. I can't. My life is out there, and I want to go back to it."

Beauty nodded understandingly. "I'm sure you miss Catherine very much."

Anthony flinched, jaw going tight. "Are you even listening? That's not—I mean, *yes*, of course, but that's not the point."

"I know just how you feel about missing someone," Beauty continued blithely, gesturing with an orange wedge. "Cesar and I were only apart for nine days but—"

"Please don't compare my relationship to yours," Anthony said evenly, gaze fixed somewhere above his sister's head.

Beauty's lips thinned into a line. "You don't like him."

"Let's say I'm cautious about liking him," Anthony said. "He kept you captive for months and we didn't know what had happened to you. It's hard to suddenly turn around and accept him as family. To suddenly believe that he's the hero in the story."

Beauty was smiling again. That hadn't taken long. "But you don't understand what it was like for those months. He did everything he could to make me happy."

Anthony's hand tightened where it held his supper knife. "He was still holding you captive."

"It's not as though I was locked in a dungeon," Beauty said with a slight laugh.

"But you *weren't free to leave*," Anthony said, knuckles turning white. "That makes you a prisoner. Just like it makes me a prisoner right now."

Connor looked up from his papers. "Actually—"

"Stay out of it," Anthony interrupted.

"Yes, do let us discuss this ourselves, Connor," Beauty said, in softer tones.

Connor's eyebrows rose. "Do you even want to know who I was going to agree with?"

"*No.*"

"Not especially."

Connor shrugged, picked up his papers, leaned back in his chair and held the pages up in front of his face to continue reading.

"I wasn't exactly a prisoner," Beauty resumed. "He did allow me to leave, after all."

Anthony shook his head. "After months. And only after you promised to come back."

"But that was because he wanted me to be with him," Beauty said. "When I told him I wanted to go home, he said that I was free to do whatever I wished, even if it meant his death."

"His death?" Anthony repeated, brow wrinkling in confusion, irritation or both. "Why would your leaving cause his death?"

Another sweet smile from Beauty. "Because he would die of grief."

Anthony stared at her. "Wait, he actually told you that? When you asked to leave, he *told* you that he'd die of grief if you did?"

Beauty nodded. "If I stayed away. It was very romantic."

"That's not romantic," Anthony growled, "that's manipulative and controlling."

"He left the decision to me," Beauty maintained.

"But he'd been living with you for months. Long enough to know that you wouldn't do something if you thought it would kill him. Which makes it *manipulative and controlling.*" Anthony tipped back in his chair and glared towards the ceiling. "Maybe you're right, maybe he's as wonderful as you say, I don't know. But I do know I would never tell Catherine that something she wanted to do was going to kill me. That's a horrible thing to say to someone."

"He was only telling me the truth," Beauty said, folding her hands primly on the table. "I told you that he was dying when I returned."

"Yes, because he was starving himself," Anthony said. "That's not romantic; it's unhealthy."

Connor coughed then, and looked over his papers to send a pointed glance at Anthony's full plate.

Anthony sent a bit of the glare towards Connor, and pushed the plate towards George. "I'm not hungry. I'm not deliberately starving myself. It's not the same."

Connor didn't comment. George took a plum off of Anthony's plate.

"The point is," Anthony continued, "separation from someone you love is not an illness. It doesn't automatically cause death." His voice dropped down to a mutter. "If it does, then someone needs to explain to me why I'm still breathing."

Beauty smiled, and the remarkable part was that there wasn't even any edge in it. She really did mean well, and she really was that nice. "Perhaps you simply don't feel as deeply as—"

Anthony's chair, tipped onto two legs, clattered back to all four. We could feel the sudden rise in tension just watching, and it must have been even more palpable in the room. Beauty stopped talking, George stopped eating, and Connor looked up from his papers.

"Don't tell me," Anthony said in a low, dangerous voice, "that I don't love her. Or that I don't love her enough. Or that it doesn't count as much because there are no spells or curses involved. Don't ever try to tell me that."

He pushed up from the table, and strode out of the room.

I didn't know about Catherine, but *I* didn't feel any better having watched this. I had known Anthony must be upset, but it was easier having that just be a vague guess, not a visible reality.

A wave of sparkles slammed into my spell, taking advantage of my distraction, and the image on the ground wavered.

"Don't break the spell yet!" Catherine said, voice ragged. I looked at her for the first time since launching this spell, was alarmed to see tears in her eyes. So much for cheering her up.

"You know he's alive and not a statue," I said, afraid this was only going to get worse if we kept watching. "Why not leave it at that?"

Catherine's gaze was fixed on the blurring image, which I kept reluctantly open but held on the dining room. I'd have to batter at Marj's spells again to follow Anthony to a new location.

"Oh dear," Beauty said. "He's obviously upset. Perhaps I should go after him."

"Or maybe I—" George began.

"I'll go," Connor said, setting down his papers and standing up.

"Let me see him for a few more minutes. Please." Catherine wrapped her arms around herself, eyes squinting from tears and the effort to see through the haze. "Let me see what Connor says to him. I need to know he's all right, and he's *not*."

I hesitated. "This is about to be a much more private conversation—and at least you know he's not going to throw himself off a parapet, that seems obvious from recent conversation, so whatever happens, he'll be fine…"

"Tarry, *please*."

I'm too soft by half. "All right, all right. A few more minutes."

I sharpened my focus again, pushed past more clinging streamers of sparkles, and reached for my sense of Anthony again. The picture cleared, bobbed about the castle a little, and centered again on Anthony, out on the front steps before a wide double-door. The front of the castle was decorated with a multitude of marble pillars, and two statues. I recognized the statues, and knew too much to feel comfortable about them: Miranda and Noreen. Anthony was standing against a pillar, arms crossed, staring at the statues. My spell steadied on him just as Connor approached.

"If you were trying to pick a fight," Connor said, "you chose the wrong person." He sat down on the top step. "You should have tried George or me."

Anthony shook his head. "You would have reasoned with me, and George would've broken my nose. Neither is something I wanted."

"What did you want?"

Anthony sighed. "I don't even know." He slid down to sit against the pillar. "What I *want* is to not be here anymore."

"Is it that terrible here?" Connor asked, resting his arms on his knees. "I mean, I understand you miss Catherine, but…"

"But that's what no one seems to understand, what I couldn't get Beauty to understand, that's it not about Catherine." He frowned, rubbed the back of his neck. "I mean, it *is* about Catherine, but it's not *only* about Catherine. It's about me, it's about my life, it's about choosing my life. Not having some fairy choose it for me in a blaze of sparkles. I had a life out there. So did you. So did George."

"True. But George has a remarkable and enviable ability to be completely content wherever he is, provided there's good food and pleasant company. And I…" Connor shrugged. "I liked being in the army; there were possibilities for the future there. But I like being here too. There's an entire country that needs to be put back together after a century of neglect. It's fascinating to be involved in that. Necessary, too."

Anthony exhaled loudly, brow dark. "Great. Give George a meal and he's happy, and you have a future career in government. Father is happy as long as Beauty is around, Beauty found her true love, and Miranda and Noreen no longer have the opportunity to feel any way about anything. So that just leaves me. Still wanting the life I used to have. Especially the way it was before the idiot prince started mucking things up."

"Was it really that good?"

Anthony leaned back against the pillar, looked up at the sky. "Yeah. It really was. It was like I'd just been wandering my whole life, and now I had it figured out. What I wanted to do, who I wanted to be. I mean, there was Catherine, and that's…" He shook his head, grinning. "I can't even describe that. But it wasn't just Catherine; I really do like running an inn. I think even if I hadn't fallen in love with Cat, I'd still want to run The Nightingale."

"Oh good," Catherine said softly.

I risked taking a little attention away from holding back sparkles and maintaining my spell to ask, "What is?"

"Sometimes I wondered if he really wanted to run the inn, or if he just said so because he knew I wanted to."

Catherine didn't seem like the sort to leave a question like that unanswered. "Didn't you ever ask him?"

"Of course. But I wasn't sure if he was just telling me what he thought I wanted to hear. There's no reason he shouldn't tell Connor the truth, though."

I was getting too distracted, and the picture was blurring. I concentrated on my spell again, while Anthony was saying, "So I had it worked out, the life I wanted, and then a sparkly, cheery fairy tells me I can't live that life. We could've dealt with the idiot prince. But this is a whole new mess."

"Maybe she'll be back soon," Connor suggested. "You can talk to her, change her mind."

Anthony shook his head. "No good, you know how fairies flit in and out of places. She might not be back for years."

"She'll probably come for the christening of Beauty and Cesar's first born child," Connor pointed out.

"Even if she is, when's that likely to be? A year? Two? More? And there's no reason to think I could change her mind anyway. She's not going to let me leave until she decides she wants to. That could be never. Or it could be ten years from now. And Cat's set to marry the prince and…" He sighed and looked down, tangling his fingers in his hair. "In ten years she could be married with five heirs."

"Can't we send him a message or something?" Catherine asked. "So at least he'd know what's going on?"

"The way Marj has me blocked out, I can't think of any way to get a message there faster than we can get there ourselves."

"I'm sorry, Tony," Connor said quietly. "It is a problem. What do you think we should do about it?"

Anthony looked at him. "We?"

Connor nodded. "Sure."

"Thanks. But I don't have any idea what we should do. I wish I did."

"Well. You could go apologize to Beauty."

Anthony sighed. "You're right. I should go apologize to Beauty."

Connor stood up first, and extended a hand to Anthony. He hauled him up to his feet, and remarked, "By the way, I was going to agree with you. You are a prisoner. It's not relevant whether it's pleasant here."

"Thank you. That makes me feel as if I might not be crazy to resent the situation after all," Anthony said as they walked back into the castle together.

Catherine leaned back. I took that as my cue to stop fighting Marj's blocking. I let go of my spell, the sparkles rushed swirling in to cut off the connection, and the image on the ground wavered away until there was nothing to be seen but dust.

"Well," I said. "He's not a statue." It was the only positive thing I could think of after that little scene. I had pretended to myself that looking in on Anthony would give us good news, but I should have known better. I *did* know better. This was why I didn't go back, to see people again and find out how their lives had turned out.

Catherine was biting her lower lip again. "You said it was going to be four or five days until we get there?"

"Approximately."

"Damn."

I shot her a surprised look. I don't think she even saw it. She was getting back to her feet, and striding over to her horse. She had mounted by the time I stood up, and was breaking into a canter to rejoin the rest of the group.

After that, I wasn't too surprised when she convinced Roderick we should keep on for another hour. We had four or five days of riding, maybe, but she was clearly intending to make it as rapid a journey as possible.

Chapter Twenty-Four

Catherine eventually agreed to camp that night, still in the mountains, with the prospect of another day or two of mountain riding ahead of us. I had to admit that Roderick had proved valuable so far. He really did know about finding a route through a mountain range, and about the best places for mountain camping. I suppose everyone's good at something. I was torn between satisfaction that I'd been right to bring him, and reluctance to admire anything at all about Roderick.

We set out early the next morning—Catherine was barely willing to allow time for breakfast—and everything proceeded well until we stopped for a midday meal. Roderick had just pulled up in a shallow, basin-like space between crags of rock and boulders, declaring it a good place to stop. He dismounted and the rest of us were about to do the same, when the scattered rocks erupted around us.

What had appeared to be lichen-covered stones uncurled themselves into small, reptilian creatures, unfurling bat-like wings and stretching out long necks. They were grayish-green in color, roughly two feet in length, and fast. The way they writhed about, it was impossible to tell how many of them there were.

And things had been going so well.

Roderick said something idiotic like "Have at ye," drew his sword, and had at them. That sounds more impressive than it was, considering that it turned into him wildly whacking about with his sword at creatures that darted here, there and everywhere, snapping at him, and wouldn't stand still long enough to be hit.

Roderick might really know how to fight, but that didn't mean I wanted to leave our survival up to him. Heart pounding, I did a flip off my horse. I wasn't showing off; it was the fastest way to get down and over to the chaos around Roderick. Once I was standing on the ground, I started throwing balls of flame at the reptiles.

"What are those things?" Catherine demanded, hanging desperately onto her reins as her horse shied.

"They're moving so fast it's hard to tell," I said, launching three more fire-balls as I spoke. "Basilisks, cockatrices, maybe something more exotic."

"More exotic than a cockatrice?" Jack yelled over his horse's whinnying. "I don't want to meet something more exotic than that."

"Too late." I gritted my teeth and threw more fire. I *knew* I was hitting some of them—my aim wasn't perfect, but it was better than Roderick's—but I couldn't see that I was having any effect. I needed a different spell, but without knowing what they were, I didn't know what to use. I tried a general binding spell, but it rolled right off of them.

Out of the corner of my eye, I saw that Emmy had gotten down from her horse and was digging through the bags of supplies on the packhorse. A few moments later she emerged with a small box that she flung at the gray-green crawlies.

Black powder filled the air, and Roderick commenced sneezing. "What—is that?" he managed between explosions

"Pepper," Emmy said, forehead wrinkling. "It works on people…"

One of the crawlies suddenly stopped short and sneezed, letting out a burst of flame. Then it went back to racing about. But a second one stopped and sneezed, and a third one did too, and all with bits and licks of flame.

Emmy groaned. "I don't think that helped."

Actually, it did. "Of course," I said with great satisfaction. "*That's* what they are. Baby dragons!"

That explained why my flames hadn't been effective. What use is fire against fire-breathers? Not bloody much. Baby dragons are impervious to flame; if they weren't, they would've flamed themselves into extinction in the first generation of dragons.

I switched tactics, and switched shapes. I turned into a dragon, filled my much larger lungs, and roared at them. Within moments, six shame-faced baby dragons were sitting in a neat line in front of me, scaly heads bowed.

"I'd've sworn—" Roderick sneezed. "—that there were twenty of them."

I glared sternly at the line of baby dragons. "This is no way to behave. Anyone would think you came out of the egg yesterday. Haven't you learned any manners at all? You can't go swarming about willy-nilly, snapping at princes and breathing fire at perfectly harmless travelers. This sort of thing sets back human/dragon relations for decades. Bite off one prince's head, and you'll have a whole parade of would-be St. Georges coming after you. Do you want that?"

Five baby dragons shook their heads in unison, and I glared hard at the sixth until it shook its head too.

"And besides," I continued, "knowing this prince, he'd probably make you sick for a week if you bit him, which wouldn't be fun for anyone."

"I wouldn't—" Sneeze. "—make anyone—" Sneeze. "—sick!" Roderick protested.

"You make me sick," Catherine muttered.

I spread my wings for emphasis. "Next time, think first and try to be a little more responsible. Are we clear?"

Six nods, and I turned back to the humans. "I think they'll be all right now. So let's get out of here before their mother gets home."

"Wouldn't she be able to control them?" Jack asked.

"Sure, but…" I glanced at the baby dragons, and lowered my voice, "but I have no idea how she feels about the importance of peaceful human/dragon relations. And I don't want to find out."

Roderick was still sneezing, but he mounted up anyway and we went. I stayed a dragon, as a precaution, and Jack led my horse.

We 'd only gone a short way along the trail before Emmy coughed. "Ah, Tarry…behind you."

I looked back over my shoulder. There were six little dragons following me in a row.

"Go home," I ordered. "I am not your mother." I had enough trouble with all these humans I'd somehow adopted. I did not need to start watching over a bunch of baby dragons too.

One of the dragons trilled a comment.

"All right, good, you don't think I'm your mo—"

He trilled another comment.

"No, I am not your father either!"

Emmy was giggling, Jack was chuckling, and even Catherine was smiling. Roderick was still sneezing.

My argument with the baby dragons went on. "I don't care if your mother is gray, and I'm green, and you're gray-green, that doesn't prove anything."

"That's actually a well-reasoned idea," Jack commented.

Oh, because that was helpful. "Stay out of it," I told him. "And go home," I told the dragons. "Now."

They weren't keen on the idea.

Talking was obviously getting us nowhere. I took a more drastic option and changed shape, wings shrinking in, scales disappearing, until I looked human again, apart from my pointed ears. The baby dragons trilled considerable astonishment, two backing up and tripping over their tails in surprise. Apparently they'd been too busy racing and sneezing and snapping at Roderick to notice when I changed the first time.

"So you see," I said, folding my arms. "I'm not related to you."

They accepted that. But then they started looking at each other, and looking at us speculatively in a way I did not approve of at all.

"Don't get any ideas just because I'm not shaped like a dragon anymore," I warned, and when they still tipped their heads thoughtfully and eyes gleamed with mischief, I took a deep breath and roared again.

"That is so much stranger when you do it while looking human," Jack muttered.

It was effective, though. The baby dragons skittered off back along the path, presumably towards home, and we continued on along the trail.

After a half-dozen baby dragons, I hoped we had fulfilled our quota of nasty encounters with magical beasts for a few days. I didn't really believe it, but I hoped.

We finished the day with no serious additional danger, except possibly for Roderick who was only in danger from the rest of us. He talked (a lot) and all of it was about him. His aura, with its shiny mirrors showing hundreds of copies of himself, had not changed when Leonard left the scene. But everyone was still alive and unharmed when we camped for the night, and I, for one, fell asleep.

I woke up shortly before dawn, with Jack shaking my shoulder and yelling my name. This was not remotely my preferred way to wake up.

"What is it?" I groaned. "It's too early; what do you want?"

"Catherine's been carried off by a cyclops, and Roderick went charging off after them!"

I woke up fast after that, bouncing up to a sitting position. "What? Why didn't someone wake me up sooner?" I demanded, heart pounding.

Jack frowned, looking offended. "It just happened. And you're hard to wake up."

That was true. When fairies do something, we really do it; when I sleep, I *really* sleep.

"I swear, these creatures have gotten stronger in the last century," I muttered, struggling out of blankets and up to my feet. Or I had just forgotten how strong they were to begin with. It wasn't like fighting monsters was my favorite occupation. "I had magical guards up, I thought that would keep them out, obviously not, which way did they go? Oh never mind. Stay here where it's safe," I ordered Jack and Emmy, focused on Catherine, and transported.

I'm lucky I didn't end up inside of a rock. That wouldn't be fatal for me, but it would be uncomfortable and take a long time to get out. Where I did end up was in a cave, and a very untidy one. There were rocks and boulders piled up everywhere, as well as less innocuous things. Things like bones. Well-gnawed bones. The cyclops had retreated to his home territory.

The scene I arrived on was in mid-action already. The cyclops, a grimy fellow at least fifteen feet high and nearly as broad, was bellowing. Catherine was standing against one wall of the cave, with the cyclops between her and the exit—but I was relieved to see her hefting a rock in one hand and glaring at the cyclops. Roderick was facing down the monster, brandishing his sword and utilizing all manner of threatening phrases, probably ones he'd rehearsed and memorized.

I let out a breath. Everyone still alive and fighting, so that was all right. Otherwise this could have been the worst oversleeping situation ever.

From the shininess of Roderick's sword, he didn't appear to have stabbed the cyclops yet, who was nevertheless bleeding in a few places. The explanation for that became clear when Catherine threw her chunk of rock, scoring a direct hit on the cyclops' left shoulder blade, and reached for another.

The cyclops bellowed again.

"Serves you right," Roderick said.

"You go away. Just want pretty girl," the cyclops growled. Not real intelligent, cyclopes.

"Yes, well, the pretty girl has her own ideas about that," Catherine snapped, raising her rock.

The cyclops turned towards her, and reached out with one hand. She backed away along the wall, and tripped over a stone. She fell onto her back, the cyclops leaning over her.

Time to get involved. I levitated two dozen rocks and sent them all flying at the cyclops' midsection, hitting with a satisfying thud. He grunted in surprise and pain, and staggered. Roderick took advantage of his moment to spring forward with his sword and stab the cyclops in the leg. That was about as high as he could reach.

That was enough for Friend Cyclops. They're usually cowards at heart. His bellowing took on a pained and dismayed tone. He shuffled past Catherine, who scrambled out of his way, and retreated into the dark depths of the cave.

Roderick took two steps after the cyclops, then stopped, apparently thinking better of pursuit. I quickly conjured up a glowing beacon to place in the cyclops' way in case he thought about coming back. That single eye doesn't handle bright light well.

By the time I'd done that, Roderick had strode over to Catherine, who was still sitting on the ground. "Are you all right?" he asked, and gallantly scooped her up.

I suppose he was trying to be gallant, anyway. She pushed against his chest. "Yes, I'm fine. Put me down."

He didn't put her down. He kissed her.

She slapped him.

He dropped her.

"Ouch," Catherine muttered, and got to her feet.

I wondered if I was now going to have to magically defend…well, either of them, from the other, but they seemed more inclined to argue.

"What did you do that for?" Roderick demanded.

"What did *I* do—what were *you* doing?"

"That was kissing," Roderick said in a superior tone. "If you don't know that, I don't know what that gentleman of yours has—"

"Why were you kissing *me*?"

"Oh, that was mostly habit," Roderick said easily, folding his arms.

Catherine stopped in the midst of straightening her skirt. "You kissed me out of habit?"

"Princes always kiss girls they've rescued. If they're pretty."

"Between you and the cyclops, it's enough to make me wish I was ugly!"

"That doesn't seem reasonable," Roderick said, forehead wrinkling. "I don't see why you'd compare me to the cyclops."

"Maybe *you* don't." Catherine looked around her and shivered. "Can't we get out of here?"

I had been judging that I ought to just stay well out of this conversation, but that sounded like my cue. "Leave it to me." I waved my hand and transported us back to our campsite.

We materialized a little way from the remnants of the fire, where Jack and Emmy were arguing. Jack was saying, "We should go after them," right on top of Emmy's, "He told us to stay here!" Oddly, I rather appreciated both Emmy's respect for my directions *and* Jack's initiative.

They caught sight of us and hurried closer. Emmy hugged Catherine, asking, "Are you all right?"

"I'm fine." She glared over Emmy's shoulder at Roderick. "Though it turned out the cyclops was only my first problem."

"I still don't see what was so awful about kissing you," Roderick complained.

Catherine stepped away from Emmy to face Roderick again, hands on her hips. "I'm engaged. You're engaged. And *not* to each other!"

He sighed loudly. "It was just a kiss. And I told you, it's what princes *do*."

I snorted to myself. No wonder Marj liked royalty, the way she always went on about How Things Are Done.

"What about Ella?" Catherine demanded. "Are you marrying her because that's what's princes do in that sort of situation?"

Roderick frowned, rubbed the back of his neck, and appeared to seriously consider the question. "I think she's pretty. And marrying the most beautiful girl at the ball *is* what's always done. So that's important, yes."

Catherine stared at him for a moment, and finally shook her head. "I didn't think I could miss Anthony more, but somehow you have that effect on me."

Roderick ran a hand through his hair, in a way that looked like a practiced gesture. "I suppose one handsome, charming man reminds you of another."

"No. Somehow I don't think that's it." She turned her head away and stared fixedly at the sunrise.

Jack had his gaze on Roderick, his arms crossed. "Why did I ever think I should be more like a prince?"

"Because we're very admirable, of course," Roderick said, with a winning smile and apparently complete sincerity.

"Sure," Jack said with a grin, and obviously no sincerity at all. "That must be why."

Emmy reached out to give Jack's shoulder a squeeze, smiling at him, and I took a peek at his aura. His aural ship seemed to be sailing better all the time.

It was a cheerful note in an otherwise very strange morning, and it made me feel lighter than I had in a long time.

At least until Catherine cleared her throat and, gaze still on the horizon, said, "It's light out by now; can't we start moving again?"

Nothing wrong with the words, but there was something in her eyes, or maybe her voice caught a bit, and I had the feeling that she wasn't as calm about all of this, about a cyclops and all the rest, as she wanted us to think. I peeked at her aura too, and her garden was still all green and growing—but it wasn't flowering, and that wall was still much higher than it used to be.

I felt like maybe I ought to hug her and promise it would be all right in the end. If I was Anthony, I expect I could have done it. But I was me, and she wouldn't have liked it, so I did what I figured she'd want me to do.

I pretended I hadn't noticed anything, and said, "We may as well start again; I don't think we'll sleep anymore anyway." How could I promise everything would be all right when I didn't know if it would be?

Roderick, as our expert in mountain riding, agreed that it was light enough to travel by. We delayed only long enough for a hasty breakfast, then continued on.

We got out of the mountains a few hours later, rode through the hills and out onto the plains by mid-afternoon. I think we all felt better with wide-open spaces around us, instead of looming and forbidding crags of rock. It did make it easier for high-flying predators to see us, but I kept that thought to myself. Besides, from what I knew of monsters and their habits, and what vague reports had filtered out of

Beaumont in recent decades, I was fairly sure the worst monsters were more prevalent in the mountains than in the plains. That I mentioned, and we all chose to take an optimistic view on the situation.

It grew harder to stay optimistic as the afternoon wore on. We hadn't seen any people in the mountains, and hadn't really expected to, mountains not being the ideal place for settlements. I remembered the plains as rolling farmland, dotted with small villages. The plains had changed.

The road was poor, pitted and pocked, and obviously not well-maintained or well-used. We passed only a few other travelers, a very few, and those handful looked at us with curiosity but no friendliness. We got as far as "good afternoon" and conversation didn't extend beyond that. The most response we received was a few perfunctory nods.

None of the people looked like they had money to spare, and most looked like they didn't even have enough. It wasn't hard to understand why, based on the country around us. We passed more fields lying fallow than planted, and what was planted looked scrabbled and best-effort, not like well-kept and prosperous farms. We went through two abandoned villages, both of them almost completely overgrown with weeds, and I would bet that many of the buildings we saw from a distance were equally deserted.

The trouble wasn't only solid features you could point to, though; it was the atmosphere of the place. An abject hopelessness, a sense that the country had given up.

Near dusk, we came to a farmhouse, with a barn behind it. Both roofs sagged and the yard was dusty, but it looked reasonably respectable and better kept than most of what we'd seen that day. After a brief consultation, we agreed we'd ask for a night's shelter.

"I'll handle this," Roderick decreed, and spurred his horse on ahead of Catherine, who had been in the lead since we left the mountains.

"Roderick, I'm not sure—" Catherine began.

"I know how to be charming," he said firmly. True, we'd seen him be charming, but it was hit-and-miss.

As we rode into the yard, the door of the house opened and a woman stepped out, leaning against the door-frame. She was tight-faced, wearing a worn, faded dress and a hard expression. Two small children peered out from behind her, both with patches on their clothes. The guilty flutters I'd been feeling all day got worse.

"And what do you want?" she asked us, voice as hard as her face.

Roderick swung down from his horse and bowed. "Good madam, we have traveled long and far on this dusty road, and having reached your pleasant home as evening draws on, we crave your hospitality for this night."

He might be overcompensating on the charmingness.

Her eyes narrowed. "You can take your fancy speeches, and your bows, and get back on the dusty road, because I've not the food or the space to share with you."

Roderick looked genuinely flabbergasted. "Do you have any idea who I am?"

"No, and I don't care," she said, moving as though to step back inside the house.

"I am His Most Royal Highness Prince Charles Henry Albert Roderick Michael Irwin Norman Gillian the Third, crown prince and heir apparent of the kingdom of Perrelda."

The woman's face didn't change. "That must be very nice for you," she said flatly.

I ducked my head to hide my grin, and behind me I heard Jack snicker.

Roderick beamed at her. "Yes, it is."

The woman rolled her eyes, stepped back across her threshold and started to swing the door shut.

"Wait, please," Catherine said, urging her horse forward a few steps. "We don't want to impose on you; we just need somewhere to spend the night. We'd pay you, of course."

The woman paused, but the offer of payment wasn't as much of an inducement as Catherine may have hoped. Instead the woman laughed, a brittle laugh, and said, "I suppose you'll give me gold? And then it'll turn to moss and leaves tomorrow night. I'm not going to be taken in by Fool's Gold."

Roderick's chin rose in shocked indignation. "Are you implying that we might cheat you?"

"No, I'm not implying it," the woman said, staring coldly at him. "I'm *saying* it. You may be honest folk; I've no way to know. But a person has to watch for oneself and one's family, and I can't be trusting strangers."

With a pang, I remembered all the parties I had once gone to in Beaumont. All the tables weighted with food, all the welcoming smiles and open hands. The country used to be known for its hospitality. A long time ago.

"We should be continuing on," I said. "We're sorry to have troubled you."

"Would you at least tell us how much farther it is to the castle?" Catherine asked.

"The castle?" The woman snorted. "You mean the site where the castle used to be. A day's ride, maybe less on those fine horses of yours. But I can't see why you'd want to go *there*. No one's had business there since the last king disappeared."

"The king is back," I said. "The castle is too." I clung to the thought. Life might be bad here now, but it was about to change.

The woman nodded. "That rumor's been flying here too. But there's often talk about a new king or a returned king or a great hero. I won't believe it until this country starts to look the way it did before."

"Was it very different?" Emmy asked softly. "Before?"

The woman's gaze drifted to the ground, some of the hard look fading from her eyes. "My mother's grandmother remembered the time before. How it used to be. Rich farmland waving with wheat. Dragons staying in the mountains where they belonged. Treaties with the centaurs, treaties that were actually kept. Hippogryphs giving rides at

Sunday picnics. But then the king disappeared. No one to enforce the treaties, no one to keep the monsters in line. It's hard to farm when dragons fly through and burn the crops. Harder still to trade or sell anything with monsters stalking the roads. The hippogryphs have their own kind of picnic nowadays, instead of giving rides."

It was a disturbing catalog, and I shifted uncomfortably in my saddle. I wanted to blame it all on Marj, for getting involved where she shouldn't have. Except Marj had cast one spell—and then for a hundred years people had been needing help, and no one had gotten involved at all.

The woman kept talking, gaze still lowered, as if it wasn't really us she was talking to. "This returned king, that's not anything new. Every few years or so someone tries to take over ruling again, but never anyone with a real claim or any magical support. All that ever means is more fighting, more bloodshed, until finally it dies away again and it all just goes on. And meanwhile, the monsters destroy the crops, carry people off. My own mother was carried away by a gryphon. Twenty years ago, but I still miss her."

There was a little silence after her words. I tried to think what to say or do—should I convince her the new king would be different this time? Maybe I could cast a spell to fix her roof. No, this woman wouldn't react well to magic. I ought to say something, but I knew how to talk at parties, not how to handle a conversation like this...

"I'm sorry," Catherine said, voice more gentle than I'd ever heard it. "My mother died ten years ago. I still miss her too."

The woman looked up at Catherine, eyes bright. "I'm sorry for your loss too." She looked away again, ran a hand over her hair. "Well. You know, if you'd split some wood for me, you could spend the night in the barn; there's space there."

Roderick threw his shoulders back, head high. "You want us to do—"

"We'd be glad to," Catherine interrupted. "Thank you."

"I haven't any food to spare," the woman said.

"That's all right," Catherine said. "We have provisions in the saddlebags."

"Good," the woman said, cold and distant again. "Stable the horses in the barn. The wood's out back." She stepped inside, shooing children before her, and shut the door.

We put the horses in the barn, where I discreetly conjured up oats for them, then we all went out to find the woodpile, some of us more willingly than others.

"This is ridiculous," Roderick hissed. "I can't sleep in a barn! Does she realize who I *am*?"

"Yeah," Jack said. "You told her."

"Besides, you slept on the ground yesterday," I pointed out, picking up the ax lying next to the woodpile. There were worse ways to earn a night's lodging than by chopping wood. I could have offered her something better as payment, but I would have had to use magic. I could guess the reception that would get me around here.

"Sleeping on the ground was different," Roderick insisted. "That was camping. This is sleeping in a barn. There's my dignity to think about."

"Your dignity can go hang," Catherine said briskly. "Tarry, give me the ax."

I hesitated. "What are you planning to do with it?"

She rolled her eyes. "I'm going to split wood. I promise."

I handed it to her, and she did use it on the wood rather than on Roderick. I hadn't *really* thought otherwise. Roderick himself stalked off to the barn, muttering about tending to Midnight. Catherine chopped several chunks of wood down to kindling size, before handing the ax off to Jack for a turn.

"I didn't know you knew how to do that," I commented, as she sat down next to me and Emmy.

"You learn useful skills when you live and work at an inn," Catherine said, but I don't think her mind was on the subject, or had ever really been on the kindling. Her gaze drifted around the yard, and I don't think she was just looking at the yard either. "It's all so sad. So terrible. A hundred *years* of this. Why hasn't someone done something?"

I jumped. "What can I do? There wasn't anything I could do."

She looked surprised. "I didn't say anything about you, Tarry. I said someone. Anyone."

"Oh. Right. Of course." I couldn't really see what I could've done in any kind of substantial way; the problems of an entire country are large ones. But it did make me feel as though I hadn't done anything of much use in the last hundred years, visiting parties and festivals, dabbling here and there, and now realizing there was a great deal the matter over here that no one had dabbled in.

"The king's back now, finally," Emmy said hopefully. "It should get better here, right?"

Catherine rested her elbow on her knee, and her chin on her hand. "I hope so." Her gaze drifted off again, and suddenly she smiled and poked me. "Look there."

I looked there. One of the woman's children was peering around the corner of the house at us. He couldn't have been more than three, with his thumb in his mouth and a smudge of dirt on one cheek.

Catherine waggled the fingers of one hand at him. "Hello."

The boy ducked his head bashfully, and retreated back around the corner.

"Cute, isn't he?" Emmy said with a smile.

"Yes. He has lovely hair," Catherine said.

The little boy had dark curly hair. I remembered who else had dark curly hair—Anthony. I didn't point it out. "Yeah. He does."

Chapter Twenty-Five

We spent the night in the barn—which had a roof and hay and not much else redeeming to be said for it—and were on the road again early the next morning. We saw more people this day, most going the same direction we were. Of the ones we spoke with, all were going to the castle.

I felt better today, more relaxed. The other travelers made the journey seem less fraught, more like a pleasant ride through a…less unpleasant country, instead of a perilous quest through a dangerous terrain. Not all of the travelers seemed as poor or as bitter as the woman at the farm. That made me feel better too. Things weren't *so* bad here. Maybe.

We also all felt more relaxed with the hope that we wouldn't be encountering any more monsters. They seemed less prevalent on the plains, and surely the odds of meeting any were dropping as we got closer to the castle.

Dropping odds, maybe, but not impossible odds.

Late that morning we were on a deserted stretch of the road, and heard hoofbeats behind us. I looked back over my shoulder, expecting another rider, and instead saw a centaur approaching. I coughed once to get the rest of the group's attention, then shook my head to suggest we ought not to engage him. I had to add a glare for Roderick to keep him quiet.

Centaurs are not like hippogryphs. Hippogryphs are animals, if extraordinary ones, and while they might be friendly, they usually aren't. Sort of like lions. Centaurs are on approximately the same intelligence level as humans and, just like humans, there are centaurs willing to be friends and others who'd rather be enemies. But as a rule, centaurs don't mix with humans, and if you meet one on the road, the best plan is to exchange a nod and let him continue on his way.

Unfortunately, this centaur didn't seem interested in continuing. He trotted up until he was alongside our party, then fell into pace with us. "Well, well, well," he drawled. "If it isn't a cute little herd of Two-Leggers, out for a ride."

I took a deep breath and mentally readied a few spells. It wasn't a *necessarily* hostile statement, but it certainly tended that way. Nor did I like the look of this particular centaur. He had greasy brown hair in a mane that reached to the point where man met horse, and his only clothing was a ragged vest that left nothing to the imagination regarding the muscles of his upper half. His horse portion looked like a match—and then some—for Roderick's enormous black stallion. Besides the vest, he was wearing a bow over his shoulder, a quiver on his back, and a grin that, like Leonard's, did not appear to bode well.

I maneuvered my horse, getting between the centaur and the vulnerable humans. "We're going our way, and you appear to be going yours."

"But you aren't going your way on your own power. Your type isn't built for walking, is it?" He cast a glance over the crowd of us, and settled an appraising look over Emmy. "Though in some ways, you're built very nicely."

"That's my *wife* you're talking to," Jack objected, tugging his reins to bring his horse closer to Emmy, and to the centaur.

The centaur pranced back a pace, but his high-held head gave no impression of retreating. "And what are you going to do about it, Two-Legger?"

Jack was turning red. "I'm—"

"We're all going to stay very calm," I interrupted, wheeling my horse back between Jack and the centaur, "is what we're going to do."

The centaur's upper lip curled. "Just because you can sit on a horse and look me in the eye, Two-Legger, don't think that makes you my equal."

I *could* throw a fireball at him, but that was hardly a good step towards renewed national peace. And trying to protect four humans from centaur arrows—yeah, that would be tricky. "We don't want any trouble," I said. "Why don't you continue on your way, and we'll continue on ours?"

"Your way to the castle, you mean?" Everyone on this road was going that way, so of course he'd guessed that correctly. "Maybe you could deliver a message to your fancy king for me."

"Maybe," Catherine said, voice cautious. "What kind of message?"

The centaur smiled a dangerous smile. "The kind of message that will be most pointedly delivered if a few of you are dead first." And then he reached for his bow, and I started hastily throwing up magical shields. The trouble was that they worked best against *magic*, not arrows. But if I had a moment to work up the best attack then—

"Now see here, I've had quite enough of this," Roderick said loudly, shattering my concentration.

"Stay out of this," I ordered. I didn't need *him* charging in and making the situation worse.

Of course he didn't listen. "Do you have any idea who I am?" Roderick demanded, back straight and chin raised.

"Why, are you someone important?" the centaur asked, with another smile. "I'd love to kill someone important."

"I...ah..." I could see Roderick being torn between his instinct to proudly declare his identity, and his instinct to stay alive. I'm not sure which would have won.

"He's no one," I said, glaring at Roderick. "Delusions of grandeur, no one of any actual importance." If he'd just be quiet and let me think for a few seconds about how best to handle a centaur—

"I object to that," Roderick told me, then told the centaur, "There's five of us and only one of you, and..."

The centaur nickered, and three more figures emerged from the trees.

"...and there's four of you," Roderick said, voice going uneasy.

I had been reasonably sure I could handle one centaur. Four centaurs made the situation more dicey. Defending four humans from four centaurs with four bows and untold numbers of arrows—that made for too many moving pieces to easily keep track of. I could transport us away, but the only places I knew to take us would mean retreating backwards along the road we had been traveling, and then there'd be centaurs between us and the castle, and...

And then that lead centaur neighed something sharp and loud and set my lizards-turned-horses prancing about and set Roderick's big black stallion rearing. Those moving pieces started moving much more frantically, and within moments were going to reach a point of frenzy that would turn very messy very quickly—and I mean "messy" in the worst possible sense of the word.

But just when mess, injury and possibly even death were looking imminent, and retreating instead began to look unavoidable, I heard more neighing and a stampeding of hooves, and a dozen more centaurs came charging up. I would have been sure this made things even worse—except that at the first sign of them, our original bold centaur froze in place, lowering his bow and his head, his three companions following suit.

I took a quick glance over our own party to make sure no was bleeding. No one was. The situation, though on the brink of a full fight, hadn't quite reached that point.

That confirmed, I turned to look over the new arrivals. Twelve centaurs, male and female and of varying ages, all armed but not all looking as fearsome as the first, and some more thoroughly clothed. Their clear leader was a female whose horse portion was jet-black, and whose hair had likely once been the same color, but was now streaked with gray.

She fixed her gaze on that first centaur. "Zanok, what happened?"

He pawed at the ground with one hoof, and muttered, "They provoked us..."

"*Don't lie to me.*" Her voice was like a whip crack.

Zanok glowered at everything and nothing. "All right, we started it. But so what, they're Two-Leggers, they're our enemies."

"Not yet," she said, voice stern. "Hopefully not at all, and I won't have a hot-blooded *pony* destroy that possibility."

Zanok ducked his head even lower, glaring at the ground between his front hooves.

The mare turned her attention to us. "I am Rajna, and I lead this herd. I apologize for these ones. Sometimes they think with their lower halves."

We looked at each other. "That's all right," Catherine said after a moment. "No real harm done." I think we were in agreement that, when you've got sixteen armed centaurs in front of you, if they're willing to be peaceful, it's best to accept that.

Most of us were in agreement. "*I* don't think it's all right," Roderick snapped. "We were viciously set upon—"

"Let it go, Roderick," Catherine ordered.

"Ignore him," I advised the centaurs. "We usually do."

Roderick's glower was as thorough as Zanok's, but he subsided into silence.

"We'll not interfere with your journey any further," Rajna continued, "but I wonder if you would tell me if the castle is your destination?"

Zanok didn't speak up then, but if we'd denied our intent to go to the castle, I'm sure he would have contradicted us. Since there wasn't much point in hiding it, we confirmed that was where we were going.

Rajna nodded. "I expected as much, and hoped you might carry a message for me." I think she saw us tense. "Not the kind of message Zanok would have had you deliver," she added, flicking him a glance.

He stamped at the ground, but didn't speak.

"What message do you have?" Catherine asked.

"I speak for four of the centaur herds who dwell in the eastern forests. Word reached us that the human king had returned, and I was chosen to represent the herds to the king. Yesterday morning, I and my fellows sought an audience at the castle." A frown crossed her face. "The guards told us that His Royal Majesty does not speak with monsters. Tell the king that we wish to know his intentions for the future, and that we hope to secure a situation of peace for both our peoples. We will request an audience once more. You can also tell him that we will not make this request a third time."

"And we're fools to ask a second time," Zanok burst out. "We were fools to ask *once*. We should approach the castle in force and—"

"If you cannot abide by the decision of the herd, you can leave the herd." Rajna fixed him with her stare. "Perhaps you would find Naron's herd more to your taste." Her glance moved to us, and she must have read curiosity there, considering she answered the unspoken question. "Naron is the leader of the fifth herd occupying the eastern forest. They do not seek peace. They have taken to raiding and violence in these years of anarchy, and would like to continue that path. The rest of us, possessed of long lives and long memories to match, remember what it was before, and know that the greatest future of prosperity for humans and centaurs alike is a future containing peace and alliance between us."

"If you're so dedicated to peace," Catherine said, voice tight, "why haven't you done something about this Naron who's been attacking people all these years?"

I winced and wished she hadn't asked that. Both because I didn't want to provoke the big herd of centaurs, and because I just generally didn't want discussions about responsibility and blame and people not stepping in when maybe they should have.

Rajna's eyebrows rose. "That is not our way. Does one of your kings tell another what laws to make? We do not tell another herd how to live. But if we were to have an official alliance with the human king, then our dealings with Naron would change. If, however, we find that the human king does not incline towards peace, that he inclines another way, then we will likely begin to see Naron's perspective. You can tell your king that too."

We promised her that we would, because what else could you say to that? After the exchange of a few more words, we parted company. They faded back into the trees, and we continued on the road to the castle. I for one was rather amazed we'd got out of that situation unscathed. Roderick muttered about his wrongs, and the rest of us ignored him.

After two miles, Catherine, riding next to me, asked, "Why do you suppose the king wouldn't want to talk to someone like Rajna?"

"I don't know," I said. Truth to tell, my attention was much more focused in the same direction as my gaze, which was towards the north-western horizon.

"It seems to me," Catherine continued, "that if she represents four centaur herds—and you can tell just looking at her that she really does have authority—and she wants to talk about peace and alliances, someone like that is exactly who a king, who's just come back from a hundred years away and has to rebuild his kingdom, would *want* to talk to. Wouldn't you think so?"

"Mmm," I said, more or less in affirmative. My gaze wasn't technically on the horizon itself. It was on the clouds of smoke rising near the horizon. They were black, with a greasy look I could see even from miles away.

"So what kind of king, instead, says, 'no, thank you, I don't want to talk to you about peace, and oh by the way, I think you're a monster too.' Who does that? And also...you're not paying any attention to me, are you?"

I looked away from the smoke. "Sure I am. Some attention. I don't know why the king wouldn't talk to Rajna. But I do know there's strange smoke in the northwest."

Catherine looked where I was looking. She wasn't the only one, because after a few seconds, Jack said, "Some kind of fire, I suppose."

"You don't think it's the castle, do you?" Catherine asked, a note of worry barely making itself heard in her voice.

"That would be annoying. It would make the whole trip sort of pointless, wouldn't it?" Roderick observed, oblivious to the glare that comment earned him from Catherine.

"It's not the castle," I said, "and that's not a fire. Not a normal one. If I know smoke patterns, and I do, that's probably where the baby dragons' mother is. I suspect that Rajna's not the only one who wants to talk to the king." At least, I hoped the dragon was here to talk. Or we were riding into a much bigger problem than a handful of sullen centaurs.

"A dragon? Really?" Roderick suddenly looked freshly interested. "Maybe I should go slay it."

"Her," I corrected, as everyone else stared at him. I was resigned to this sort of thing from him, and I had loads of time to stop him before he got in stabbing distance of the dragon.

"*Why* would you want to do that?" Emmy asked.

"That's what princes do," Roderick explained. "Slay dragons. Among other things. It could be holding a fair maiden captive."

"Who, I imagine, you'd want to kiss after you rescue," Catherine said in scathing tones.

"If she's pretty."

"You're supposed to be getting married!" Catherine said, voice growing even more irate.

"I don't see what that has to do with anything."

"You don't want to go fight the dragon anyway," I said, "because I'm guessing there's at least three adult dragons gathered over there. Based on the smoke patterns. That's interesting. Dragons don't often come out of the mountains." Once in a while you saw a solitary dragon winging over cropland, and apparently there'd been some raids going on in the last century, but three dragons sitting on a plain long enough to send up that much smoke—that was something significant.

"Do you get the feeling that the king's return is attracting attention?" Emmy asked, staring at the distant smoke. "It's slightly unnerving."

"But to be expected too," I pointed out. This was good. Change was good. Something needed to change around here, that was clear, and I liked the idea that the king returning was already starting to make things different. It made this one crisis that *I* didn't have to deal with.

Within a couple more hours, we were able to catch glimpses of the castle in the distance, the tallest towers rising up above the trees. I had a horrible premonition right along that Marj's spell was going to stop us—or at least me—but it didn't. I don't think it ever occurred to her that I might try to approach the castle by human means, rather than magical ones.

By midafternoon, we reached the outermost gate of the castle, guarded by six burly men in uniforms. If I'd been human, I wouldn't've wanted to argue with them. If I'd been Rajna, on the other hand, I would have felt confident about my ability to force my way past them if necessary. For us, we were hoping that wouldn't be necessary. We dismounted from our horses, as one of the guards separated from the group at the gate to walk the dozen feet down the road to meet us.

He gave us only the most cursory of glances before saying, "If you three men are here to join the king's guard, go around to the back. The rest are pitching tents there. Sorry, girls, we don't have any space on the castle staff." His glance lingered just a moment longer on Catherine and Emmy. "Though depending what you're here for, you could go around back too and—"

"We're not here for *that*," Catherine said sharply. "Or to join the castle staff, or to join the army."

I tried to ignore an uneasy qualm. Of course a returned king would start gathering an army. That was only natural, countries all had armies. And not every monster could be expected to talk about peace. It wasn't…necessarily a bad sign.

"Petitioners, eh?" the guard said, hooking his thumbs through his belt. "You'll have to come back tomorrow. Gifts and tribute you can leave with us. If you've really got to see the king, you can join the crowd tomorrow. That's when he's addressing his subjects. He might see individuals too, but I wouldn't hold my breath over that."

"He's addressing his *human* subjects?" Emmy said softly.

The guard's gaze grew darker. "The king only has human subjects. Anyway, you'll have to come back tomorrow. You can't come in today."

It was harder not to see that human subjects remark as a bad sign. I tried. Technically, the non-humans always had been sort of independent of the human government…

"We're not going away and coming back tomorrow," Catherine said, hands on her hips and glare in full force. "We've been riding for days to get here. And we're not here to see the king anyway. I have to see Anthony Maurier, your new queen's brother."

Suddenly all the guards were smirking. "Oh," the lead guard said knowingly, "you're one of *those*. What are you, his fiancée?"

Catherine looked puzzled. "Yes."

He nodded. "Uh-huh. Another one."

"What do you mean, *another one*?" Anyone who knew her would have known that Catherine's expression just then was very perilous indeed.

The guard seemed oblivious. "Word got out that the queen has three young, unmarried brothers. Be sensible about this. You can't really think you're the only one who thought of this idea. We don't let people in to see anyone in the royal family and that's final."

This was an obstacle I had never considered. I never talked my way past royal guards; I always used magical means to get into castles. Surely we hadn't got past all the monsters just to be stopped by a human with a bit of braid on his jacket?

Catherine's mouth dropped open. "But I'm really—!"

"This is all absurd," Roderick interrupted, pushing his way to the front of the group. "Never mind who she is. Do you have any idea who *I* am?"

The guard looked at him with frank curiosity. "No. Who are you?"

Roderick puffed up his chest, and launched in. Just this once, it seemed like a good idea to hang back and let him go ahead. "I am His Most Royal Highness Prince Charles Henry Albert Roderick Michael Irwin Norman Gillian the Third, crown prince and heir apparent of the kingdom of Perrelda."

The change in the guards was remarkable. Letting Prince Roderick of Perrelda and his companions into the castle was a different matter entirely from letting in a group of miscellaneous probable nobodies.

"Would you like an escort, Your Highness?" the guard asked anxiously, as a few of his fellows led our horses away to the stables. "We march very well. Though it'll take us a while to form up."

"We don't need an escort," Catherine said.

"I might want an escort," Roderick objected. "It's the proper thing to—"

"I don't want to wait, so you don't need an escort."

Roderick still capitulated easily at least half the time. Instead of an escort, we just received directions on how to get in past the outer grounds and gardens to reach the main part of the castle.

Chapter Twenty-Six

The five of us walked through the outer reaches of the castle grounds, past many gardens and far more archways than I thought were strictly necessary. I recognized the last courtyard when we came to it, though the only other time I'd seen it had been from a different angle, through my spell to look in on Anthony. At the far end of the courtyard was an elaborate wooden door, up several marble steps. Clusters of pillars stood on either side of the door, and on either side of the steps stood a stone statue of a woman.

There was only one living figure in sight. A man was sitting on the steps, leaning back against a pillar. With the sun overhead the shadows were small, but still enough to hide his face. Being magical, I could sharpen my eyesight to see not just his face, but also that he had it tipped up, his eyes shut. The rest of our group not having my abilities, I don't know how many of them even knew who it was. But Catherine was smiling, and it was the smile she only wore for Anthony.

Already in the lead, she stopped in the middle of the courtyard, and called, "Hello, stranger"—and the tone was the one she used for Anthony too.

He opened his eyes and looked out. "*Cat!*"

An instant after that, Anthony was down the steps and across the courtyard. He caught her in his arms, held her tightly and spun around with her twice. She wrapped her arms around him and buried her face against his shoulder. I focused my magical eyes and watched the branches of their auras intertangle.

"Do you suppose he noticed the rest of us are here?" Jack asked with a grin.

"I doubt it," I said, grinning too. Whatever else happened, whatever problems there were to be dealt with, the world still felt so much more *right*. At least I'd helped fix things this much.

Roderick sniffed. "Bit rude, really. Don't you think so?"

"No," Emmy said, leaning her head on Jack's shoulder.

Anthony set Catherine down, looking into her face with his hands on her shoulders. "What are you—how did you get here?"

"Horseback, mostly," she said, eyes dancing. "Some magical transportation near the beginning."

"Magical..." Anthony looked past her to see the rest of us. "Oh. Hello, Tarry." His gaze moved along the line of us. "Jack, Emmy, and..." He stopped on Roderick, eyes narrowing. "You."

Roderick had his chin in the air. "You ought to have greeted me first. I'm the highest ranking."

I sighed. Sometimes, I regretted not turning him into a toad too.

"I'm going to kill him," Anthony announced. "I swear I'm—I don't know how yet, but I'm going to—"

"No, it's all right," Catherine said, tugging on his arm. "I promise, it's all right."

"Really? Is it?" Anthony snapped, which would have worried me more if I couldn't see that his aura was still all interlocked with hers. "Please, by all means, explain to me how him being here, with you, is all right...*Catherine*."

"Don't," she said in clipped tones, "call me that."

I tried to swallow a sudden laugh, while Anthony turned away from Roderick to look at her, eyebrows raised.

She looked steadily back at him for a moment, before a smile blossomed. "We found the girl who owned the glass slipper. Roderick's marrying her instead of me. So...I suppose that means I'm a free woman again." She looked up at him, archly. "Am I?"

I think it took a second to sink in, and when it did Anthony grinned. "No. You're not," he said, pulling her back into his arms to kiss her.

I do like being around couples who are in love.

Eventually, and it took a while, Anthony woke up to the idea that maybe he ought to show us inside, and introduce us to the rest of his family. The two nearest were not at their best; Anthony pointed out which statue was Miranda and which was Noreen, no one wanted to linger on the subject, and we went on inside instead.

The next meeting was better. With my magical orienting, we located Beauty and George in a sitting room with a big western-facing window and poofy couches. Beauty was sitting on one of the couches reading, and George was at the room's small table, eating what I supposed was a between-meal snack but included most of a chicken. Anthony introduced both of them, but didn't need to introduce all of us.

He was holding Catherine's hand and, from the way he was looking at her besides, it took no great insight when Beauty said, "You must be Catherine."

"The way he's looking," George said, pushing up from his table, "she'd better be Catherine."

"George," Anthony groaned.

"I'm just saying, you can't be sure about these things. Great ladies man that you are—"

"*George!*"

"George, really now," Beauty admonished sweetly, hugging Catherine.

George hugged her next, less politely and more enthusiastically. "Good to meet you! Glad you're here. Maybe now Anthony'll stop glowering at everyone."

I grinned. I always enjoyed the atmosphere George put into a room. And the reliability of finding food near him. I sidled toward the abandoned table.

Even Anthony's glower didn't dampen his brother, or the pervading cheerfulness in the room. "George, could you just not talk? Could you do that?" It wasn't really much of a glower, as it was overlaid with his clear delight at having Catherine here. Taking her hand again, he said, "Cat, you have to promise not to judge the family based on Brother George the Bear here."

"That's all right," Catherine said, and her eyes glinted with mischief. "Glad to meet you, Brother George. I've heard *so much* about you."

"You have?" George's forehead wrinkled. "Anthony, what have you been telling her?"

"Oh, nothing much," Anthony said with a nonchalant shrug. "Just the truth."

"I was afraid of that," George sighed, and turned back to his table and his plate. He frowned. "S'funny, I thought I had a drumstick left."

"Sorry," I said through a mouthful of chicken. "It looked good."

Anthony went on to introduce me, Jack, Emmy and as a near after-thought, "Oh, and that's Roderick."

"A*hem*," Roderick said. He had been standing off from the rest of the group, arms crossed, not looking at all happy to be out of the center of attention.

"Prince Roderick," Anthony amended.

"Honestly, if you want something done right," Roderick muttered. He swept a bow. "I am His Most Royal Highness Prince Charles Henry Albert Roderick Michael Irwin Norman Gillian the Third—"

"You ever get those names out of order?" George asked.

The set of Roderick's jaw got tighter. "—crown prince, heir apparent and future *king* of the noble and most excellent country of Perrelda."

Unless I was mistaken, he'd managed to fit an extra title or two in there. Figured.

"It's a pleasure to meet you," Beauty said, extending one hand.

He bowed again and kissed her hand. "And it is a pleasure to meet you, most beautiful lady," he said, tone shifting into that disconcerting charming quality again.

Catherine cleared her throat pointedly. "She's engaged and so are you."

"I was being courteous," Roderick protested. "Don't you understand courtesy?"

"Hey, weren't you engaged to Catherine?" George said, gesturing with a chicken wing.

"Not anymore," Anthony said, beating Catherine to it by a half-second.

"Oh good," George said, took a bite and added, slightly garbled, "So we don't want to send a hippogryph to kill him after all?"

"You don't want to *what*?" Roderick said, head rising and shoulders going back.

"Well…" Anthony said, studying Roderick thoughtfully.

"No, you don't," Catherine said, and finished that question. Pity. Though maybe it wouldn't be very fair to the hippogryph.

"Do you know where Father is?" Anthony asked.

"He's upstairs resting," Beauty said. "He's not very strong, you know."

Anthony's expression darkened, and he muttered, "Hasn't been for the last year, anyway."

Beauty smiled, this sugary but oh-so-sincere smile. "I don't think assigning blame will do anyone any good."

"Did I assign blame? Did I name anyone?" Anthony asked, and from the edge in his voice this couldn't be a new conversation. "No, I didn't. You read into it."

She kept the pleasant expression. "But you were being obvious. We all know what happened approximately a year ago, and you have made it abundantly clear how you feel about Cesar. I do hope you'll eventually come to a more forgiving attitude. Now let's go locate Cesar and Connor, shall we?"

She really must have been exhausting to grow up with. A few minutes with her made me feel like I'd eaten too much dessert—and that's not easy for me to do. Anthony looked like he wanted to keep arguing the point, but Catherine tugged on his hand and we all followed Beauty out the door. George and I both managed to pass the table on the way out, giving each other a nod as he picked up the remaining wing and I pocketed a few rolls sitting next to the chicken.

As we walked down a long, sun-drenched hallway, I heard Catherine comment quietly to Anthony, "She really doesn't ever argue, does she?"

"No. Not ever."

If Beauty heard them—doubtful, considering I have better ears and barely caught it—she didn't indicate it. As we turned down a branching corridor, she told us, "I believe we can find Cesar and Connor in a meeting with the advising council at the moment. When Cesar was enchanted, everyone in the castle was enchanted too. Now that the spell has been lifted, they've reassembled the same advising council."

"I have fresh understanding why no one's been running this country for so long," I muttered. Leave it to Marj and her thoroughness. Taking out the king wasn't enough; she had to put *everyone* who might do anything useful out of commission. And of course she wouldn't take any responsibility for the resulting chaos. At least *I* never caused this kind of havoc. Going to a few parties and christenings never ruined any countries.

Yeah, it didn't help much either, but it didn't do any *harm* at least.

We followed Beauty to an echoey chamber that was bigger than it needed to be, where the advising council were holding session. The room held a vast wooden table in the center, which nevertheless left wide reaches of empty space around its perimeter. All eight of us were able to enter and stand at one end, without getting close to the table or the twelve men sitting around it. I assumed the ten harried-looking individuals were the advising council. The only ones talking were Cesar at one end and Connor at the other, and it didn't require magical sensitivity to know that we'd walked into the middle of a heated disagreement.

Connor was speaking when we entered. "If you wanted to kill all the hippogryphs, I still would have objections, but at least that would be an attack on animals with an intent to protect humans. But you're talking about killing dragons, gryphons, centaurs; those are intelligent, sentient creatures. It would be murder." It was his tone as much as the words that told me this was an intense debate. From what little I'd observed of Connor, he didn't lose his temper much more often than Beauty. He was skirting close to it now, though.

Cesar glowered down the length of the table. He didn't look as handsome, with that expression. "You call it murder. I call it justice against creatures who have been preying on my people for the last century."

"But that's the point." Connor leaned forward, picking up his papers from the table. "That's the question I've been trying to work out for months, ever since I joined the army." His voice took on a scholarly air. "How do species, formerly peacefully coexisting in mutual prosperity, turn to outright hostility and depredation in a relatively short time, without apparent provocation? I've looked at reports, I've studied the history, I've talked to people coming out of Beaumont, and from all of it I'm convinced that not all the magical creatures have been attacking humans.

"I believe you can subdivide the magical creatures into three groups. The ones who'd cause trouble regardless of external circumstances; those existed even during peaceful times, and I agree they have to be contained or, if no alternative can be found, killed. Then there are the ones who cause trouble now only because they believe there are no repercussions. Institute laws and enforce them, and those creatures will abide by them. In the third group are the ones who want to live peacefully and *do* live peacefully now, and I don't believe those are in the minority. The ones who are rampaging and destroying receive more attention, making them seem more dominant than they are."

Did that mean the situation in Beaumont wasn't really as bad as it seemed? I liked that idea, wanted to believe that idea—except that I'd seen all those fields lying fallow, heard the story from the woman who'd lost her mother to a gryphon. A few rampaging monsters could still wreak a lot of harm.

Cesar shook his head. "That's only your theory."

"Perhaps, but I have extensive facts supporting it." Connor sorted through his papers and drew one out. "Take the dragons, for instance. Every report and story I have been able to find points to one of two dragons as the cause of every disturbance; I believe only those two have caused problems, while the rest continue to live peacefully in the mountains the way they always have. Two dragons can cause so much damage that it creates a sense of widespread attack when, in fact, the hostility is isolated. Or the centaurs. There are very few, very limited stories of attacks by centaurs. I believe there is one rogue, extremist group while the majority are not dangerous."

That tallied with what Rajna had said. But I didn't feel I ought to interrupt the conversation at that moment to bring it up. This was not the sort of conversation that invited outsiders to join in. Everyone else must have thought so too, as they also remained silent.

"That's what you say," Cesar said, voice harsh. "But *I* say the only way we can be sure of containing the problem is to destroy them all. We've had floods of volunteers for the army in the last few days alone. We can fight the centaurs, the dragons, and all the rest of them. The only way we're going to make this country safe for humans is to get rid of anyone who isn't human."

Connor set his papers down, and folded his hands together on the table. It could have been a casual gesture, but his knuckles were white. "This is a hard problem, but that is not the answer. You need laws, you need treaties, you need an army to enforce them and to deal with the radical elements. Be ready to act on future violence, but you can't slaughter everyone based on what they might have done or might decide to do. Judiciously target the ones we know are guilty of attacking humans and make agreements with the rest. We have indications that some are interested in discussing peace and cooperation. You can't simply ignore that. Follow the plan I suggest, I believe there will be peace, and I believe it will be soon." His voice grew cold. "Hunting down and killing every magical creature in this country is a path that will never come to an end. The killing, the counter-attacks, the bloodshed will go on and on. And you will be beginning your reign with violence and without ethics."

"I will be keeping my people safe!" Cesar roared.

By contrast, Connor's voice was very quiet. "Many horrible things have been done in the name of safety. You don't need to add another to that page of history. There's a better way to do this."

The tension in the room was making me uneasy. It couldn't have all stayed cheerful and happy for a *little* while? I focused my magical sight, hoping to find out how dangerous this situation really was. I had already seen Connor's aura with its grove of oaks, and was reassured now to observe the steady firmness of his trees. He might be tense, but there wasn't any serious storm going on.

Then I turned to Cesar's aura, at the same moment that he sneered and demanded, "And by your plan, how many humans do we sacrifice to the dangerous monsters we miss? Five? Ten? A hundred? How many people are those monsters' lives worth?"

A prickle ran down my spine, partially at the words (after all, I might well fall into his definition of a monster myself) but also because I didn't like Cesar's aura. I didn't like it at all.

"You can't calculate it that way," Connor said evenly, gaze steady on the king. "Counting up numbers, letting the ends justify the means, it never works. I am talking about right and wrong, and killing entire populations without any regard for the individual's guilt or innocence is *wrong*. We have to have a line that we will not cross, if we intend to be men and not beasts."

Cesar grew still.

"I don't think he should have put it that way," Beauty whispered.

"I think it was deliberate," Anthony said.

Cesar slammed his fist against the tabletop, making everyone jump, even me. Solid hardwood though it was, I half-expected it to crack. "How dare you say that to me! I am the king, and you will treat me with respect!"

"And the king is not above the law," Connor said, volume finally rising. "Not the country's law and not God's law."

Cesar rose to an impressive height and pointed at Connor. "I want him executed. At once!"

The prickle in my spine was a whole lot worse now, but it wasn't mingled with surprise. Cesar's aura was a lion, and not a noble, majestic lion. A wild, untamed lion who would fight any challengers, ask no questions and maintain rule by tooth and claw.

If I had to, I could transport Connor and all the rest of us out of here, except for Anthony. But if I *had* to, I could take the rest of us out and down the road a bit—but would Cesar let us back in if I tried that?

Beauty said, "Oh dear," and hurried across the room to tug on Cesar's arm. She leaned in close to murmur in his ear.

Catherine's frown was half worried and half annoyed. " 'Oh dear' seems a bit mild."

"Beauty's always mild," George commented.

"I should yell more," Roderick decided. "It sounds so authoritative."

Meanwhile, mild or not, Beauty was accomplishing something. "Oh all right," Cesar said grudgingly, "I won't have him executed."

Well, that was simpler than magically whisking everyone away. Which was about the only reassurance I found in the situation.

"His Majesty is gracious," Connor said, voice skirting just this side of sarcasm.

"There, you see, dear? No reason to get so upset," Beauty said with a smile. She tucked her arm through Cesar's. "Let's go for a stroll in the rose garden. Wouldn't that be nice?"

His expression still looked grim, but they walked out together. I relaxed slightly, once the mad lion monarch was out of the room.

"What she thinks she sees in him…" Anthony muttered.

"It appears we're done for the moment, gentlemen," one of the council members said. He had a haggard look, one shared by all his fellows. How long had they been trying to work with Cesar? With a series of mutters and mumbles and comments to each other, all ten stood up and made their way out of the room, taking a different door than Beauty and Cesar. A few looked back at Connor, expressions guilty. Connor himself had leaned back in his chair, eyes closed, pinching the bridge of his nose, and didn't move.

"That's already the second time he's decided to execute you," Anthony observed, walking towards the table. The rest of us followed.

"I know," Connor said without moving.

"It's been *four days*, Connor. At that rate, she won't be able to talk him down forever."

"I know," Connor said again. "But unlike the rest of his supposed advisers, I will not sit by and say nothing while he plans genocide." He straightened in his chair and opened his eyes. "I see we have company," he said, firmly moving to a less charged tone of voice. He looked at Catherine first, who was still holding hands with Anthony. "You must be Catherine."

"That's putting it more politely than George did," Anthony said with a trace of a smile.

"I get no respect," George muttered. "The oldest one, and I get no—hey Connor, don't they ever serve food at these meetings?"

I'd be lying if I said that hadn't occurred to me too. The table was sadly bare of anything but papers.

Connor ignored the question, continuing to look over our group as we found nearby seats at the table. "And you, of course, are Anthony and George's magical friend. I remember you from the day we were all transported here."

"You do?" I said, sliding into a chair. There'd been plenty to distract him at the time.

"I have a good memory. If you're lucky, Cesar won't recognize you. You can pass as human if he doesn't, and that would be simpler for everyone." He studied Jack and Emmy a moment, then correctly guessed their identity. "Anthony's mentioned you." He studied Roderick longer, and finally shook his head. "I can't place who you could be."

Roderick puffed up, chest out and chin up. "I am His Most Royal Highness—"

"That's Prince Roderick," Anthony said.

Connor's eyebrows rose. "Really."

"They're not engaged anymore," Anthony clarified.

"Ah. In that case, welcome to Beaumont, Your Highness. I would love to discuss trade arrangements with you. There has been no organized trade between Perrelda and Beaumont for a hundred years and that's had a detrimental effect on the economies of both countries. We could do something about that."

"Sure, if you think it's a good idea," Roderick said.

Seemed a little inadequate to me (but typical Roderick) and maybe to Connor too, since there was a distinct two second pause before he said, "We can discuss it later. I'm sure after a trip from Ryvideau, you aren't ready to launch into business immediately. Did you have a pleasant journey?"

"It could have been worse," I said, aiming for a diplomatic view.

"It could have been better," Roderick countered, hitting one fist against the table. After Cesar, it was exceptionally unimpressive, and ignored by all. "Practically everyone we met was hostile. Like those centaurs this morning."

"You met hostile centaurs?" Connor said, eyes narrowing with interest.

"Only a few of them were hostile," I said. "And the ones who were hostile weren't actually important or anything."

"We have a message from the leader of the centaurs," Catherine volunteered, idly straightening the stacks of paper in front of her. "It's supposed to be for the king."

Connor shook his head. "He won't listen. What does the message say?"

We conveyed what Rajna had told us, that they wanted peace but would change their minds if Cesar wasn't open to speaking with them.

Connor seemed unsurprised by the news. "A messenger came running into the council meeting this morning to say a delegation from the centaurs was at the door. Cesar refused to see them. His standing policy is that he won't speak to non-humans, and he saw no reason to change that. I'd like to be encouraged that they're willing to come request an audience a second time, but he'll just refuse again." He rubbed one temple. "And that will be the end of any possible treaty with the centaurs."

"Do you know you've got dragons outside too?" I asked. "There's a few of them a couple miles west of here."

"I did know," Connor said. "We can see the smoke."

"And everyone went into a panic when they arrived early this morning," George added.

"Yes, until Cesar made a lot of noise about how strong his walls are," Connor said, "and everyone calmed down when the dragons didn't attack. They haven't sent a message yet, but since they're still here, not fighting, they probably want to talk." He sighed. "Or at least, they will until Cesar refuses to meet with them."

"What is he, insane?" Jack asked, folding his arms. "Who doesn't *talk* to dragons when they give you the option?"

Roderick stuck his nose in the air. "That's not How Things Are Done."

Come to think of it, I'd never heard Marj advocate for negotiations with dragons either.

Connor shrugged. "I'm sure that being under a spell made him feel hostile towards magic, and then he came back after a century, heard a score of stories about magical attacks, and…you heard what he's planning. He's king, so he has an army that will let him do something with his hostility."

"It doesn't seem fair," Emmy protested. "Just because he's got a crown and the right ancestors, he can do whatever mad thing he wants. Start a war or…burn an entire country's worth of spinning wheels!"

"That's How Things Are *Done*," Roderick said, as though it were patently obvious.

"Well, it shouldn't be," Emmy said, glaring at him. "Someone ought to rein in monarchs when they go off on mad schemes."

Roderick waved a hand. "Yes, well, that's what advising councils are for. And fairies."

I jumped. He was Roderick, so he couldn't possibly be having a useful insight. Right?

Everyone else seemed to feel that way, since they ignored the comment. "Where did the army come from?" Catherine asked. "I thought there hasn't been an organized military in Beaumont for years."

"There hasn't been, until this week," Connor said. "There were rogue groups, half of whom probably did as much pillaging as any centaur. Some have shown up here, thinking they'll throw in with the reigning power. Cesar's happy to make alliances with humans. Then there are the droves of young men who haven't had anything better to do their whole lives, because there's been no future for anyone in this country for decades. They've come looking for what's probably the first opportunity they've ever seen."

Emmy's lips were tight. "So he really does have enough people to pursue this idea of killing everyone and everything that's magical."

"Yes," Connor said simply. "I doubt he can really accomplish it, but he can get all the magical creatures good and mad at us, and then it's all just..." He looked down and ran a hand through his hair. "Then it's all just going to get worse."

Just once, just *once* it would be nice to solve one problem before the next one popped up. Especially when the 'next one' kept looming ever larger. Once I started getting involved, where did it all end? "And I thought Anthony being trapped here was a big problem."

"That *is* a big problem," Catherine protested.

"Agreed," Anthony said quickly, then glanced at Connor. "Although Tarry's right too, it kind of pales next to civil war."

"So what are we going to do?" Catherine asked.

"About which problem?" I asked.

"Either. Both."

We talked about both, but we didn't solve either. Connor had more theories and angles on affairs of state and potential war than the rest of us combined, by a wide margin, but Cesar was the only one in position to make decisions. The army was starry-eyed by the return of the king and clearly ready to follow him into anything. The advising council was too cowed to oppose him. The only one who even might be able to get through to him was Beauty, but so far she'd shown more interest in wedding plans than plans for the country.

As to Anthony and his problem, I needed time to study and sort out Marj's spell. I couldn't just undo it, not legally. But if I stared at it long enough and poked at it hard enough, I might find a loophole, a way to alter it sufficiently to solve the problem; I was allowed to do that. Kind of like turning a magical death sentence into an enchanted sleep. That was a standard modification though, while this situation didn't have any standard response—so I'd need some time.

It grew evident to everyone that we were not going to get to any conclusions in the immediate moment, and when the chimes rang for supper everyone agreed—with particularly strong urging from George—that we ought to go eat.

The meal was served in a grand banquet hall near the center of the castle, high windows letting in the evening light, with candles racked along every wall to provide extra glow. One table stood at the head of the room, while two long tables ran perpendicular to it, down the length.

When our group entered, joining the crowds straggling into the half-filled room, Cesar already sat at the center of the head table, in a tall-backed chair clearly designated for the king. Beauty wasn't with him, and he sat in brooding solitude. The advising council was present, along with a number of people who were clearly nobility (I couldn't be sure where they'd come from, but my guess was that they'd been enchanted with all the rest when Cesar was—no one else in Beaumont was that well-to-do anymore). Some sat at the head table, some at the longer ones, but no one sat too close to the king.

One of the longer tables was half-occupied by a group that looked rougher around the edges—though they also seemed to be having the best time, from the boisterous laughter and the litter around them of already-empty mugs. Those turned out to be the leaders of the various bands who'd sworn allegiance to the king and joined the army; some looked less respectable than Rajna.

We were still looking for places to sit when Anthony's father walked in the door behind us. Anthony immediately pulled Catherine over to be introduced, pride evident in his wide grin.

"He might have introduced me," Roderick said with a sniff.

"He's not marrying *you*," I snapped.

The prince's eyebrows rose. "Certainly not. But what does that have to do with protocol and proper respect for the crown prince—"

"Why don't you go sit down?" I interrupted. I could not stand listening to him recite his title yet another time.

He shot me a look that clearly conveyed I was beneath notice—and then he went to sit down, among the nobility of course. The rest of our party was also seeking out chairs, but while I was eager to see what the staff would provide for supper, I lingered where I was for a moment. I wanted to read Mr. Maurier's aura.

Introductions finished, Mr. Maurier took Catherine's hands with a smile. "It's so good to meet you. My son has told me about you. How did you come to be here?"

She gave him the brief version of the trip, leaving out the details—especially the unpleasant ones—and essentially described it as coming to visit Anthony. While she spoke, I focused in my magical senses, looking at his aura. I had trouble with it; his aura had a shiny quality I hadn't expected, and it was making the read hard.

"How nice," he said. "And I understand you run an inn?"

I could see flowers bloom in Catherine's aura clear as day as she talked about her inn. "Yes, The Nightingale, it's a wonderful place. My father and I have been running it for years—and now it's mostly me and Anthony."

Mr. Maurier was just saying that that was nice too, when Beauty walked up. "Oh, how lovely that you two have met," she said.

Her father turned towards her at once. "Beauty, my dear, how was your day?"

"I've had a lovely day, Father," she said, kissing his cheek. "Cesar and I went for a walk in the rose garden this afternoon."

Seeing the two of them together, the pieces fell into place for Mr. Maurier's aura. Like Roderick's, his aura was a mass of reflections—but where Roderick's aura showed himself over and over, Mr. Maurier's aura was all reflecting Beauty.

"That sounds delightful," he said, and soon the two of them were walking off towards the main table together, Mr. Maurier casting an absent "very good to meet you" over his shoulder. And the way his aura looked, it was remarkable he even bothered with that.

Catherine watched them go, head tilted slightly to one side. "Hmm."

Anthony sighed and put an arm around her shoulders. "Maybe we should view it in a positive way. He's treating you like one of the family." His tone was much more bitter than positive.

"It's all right, Anthony," she said, leaning her head on his shoulder. "I don't mind."

"*I* do. And it's not all right. But it's just how he is."

I'd lost track of Connor and I didn't care about Roderick, so when Catherine and Anthony headed towards the table where Jack, Emmy and George were sitting, I followed them. I claimed a chair between George and Jack, while Anthony sat down on George's other side, Catherine next to him.

We were still waiting on most of the food, but I immediately spotted the baskets of bread and of fruit on the table. I began snatching up breadsticks and apples. It had been a long day, and I did not want to deal with any of our current problems, let alone any new ones that were sure to pop up, on an empty stomach.

Next to me, George was studying his brother. "You look all set to start moping again," he said, and tousled Anthony's hair. "Don't do that."

Anthony grimaced at him and tried to flatten his hair. "Don't do *that*. And I'm not moping. I'm frustrated."

George couldn't have heard the recent conversation, but if he had seen Anthony talking to their father, he could probably guess what had happened. George wasn't that insightful, but his father wasn't subtle either.

"Brooding on your frustrations won't do you any more good than moping," George said, picked up the nearest basket of breadsticks (I'd only taken half) and selected three. "And why would anyone want to mope when there's good food to eat? Much pleasanter way to spend the evening, Tony-boy."

Anthony looked pained. "George, you really didn't need to..."

"*Tony-boy?*" Catherine's eyes were lighting.

"You don't have to—I mean, really, you don't want—there is no conceivable reason why you would ever—"

"But I thought you *liked* nicknames," Catherine protested merrily.

"Cat..."

"Tony-boy..."

"Don't do that."

"Right. Mm-hmm. Sorry."

I grinned, munched my breadsticks, and wondered if George was more insightful than I had thought. Anthony may have been protesting, but he was smiling again, and Catherine was clearly enjoying herself too. And that meant I could settle down to enjoy the meal.

The guards at the castle gate had been right when they said the staff didn't need any more help. Based on that supper, everything was under control. There was chicken, lamb, beef, three kinds of fish, tarts, meat pies, roast vegetables, pastry puffs, candied yams…plate after plate after plate. It was *wonderful*.

After three servings of every dish (maybe four—I lose count), I felt ready to pay more attention to what else was going on, outside of the immediate circle of Jack, Emmy and George. Catherine and Anthony were deep into their own conversation which, from the way their heads leaned together, did not look like the sort I ought to eavesdrop on. In a loud banquet hall, it was surprisingly easy to have a private conversation, if no one around you had magical ability.

I looked farther afield. Roderick was regaling the local nobility with stories about himself—not interesting. More interesting was the head table. Beauty had joined Cesar, sitting on his right; he was currently turned to the left, in discussion with someone who looked like a military official. Mr. Maurier was seated on Beauty's other side, but Connor was standing between their chairs, talking to Beauty. I sharpened my hearing—*that* was a conversation I wanted to eavesdrop on. Maybe we'd get very, very lucky and the whole civil war mess would be averted after all, by way of Beauty's influence on the unstable king.

"You're the only one he might listen to," Connor was saying as I tuned in, his voice urgent but even. "If you'd just have a conversation with him, maybe he'd see the other side of this."

"But it sounds to me like you've already laid out your argument quite clearly," Beauty said, hands folded before her. "He obviously disagrees with you, and has chosen the course he considers best."

"Yes, I know," Connor said, voice getting tighter. "But his choice is going to lead to war."

"But that's what you disagree about," Beauty said placidly. "I don't see how you can be so sure that your view is the correct one. Perhaps you should try to see his side. You know it's always best to see both sides of a question."

I should have known. We couldn't be that lucky. I reached out for another pastry puff, bit into a corner as I kept listening.

"Yes," Connor said. "That's fine. But I don't think you quite see—"

"And considering that Cesar's only just come back from a long and difficult time," Beauty continued, tone kind and smile firmly in place, "and is trying to adjust to ruling a kingdom again, I really don't think now's the appropriate moment to be questioning his decisions. He's under enough pressure already. I don't want to add to that, of course, and perhaps you ought to think about that too."

Arguing with this woman had to be like punching at clouds. There was nothing to *hit*. Come to think of it, Marj was like that sometimes—so blatantly off-course, while professing kindness and light. In a way, I felt strangely grateful that Marj was at least a little more obviously self-serving and inconsiderate. It made being angry with her simpler.

Based on the edge coming into his voice, Connor was finding it possible to be angry with his sister. "Beauty, I really don't think you understand the gravity of this situation. Cesar's emotional well-being is not on an equal magnitude with the destruction of entire species who—"

"Is he bothering you, Beauty, my dear?"

To my magically-enhanced hearing, Cesar's voice was like the crack of doom. I flinched, hastily toning down my magical senses. Maybe too far, as everything went silent. I hit my ear with one open palm, trying to make sure I hadn't gone deaf, then realized by looking around that the room really had gone quiet. Apparently I wasn't the only one who had heard Cesar.

Connor straightened from his position leaning over Beauty, as she smiled at Cesar and said, "No, dear, we're just having a small discussion. Connor, weren't you going to go have a word with George?"

"I suppose I was," he said, nodded slightly to Cesar, and walked away.

Conversation resumed, if with a more subdued tone, and was flowing freely again by the time Connor pulled up a chair between me and George.

"That didn't go very well," I observed. "Good idea though, trying to get her to talk him around."

Connor blinked at me. "How did you…oh. Magical hearing?"

I held up my hands. "I promise I only eavesdrop for benevolent purposes." Well, mostly. Unless I was *really* curious.

"It doesn't matter," Connor said, staring at the empty space on the table in front of him. "So you heard that Beauty is convinced Cesar is good and kind and perfect, and she refuses to see anything that indicates otherwise."

George pushed a meat pie towards him. "Eat something. You'll feel better."

"I highly doubt that."

"Eat anyway."

Good advice. I had two more meat pies myself, and Connor did eat something, although I don't think it made him feel better. After the last round of dessert, there were several rounds of musicians as entertainment, and the whole affair broke up late. The humans went to bed, and I went up to the roof, where I didn't expect to be disturbed.

Fairies don't have to sleep as often as humans, so it was easy enough for me to sit up one night. I had work to do.

It was a beautiful clear night, and the castle roof gave a better view of the stars than it did of the landscape. The surrounding hills and plains were largely lost in the darkness, though I could see a glow where the dragons were camped. The stars shone down brilliantly from above. What I could see with my physical eyes, however, was only of secondary concern. The castle roof was also a convenient place to study Marj's spell.

I settled down cross-legged in the center of the roof and closed my eyes. I opened my magical eyes to focus on the great swirls and swathes of pink sparkles wrapping all around the castle, and went to work hunting a loophole for Catherine and Anthony.

Chapter Twenty-Seven

I came down from the roof in time for breakfast, even though I was tempted to stay up there permanently. I had studied Marj's spells from every angle that existed, and whatever answers there were, I had them.

There weren't many.

I was barely into my fourth helping of eggs when Catherine and Anthony arrived in the main hall and came straight over to me.

"Did you find out anything about the spell keeping Anthony here?" Catherine asked.

They hadn't broached the subject last night, but I couldn't expect them to hold off on it for long. I knew that. It was why I had been so reluctant to come down. "Good morning," I said. "Why don't you eat something?" I offered them a basket of rolls.

"Never mind that," Catherine said, waving the basket away. Anthony took a roll. "What did you find out?" she asked again.

"Why don't you eat breakfast and then we'll talk about it?" I suggested. It did not help at all that I could see both their auras were all flowering and happy and hopeful.

Catherine dropped into a chair opposite me. "That's not a good sign. If you had good news, you'd just tell us." She said that as though she was bracing herself for bad news—but her aura was still all cheerful and sunlit. For now.

"Tarry insisting on breakfast doesn't necessarily mean he has bad news," Anthony said, taking the chair next to her. "Tarry just likes breakfast."

"Right," I agreed. "I do. Breakfast is great, breakfast is a very important part of—"

"So do you have bad news?" Anthony asked.

I sighed, shoulders slumping. Dodging around this for a little while was plainly not going to work. Too bad, because I hate to give bad news to someone who has an empty stomach. "I wouldn't call it *bad* news," I hedged, "I don't think I'd call it that. I wouldn't call it *good* news either, precisely, but..."

"Can you break the spell or can't you?" Catherine asked.

I winced. "Not so loud! I'm trying to keep my magicalness discreet, remember?" I looked around, but no one seemed to be paying attention. "If we've really got to have this discussion right away, let's take it somewhere more private."

We took the discussion to a sitting room not far from the banquet hall. Every castle I've ever been in has had an inordinate number of sitting rooms. I insisted on bringing the basket of rolls too. We sat down on opposite couches, and I tried to think of the best way to get into this conversation.

"So I assume you've tried to leave?" I asked Anthony. "You know, just walk away?"

He nodded. "Of course, the first day. I got as far as the farthest archway and there was—it was like an invisible wall that only got in my way, no one else's. And it gave off pink sparks when I touched it."

"It would," I muttered, glaring down at my feet. "Marj likes pink sparks. Well, that about fits."

"Fits with *what*? Tarry, what did you find out?" Catherine demanded, hands in fists in her lap.

I sighed again. "Unfortunately, I found out that Marj wasn't creative with this. She just created a standard shield spell."

"Why is that bad?" Anthony asked. "If it's standard, how complicated can it be to get past?"

"See, that sounds reasonable, but in actual practice, simple spells are harder to get around." I rubbed the back of my neck, tried to explain this without rambling off too far. "Complex ones are much more likely to have a loophole in them somewhere. This particular spell is among the most basic, and one we all use. So any obvious flaws in it were discovered and adjusted for centuries ago."

"So can you break the spell or not?" Catherine asked for the second time.

"I've told you this, it doesn't work that way. Fairies can't just undo each other's spells. It's against the rules." I picked up a roll from the nearby basket and tore it nervously in half. I didn't *like* this conversation, and I saw no reason to think it would get better. "What we're trying to do is modify the spell in a way that will solve the problem. Like Marj did with Princess Rosaline. She couldn't undo Echinacea's spell, but she modified it into sleep instead of death."

Anthony frowned. "I don't want to sleep for a hundred years."

"No, that wouldn't help much," I agreed. "It wouldn't work on this spell anyway. Death relates naturally to sleep and..." And I was stalling. "Well, it's not relevant here. So I spent last night trying to work out what would be relevant."

"And?" Catherine prompted.

I took a bite of bread, chewed, swallowed. Stalling again. "First off," I said at last, "I think we ought to keep firmly in mind that this is just the first and most obvious option, modifying the spell, I mean. It's completely possible, probable even, that we're going to think of other options as time—"

"Just tell us what you found out," Catherine interrupted, face tight with impatience.

"*Can* you modify the spell?" Anthony asked, leaning forward from where he sat on the couch.

"Ye-es...but I don't think you're going to like any of the options." I didn't like any of them.

"All right, understood," Anthony said. "So tell us about them."

"Well." I tore off another chunk of bread. "I can get you out of here if you're willing to permanently transform into something else. A bird, say."

Anthony shook his head. "I don't think that's exactly..."

"I didn't think so either." I stared at the torn piece of bread, and was not at all hungry. I tossed it up in the air, flicked a bit of magic and shaped it into a bread bird that flew out the window. "Or I might be able to modify the spell to just keep part of you. So if you cut off a hand, the rest of you could leave."

Anthony flexed his fingers. "That seems drastic. I couldn't just leave a lock of hair?"

"That wouldn't be enough. It would have to be a hand at the minimum. And that would be a bad idea even if you were willing, because in all likelihood the, ah, removed appendage could react strangely to the spell, take on its own activities, it could all get very weird and unpleasant and I don't recommend it." I had debated even mentioning that idea but it was an option, if a bad one. In among a lot of bad ones. "Or there's the Persephone-clause. You'd only have to stay here for nine months out of the year instead of twelve, but it would lock out any possibility of ever leaving during those nine."

Anthony shook his head. "There's no long-term future in that. How can you have a life somewhere if you can only spend a quarter of the year there?"

I stared at the remainder of the roll in my hand. "See, I knew you wouldn't like the options."

"Those are *all* the options?" Catherine said, voice rising. The flowers in her aura were pulling themselves closed again as the situation sank in.

I forced myself to nod. "I hate to say it, but Marj is actually effective with her magic. She uses it for silly things mostly, but when she casts a spell, there's no easy way to circumvent it."

"But *she* could lift it," Catherine said, hands lacing together so tightly her knuckles were white. "If we could just talk her into doing it."

Anthony's shoulders had slumped. "I have this feeling that no one ever talks Marjoram into doing anything."

I hesitated. "It's not *unheard* of. It's happened. I'm almost sure of it."

"That's about what I figured," he said, with no animation in his voice at all. "Maybe Beauty's right. Maybe I should try to accept being here."

I instinctively wanted to tell him not to give up, but I couldn't honestly think of any reason not to. I wanted to be encouraging just for the sake of not dealing with despair, not because I had any good reason for him to be hopeful.

"No, you shouldn't," Catherine said. I doubt she cared whether there was a good reason to keep fighting or not. "I'm not prepared to spend the rest of my life here."

Anthony didn't look at her. "I didn't say anything about you staying here."

Catherine's eyes narrowed. "Anthony…"

"Just because I'm trapped here, there's no spell holding *you* here."

"*Anthony…*"

"There's no reason you can't go back to your life."

"No, only that a significant part of my life is trapped here!"

I coughed. "Maybe I should step out for a minute?" How did I keep getting stuck listening while they argued?

Maybe because they kept ignoring me whenever I tried to leave. "I mean it, Cat," Anthony pressed on, "you can just—"

"I did not travel for four days, camp in the mountains, sleep in a barn, fight with baby dragons and centaurs and a cyclops, and be kissed by Roderick, just to turn around and go home again!"

Anthony blinked. "Roderick kissed you?"

No, I didn't want to stay for this. Storms were raging through both their auras by now. I quietly got to my feet, started moving towards the door,

Catherine's eyebrows rose. "Baby dragons, centaurs and a cyclops, and that's the part that bothers you?"

"No—I mean…" Anthony shook his head. "None of you seemed hurt, are you…"

"No, we're all fine," she admitted. Because I was *some* use as a magical protector.

"So what happened when Roderick kissed you?"

Her eyebrows rose archly. "Considering you think I ought to just go back home and carry on with my life, I don't see how it's any of your concern what happened when Roderick—"

"She slapped him," I said, stopping short of the door because I couldn't let that one just go by.

"*Tarry!*"

"Don't yell at me," I protested, "that's what happened. And pretending that something else happened with *Roderick*, of all people, is just ridiculous. Now I'm going to go finish breakfast while you two talk—"

"You don't have to go, there's nothing to talk about," Catherine said, "because I'm not leaving."

Anthony's lips pressed into a line. "Can you at least consider the idea? Can you try for once to be open to another view?"

She glared at him, an expression alarmingly similar to how she'd looked at Roderick any number of times. "I suppose you'd rather I was one of those horrid simpering girls who doesn't have any views."

"Considering that girl would probably go home when I said that she should, then yes, at the moment, yes, I think that—"

"How much is it not about me?" she asked abruptly.

"What are you talking about?"

I understood better than Anthony. "Could you not go there? Really, I don't think that's a good place to go."

They were still ignoring me. "You sat out on the front steps and told Connor that your trouble with being trapped here wasn't entirely about me. *How much* is it not about me?"

Anthony's general exasperation had been overlaid with confusion. "How do you know that? You can't know that."

She waved a hand at me. "Tarry cast a spell."

I winced. I should have just walked out the door two minutes ago. "Why do you have to drag me into this? She was *worried*, and—"

"Never mind that," Anthony said, "this whole thing is absurd—"

"Do you not really want me to be here?" Catherine demanded. "I thought it was *nice* that you really wanted to run The Nightingale, but maybe I was reading that wrong. After all, suppose someone wants to run an inn, why not marry an innkeeper's daughter?"

"That's ridiculous and not what I meant and—I was talking about how I want to live my life, it wasn't about you!"

"I can see that," she said coldly.

He groaned, pressed one fist against his forehead. "That's not what I—"

"You go right ahead and live your life however you want," she snapped, "why should that have anything to do with me, just do what you like and don't let me stop you."

He lowered his hand, glared at her. "Fine. I will. And you can just go kiss Roderick if you'd like to!"

"Maybe I will!"

"I don't care if you do!"

And then there was silence. I was still hovering by the door, while the two of them sat on the couch, both with arms crossed, neither looking at the other.

I coughed again. "So. I'm just going to go. We can talk more later." I reached for the door handle, pulled it open.

"Tarry, wait," Catherine said.

Why didn't I pop out the moment their voices got heated? I was positively crawling with awkwardness by now, and she wanted me to stay? "Oh come on, you don't want to talk to me right now."

"You said you can't break Marjoram's spell because of the rules. So you *could* do it?"

I blinked. Yeah, I had said that, way back at the beginning of this conversation. How did she keep track of so many ideas at once? "Well, yes. Technically. But I told you, the rules—"

"*Please*," Catherine said, looking at me with eyes alarmingly bright. "This is—this…" She trailed off, waving a hand between herself and Anthony, somehow conveying everything that had just happened and the larger problems too, and why it was all so very, very bad. "Can't you break the rules? Just once?"

And then Anthony was looking at me too, trying not to look hopeful but he couldn't keep it out of his eyes or his aura.

My stomach sank right down to my boots as an awful conversation got so much worse. "You don't understand," I said feebly. "It doesn't work that way, I can't just…I *can't*."

Anthony shook his head. "Cat, we can't ask—"

"Yes, we can! He's our friend and this is our life we're talking about. It's more important than some silly rule that—"

"The rules aren't silly," I said. My stomach seemed to be back in its place, but guilt and anger were twisting it into knots. "And they can't be broken lightly or without consequences. Believe me, *I* know."

For a moment, silence. Then Catherine asked the obvious question. "How?"

How did I know? I didn't want to talk about how I knew. I never talked about this. Five hundred years, I hadn't talked about this. But no one had ever asked either, and if I didn't answer now, she was going to keep looking to me for a solution that I didn't have. I walked away from the door, sat down on the couch again. "I broke the rules once," I said, staring at my toes. "The Fairy Court banished me to live with humans. As a human."

"We're not so bad, are we?" Anthony asked, with a forced light tone.

They still didn't understand. I still didn't look up from my feet. "They banished me for a *hundred years*. And it wasn't living with humans that was bad, it was…" I rubbed a hand over my eyes. "It was actually good, at first. I had—friends." Family. I had thought of them as my family. And I had avoided thinking about them for centuries now.

"But then…bad things started happening. Not big, epic bad things, nothing anyone would write a legend or a ballad about. Just normal things. Nerissa got sick with fever. Jerome didn't have the money to marry his childhood sweetheart, so her father made her marry someone else. Octavia lost her baby. A magician got into a fit about something and sent a storm that ruined everyone's crops that year. Normal things. But I couldn't *do* anything. I didn't have any magic.

And I promised myself, when I got my powers back, I'd fix everything."

I sighed. "But then more years passed and…and by the time a century had gone by, *everyone* I knew, everyone I'd known when I first arrived…they were gone. Young or old, they still died eventually. And the bad things, they just kept happening. No one could stop all of them, and in the end, it didn't matter anyway because nothing lasts forever. So what's the good of anything, and if you have a choice about it, why not just eat, drink and have a good time?"

Catherine was shaking her head. "No, I don't believe that. The things we do matter."

"But the problems never stop." I clenched my hands in my lap, stared down at them. "You think if we solve this problem, you two will live happily ever after together. But life just isn't like that."

"I'm not asking to live happily ever after together," Catherine said in a low voice. "I'm just asking—"

However she finished that sentence, it was drowned out by the sudden, deafening roar from outside. The castle didn't actually shake, crack apart and topple over, but for a few seconds it felt as though surely it was going to.

"What was that?" Catherine asked, gaze darting towards the window. The window showed nothing of consequence, clearly facing the wrong direction.

I took a deep breath, tried to re-bury dug up memories, and focus on the present. On the latest problem. "That, unless I'm gravely mistaken, which I'm not, was a dragon."

"And I don't suppose that was dragon language for 'hello, lovely to meet you?' " Catherine said, hand reaching out to clutch Anthony's hand resting on the couch next to her. He looked down with something like surprise, but his fingers wrapped around hers too.

"No," I said, "that sounded more like Draconian for 'hello, I want to talk to you and I'm already not happy with you, so you had better have something good to say.' "

"All that in one roar?" Anthony said.

"Draconian roars are complex."

"Can we not talk about dragon linguistics while there's a dragon roaring at us?" Catherine said. "What are we going to *do*?"

"First, we're going to be thankful that at least it didn't mean 'hello, I'm here to kill you,' and second, we're going to get a better idea of what's going on." I snapped my fingers and transported all three of us to the roof of the castle. It had been a rotten conversation anyway, well-worth interrupting. Not that this was likely to get any better.

The view was less pleasant than it had been the previous night. To the south, a long lawn sloped down towards the trees. A number of those trees were bent double by the weight of three dragons perched in their upper branches. The dragons all had their wings at least half unfurled, they were sending up considerable tendrils of smoke and though they said they were willing to talk, they did not look friendly.

The dragons were only part of the problem. On the lawn, dozens of centaurs were massed in neat rows. I sharpened my eyesight enough to recognize Rajna at the head of the foremost column. Considering she was only conditionally friendly, that was only conditionally comforting.

That was the south, the front of the castle. To the north, at the back, the newly-created army was camping. Men were currently falling out of tents and stumbling into formations, while officers yelled directions. Not comforting either.

And just to add to the confusion, there were a lot of milling civilians in every direction—none all that close to the centaurs and dragons, but close enough to be likely casualties if a fight started. I remembered that Cesar was scheduled to address his subjects today. Obviously people had come for the speech.

"This is bad," Catherine was murmuring, "this is so bad."

We didn't have time for more analysis in the immediate moment, because company arrived. I wasn't the only one who thought of coming to the roof to see what was going on, and the door opened to emit a stream of people. Cesar was at the head, followed by Connor, as well as the entire advising council. I could only assume they'd been in conference when the roaring started. They must have had guests at the meeting too, because George and Roderick turned up right behind the rest, George munching a pastry as big as his head and Roderick fussing about whether his sword belt was straight.

For a long silent moment, everyone stared at the forces arrayed to the south.

"What do you suppose they want?" Cesar said finally.

That was probably rhetorical and definitely wasn't directed at me, but I answered anyway. "The dragons want to talk, but they don't sound happy. I think it's fairly obvious they've been talking to the centaurs."

"We just had a message from the centaurs," Connor said. "They asked if we're willing to meet with them to discuss an alliance."

"That's what they said when we talked to them yesterday," Catherine said, "but they also said they'll fight if we aren't willing to talk."

Connor was pacing. "All right, so it's not a disaster yet. They aren't determined on attacking yet. The dragons are open to talking, the centaurs are open to talking, and we..."

He trailed off. Every gaze went to Cesar. He looked back without apparent trepidation, feet firmly planted, and clasped his hands behind his back. His face was calm, but his aura was roaring defiance. "I don't negotiate with monsters."

I wanted to push him off the roof. I wanted to turn him back into a Beast. I locked my fingers together behind my back, resisting the urge to hurl magic around.

"You don't have a choice anymore," Connor said, voice flat. "Those are dragons out there. Three fully-grown dragons. And dozens of well-armed centaurs. If you don't talk to them, they are going to attack us."

"Let them." Cesar waved a hand towards the army behind the castle. "We have a defensible castle, and a military force to defend it."

Connor's hands closed into fists at his sides. "Your military force consists of farm boys and mercenaries, half of whom know nothing about fighting and none of whom have been trained to fight together. If you choose to fight today, we are all going to die. You, me, Beauty, those men out in the field who swore loyalty to you, the people who came to see their new king today, and probably even a lot of centaurs and a dragon or two. There's no reason for this."

And yet it was the way life was. Terrible things happened every day. This was exactly why I had spent centuries going to parties, and trying to ignore the other side of life.

Cesar was impervious to Connor's argument. "Nonsense. Everyone knows one human soldier is worth five monsters." He turned, and headed for the stairs. "I'll find a messenger to tell those creatures I will not be speaking with them. And I need to find my general to plan a strategy. I believe bringing the army within the walls of the castle and fighting from the main gate would be best." His voice and footsteps faded away as he disappeared down the stairs, evidently completely confident that we would follow him.

After a few seconds, the advising council did.

"If any of you," Connor said tightly, "had supported me, this might have been averted."

The last one paused at the head of the stairs to look back with a guilty expression. "It's just that—you don't know what it's been like, a hundred years enchanted and..."

"I don't care about your excuses, go," Connor said, waving him away. He went.

The rest of us remained on the roof, staring at each other—except Roderick, who was leaning on the low wall and studying the dragons.

"So what are we going to do?" Anthony asked, after several seconds of silence.

Connor shook his head, running a hand through his hair. "I don't know. I really don't. Go get a sword and join the army, I think. I don't know what else to do. If that band of farm boys can actually defend the castle, this might turn into a draw instead of a slaughter, which might keep a few more people alive at the end of the day."

"You don't think the humans have a chance, do you?" I asked. Even though I could assess the situation well enough myself. I avoided fights, but it didn't need a military genius to calculate the odds here.

"This army, against those forces?" Connor said. "No." And then his head rose, looking at me with eyes widening. "Although, if we had some magical support..."

I shifted, looked away. "I can't. This is a war. There are rules."

Out of the corner of my eye, I saw Connor nod slowly. "Cesar wouldn't have accepted your help anyway."

"No rules getting in my way," George said cheerfully. He popped the last bite of pastry into his mouth and asked, "Where do you s'pose we could find the swords?"

"I can't leave the castle, but I can defend from inside a gate," Anthony volunteered, mouth set into grim determination. "Not very well, maybe, but a little better than most farmhands."

"Wait, there has to be something else we can do," Catherine said, voice rising in desperation.

"If I'm going to slay a dragon, I really should be wearing black," Roderick said, inspecting his red shirt. "But I suppose this will have to do." He stepped up to stand next to Connor. "Lead the way."

Connor grinned at him. "Good to have you with us, your highness."

"This is insane!" Catherine protested, head turning to look between them. "This is practically suicide, there has to be a better plan than this!"

"Tarry, can you get her out of here?" Anthony asked.

I jumped, not expecting to be addressed. I was so clearly superfluous to this conversation. "I can do that. Yeah. That I can do." It was all I could do. It was so little.

"Good," Anthony said with a nod. "Cat, don't argue with me this time. Go home. Find Jack and Emmy, and all of you go home. Your father and The Nightingale need you."

"But I need *you*," she said, catching his arm as he turned to follow George, Connor and Roderick towards the stairs.

Anthony looked back, and half-smiled. "I thought you were mad at me anyway."

"I am. That doesn't mean I don't still love you."

Anthony lifted her chin with one finger. "I don't not love you too," he said, kissed her swiftly, and was gone, clattering down the stairs after the others.

Catherine looked after him, looked at the massed armies in either direction, and looked at me. "How can you stand there and do *nothing?*"

It wasn't like it was easy for me. "These are armies, I can't interfere with the military. And Anthony, Connor and George just rejoined the army, so I can't interfere with them either. That's just the rules and I—"

"I know about your rules and I know they're important, but…" She blinked hard, looked out at the dragons again. "People are going to die. People I care about." Her voice broke on the last phrase and she sniffed. "People I thought you cared about."

Well, yes, that was the problem. If I didn't *care,* I could just walk away. I had spent centuries trying not to care. Spent centuries walking away. "In a hundred years," I said slowly, "it won't matter."

I was mostly talking to myself, but Catherine lifted her head to stare at me, tears and anger mingled in her eyes. "It matters *today.* It matters to *me!*"

I stared back at her, jaw tight and guilt writhing through me and—and suddenly I was remembering Nerissa. Nerissa who had died of a fever centuries ago, who no one except me remembered anymore. She'd had a lot of the same defiance, the same determination, the same fierce caring for others. Maybe that was why I had liked Catherine; I had pushed away thoughts of Nerissa for years, but Catherine reminded me of her. Nerissa had been my friend, and I knew I would have saved her if I could have.

Maybe it wouldn't have made much difference in the end, but it would have been different for her. And *that* mattered. Because people mattered.

You know something, something I never admitted even to myself? All those centuries, I was never very good at not caring anyway. Why else would I spend so much energy haranguing Marj about all the people she was trampling over?

I let out a long breath. "I can't promise you'll live happily ever after together."

The first glimmer of hope came back into Catherine's eyes. "I wasn't asking for that," she whispered. "I just wanted us to be together."

I nodded. "Then I think it's time to break some rules."

Chapter Twenty-Eight

I crossed to the edge of the roof, and leaned over the wall to look at the activity below. Cesar's army had swarmed in from the back and was gathered in the various courtyards near the front half of the castle, ready to march out through the main gate. Assuming they could get organized enough to march, which currently looked doubtful.

Beyond the gate, the centaurs were lined up with their weapons drawn, and the dragons were wheeling and circling and getting themselves into a V high above, preparatory to diving actions. Anyone not involved in either army was scattering into the distance—but not as far as I would have considered sensible. Entirely too many of them were stopping and looking back and even sitting on the grass to watch. This was a terrible idea. But then, so was everything else going on right now.

"I think," I said, "that everyone needs a bit of a rest."

I reached over the wall, spread my hands out palms down, and concentrated. Dark green smoke poured from my palms, growing thinner and fainter as it spread, until it was hardly more than a shimmer (which is *not* the same as sparkling). It drifted down into the castle, over the army, out beyond the main gate and over the centaurs too.

In the courtyard, everyone the shimmer passed slowed, began to yawn, and after a few seconds settled down to sleep. A few stayed awake just long enough to open the main gates, only to then fall asleep sprawled half inside the castle and half on the road outside. Out on the plains, some of the centaurs curled up on the grass, while others fell very contentedly asleep standing up. Horses can sleep in either position, you know. The spell kept spreading and reached to the onlookers too, until the surrounding lawn was covered in sleeping bodies.

When everyone on the ground was accounted for, I lifted my hands and sent my magic up toward the dragons who, based on the way their heads were swinging, were just beginning to notice that something strange was going on. The shimmer hit them and they stopped thinking about it. They circled down to settle in a clump of tangled wings and tails, all asleep in one big pile. Considering that's how baby dragons sleep, this could have been adorable, but…well, there were a few too many wickedly clawed feet visible.

"What did you just do?" Catherine asked from behind me, voice faint.

"I put everything on hold for a while."

"I didn't know you could do that."

"I usually choose not to use world-altering spells. It doesn't mean I can't. But I promise they won't sleep for a hundred years. A few hours, maybe."

I rubbed my hands together. It probably looked like I was just anticipating next steps, but also my hands had a funny tingle going on. Funny tingles happen when you're casting spells that you're not allowed to cast. There was a funny tingle running up my spine too, because I knew exactly how much trouble this was going to get me into. But never mind that now, I had work to do.

I turned my back on the sleeping crowds, looked at Catherine who was looking back with very wide eyes. "So while everything's holding still, I'll find Cesar, wake him up, and convince him that he needs to talk about peace, and right now. If he's less than agreeable, which is probable, I'll turn him back into a Beast, and we'll figure out what else we can try." I wasn't sure what else, but the sky was the limit—I was breaking the rules, I couldn't get into any more trouble than I was already in.

She cleared her throat. "Can you do that? Turn him into a Beast?"

"Legally? No. Marj has prior jurisdiction because she enchanted him first, so I'm not supposed to cast major spells on him. At the moment, that's irrelevant." The funny tingle in my spine was joined by nerves in my stomach—but you know, while some of them were worried, there was something thrilling about all this too. After centuries of doing nothing, I was going to do *everything*. "Speaking of spells I can cast but not legally..."

I snapped my fingers once and sent a single spark out questing in amongst the slumbering soldiers until it found Anthony. Once I located him, I sent a flood of magic at the spell wrapped around him, and felt a very satisfying snap as Marj's sparkly streamers of magic stretched, strained and broke. "Anthony can walk out of here when he wakes up. I can't promise Marj won't re-enchant him, but I'll try to talk her out of it. And while I'm at it..." I leaned over the wall until I could see the two statues standing in front of the door. I darted a spell at each of them, and the stone statues shimmered and turned back into flesh. Miranda and Noreen looked around in confusion for a few seconds before my sleeping spell caught them too, and they sank down onto the steps. "There, that's taken care of too."

Catherine took a few quick steps forward and hugged me.

"Oh. Um..." I gingerly patted her back. Fairies aren't really huggers.

"Thank you," she said. "If they banish you again, I promise you can come live at The Nightingale."

I felt a strange warmth in my chest. "Thanks," I said, and coughed. "That's, um...thanks."

It was just about the nicest offer anyone had made to me in a long, long time. Nicer even then, 'how about a fourth helping?' Except if I took her up on it—I'd have to watch whatever bad things life sent at them.

But I'd get to see the good things too.

I backed a careful step away from Catherine. "Right, so, right now, I need to find Cesar and—" I broke off as all my magical senses went pinging all over the place. New arrivals had appeared on the rooftop behind me. Catherine's eyes widened again as she looked past me.

"Ooh, Tarry, you're going to be in *trouble*," a voice trilled gleefully.

I sighed, and said, "Hello, Sage," without turning around. I had really hoped this wouldn't happen so soon. I wasn't *done* yet.

"You know you weren't supposed to do that," Sage scolded.

"I had reasons," I said, turning to face her and her two companions. I nodded to them. "Collinsonia. Aniseed. Always a pleasure." They weren't my favorite people, but we usually got on. They were better than Marj and her friends. If a group of Good Fairies had come to arrest me... Maybe the Fairy Court knew that would just guarantee I'd resist arrest.

"You have broken very serious rules, Tarragon," Collinsonia said in her gravelly voice. "There will be consequences."

I rubbed the back of my neck. "Yeah. I know."

"Who *are* you?" Catherine asked, voice slightly unsteady.

Aniseed focused his usually dreamy eyes on her for a moment. "I believe what you really mean is: what are we," he said in a distant tone.

"We're fairies, of course, little human," Sage said happily, flitting over to peer at Catherine from an inch away. "You're kind of pretty. Not colorful, though."

Catherine leaned back but didn't actually take a step in retreat. "If you're all fairies, why don't you look the same?"

I couldn't blame her for being taken aback. Sage especially doesn't look much like anything humans are familiar with. She's shaped like a human, basically, but her skin is a multicolored pattern of patches, mostly purple, orange and pink. Her hair, if you can call it that, is black and short enough to be little more than fuzz. Collinsonia, on the other hand, is just the opposite, short and solid and compact, and faintly blue-gray in color. Aniseed is always swathed in pearly, faintly luminescent robes that match his skin. His eyes and sweep of shoulder-length hair are both silver. Altogether, they look much more extraordinary to humans than I ever do.

"We look different because we like different things, silly!" Sage exclaimed, hands on her hips. "I like butterflies. Don't you?"

"Fairies usually look sort of like what they're interested in," I explained. "Collinsonia is a stone fairy, and Aniseed—"

"I am attuned to the celestials," he intoned.

I rolled my eyes. "He likes the stars."

Collinsonia cleared her throat, sounding like a patter of stones. "Now is not the time to explain the nature of fairies to the human. The King and Queen are displeased, Tarragon."

I scratched behind the point of one ear. I knew that, I'd just sort of been stalling. "I figured they would be. Look, can't you three turn a blind eye for just a few more minutes? There's this king I need to deal with." If they hauled me off and woke everyone up now, everyone would just go back to fighting with each other. If I could just have a few more minutes…

But before I could get any farther with a negotiation, my senses pinged again—more like a shrill whistle this time, and Marj arrived in a mass of pink sparkles and fury.

"Tarry, you broke my spells!" she shrilled. "You're not supposed to do that and..." She trailed off, looking around at the slumbering armies. "Oh dear. You did more than just break my spells, didn't you?"

"You could put it that way." My shoulders sagged. Marj would never stand by while I turned Cesar back into a Beast. Meaning all of this wasn't even going to stop the disaster from happening. I was probably going to spend a hundred years as a toad, and I hadn't even done any good.

"The King and Queen have sent us to bring him back to the Royal Court," Aniseed told Marj, seeming especially slow and remote next to her frenzied sparkliness.

"But this is ridiculous," Catherine broke in, "all he did was stop people from killing each other for stupid reasons. How can you object to that?"

"We are not to interfere in wars," Collinsonia said, somehow contriving to look down at her, even though Catherine was the taller of the two.

"No, you just interfere with everything else," she snapped.

"And who are you?" Marj asked, in her distantly polite tone of voice, nose in the air.

"Catherine Williams," she said, dropping half a curtsy. "You decorated my inn once for—"

"Oh, you have an *inn*," Marj said. Her nose rose even further. "You're not a princess, then?"

"No, definitely not," Catherine said with some puzzlement.

"I see," Marj said, and turned to me. "Tarry, you should have known better."

I could not deal with her right now. "Don't even start, Marj." I *should* have known better—not the way she meant, not about not breaking the rules, but I should have had a better plan. I should have made sure I could actually fix things.

Now my only chance was to argue the case to the King and Queen. And there was no predicting how *that* would go, no matter what I said to them.

"We don't have time for this," Collinsonia said. "We need to gather up all involved parties and get to the Court."

"Me, that's me," Catherine said quickly. She stepped forward to stand next to me. "I'm involved."

My stomach, already twisted, did an extra flip. Oh no, this was just going to make things so much worse. I had known I was done for from the moment I cast the first sleeping spell, but I had never meant to drag Catherine down with me. I hurriedly stepped in front of her. "No, she's not involved," I contradicted. "She had nothing to do with any of this."

"Yes, I did, I stood right here and said—"

"You are *not* involved, you are not coming with us." I dragged her aside a few steps, and hissed, "You don't want to do this. This is how people get turned into toads. Or kittens. Or worse."

"There's something worse than being turned into a kitten?"

I glowered at her. "That's not funny! Trust me, you don't want to get mixed up in this."

She shook her head, mouth set in a determined line. "I'm already mixed up in this. You got into trouble trying to help us, because I asked you to. I'm not walking away now, and that's final."

I let out a breath—and gave up. It would be easier to defend her to the Court than to argue with her, when she got that look. I turned back to the cluster of fairies. "All right. She's involved. Cesar, the king, he's involved too." This really was all his fault. And if I couldn't get away with turning him into a Beast, just maybe I could convince someone else to, which *might* be enough to keep this war from re-starting when everyone woke up. It was a long-shot, but it was the best I could think of. "That's it. No one else."

"I don't think he's telling the truth," Sage announced, hopping up onto the nearby wall to perch with her elbows on her knees.

"Yes, Tarry, you don't really think we'd believe that?" Marj said, crossing her arms and jetting off silver sparks.

If my life had to explode, was it too much to ask for the explosion to not be accompanied by sparkles? "You know who else is involved?" I snapped. "*You're* involved. You started the whole mess."

Marj sniffed. "That is simply nonsense."

"There's an easy solution to this," Collinsonia said. "We'll bring the entire royal family—they're surely involved—and we'll bring anyone else he's been spending time with lately. We'll be able to sense traces of his aura on them."

"That's a bad solution," I objected. "I don't like that solution."

"Because you know it will work," Aniseed said serenely.

Yes, that was exactly why I objected. Because it was going to work, and it was going to drag along everyone I had been hoping to keep away from the Fairy Court and potential toad transformations. Over my objection, they went ahead anyway. That led to identifying the entire Maurier family, plus Cesar, Roderick, Jack and Emmy. Catherine was willing to back me up that none of these people were involved in anything, but the other fairies didn't believe us. Finally I had to give up, wave my hands, transport the involved parties to the roof and wake them up.

There followed a multitude of exclamations and mutters and queries, depending on the individual. Most of them were along the lines of "what just happened?" and "where are we?" and at least one, "but I was going to slay a dragon." Catherine threw her arms around Anthony and there was a fair bit of hugging going on around Miranda and Noreen too. In the middle of all the hubbub we got enough explanation out for most people to have some notion of what was going on, though I wouldn't swear Roderick followed much of it.

All his royal highness came back with was, "You mean I don't get to slay a dragon?"

"No," I said, "you don't." Then I waved my hands again, and we were off to the Fairy Court.

Chapter Twenty-Nine

I had only the haziest idea how I was going to explain anything to my monarchy, and the instantaneous trip there gave me no time to think about it.

It's slightly simpler but still difficult to explain exactly where the Fairy Court is. Don't even get me started on *when* it is. For where, the Fairy Court is only in some sense in the world that humans inhabit. You can get there many ways from many places, and they don't make any geographic sense from a human perspective; there's a mountain in Greece, a garden in Britain and my favorite orange grove on the western coast of a distant continent, from all of which you can reach the Fairy Court by a short walk. It doesn't make my brain hurt because I'm a fairy and I understand temporal, magical and spatial relationships, but it tends to give humans headaches.

If you ever happen to take a wrong turn while in a British garden or on a Greek mountain and find yourself at the Fairy Court, it doesn't make much difference how long you stay. All you can do is hope that five minutes will have elapsed, or maybe a year and a day, instead of seven years or seven times seven years. And, piece of free advice— don't talk unless someone talks to you first.

The entire crowd of us arrived, fairies and humans, in the front entrance hall of the Court. The area around us was deserted, with all the activity in the next room (though 'room' is a loose term in this case— so is 'hall'). The other fairies immediately headed off down the hall— Marj floated, Collinsonia stomped, Aniseed glided and Sage skipped. The humans stayed planted in a muddled and hesitant clump.

"I promise you can walk forward," I said. "The floor is much more solid than it looks." I took a few steps forward myself. "The place also isn't as big as it seems. In some senses."

It's almost as hard to describe the Fairy Court as it is to explain where it is. Parts of it humans don't have the ability to see the way I do, which means they don't have the vocabulary for me to explain it to them. For what humans *can* see…golden columns line the front hall on either side, each column encircled by jeweled vines. Between the columns you can see the blazing pinks and reds of the sunrise to the east, and equally blazing oranges and golds of the sunset to the west, both at once and all the time.

The floor tends to give humans the most trouble. Some say it looks like you're looking down at the ocean, while others insist it looks much more like the entire night sky circling below, stars and galaxies and all. Up above, there's a perfectly natural blue sky, with just a few decorative white clouds.

I managed to herd my humans forward, at varying paces and with varying degrees of confidence, towards the archway at the far end of the hall. That opened onto the throne room, where all the activity was. From the hall, all you can see through the arch is a flurry of color and light and not much else, in part because the archway gives the impression of being at least a mile away. And in one sense it is. And in another sense it's not. But you can cross the hall in a dozen or so steps, and from a practical perspective, that's all that really matters.

We entered at the southern end of the court (as much as you can talk about directions at the Fairy Court), while the royal thrones are at the northern end. The landscape in there is slightly more manageable for humans, essentially marble pillars, a high vaulted ceiling, and an expanse of blue sky in all directions between the pillars, including the direction we'd come from.

A vast crowd milled about between us and the thrones, but that didn't matter. Communication amongst fairies is different than it is amongst humans. We didn't have a herald or need one. When you arrive at the Fairy Court needing an audience with their Majesties on urgent business, everyone knows it. Space had cleared for Sage, Collinsonia, Aniseed, and Marjoram, and remained cleared for us, only closing behind our group as we moved forward towards the thrones.

Beyond being basically human-shaped, fairies resemble what we're interested in, but for the King and Queen, it's hard to find anything they resemble. Moonlight might be the closest. Silvery, distant and cold. Thin and tall and remote. The King and Queen are only interested in fairies, so some speculate that they're what we would all look like in our most essential way, if we weren't affected by outside influences. But that kind of speculation makes even my head hurt.

I stopped a respectful distance from the thrones (not that the distance would be any protection if spells started flying) and bowed deeply. The last thing I needed was to offend them now. More than recent events had already, I mean. Still, if I was going to scramble my way out of this, a respectful attitude couldn't hurt. Behind me, I sensed the humans bowing or curtsying a heartbeat after me. Roderick didn't go as low as he should have.

The Fairy Queen lowered her chin perhaps half an inch, her eyes a comparable distance, and still gave me the impression that she was standing atop a high mountain peak, sending her gaze down over rocks and ridges and valleys and streams, down to the very base of the mountain, to look at me.

"Tarragon," she said in a voice that sounded like the wind between the stars, "you have broken our laws by interfering in large-scale hostilities among the humans."

"And by overturning my spells," Marj put in, sounding especially shrill coming right after Her Majesty.

I ignored Marj, because talking to Marj would just lead to yelling and in-fighting and that would be totally counter-productive towards my goal of convincing the King and Queen that I was calm, rational and acting from justifiable and laudable motivations. "With all due respect, your Majesties," I said, "I had impeccable reasons for my actions."

If someone had told me a week before that my future would depend on convincing the Fairy Court that I was a responsible, conscientious and upstanding citizen…yeah, I probably would have run away to my orange grove on the spot. Too late now. Now this was my only last gasp hope, because if I could talk the King and Queen around to the idea that my actions were acceptable, maybe they'd actually let those actions stand.

"Really?" the King said, and in a single phrase evoked the call of hunting horns and the baying of hounds. "And what reasons were these, which were more important than our reasons for imposing the law?"

A difficult question to answer, to say the least. Fortunately, I hoped I had landed on the one argument that might carry weight. I kept my chin up, my back straight, and answered, "I was defending True Love."

My best and likely only chance was Catherine and Anthony. Directly or indirectly, I had been trying to help them. I had also been trying to prevent a war but, strange as it might sound to humans, that would probably mean much less to the King and Queen of the Fairies.

War is a uniquely human concept, and fairies avoid it because we don't really understand it. Rocks and animals and celestial bodies don't go to war. True Love, on the other hand, is universal. It looks very different among trees and stars than it does among humans, but at its heart it's the same. Every fairy understands the concept of True Love, and few ideas are held in higher regard.

"An intriguing claim," the King said, a ripple going through the crowd in response to my assertion. "Are you prepared to explain in what manner your actions were in the defense of True Love?"

"I am, Your Majesty," I said, and kept my voice steady. Even though 'prepared' was overstating it to an extent that made my response just a hair-shy of an absolute lie. But it's not like I had time to come up with anything better.

"But that's ridiculous, Tarry," Marj protested—completely out of turn. "How can you claim that breaking my spells had anything to do with helping True Love? That's what my spells are all about."

There she went, shoving her wings in where she wasn't needed, once again. But neither the King nor the Queen reprimanded her, so I figured I'd better answer her. "Like I said already, Marj, your spells are what caused most of the trouble. I had to interfere to fix the mess you made."

She sniffed. "Impossible."

"Marjoram is noted for her concern for mortals," the Queen observed.

I dearly wanted to mutter "*some* mortals" at that moment, but you don't interrupt the Queen. You just don't.

"What have you been engaged in recently?" the Queen asked Marj.

Marj looked up at her with the most innocent of expressions. "Only good, kind deeds bringing together people who were meant to be joined."

I controlled my urge to gag, but it was narrow.

Marj looked at my cluster of humans, and seized on Beauty and Cesar, pulling them forward from the crowd. Her madly flapping wings set up a cloud of sparkles around them. "Like these two! You see? I brought them together. And aren't you happy, dear?"

"Perfectly," Beauty said, smiling at Marj.

I thought I heard Anthony cough at that one. Cesar's glower was also rather at odds with the idea, although it seemed to be in response to the general situation, rather than Marj's question.

"And I fail to see, Tarry," Marj continued, "how your little display did anything at all for them."

Right, because no one else could possibly matter. "I wasn't trying to help them. I don't care about *them*. I was trying to help *these* two," I said, pulling Catherine and Anthony forward in turn. They were holding hands.

Marj's nose wrinkled. "The innkeeper? And the one who didn't want to spend time with his family?"

"That's not exactly—" Anthony began.

She talked over him. "And he's not even really royalty. I mean, in a distant, related sort of way, but that hardly counts."

"Why should it even matter whether we're royalty?" Catherine demanded.

I opened my mouth to tell her she'd better not talk here—then closed it again. Because if I was going to convince the Fairy Court that these people should be allowed to decide their own fates, without fairies interfering…well, my interfering wasn't going to help my point. Besides, if Catherine had recovered enough from the general shock of the surroundings to argue with Marj, it wasn't likely anything *I* could say would silence her.

Marj was all patronizing as she looked down her nose at Catherine. "We generally only expect to see True Love among royalty, and possibly certain very *special* commoners. You don't seem like the right type."

Catherine's eyebrows rose. "Not the right type."

"Only people like Beauty, right?" I prompted Marj. "Sweet and mild-mannered and refined and apt to fall in love with princes?" Give her enough rope, maybe I'd be able to tie her up in it…and get her to support my argument in spite of herself.

Not being able to read my thoughts, Marj looked at me with pleased surprise. "Why yes, Tarry, that's a very succinct description. Of course, great beauty and proper prioritizing of love are also very—"

"You're saying I'm supposed to sit around quietly until a prince comes along," Catherine said, arms crossed as she glowered at Marj.

"You could put it that way," Marj agreed without a trace of sarcasm.

Catherine appeared too stunned for words at that, so Anthony picked it up. "And you're also saying only princes are supposed to fall in love?"

Marj patronizing smile expanded to take in Anthony too. "To fall really, Truly in—"

"You mean princes like him?" Anthony asked, jerking a thumb toward Roderick. "The idiot who had to find his bride by her shoe size?"

"And who still can't remember her name?" Catherine added.

"I remember it," Roderick protested. "It's…Eleanor."

"*Ella*," Catherine, Jack and Emmy chorused—and me too.

Roderick shrugged. "See, I was close. What's in a name, anyway?"

We were getting some ripples of laughter from the crowd, but Marj's patronizing expression hadn't even taken a hit. "I've had centuries of experience with this situation, and with very rare, select exceptions, we only see True Love among *royalty*."

"What stories we have heard," the King said, everyone else falling silent as soon as he opened his mouth, "do have a tendency to describe royalty as experiencing True Love."

"If I may say so, Your Majesty," I said with half a bow, "that's because you only hear stories about humans who are royalty. My fellow fairies with an interest in humans only see True Love among royalty because they only *look* at royalty. I, however, pay attention to other people. And I have evidence on this subject."

I turned and beckoned Jack and Emmy forward. "You remember them, right, Marj? You decorated their wedding. With all the doves."

Emmy waggled her fingers in a tiny wave while Marj's sparkles took on a blessedly muted shade. "Oh," Marj said. "Yes. The kitchen maid and the goatherd."

"The goatherd who chose her over the princess," I added. "He chose the kitchen maid, who gave Echinacea *and* you a lecture on morals. How's that fit in with your 'meek girls waiting for princes' theory of special commoners?"

Marj harrumphed. Sure sign she was rattled, if she made a sound less refined than cooing. "Yes, *well*. I acknowledge the possibility of exceptions, but…"

"If you accept *they* have True Love," I said, and turned to point to Catherine and Anthony, "then you have to accept it's possible for *them* too. And come on, I can't be the only one who can see their auras, right?"

A lot of magical eyes focused more fixedly on Catherine and Anthony, and they had to be seeing some variation of what I could see: the trees in her garden and in his forest were so interlaced you could hardly tell which branches came from which.

I held my breath, and after a long moment, the Queen decreed, "I believe we can acknowledge that there is True Love between Catherine and Anthony." No one had told her their names, but—well, she's the Queen of the Fairies.

And at that pronouncement, I felt almost gleeful enough to sprout wings and fly. I was never, never going to let Marj forget this. Because if the Queen of the Fairies believed in True Love among commoners, Marj and her lot *had* to accept it. And that had to change things, that had to mean handling situations differently and—

"This fact alone, however," the Queen continued, "does not explain how your actions were justifiable, Tarragon."

My heels had actually begun to lift an inch off the floor, but they bumped right back down now. I'd got so caught up in the principle argument that I'd almost forgotten the more immediate issue, my rule-breaking and the consequences, for me and for Beaumont.

So I took a deep breath and began sketching over recent events, trying to show how my actions were relevant to keeping Catherine and Anthony together. Freeing Anthony from Marj's spell should have been the easiest to justify, though Marj didn't think so.

"I was not preventing them from being together," she protested, hands on hips and sparkles brightening again with indignation. "She could live in Beaumont."

"She has a life in Perrelda," I said flatly. "So did Anthony. And your little stunt about family togetherness was tearing them apart."

I would like to believe that Marj knew, on some level, that she was being ridiculous. I would like to believe that no one even distantly related to me could be that dense. Just stubborn about backing down. "But this is How Things Are *Done*," she insisted. "How They're *Always* Done."

"And they're always ridiculous," Catherine snapped. "You try to control everyone's lives, but we have a right to make our own choices."

"Intriguing," the King intoned. "Trees and stars do not speak of choices."

"Humans aren't like trees and stars," Catherine said. "Trees and stars are what they are and they don't change, not really. Humans change, and the choices we make are what make us who we are. But we have to be free to make those choices."

"So it doesn't work as well if someone comes along and turns you into a statue," Miranda spoke up. "Because then you can't make any choices or become anyone."

Marj shot her a cold look. "You and your sister needed to learn a lesson about jealousy."

Miranda's look was equally frigid. "I've never felt more jealous than when I could see everyone else walking around living and *I* was trapped in stone."

"Freeing these two had little to do with True Love, did it?" the Queen observed.

She'd just pointed out the big gaping hole in my defense. "Ah, yes, well, actually, you see..."

I had nowhere to go with that, so it's just as well she interrupted me to say, "But it does seem to have been a poorly taught lesson."

If anyone else had said that, Marj would have squawked indignation, but since it was the Queen, she lowered her eyes and said, "I'm afraid that may be so, Your Majesty."

Whatever else happened, whatever other consequences still awaited, I was going to forever cherish the moment when Marj was forced to admit she was *wrong*.

"Let us say that in this case, two negatives create a neutral situation, and clear the incident from the proceedings," the King decreed, which was just a fancy way of saying that neither Marj nor I were in trouble for it. So that made one charge dropped, two bigger ones still to deal with.

"As to the matter of the gentleman separated from his True Love." The King cast his gaze upon Catherine and Anthony for so long that neither one could match his stare and even I, with my fairy lung capacity, still had to let out the breath I was holding. If I had at least made *this* right—if this at least had been made better...

After what felt like a century or two, the King finally said, "I believe we can affirmatively state your intentions were good, Tarragon, and in keeping with the highest ideals of this Court. Therefore we will allow the effects of your actions to stand."

I let out my second breath, felt my heels start to rise again. All right, they still might turn me into a toad—but it was going to be *worth* it.

"So Anthony doesn't have to stay in Beaumont?" Catherine said, hopeful but cautious in that hope.

"I believe one could say that," the Queen said—and when she believes something, it's true. Sometimes because she believes it.

Catherine promptly hugged Anthony. This was not exactly proper decorum while having an audience with the King and Queen of the Fairies, but when it's True Love everyone looks tolerantly at that kind of activity. My grin probably wasn't proper decorum either, but I was having trouble tamping it down.

"But as to the most pressing matter." The Queen folded her hands before her. "Your interference with the military."

There went my grin. "If he went off to get himself killed, wouldn't that interfere with True Love?" I hazarded.

The Queen stared down at me, eyes narrowed. "No. True Love is entirely capable of surviving death," she said. "Nor did you need to interfere with an entire army to protect one man."

"And after all that fine talk about freedom, you were interfering with *my* choices." Cesar pushed his way through to the front of the group. "They're my army, my choice what they do, and you and your dirty magic interfered."

My shoulders rose on instinct at his tone. Even though, really, this was exactly what I wanted him to do. I very carefully kept my mouth shut.

Cesar wasn't a Beast anymore, but he still had a fierce glare, one he employed very unwisely as he leveled it at their Majesties.

The King and Queen met that glare without a trace of discomfort. "Cesar of Beaumont," the King observed. "You escaped your enchantment recently, didn't you." It wasn't a question. The King doesn't need people to tell him news like that. He always knows it already.

"I did," Cesar said with a scowl. "And I came back to find out that monsters had been terrorizing my country while I was gone. Which is why I'm going to get rid of all of them. Centaurs, hippogryphs, dragons, they're all going. They're unnatural, all of them."

The Queen's expression, always cold and remote, was now resembling ice capped mountains half a world away. "And would you include fairies in that number?"

I'd've backed down in front of that expression. He didn't. "Unnatural, dirty, *magical* creatures are not welcome in Beaumont. They leave, or they're dealt with."

"Killed, you mean," I prompted, just to make sure the full import was coming home to the audience. Though really, this little display couldn't have been better if I'd scripted it myself.

He nodded, fists tight at his side. "If that's what it takes."

The ripples going through the room at this moment were even more pronounced than the ones produced by my claim of defending True Love.

"He doesn't really mean it," Marj trilled, hands fluttering almost as madly as her wings. "He's just been under a small amount of pressure lately..."

"I mean every word," Cesar snapped.

The King and Queen exchanged a glance, and I got the distinct impression there were entire libraries of meaning in that single glance. "Obviously," the King said, "a century as a Beast has done nothing for his temper." If you ask me, it hadn't done anything for his intelligence either.

"It may even have exacerbated the problem," the Queen said. "Clearly he is posing a direct threat to this court through his assault on magic. That constitutes a situation which must be...dealt with."

Those last two words sent a shiver up my spine, and that was even though I *wanted* her to deal with Cesar. But there was such significance weighted behind two little syllables—and I couldn't help remembering that they'd still want to deal with *me* next.

"A return to his former state seems unwise," the King reflected. "A Beast was evidently not the best choice to encourage appropriately regal characteristics."

"Wait a minute, don't even think about turning me into something else," Cesar protested, with real alarm in his eyes for the first time. "I already spent enough time enchanted, you can't do that to me again!"

"Cats are regal," the Queen said, and waved one hand at him, almost lazily.

A pale blue glow suffused Cesar. He tried to brush it off his arms with frantic motions. "You can't—this isn't—you *can't*—"

He shrank, down and down and within seconds, where Cesar had been standing, there was a cat. A large brown cat with fur sticking out in every direction, back arched, spitting angrily.

"That should do nicely until he sorts through his temper problems-," the King said.

"Cesar?" Beauty whispered, and knelt down next to him.

He hissed and crouched into a fluffy ball, grumbling in cat-language.

"One could argue that we are interfering with his freedom," the King said—although no one would have argued, because you just don't argue with the King and the Queen if you can possibly avoid it. "But as he was posing a direct threat, interference becomes warranted."

And that was my *answer*. My escape clause. My excuse. If they accepted it.

"And that was just what I was thinking when I interfered with him too!" I said with great show of confidence. "He was threatening the survival of magical races when I cast my spell on his army. Making it warranted."

The King stared at me, maybe for even longer than he had stared at Catherine and Anthony. Long enough that I felt sure he knew this had not really been my uppermost thought when I cast that sleeping spell and that I had now made a terrible, terrible mistake trying to trap the King of the Fairies. Because it *was* a trap. If he said I was wrong now, he'd have to admit he was wrong too, and the King of the Fairies is *never* wrong.

When enough time had gone by for two or three Ages of Men to pass away, the King nodded. "We accept your justification. I expect you to bear in mind, however, that you are on very thin ice with this Court. This has not been your first offense either, and if any complaint brings you before us again within the next millennium, I assure you the consequences will be dire."

When the King of the Fairies threatens something dire, he's not kidding. Try continents sinking or mountains exploding—those *might* be bad enough to qualify as dire by the King's definition.

But that was all right, I could face that some other day, if it ever came at all. *Today*, I was getting away with everything. I felt good enough to—not to sparkle, never that, but shooting off fireworks would have felt about right.

The Fairy Court expects a certain amount of dignity and restraint, however, so I just bowed and murmured, "Thank you, Your Majesty."

Now if we could all get out of here before anything else—

"I want you to change me too," Beauty announced. She was standing beside Cesar, back straight and head high. "If you're leaving Cesar as a cat, I want you to change me too."

This sent Marj scurrying back from wherever she'd retreated after Cesar's enchantment (which had to be another puncture to her pride). She hovered beside Beauty, hands pressed to her chest and sparkles turning violently pink. "Beauty, my dear, do you know what you're saying? Do you realize they may actually enchant you?"

"Good," Beauty said, voice steady. "I want them to."

I winced, rubbing my temple. Why had I dared think, even for a moment, that all the problems were solved?

A tumult of protest was rising from the rest of her family, at least most of them. Connor had a grim expression, but was silent.

"I know what I'm saying," Beauty said over all the chaos, "and I mean it and if you're turning Cesar into a cat than I want to be one too. I love him, and I can help him, and this is what I want."

"Oh Beauty my dear," Marj said again, with a sob in her voice, "this is so *romantic*!" She plucked a lacy handkerchief out of the air and dabbed at her eyes.

"It's not romantic, it's insane," Anthony fired. "Beauty, he's not worth it!"

"That's up to me," Beauty said, gaze on the still-grumbling cat. "It's my life, and I know what I'm doing."

"But you can't—"

"Better let it go, Anthony," I said quietly. "She's right; it's her life."

"How can you be all right with this?" he demanded, wheeling towards me.

"You know all that talk about freedom?" I said. "You have to let her have the freedom to choose her life too."

"But she's making a bad choice!"

"And Marj thinks *you're* making a bad choice," I pointed out.

For a second, I thought he was going to keep arguing. But he clenched his teeth and Catherine slipped her arm through his and Anthony subsided.

One member of the family was not willing to let go. Mr. Maurier separated himself from the group and stepped forward. "If you change Beauty, I want you to change me too."

"Father, you shouldn't," Beauty protested.

"This is what *I* want. I want to be with my daughter."

Which, it seemed to me, made a clear statement on how he felt about being with the rest of his children. They all looked at one another, Miranda and Noreen reached out for each other's hands, and George shrugged in a resigned sort of way, which seemed to sum it up for all of them.

"If that is your wish," His Majesty said, "granted." There was a wave of the royal hand.

Beauty turned into a pretty Siamese with vivid blue eyes. Mr. Maurier was a venerable gray cat with short fur and a long whippy tail. Beauty padded over to Cesar and bumped him with her head. He hissed once. She bumped him again. He grumbled a little more, then gave something remarkably near a sigh, for a cat, and licked her nose.

Marj probably considered this a happy ending for her chosen couple. I couldn't see it, but I never could get very invested in the couples Marj considered the epitome of romance.

"There being no further pressing concerns—" the King began.

"I have a concern," Connor said, and somehow hit just the right tone so that he managed to interrupt the King of the Fairies without it sounding rude.

Even despite that, I definitely wanted to grab him and hustle him out the archway, because this good luck we were having couldn't possibly last. But the King and Queen were looking at him intently and you can't haul away someone the King and Queen want to talk to.

"Your family members chose of their own free will," the Queen said.

"Not that concern, Your Majesty," Connor said with a nod in her direction. "My concern was on a broader scale. The King of Beaumont is once again in animal form, leaving no one to properly run the country, which has already suffered under a century of anarchy."

I have to admit I hadn't thought that far ahead yet. I had been concentrating on preventing interspecies war—but now that Connor brought it up, I remembered the woman with her children, with the barn we stayed in. She had mentioned that a new king arose every few years but it never lasted and nothing changed. I had been so sure that this time would be different…but remove Cesar, and maybe it wouldn't be.

Again with the constant popping up of problems. When did it end? When did I get to go back to attending parties and having a good time?

Some people didn't feel this was their problem to handle. "Political affairs are not our business," the King said.

Connor's eyebrows rose in polite incredulity. "But I believe they are, Your Majesty. Fairies often involve themselves in matters of succession, in matters of royal matrimony, even in the qualities that future monarchs possess, as we can see in the example of Cesar. In this matter it is particularly your concern, as you have deprived the country of its previous king."

My shoulders rose up around my ears. He had contradicted the King of the Fairies. He had made a valid argument and he had done it politely but *still*.

And then I saw something I had *never* expected to see on the face of the Queen of the Fairies. A smile. It was tiny, barely a quirking of one corner of her mouth, but it was there. "An interesting argument," she said, and her voice was still like the breeze in mountain reaches, smile or no. "Who can we put in as king?"

"It should be someone related to the royal family, so as to have a proper claim," the King said. "But the last of the royal family was Cesar."

"His intended consort, on the other hand, has relatives." Her gaze turned to Anthony. "You are the youngest son, yes?"

He stared back, suddenly tense. "...yes."

I knew where this was going and I *knew* we should have run as soon as they decided not to turn me into a toad.

"Fine. You can be king." The Queen clapped her hands. "I believe that's settled."

"No, wait," Anthony protested, "I can't be king, I'm not—I don't even want to stay in the country, let alone run it, and besides, how would I possibly run a country? I can run an inn, I wouldn't know where to start with a country, you can't just throw someone into kingship without even considering whether they're qualified!"

I hurried to get half a step in front of Anthony. "He didn't mean that, he's not really thinking about what he's saying." Because you don't tell the Queen of the Fairies that she can't do something.

The Queen blinked a long, slow blink. "This is how succession often happens. No one asks if the man waking the sleeping princess knows how to manage a government."

Anthony was looking flabbergasted. "But that's—but I'd mess it up. And why would you make *me* king anyway? I'm the youngest, youngest sons don't inherit."

"They do by fairy law," I said. "Why do you think fairies are always helping youngest sons?"

"That doesn't matter, I wouldn't be good at it, and youngest sons don't inherit by human law anyway. Oldest sons do."

Heads starting turning towards the oldest son of the Mauriers.

It took a second longer for it to dawn on George. "Oh wait a minute. Oh wait, no, I wouldn't be good at being king either. I mean, not that the power and the wealth and the luxury don't look nice, but there's work and responsibility mixed up in there too and I don't think I want it. I just like to spend time with cheerful people and enjoy good meals. Kings do that but they also have to think about things like...taxes. And diplomacy. And I don't know what else. But all of that. I mean, I've heard Connor talk about it and I don't even understand half of what he says." A new idea visibly dawned across his face. "Oh, but maybe if I had Connor to advise me...but no, that doesn't make sense. Why should *I* be king? He's the one who knows how to do it; make Connor king."

"Middle sons never inherit," the Queen said. "Not by human or fairy law." I was staring hard at her, and I thought that very tiny smile might still be there. Hmm.

"They inherit when every other son abdicates," Anthony said, and looked at George. "Are you abdicating?"

He nodded. "Definitely."

Anthony nodded too. "So am I. That leaves you, Connor."

Connor, for a rarity, actually looked rattled. "But I wasn't—this isn't what I had in mind when I brought the subject up."

But there was a lot to recommend the idea. Connor could take over Beaumont, solve all those problems. Anthony and Catherine could go back to The Nightingale, solving their problem. And I could go back to looking for the next party. Maybe everyone wouldn't actually live happily ever after, but it would set us all up with a good chance at it.

Maybe I could tip this scale a little. "If you weren't making a bid to be king, that means there's no pride issue to deal with," I pointed out. "Which was Cesar's original failing."

"You'd be good at it, Connor," Anthony insisted, perhaps following the same line of thought as I was. "You're the one with all the plans and the ideas about what to do in Beaumont."

"Sure, you were already telling Cesar what to do," George agreed.

Connor looked pained at that. "I wouldn't put it that way, George."

George beamed. "Because you're diplomatic too."

"He's the one you want," Anthony said. "He'd be much better for Beaumont than George or me."

"It may be possible," the King said slowly, "but only with a certain condition. If we are going to engage with this situation at all, we cannot do so in a half-hearted way. A middle son with tenuous claim to the throne is a situation requiring close magical involvement, both as support and as overseer. Who will volunteer to attach themselves to the royal court of Beaumont?"

He had pointed out what I, in my enthusiasm for a solution, hadn't wanted to consider. That 'tenuous claim' part. The woman who told us about the last century's history had told us about previous claims to the throne too, none of them successful. But that was all right, some magical oversight would solve that, everything was fine anyway. I stuck my hands in my pockets, tried to look nonchalant, waited for all of this to get resolved.

Except no one was volunteering. Across the Fairy Court, wings and scales and fur and leaves rustled, but no one raised a hand. Very few fairies find such a position desirable. Attachment to a royal court can last through several royal generations, depending on the situation. This situation almost guaranteed it; not only was someone with uncertain claim taking the throne, the old king was still hanging around as a cat, and could revert to human any time—but probably not for several decades. This was going to tie someone down for a century, minimum. Good Fairies like to flit about without any commitments more binding than that of godparent, and Evil Fairies never do anything that hints of altruism.

And me, I didn't make commitments. Obviously. This whole tangle for the past few weeks had been a temporary situation, one I was going to extract myself from as soon as possible so I could go back to my proper life, the one where I visited parties and buffet tables and never did anything more serious towards changing the world than occasionally sniping at Marj.

Which, when I put it that way, seemed a bit...inadequate.

A long, long time ago I had talked to Nerissa about all the things I was going to do someday, the ways I was going to change people's lives. I hadn't done any of them.

I fought it for a minute longer, but after a minute I said, "I'll do it."

Both the King and the Queen looked at me then, and that very tiny smile on her face was just a bit larger.

"You, Tarragon?" the King said. "How very out of character."

"Yeah, well." I scowled. "Someone has to do it." Maybe it was about time it was me. And anyway, I was going to make good and sure Connor held plenty of parties.

"Very well," the King intoned. "Connor Maurier, you are hereby given the approval of the Fairy Court to reign over the kingdom of Beaumont. The Fairy Tarragon is hereby given responsibility to oversee said-court as long as the situation remains unstable." He clapped his hands once. "There now being no further matters..."

"I was wondering how important you consider names," Roderick said, pushing his way forward to the front of the group.

Why had I even *brought* him?

Oh right, that hadn't been my choice, had it?

The King and Queen both looked at Roderick, but it was with an expression of cool disinterest. Since they usually looked remote, that was saying something. "Names," the Queen said.

"We'll just be leaving now," I announced, reaching out to seize Roderick's arm.

"Right, names," Roderick continued, trying to shake me off. "Do you two even have names? No one's mentioned them."

"We do not have names we share with humans," the King said, a hint of thunder in his voice. And that's as good as a dismissal.

I hauled Roderick back and shoved him towards George, who got the message and seized him by the shoulders. "Really, we're going now," I said, and bowed. "Your Majesties. It was an honor, as always. Thank you. Very much."

I shooed all the humans—and cats—towards the archway, back towards the entrance hall. George pulled Roderick along.

I would have just transported us all out of the throne room and back to Beaumont directly, except that you can't do it. It's not just against the rules. You literally can't. And I literally can't either. Once we were in the entrance hall, I delayed a moment longer so that I could breathe a general sigh of relief.

Quite frankly, it was nothing short of miraculous that I hadn't been stripped of my wings. I don't usually have wings, but speaking symbolically. The King and Queen must have been in particularly good moods. Or maybe they were just so irritated by Cesar that they were more inclined to forgive someone who'd been making trouble for him. That seemed probable too.

So I wasn't banished for a hundred years, though I *was* stuck guarding over Beaumont for at least that long. To some extent, that made banishing me unnecessary, but they hadn't known it would turn out that way...I assumed. But I also remembered that tiny bit of amusement on the Queen's face. If they decided not to banish me because they *knew*—but no, they couldn't have anticipated that entire chain of events.

I tried telling myself that, except that of course they could, they're the King and the Queen of the fairies.

And at that point I decided I'd rather not think any more about how much I had or hadn't been manipulated, because it just wasn't going to pay, whatever I decided.

Only a few seconds had passed, and around me my crowd of humans were still trying to process both recent events and the local geography.

Emmy had a tight grip on Jack's arm, and was looking down at the swirling eternity below her feet. "This place is so *strange*."

"Not as strange as this," Miranda said, picking up Beauty and holding her high to look her in the eyes. "You just always have to be better and more loyal and more self-sacrificing than everyone else, don't you?" The words were scolding, but the tone was sad.

Beauty just purred at her.

Noreen, standing next to Miranda, groaned. "She *still* won't fight."

Roderick probably would've been willing to fight. He was willing to complain, at least. "I never ask anyone for their name and everyone gets upset, so then I ask people about their names and everyone *still* gets upset."

No one was paying much attention to Roderick. Catherine and Anthony in particular weren't paying any attention at all to Roderick, the cats or the swirling eternity around them. If I was any judge of kisses, they were absorbed with some swirling eternity of their own.

George was crouched down and trying to get Cesar to sniff his hand. Cesar still had his fur arumple and was turning his back to George; becoming a cat had not made him any friendlier.

Connor was frowning.

I focused over there. "Cheer up, man," I said, walking over and clapping him on the back. "You were just made king. That's good."

"Yes, I suppose," he acknowledged, frown remaining. "But I'd feel more cheerful about it if I wasn't taking over a country that's about two minutes away from large-scale civil war."

It appeared I was going to be working with a pessimist. On the other hand, he had a point. "Yes, there is that," I admitted. "I suppose it's time we got back and did something about it." If I was going to be responsible, I'd better go ahead and *be* responsible. So with that, I waved one hand and transported us all back to Beaumont.

Chapter Thirty

I took everyone back to the main courtyard of Cesar's castle—though I don't know that it could exactly be defined as *his* anymore. Because I'm a fairy and I understand spatial, temporal and magical laws, we arrived exactly seven minutes after we had left, which was not how long we'd been at the Fairy Court. Nothing had changed at the castle. Slumbering soldiers sprawled everywhere and, though I couldn't see them from the courtyard, I could sense the sleeping dragons, centaurs and onlookers outside.

"Do you have a plan for what to do after I wake everyone up?" I asked Connor.

He was still frowning, but it was a thoughtful frown. "Possibly. Start with the advising council. We'll begin there."

I started with them. Connor told them what was what, and that was that. They all swiftly and wholeheartedly pledged loyalty. They may have lacked backbone, but they weren't stupid. They knew as well as the rest of us that Cesar had been making a muck of running the country; they just hadn't had the nerve to do anything about it. And really, a spineless council was just as well when you're trying to bring in a new king, though it wouldn't be much use in the long-term. I made a mental note that we needed a new council and soon, but not until after the current crisis was resolved.

After we had the current council in line, I transported everyone who was awake up to the wide stone walkway above the main gate. It was the best location to address both the courtyard and the crowds outside.

I was raising my hands to lift the sleeping spell off everyone else when I realized we had one more problem.

"I really hate to say this," I said, rubbing the back of my neck, "but you're not dressed right, Connor. None of us are."

Connor looked down at his shirt. It was a perfectly nice linen shirt, but not exactly regal. "I could go change."

"No, don't bother, it'll take too long." I waved my hand once in negation, and then waved it several more times to transform everyone's clothing.

One thing about attending parties—you see a lot of fashion. It was easy enough to conjure up elegant silk dresses for Miranda and Noreen, full of bows and frills and ribbons because that seemed like their type; an emerald green dress for Catherine with little flowers that matched her aura; and a blue dress for Emmy the color of her eyes. For the men I magicked up jackets in the latest cut of fashion: dark brown for George the Bear, green for Anthony to match both Catherine and his aura, blue for Jack with his sailing ship aura (incidentally, I'd never seen his sails looking better), and for Roderick—well, I couldn't resist giving Roderick a vivid purple jacket, which then he ended up liking anyway.

And for Connor, a red robe lined with fur, and a gold circlet with extra shine.

I only do clothing spells in emergencies, but that doesn't mean I *can't* do them.

For myself, I conjured up a long blue robe and, with a sigh, grew wings out of my shoulder blades. They were manly wings. Very tough-looking. Big and feathered and dark green. And I absolutely and adamantly drew the line this side of sparkles.

Once we were all suitably arrayed to impress, we arranged ourselves on the walkway, and I set about waking everyone else up.

One convenient aspect to that spell—everybody wakes up a little sleepy and groggy and it takes a few minutes for them to really get fully back on top of everything, like chasing each other with swords. So that gave Connor the minute he needed to stand up above the castle gates and get everyone's attention with a speech that started with the phrase, "People of Beaumont"—and he managed to gesture just right to suggest that he meant everyone, centaurs, humans and dragons alike.

I cast a neat little spell to make his voice carry, then let him talk. For being impromptu, it was a good speech. It went over the fresh indisposal of His Majesty, King Cesar, while not actually pointing out the angry brown cat in our midst, and said a few words about how this ought to be taken as a sign or maybe an inspiration towards friendliness amongst ourselves. This set the right tone for when he also announced he was the new king—although I like to think the robes and circlet had suggested the idea already.

That was when the first snag arrived down the current (although snags don't actually move, it's whoever's in the current who moves to catch them...but you get my drift). The snag was from among the human soldiers, and someone high up, based on his coat and his attitude. I haven't the least doubt he was a mercenary leader who'd brought his men to join the army, and who Cesar had promoted to general.

"So whose authority made you king anyway?" Mercenary asked, thumbs hooked in his belt. He managed to swagger while standing still. "Just because you're almost related to the last king, that's not much of a claim."

"I can answer that question," I said, stepping forward. "Their Most Royal Majesties, the King and Queen of the Fairies did." I leaned over the wall of the walkway and grinned, fiercely. "Please, by all means, tell me you don't believe me."

He didn't even blink. "I don't believe you."

"I really did hope you'd say that," I said happily. I keep a low profile mostly, but every now and then I like to be dramatic.

I started by launching clouds of blue smoke all around us. Then I set off a nice wind whipping over the plains and through the courtyard and blew everyone around. Finally I spread my arms—and my wings— and shot fireworks up into the sky, great flaming lights in blue spirals and green showers. That's as close as I get to sparkles.

"Do you think that was overdoing it?" Connor asked in a low voice.

"Not at all," I answered, then pitched my voice out over the crowds. "Any more doubters?"

There were no more doubters, of any species.

And that pretty much settled the question. Magic goes a long way towards securing rights to a throne. Whether it's magically killing a dragon or having a magical bird land on your head or because magical forces gave you their approval, if there's magic involved, it seems to be all right by most people if you rule their country.

If I wasn't on thin ice with my monarchs, I might point out that this prevailing attitude among humans says interesting things about whether royal succession has been the business of fairies in the past. But that ice is less than thick, so I won't even make that observation.

After the smoke cleared and the fireworks faded, Connor resumed his speech with some stirring words about community and cooperation and communication and mutual respect and appreciation, and by the time he was done Rajna of the centaurs and Grwnoiren of the dragons and all of Cesar's generals and advising council were feeling amicable towards sitting down and having a conversation about mutually beneficial plans for the future of the kingdom.

I couldn't tell, at this point, whether a capable, plan-making king would mean more or less work for me as the magical adviser, compared to a king who never did much of anything. It was a toss-up. But at least this new position gave me a lot more leeway to cast legal spells, should situations come up where I wanted to. I was musing over possibilities as we all headed down the stairs from the balcony and into the hallway below.

Connor was deep in conversation with his advising council. "One of you—you, find some footmen, get one of the long tables from the dining hall moved out to the west meadow, right away. And some chairs, but only along two sides. And you, go up to my rooms, find my notes, the ones in the leather folder, and as much blank paper as you can get your hands on. And ink, don't forget ink. You, go find the cook, tell her we need food suitable for humans, centaurs and dragons out to the west meadow within half an hour."

I perked up at the prospect of food, while the third adviser so pointed at looked at Connor with something like petrification. "What do centaurs eat?"

"All the food humans eat, and the food horses eat too. Apples, oats, hay."

"And dragons?" That question was barely a squeak.

"Anything," Connor said. "As long as it's moving. By the way, Prince Roderick, I think it would be wise if you attended this meeting, as a sign of international ties. We don't have a formal agreement between our countries yet, but a symbolic gesture at this point would be valuable."

"Sure, all right," Roderick agreed, busy smoothing out the cuffs of his purple jacket. I regretted not making it a brighter shade.

Connor just nodded, and turned to a fourth member of the council. "Now, about the dismal state of the royal treasury, I do not want that kind of information coming up in the discussions today..."

"It's good not being king, isn't it?" George said, watching Connor and elbowing Anthony. "So many things to not have to think about."

"That's one way of looking at it," Anthony agreed. "Lots to not worry about."

But a moment after that, we all encountered a small, unimportant, really not material worry. But an inconvenient one. We'd all been moving towards the door leading out to the courtyard, but before we reached it there was an explosion of pink sparkles in the doorway.

"Oh no," I groaned. "I thought I left you at the Court."

"You did," Marj snapped. "I followed you."

"And what, you spent the intervening time reapplying your make-up?" I suggested.

Not surprisingly, she ignored that. "You've ruined everything and it's terrible and it's all your fault!"

"Some of it's my fault," I acknowledged. As good as things were going, I had no objection to accepting the responsibility for it. "Very little is ruined. Much more is fixed."

Connor cast her one glance, then continued his discussion with his advisers. That apparently left me to deal with the Good Fairy, which did seem reasonable enough.

Marj looked down at Beauty and Cesar, who had just drifted along with the rest of us, though much closer to the ground. "This is very romantic but *not* what I had planned—and they were so perfectly happy together!"

"That's putting it strongly," Anthony muttered.

"You stay out of it," she fired at him, "or I'll turn you into a toad."

"Ignore that," I advised Anthony. I was feeling too good about everything to be bothered by Marj's totally meaningless threats. "She never turns anyone into toads. Besides, you're even more firmly part of the royal family now, and I'm now in charge of magical matters pertaining to the royal family of Beaumont. So that means no kittens either, Marj."

"Speaking of kittens and cats..." George picked up Beauty, and beckoned to Cesar and Mr. Maurier. "Why don't we get away from the scary sparkly lady and go find some nice cream, hmm?"

"How dare you refer to me that way?" Marj shrilled, forced by his height to look up at a sharp angle to address him.

George ignored the comment, said a polite, "Excuse me," and edged past her and out the door, I assume towards the kitchens. "And we'll find some fish, and maybe figs, and stew, or a nice steak, and some meat pies..."

"Wait for us," Miranda said, following him with Noreen following her. "After days trapped in stone, I'm dying for something to eat."

I knew I liked this family.

Marj glared after all of them for a moment, then turned back to me. "You ruined everything!"

"You said that already," I pointed out, grinning at her.

"From now on, I want you to stay out of my life! Stay out of my business!"

I cocked an eyebrow at her. "So you followed me to tell me to leave you alone? How...logical."

Marj was as pink as her sparkles. "I am never speaking to you ever again!" she announced, and disappeared in a veritable explosion of sparkles and hearts and pink bubbles.

"In that case, maybe now I'll get some quiet," I muttered, using magic to clear the sparkles off me, each fleck vanishing with a crackle. That spell's usually more trouble than it's worth, but I had a reputation to think about now. I couldn't start my career as the Magical Adviser to Beaumont with sparkles on me; it would give the wrong impression.

I was still chasing down sparkles on my sleeves when Catherine said to me, "I'm sorry about Marjoram."

"So am I," I said, with feeling. "Often. But why should you be sorry? You're not related to her."

Catherine smiled slightly, but her forehead creased in puzzlement. "No, I meant...she *is* your family, even if you don't get on well, and she just vowed never to speak to you again."

"Oh, that." I waved a hand dismissively. "She'll get over that in a decade or two."

Marj had vowed never to speak to me at least twenty-seven times, give or take. We have a volatile relationship. But when you live for millennia, that always gives you plenty of time to bury the hatchet. Also to dig it back up again.

Besides a bit of quiet, I could see another up-side to this current fight. "You know, since Marj is mad at all of us, you should be safe from an invasion of doves at your wedding."

"Oh good," Anthony said, a heartfelt comment.

"That's right, I forgot," Catherine said, poking his shoulder. "Doves would scare you off."

He nodded deeply. "Right. The dim-witted prince and his insane magician adviser and the sparkly pink fairy and the entire Fairy Court didn't scare me off, but *doves* would do it."

And Catherine giggled. I wouldn't have expected Catherine to giggle, but there it was, and it was adorable.

"Why are you two still hanging around here anyway?" I asked. "Go walk in the rose garden or something."

"Tarry, you're a man of good ideas," Catherine said, and tugged Anthony's hand. "Let's go do that."

"Is it a very big rose garden?" Jack asked, his own fingers around Emmy's hand.

"Enormous," Anthony said. "Cesar was passionate about roses."

I could think of worse ways to spend the afternoon than wandering around a rose garden, even alone. Or better yet, I could go after George and see what he found in the kitchens. But... I looked at Connor. "You sort of need me at this summit meeting, don't you?"

He looked up from his discussion. "Sort of? No. Definitely? Yes. And there are a number of points I need to discuss with you, about the meeting and on a few other subjects."

"I thought you might say that." I sighed, shoving my hands in the pockets of my robe. "You're going to make me work, aren't you?"

"I don't know how I could *make* you, but I will expect it of you."

"I thought you might say that too. But you know what would be nice?" I said, pitching my voice louder. "When we've been doing lots of good work saving the country, and need some time away, it would be nice to have a charming little inn somewhere to go visit."

From the doorway, Catherine looked back over her shoulder and smiled. "I know just the place. Drop by any time."

It was uphill work for a few years in Beaumont. But the council, after quailing before Cesar's temper, was eager to accept Connor's calmer and more thoughtful reign. The general populace had misgivings, but those faded quickly as the world around them improved.

The country *did* improve. I made judicious use of magic—and, to be honest, sometimes not so judicious—and Connor had good ideas and knew how to carry them out. Where necessary, the monsters were contained, and where possible, treaties were made. In time, not without difficulties, relative peace and prosperity returned to Beaumont.

And I stayed on, because even if the world had settled down for now, there was still a former king stalking around the castle as a bad-tempered cat, and I was bound to provide magical support until that sorted itself out. But it wasn't so bad, somehow, having responsibilities and necessary work to carry them out. Connor was a king who did actual work, which meant actual work for me too—but also more *accomplishments* than I'd managed on my own in five centuries.

Besides, I got my fair share of time raiding the royal kitchens with George too, and insisted that we throw frequent parties.

Besides—it wasn't such a bad thing, solving problems for people. I didn't like the *problems*, but I liked the solving. And even the parties were much more fun, when I was attending them with friends.

I also found time to attend Catherine and Anthony's wedding, where there were eight kinds of pie and no doves at all.

Now that I could magically transport between Beaumont and The Nightingale, I was still a regular guest in Catherine's kitchen, where Jack and Emmy frequently came to dinner too and I never got tired of seeing the way Catherine's and Anthony's aural branches intertwine.

I went back to the Perreldan castle too, to attend Roderick's wedding. There were doves, but at least Roderick managed to memorize Ella's name in time for the vows. Roderick went on blissfully pleased with himself and not especially worried or concerned about anything else, so I suppose you could say that he lived happily ever after. Princes and princesses often do.

As for my less royal friends, Jack and Emmy, Catherine and Anthony, they lived on in fairly ordinary lives, if any life can really be said to be ordinary. No one with any depth is purely happy all the time, and no one escapes all the problems of life, but they lived lives full of love and laughter, good companions and good work, and ultimately, that's all any of us, even me in the end, can ask of a life.

Looking for More Tales?

Now available in paperback and ebook:

The Wanderers

Meet Tarry's friends Jasper, a wandering adventurer, and Tom, a snarky talking cat, as they fight monsters and wander through familiar—but slightly slanted—fairy tales. When they rescue Julie, a witch's daughter, it sets off conflict with her very familiar, very sparkly Fairy Godmother.

The Storyteller and Her Sisters

Lyra and her eleven sisters must dance every night to rescue twelve princes from a curse, while keeping an enchanted forest from falling into the hands of their mad father. And naturally their Fairy Godmother is no help at all…

More Books from Stonehenge Circle Press

Secrets in the Dark
by K. D. Blakely

Hiding from bullies in the town cemetery seemed like a good idea. Right up until we fell through a creepy secret doorway into a magic land called Chimera. My friends and I promised to keep Chimera a secret, but that's hard when we go there every month. Who knew being born in THE STRANGEST YEAR EVER could change...everything!

Pucker Up
by R. A. Gates

Ivy always thought that breaking a curse with True Love's Kiss was the ultimate romantic gesture in fairy tales. But when she has to plant one on a prince who's been dead for 200 years, it's just gross.

Find more of Cheryl's favorite books:
http://marveloustales.com/recommendedreads

Acknowledgements

This book would not have been possible without the support of friends, family, and everyone who said, "oh, what a cool idea" when I floated this plot past them. Every book is a journey, but this one has been a particular saga! Thank you to Dennis and Meaghan, my earliest readers, and to Karen, Kelly and Ruth for their final-round feedback. As always, thank you to the entire writing group at Stonehenge—you continue to make me a better writer every week!

I owe thanks also to the great retellers of tales: the Brothers Grimm, Charles Perrault and Jeanne-Marie Le Prince de Beaumont—as well as to Walt Disney, Gail Carson Levine, Patricia C. Wrede, Juliet Marillier and Robin McKinley.

About the Author

Cheryl Mahoney can't remember when she began her love affair with stories. She never goes anywhere (including the grocery store) without a book and a pen. She loves gathering with good friends to eat good food, but she would never want to spend five centuries going to parties with strangers!

Cheryl also writes a book review blog, Tales of the Marvelous (http://marveloustales.com), and is on Goodreads (MarvelousTales). Her first novel, *The Wanderers*, was published in 2013, and its companion novel, *The Storyteller and Her Sisters*, in 2014. She has completed NaNoWriMo three times.